STILL LIFE WITH SHAPE-SHIFTER

"A triumphant tale of love and loss . . . The everyday relationships—the love shared by siblings, friends, and romantic partners—shine with even more wonder than the magic . . . This series is not to be missed."

—*Publishers Weekly* (starred review)

"Book two of the Shifting Circle series expands the scope of the story yet loses none of the character depth and poignancy. While *The Shape of Desire* hinted at shape-shifters' generally shortened life spans, this examines the issue in greater detail with the benefit of taking the tale in new directions. A sweet secondary story twines throughout the book, culminating in a haunting, bittersweet conclusion that again poses the question, what would you do for love?"   —*Monsters and Critics*

"An incredibly poignant and bittersweet story of love, loss, and family. As always, Shinn's calm yet powerful voice tugs at readers' heartstrings . . . Smoothly written and emotionally charged, this story takes us beyond the horror and carnage normally found in paranormal stories and instead focuses on the humanity of those who straddle the line between the human and immortal worlds—and those who love them."

—*RT Book Reviews* (top pick)

"This is a wonderful fantasy story about family, sisters, and their bonds. It's warm and wonderful and will keep readers enthralled."   —NewsandSentinel.com

"Shinn takes her subject matter seriously as she delves into universal issues of love, trust, and family . . . A sure bet for most fantasy readers, but this novel should also appeal to those who prefer only a touch of the supernatural in their fiction."

—*Library Journal*

continued . . .

THE SHAPE OF DESIRE

One of *Publishers Weekly*'s Best
SF/Fantasy/Horror Books of 2012

"If you enjoy a book with great characters, mythology, and the more normal side of the paranormal, then *The Shape of Desire* is one book you won't want to miss!"   —*A Book Obsession*

"Ms. Shinn's way of painting a picture with words was fully evident in her latest work . . . It was a deeper-resonating book that I think will stay with me for quite a while."
                                                    —*The Book Pushers*

More praise for the novels of Sharon Shinn

"Shinn is a master of world-building, plotting, and characterization—I loved *Reader and Raelynx* so much that I immediately started rereading the series from the beginning! Not to be missed."
                        —Mary Jo Putney, *New York Times* bestselling author

"A vivid, spellbinding addition to the superb Twelve Houses saga . . . A beautiful adult fairy tale that readers will appreciate."   —*Alternative Worlds*

"A chocolate truffle of a novel: richly indulgent, darkly sweet, and utterly satisfying."   —*Kirkus Reviews*

"The whole series is highly recommended for romance readers interested in dabbling in fantasy or fantasy readers who do not mind some mingling of the genre boundaries."   —*SFRevu*

"Shinn continues to demonstrate her ability to write epic fantasy that leaves the reader wanting more."
                                        —*The Southern Pines (NC) Pilot*

"Combines storytelling expertise with a richly detailed fantasy world. Recommended."   —*Library Journal*

"Outstanding . . . A lyrical grace and deep appreciation of camaraderie reminiscent of Diane Duane at her best . . . [A] superior fantasy series."   —*Publishers Weekly*

"Engaging . . . An enjoyable yarn with characters who leave you wanting more."   —*Locus*

STILL LIFE WITH
SHAPE-SHIFTER

SHARON SHINN

ACE BOOKS, NEW YORK

THE BERKLEY PUBLISHING GROUP
Published by the Penguin Group
Penguin Group (USA)
375 Hudson Street, New York, New York 10014, USA

USA I Canada I UK I Ireland I Australia I New Zealand I India I South Africa I China

Penguin Books Ltd., Registered Offices: 80 Strand, London WC2R 0RL, England
For more information about the Penguin Group, visit penguin.com.

STILL LIFE WITH SHAPE-SHIFTER

An Ace Book / published by arrangement with the author

Ace Books are published by The Berkley Publishing Group.
ACE and the "A" design are trademarks of Penguin Group (USA).

For information, address: The Berkley Publishing Group,
a division of Penguin Group (USA),
375 Hudson Street, New York, New York 10014.

ISBN: 978-0-425-25635-0

PUBLISHING HISTORY
Ace hardcover edition / November 2012
Ace mass-market edition / October 2013

PRINTED IN THE UNITED STATES OF AMERICA

10 9 8 7 6 5 4 3 2 1

Cover illustration by Jonathan Barkat.
Cover photographs: filagree © iStockphoto/Thinkstock; leaves © Maksim Shmeljov.
Cover design by Judith Lagerman.
Interior text design by Laura K. Corless.

ALWAYS LEARNING   **PEARSON**

For Ramona, Rebecca, and Rachel
Sisters of a different mother

CHAPTER ONE
MELANIE

I'm sitting at one of the three stoplights in Dagmar on Monday morning when Kurt Markham strolls down the crosswalk in front of me so slowly that he's only halfway across the street before the light turns green. It's all I can do to keep from flooring the Cherokee and running over him, backing up, and running over him again. I can tell he recognizes my car because he gives me a grin and a thumbs-up as he finally steps onto the sidewalk, into a zone of relative safety. It's the grin that gets to me. I have to tighten my hands on the wheel to keep from swerving to the right, jumping the curb, and chasing him down anyway. What's the point of having an SUV, after all, if you can't take it off-road?

My more civilized instincts keep me in my lane, however, and I don't even blare the horn at Kurt as I drive on past. But I'm in a temper when I finally pull into the small parking lot outside of the office, and it's not too much to say that I *stalk* inside. Chloe and Em take one look at my face and find something fascinating to read on their computer screens. Only Debbie has the nerve to step into my office as I'm throwing my purse to the desk and ignoring the shrill summons of the phone and cursing because I've spilled the last of my cheap McDonald's coffee an inch away from the keyboard.

"Bad morning?" she asks as she stands in my doorway. As always, her sleek black hair lies smoothly against her cheeks and she's impeccably dressed, with a style more suited to a city of two million than two thousand. Well, she has to present a certain professional air; she's the owner and public face of Public Relations by Zimmer, PRZ for short. I'm just the bookkeeper-slash-office-manager. I can get away with nice pants and cute sweaters and the occasional bad-hair day.

"Not at all," I say in a voice of exaggerated politeness. "I like it when I wake up a half hour late because the power's gone out at midnight, and I can't dry my hair because the power's gone out at midnight, and I can't see to put on makeup because the power's gone out, and I can't make coffee because—oh yeah, the power's gone out and—"

"Got it," she interrupts. "You can stay at our house tonight if you want."

"No, the electricity came back on just as I was walking out the door."

She nods. "And how was the weekend?"

"Not too bad till the mail came Saturday with an offer from Kurt Markham. He'd give me two hundred thousand dollars for the house."

She raises her eyebrows and sips her tea but doesn't make any other reply. I am so tense and so angry that I think, at this point, if she'd said anything, no matter how insightful or sympathetic, I'd have wanted to slap her perfectly made-up face. And Debbie is my best friend in the entire world.

"So," I say in a summing-up kind of voice, "it wasn't so great. How was *your* weekend?"

"Simon ended up in the ER because he fell off his bike and he wasn't wearing a helmet, so in addition to worrying that he had a concussion, we had to answer all sorts of searching questions about whether or not we're bad parents.

He's fine, by the way," she adds, almost as an aside. "And Stevie flushed God knows what down the basement toilet, but at any rate it overflowed and sent some truly disgusting sewage over the bathroom floor and into the laundry room."

"And everyone says boys are easier than girls." To my surprise, I find myself smiling just a tiny bit. "How did Charles handle everything?" Charles-reaction stories are often even funnier than Simon-and-Stevie stories.

"He was totally calm and focused during the whole hospital adventure, but he kind of lost it when the toilet overflowed. Made the boys sit with him for an hour while he Googled the history of plumbing and talked about the first indoor toilets ever installed and traced the outbreak of some horrible cholera epidemic to a badly designed sewage system. I think Simon's now afraid to even flush toilet paper, but I'm betting we won't have any blockages for a while."

"I love Charles," I say with a sigh.

"Yeah, so do I, but it's not like he's perfect," Debbie replies.

"Oh, please. Tell me a Bad Charles story."

"Well, remember when I was out of town a couple of weeks ago? Apparently Charles kept forgetting to run the dishwasher. And he didn't want to leave dirty dishes on the counter. So he started piling them up in the refrigerator because he figured they wouldn't mold while they were in there. So of course when I got home, every plate, every bowl, every glass, and every piece of silverware was dirty. And most of them were in the fridge."

I actually think this is a creative solution to a challenging situation. "He's a prince among men," I say. Charles is a big, gentle, brilliant man with a quirky streak, and I never let Debbie forget how lucky she is to have him. Though she doesn't need reminding.

For about six months in high school, Debbie and Charles and Kurt and I double-dated.

There are days I still can't believe that's true.

Debbie has clearly decided that her family-drama stories

have improved my mood enough that she can risk a question. "So what are you going to do about Kurt's offer?"

"Write 'Only when I'm dead' across it in red Magic Marker and mail it back."

She nods, but I can tell she doesn't agree with me. "Still. Two hundred thousand dollars."

I know what she means to imply. *That's a lot of money for such a modest property.* There are only two tiny bedrooms, a bathroom scarcely bigger than the one you'd find on an airplane, a small kitchen just inside the front door, and one largish open space that contains some living-room furniture and a scuffed old square wooden dining table and mismatched chairs. There's no basement. The yard is extensive, more than twelve acres, but that's not the real reason Kurt wants the place. It's situated smack in the center of two growing housing developments, both of which he owns. He wants to buy the property, raze the house, improve the land, and make a fortune.

My voice is scornful. "He'll make ten times that much on Markham Family Estates or whatever he decides to call his subdivision."

"So tell him you want half a million dollars."

I hunch my shoulders. My bad mood has come back. Except it's not just situational irritability or a head-swimming rage that even I realize is inappropriately proportioned. It's flat-out, ungovernable, all-consuming fear, and for the last few weeks it has colored every aspect of my life. I feel it thicken my throat as I say in a surly tone, "I can't sell the house."

Debbie's voice is so soft she might be murmuring to one of her boys as she coaxes him to sleep at night after a harrowing dream. "Ann will understand."

My reply is immediate. "No, she won't."

"Have you *asked* her?"

I turn on her with another flare of anger. "No, I haven't asked her! *I* don't want to sell! *She* wouldn't want me to sell! It's the house she grew up in—I can't just all of a sudden tell her to look for me somewhere else—"

"And why can't you?"

Now I gesture with short, sharp movements, my fingers spread as wide as they will go, as if I am trying to juggle something so large and so overheated that I constantly fear I will not be able to catch the next bounce. "I'm not sure I can explain," I say in a ragged voice. "I just have this feeling. If I moved. No matter how many times I told her where my new house was. I'm not sure she'd be able to find me again."

Debbie listens in silence, her face wearing an expression of complete understanding. Debbie is the only one who knows about Ann, is the only person, since my father, with whom I have ever been completely honest about my sister. There are many other reasons Debbie is my closest friend, but this single one would be enough. "And when's the last time you saw her?" she asks quietly.

I turn away to boot up the computer because I don't want even Debbie to see the fear on my face. "A month. Maybe five weeks."

She waits a moment because she can always tell when I'm lying.

"Almost exactly two months," I say at last. "She came home at Christmas and stayed for a while. She hasn't been home since."

For a long time, neither one of us speaks.

Is she hurt? Something happened to her last autumn, I know—she got into a fight, or had a nasty fall—because I saw the healed scars on her ribs when I brought her a fresh towel after her first bath. But she had laughed away my concern, and she hadn't moved with any particular evidence of pain. Still, given her lifestyle, she could be prey to so many accidents! I have to shut my mind to the constant cascade of images of Ann lying hurt and bleeding in some lonely landscape, solitary, helpless, and afraid.

Is she dead? That's my greatest fear, of course—that she will pass on, and I will never know, though a part of me believes she could not, *could not*, die without leaving such a powerful vacuum on the Earth that my own soul would be sucked into it. I would know, surely I would know, if such a calamitous event had occurred.

But if she is not dead, if she is not injured, what has happened to her? Has she merely forgotten to be human?

And wouldn't that be just as bad?

The day doesn't get much better. It's Monday morning, so the phone never stops ringing with questions people have stored up all weekend. Even though I managed *not* to spill coffee on my computer, it has decided to throw a tantrum, and it crashes four times in as many hours. When I go out at noon, deciding I deserve ice cream for lunch, I find my right front tire is flat. My last experience trying to change my own tire didn't go so well, so I call AAA, where I'm informed that no one will be able to help me until five o'clock. It's enough to make me want to walk a mile to the nearest railroad tracks and pillow my head on the unforgiving steel, waiting for the next locomotive to chug by.

I didn't used to be this way.

I was never exactly a *carefree* sort of girl. I took everything seriously, studied hard, didn't bother with teenage rebellion or adolescent angst. But I wasn't grim. I wasn't angry. I had a sense of humor and an appreciation for fun. Hell, I was a *cheerleader*—I wore short skirts and kicked up my legs and exhorted my fellow students to roar out their love for Dagmar High. I dated Kurt Markham, for God's sake, and you can hardly be more shallow than that.

Ann's the one who changed everything. Even so, at the beginning, she didn't fill my heart with such apprehension. In the beginning, she was nothing but joy.

My own mother died when I was five; it's hard to tell which of my memories are true and which ones I invented from photographs and my father's stories. The older I get, the more I look like her, especially now that I wear my oak-brown hair in a simple shoulder-length style. I have her green eyes, her surprised expression, her sturdy build. My smile is my father's, though, a skeptical and provisional expression until I am completely won over. Then I laugh with my whole body. Or I used to.

My dad was a quiet guy, tall and stooped and perpetually thinking about something; he taught physics at Maryville University for thirty years. He was not particularly well suited for taking care of himself, let alone a small girl, so we bumbled along for a few years, living on pizza and frozen pot pies and the occasional feasts prepared by his mother when she would come up from Texas. I used to secretly wish she would take me home with her so I could live always in the guest bedroom with the fuzzy pink bedspread and the pictures of seashells on the walls. I almost asked her once, when I was eight, but then I thought about how lonely my father would be if he lived all by himself. At the time we owned a rambling ranch house in the St. Louis suburb of Kirkwood, nine rooms if you counted the ones in the basement. It was too big for two; I could imagine how empty it would seem for one. So I didn't ask.

And just a few months later, my father married Gwen. He called her Guinevere, though her legal name was Gwendolyn. Her hair was so blond you could hardly believe it was natural, though it was; her eyes were a dreamy blue. She was short, delicate, affectionate, full of laughter, full of warmth.

Full of secrets.

She changed our lives in so many ways, and at first those changes were largely positive. For one thing, she could hold together a household, so that rambling ranch house became tidier, more comfortable, and better stocked with edible food. For another, she was mostly a happy presence. Even when you couldn't see her, you could hear her laughing in another room, or singing the chorus of some popular song. She would swoop in and give me a kiss when I was doing homework or coloring artwork. But there were downsides. She absorbed more of my father's attention than I liked, and that took some getting used to; and she had occasional days of gray funks, where she sat around the house and wouldn't speak and wouldn't eat and wouldn't say what was bothering her.

Now and then, she would disappear.

It happened twice during the first six months they were married. We would wake up, and Gwen would simply be gone. No note, no phone call. My father, usually so placid, was wild with anxiety. I remember him shouting on the phone to the police, who apparently were not as concerned as he was that his wife had gone missing. These days I can reconstruct part of the conversation I did not understand when I was a child. They were probably telling him that they wait forty-eight hours before opening missing-persons cases on adults, especially adults who vanish from their own homes in the middle of the night. They were probably asking him questions he could not answer. *Could she be visiting with a friend or a relative? Is an old boyfriend in town? Could she be meeting a contact somewhere and buying drugs?*

I remember my father yelling, "Of course not!" into the phone, but surely the questions made him uneasy. The truth was, as I realized when I was a teenager, he had married Gwen without knowing very much about her. He'd never met any of her family members, even at the wedding; she only had one or two friends, and those she practically left behind once she became his wife. She was a deep mystery in a charming package, and the police were right to believe there were secrets in her life that would explain her disappearance and that she would come back on her own.

I have no idea what she told my father about those early absences, how she explained her actions and convinced him to trust her again. I'm certain she continued lying about her motivations until finally, left with no other options, she unwillingly told him the truth. But for a while, her strangeness, her erratic behavior didn't matter. Because eighteen months after she married my father, when I was ten, Ann was born. And she became the center, the heart, the lodestone of everyone in the house.

I had never been around babies before and I wasn't sure what to expect. I knew from TV shows that they cried all the time and from commercials that they smiled when you put them in fresh diapers. And Ann did indeed wail whenever she was unhappy, and she did indeed go through an astonishing number of Huggies. Gwen had had an uncomplicated delivery but she recovered slowly, so I quickly learned how to change the baby, how to calm her, how to feed her. From the beginning, I considered Ann my responsibility at least as much as she was my father's or Gwen's.

And I loved her more than I loved anyone else in the world.

I was probably eleven or twelve the night I lay awake thinking fairly deep existential thoughts. I had heard noises downstairs—which turned out to be my father and Gwen talking in the kitchen—but I had initially worried that the sounds were caused by burglars. My first thought was that I would hide in my closet so they wouldn't find me. My second thought was that I must get Ann and hide her in the closet with me. Otherwise, I knew, they would steal her; there could hardly be a greater treasure in the house.

From imagining criminals breaking in to rob us, I went to thinking up other disasters. Fires, tornadoes, unspecified apocalypses that leveled the house and rendered the whole neighborhood a smoking ruin. In every scenario, I was the one to grab Ann and flee with her to some compromised haven. Gwen and my father were left behind to blow away or burn.

In the years since then, I've heard other people talk about their own complex childhood fantasies, in which they run away from home or find themselves tossed out without a penny. They describe elaborate story lines of camping in the woods, living on ants and mushrooms, building huts, finding water, carrying on their lives unencumbered by parental supervision. I'm sure it's some kind of ritual of passage; I'm sure it's the child's way of testing out the ways he or she will behave as an adult.

But mine feels different to me. It is not so much a wishful fantasy as willing acceptance of a clear-cut duty. Ann needed someone to take care of her, watch over her, protect her, guide her, love her. I was obviously the only one qualified for the job. I'm not sure there was a time you could have asked me, from the minute she was born until this very day, when I would have given a different answer to the question *Who does Ann belong to?* She's mine.

And that's why it is killing me to think she is in danger and I cannot help her and I cannot find her, for I cannot live if she is lost.

Debbie offers me a ride home, but the AAA guy shows up at five minutes to five and changes the tire with no fuss. I'm on my way home a half hour later, squinting against the setting sun. I make three turns through the heart of Dagmar, then I'm on the first winding loop of Bonhomme Highway, the two-lane road that will take me all the way to my door. It's early March, so the trees that crowd up against both sides of the road are still mostly bare, but I'm starting to feel a little hopeful. It can't be much longer until spring, can it? One day soon, the branches will bud and blossom and explode into greenery. One day soon, winter will surely be gone.

Ann has been in my mind so strongly all day that I start wondering if there's a reason. Is she on her way home? Will she be waiting for me when I pull up in front of the house? Will she be sitting on the front porch, curled up in the chilly spring sunshine, or will she have remembered where I keep the spare key and let herself inside? You'd think the hope, or the uncertainty, would have sent me home at a faster rate, eager to see her and hug her thin body to mine, but instead I dawdle. I stop at the grocery store to pick up coffee and fruit and bread, items I don't really need; I pause at a service station for gas though I still have half a tank left.

I don't *want* to go home, that's the truth. I don't want to get closer and closer to my house and feel my chest tighten with hope. I don't want to skid onto the gravel bed at the edge of the lawn so fast that the rocks spew up from my tires. I don't want to run to the door, almost dropping the keys in my nervousness, calling out her name. I don't want to dash from room to room, checking, just making sure, thinking maybe she's asleep in her bedroom or maybe she's outside, running barefoot across the back acres. I don't want to go home because until I know for sure she isn't there, I can still believe she might be.

But just in case she's there, I have to go home.

The last mile of my journey takes me past Markham Manors, Kurt's new development, where more than half the homes are still under construction. As I always do, I drive straight past, keeping my eyes fixed on the road. When I swing the Cherokee onto the gravel patch, I note that parts of the lawn are starting to show green, the front gutter looks loose—and Ann is not perched on the small front porch, waiting for me. My groceries are in two sturdy cotton bags, and I carry them in one hand while I shake the house key loose in the other. I've promised myself I won't call my sister's name as I step into the house, but I can't help myself. *Ann? Ann? Are you here?*

There's no answer. There's no blond girl sleeping on the sofa, in her room, in mine. There's nothing in the house at all but old furniture, older memories, useless worry, and helpless love. I feel my chest cave in with the oppressive G-force of disappointment. Grocery bags still in my hands, I lean my head against the chilly white surface of the refrigerator and forbid myself to cry.

I have not been home for more than fifteen minutes when there's a knock on the front door. My heart gives a painful squeeze. Could that be Ann? Was I right, after all, to expect her home tonight, simply wrong about the timing? I lay aside the newspaper and jump up from the couch, trying not to run, reminding myself that Ann would not be content with a single polite knock but would be pounding the wood, ringing the doorbell, calling my name. This will be a local kid selling magazines or a siding salesman here to tell me my house looks like it needs a lot of work. No one I want to talk to.

So I'm already wearing a closed and somewhat forbidding expression as I open the main door, keeping the screen door shut and latched. "Yes?" I say coldly.

The person I see through the mesh is a stranger, a man who might be in his early thirties. He's not too tall and so good-looking that I instantly think I've seen him somewhere, maybe in a movie or television show. His hair is dark and just a little shaggy, but the careless style softens a face that is classically handsome—straight nose, firm chin, molded lips, the eyes a soulful brown. He's wearing jeans and a bulky fisherman's sweater, but I can tell he's got a slim, wiry build. He's in good shape. Not a jock, like Kurt, but he takes care of himself, works out at the gym, maybe runs, plays volleyball in a neighborhood league.

"Are you Melanie Landon?" he asks.

Dagmar is a small town. Even when strangers come to your door, they're usually related to someone you work with or went to school with or meet every week at the store. The fact that this guy has to ask the question means he's a true out-of-towner. There seems to be no point in denying my identity, but my voice is frosty as I reply, "Who's asking?"

"I'm Brody Westerbrook."

The name is as teasingly familiar as the face, but I can't place it. "And what do you want, Brody Westerbrook?"

"You're Melanie Landon, aren't you?" he says. When I don't answer, he steps a little closer to the door; I get the impression he wants to press his nose against the screen and peer inside. "The sister of Ann Landon?"

My breath catches in my throat, and then, before I know what I'm planning, I've pushed through the screen door to join him on the porch. "What's wrong with Ann? Is she hurt? Where is she?" The words come so fast they trip over each other like clumsy puppies.

His face shows comprehension and dismay as he realizes what he's done. "No—no, I'm sorry, I don't have any news about her, I was just—I'm sorry. I didn't mean to upset you."

For I've turned aside to hide my face, but I can't stop the tears from welling up, and they're followed quickly by great tearing sobs that feel as if they're ripping my ribs apart. I put one hand over my eyes, one hand over my mouth, trying to stuff the tears back inside, but they won't stop. I hear the ragged, forlorn catch of my breath, and if I had any energy left to be embarrassed, I would be mortified at the display I am making before a total stranger.

He's mortified enough on his own account. "Miss Landon—Melanie—I am so, so sorry. Could you—would you—why don't you sit down? Can I go into the house and get you some water? Would that be okay?"

I can't speak an answer, so I shake my head and try to blunder back inside, but I'm crying so hard I can't even manage that much. I stumble into him and he automatically raises his arms to help me catch my balance. And then, as if he doesn't know what else to do, he tentatively puts his arms around me and draws my head against his shoulder.

God help me, it has been so long since I've allowed myself to weep in somebody's arms that I rest my cheek against his sweater and let myself cry. He smells like cotton and aftershave and some kind of deodorant soap. He's just the right height to comfort me, taller than I am by three or four inches, and I can feel how easily he braces himself to take my weight as I sag against him. He's not hugging me, not exactly, but he's wrapped one arm loosely around my waist and he's patting me with his free hand, and for a moment, just a heartbeat or two, I believe that maybe everything will be all right.

And then I pull back and straighten up and spare a moment to think how horrific I must look, with a splotchy face, reddened eyes, and running nose. "I'm so sorry," I say with the shreds of dignity I can gather. "I've had a very bad day."

"I'm the one who should be apologizing," he replies. "If

I'd thought—I just didn't realize—maybe I should come back some other time."

Once you've wept in a man's arms, it's hard to rudely demand that he state his business or vacate your property. "Some other time might not be as different as you'd hope," I say with an attempt at lightness. "If you promise me you're not a serial killer, I'll invite you in for a soda or a glass of water."

He hesitates, which I think is interesting. He's obviously come here looking for something, and my breakdown has no doubt led him to believe I'm in a vulnerable state; now would be the perfect time for an unscrupulous man to push his advantage. "I'd love a soda," he says after a moment, "but I'm not so sure you're going to feel like talking to me once I tell you what I'm here for."

I raise my eyebrows, but a sense of foreboding acts within me like a wash of adrenaline. I feel my tears start drying, my muscles cording to land the punch or withstand the blow. I wipe my sleeve across my face to clear away the last traces of moisture. "So why don't you tell me why you're here?" I ask in an even voice.

He gazes at me steadily. He really does have a beautiful face, and the earnest expression just makes it more appealing. "I'm a journalist," he says. "Well, I used to be. I quit my job a couple of months ago so I can work on a book. I want to write about something most people don't even believe exists."

"Oh God," I say.

I recognize him now. Brody Westerbrook, of course. He was the Channel 5 news reporter who broke that awful, that terrible story about a series of murders that happened last year in the western St. Louis suburbs. All the deaths were attributed to some kind of mysterious animal that forensics guys couldn't identify and eyewitnesses couldn't describe. When the police and the park rangers finally tracked down the marauding creature, it was loping through the cluttered wilderness of Babler State Park. A news helicopter offered a live feed as the animal experts trapped it and shot it with tranquillizers and who knows what other kinds of drugs.

And right there, on-screen, on television sets all over the metropolitan area, that wild animal transformed into a human being.

"I want to write about shape-shifters," Brody Westerbrook says. "And I think your sister Ann is one of them."

CHAPTER TWO

I invite him inside after all. I am too tired and too forlorn to do anything else. For a moment, I debate getting out the bottle of leftover wine in the refrigerator, uncorked just last weekend when Debbie and Charles were over and maybe holding two more small glassfuls, but I'm already thinking badly, and I don't need to cloud my mind any further. I pour Cokes for both of us, and we sit, warily, on either side of the old, scarred, oak table. I see Brody Westerbrook surreptitiously glancing around the room, noting the shabby furnishings, the scratched hardwood floors. This isn't a place you'd live if you had any money.

If he's done enough research to find me, he knows that I can afford to move to a bigger house or simply install a few upgrades. A new couch, new curtains, refinished floor, modernized kitchen—all these improvements could add a great deal of charm to this old place.

He catches me watching him, and smiles. "It seems like a comfortable sort of house," he says.

"That's not what you were thinking," I challenge him. I might have invited him in, but I'm still armored to the hilt; my guess is I'll be challenging him a lot. "You were thinking it's a dump."

He regards me with interest. "I pretty much always say what I mean," he answers. "So why do *you* think it's a dump?"

Now I bristle. "I haven't had time to pick out fabrics and—and interview general contractors and deal with all the *mess* of renovation."

He nods, as if I had actually answered the question he asked. "You should see my place," he says. "I live in a studio apartment, and I'm never home, so there's stuff just strewn from one end to the other. I pay someone to come in and clean, but there's nowhere for her to put things, so she just makes the piles neater and scrubs the bathroom and goes home."

I raise my eyebrows. "Seems like a television reporter would be able to afford something bigger than a studio apartment. Maybe even a house."

He smiles. "I don't have time to look at real estate and pick out furniture and deal with all the *mess* of moving," he replies.

It makes sense that a journalist would perfectly recall your own words and use them against you at the first opportunity. I scowl.

He goes on, "Anyway, like I said, I'm not a reporter anymore. I'm a freelancer. Lot less money. Mostly I'm living on savings. Not the best time to go house-hunting."

"I thought you were writing a book."

He nods. "Yep. But it's going to be a while before that brings in any money, if it ever does. So I'm writing a few articles when the opportunity comes along. Editing a manuscript for a professor at Wash U. Stuff like that."

I open the bag of pretzels I got out along with the soda and shake a few thin salted sticks into my hand. "So tell me about your book," I say. I can't look at him when I speak the words.

"I don't know if you remember this," he says, slowing his words to a storyteller's cadence. Now that I'm not looking at him, I realize that his low-pitched, mellow voice is as attractive as his face. It would have to be, I suppose, for him to be an on-air reporter. "But last November there was this extraordinary event. I was in a news helicopter as authorities caught an animal they suspected had been responsible for five human deaths in about three months. My cameraman had his lens trained on the animal as they brought it to the ground, and I could see the monitor. While it was lying there—while we watched—it changed. From an animal to a person. We caught the whole thing on tape."

I nod. "I saw it," I say very quietly.

He waits, but when it's clear I'm not going to add anything, he goes on. "There was a firestorm of publicity, if you remember. I thought there would be panic, crazy folks wailing about the apocalypse, or aliens, or mad scientists conducting experiments on innocent people. But that's not the way it went. Most people thought we'd doctored the tape. I mean, I saw some so-called technical expert do a whole segment on one of the other stations showing, frame by frame, how we had digitally turned an animal into a human being. It was jaw-dropping. We almost got cited by the FCC. None of the legitimate news sources took us seriously. They either ignored the story completely or condemned us for trying a sensational trick to bring up our ratings.

"The *bloggers* liked it," he adds. "That clip was the most downloaded video on YouTube for a solid month, and everyone with a website and an agenda posted it. Then they posted their own 'true footage' of shape-shifters and Bigfoot and Loch-Ness-style monsters that lived in the murky old ponds down on the lower forty of their grandfathers' abandoned farms. There was a whole contingent of people who believed we'd filmed a werewolf, and they kept issuing 'health advisories' about how to survive a werewolf bite without being turned into one yourself. We were even on the cover of *National Enquirer* a time or two. But the truth was, most people simply didn't believe the event had occurred."

I force myself to look at him fleetingly. He still appears a little annoyed, but mostly resigned. This is someone who long ago stopped being surprised by the unfathomable decision-making processes of the general public. "But there were a bunch of other people there when it—supposedly—happened, weren't there?" I say.

He nods. "Sure. The cops and the animal-control guys were there on the ground, and my cameraman and I saw the same thing from the air. And you can bet all of them were interviewed at one time or another. But, you know, three of the cops said they were too far back to see clearly enough to make a statement in court, and one of the animal-control guys explained how there's a long history of bears being mistaken for humans or vice versa. Such a bunch of bullshit. They were just too unnerved by reality to speak the truth. They didn't want it to be true. It seemed too impossible. So they convinced themselves they were mistaken."

He shakes his head.

Despite myself—despite my own worries, which at the moment revolve around what Brody Westerbrook plans to do to destroy my world—I am a little intrigued by this story and how it affected his life. "Did *anyone* believe what happened?"

"Sure. My cameraman, my producer, the station manager—I mean, it was a live feed, and they *knew* we weren't sitting in the studio doctoring footage. But as soon as they saw how the rest of the world was reacting, they pulled the plug. I wanted to do a long series on the topic of shape-changers and how they've been portrayed throughout history and how they live among us today, but they wouldn't go for it. Too self-serving, they said—make us look like we were trying to legitimize a hoax. I brought it up every day for about three weeks, and they always said no." He shrugs. "So I quit."

"To write your book. About shape-shifters?"

"That's right."

I snap a few pretzels between my fingers. "And what have you learned so far?"

He doesn't answer at first, so I glance up at him again. He's watching me, a faint smile on his face. "Not so sure I'm going to tell you what I've learned," he says. "I need to protect my sources."

"You haven't learned anything," I say bluntly. "You haven't met a single shape-shifter."

He waggles his head from side to side in a *maybe-yes-maybe-no* motion. "I've seen some things. I've talked to people who know shape-shifters. A lot of my evidence is anecdotal so far, but the anecdotes are pretty compelling."

"Sure. Alien-abduction anecdotes are pretty compelling, too, but they still don't make me think there are spaceships hovering over the planet and scooping up random people to run biological tests on them in the middle of the night."

His grin intensifies. "See, you just did it," he says.

I feel immediately hostile. "Did what?"

"You linked my shape-shifting premise to an even more preposterous one so that you could discredit my theory just by association. That was a common tactic used by the media and the bloggers back when my story was first aired."

"Sorry," I say tartly. "I'll try to be more original next time I mock you."

"And you're only mocking me because you're trying to keep me at a distance," he adds. "You don't want me to win you over. You don't want to feel comfortable enough to confide in me. You've set yourself against me. And here I thought you were going to be a friendly girl, offering me pretzels and soda. I was even starting to hope for dinner."

I can't help it; I laugh, as he surely intends me to. I suppose journalists must have a knack for making people like them, or they'd never secure any interviews, but Brody Westerbrook has certainly developed the skill to a high degree. "I've dropped cyanide in the Coke and sprinkled arsenic on the pretzels," I say. "I know how to get rid of pushy reporters."

He smiles again, and says casually, "Tell me about your sister Ann."

My laugh turns to dust in my throat. I just stare at him and don't answer.

"I know a little bit about her," he goes on. "She was born twenty years ago at St. John's in Creve Coeur. Nothing particularly unusual about the birth. She lived with you and your father and her mother—your stepmother—in a house in Kirkwood until she was five. Then your family abruptly sold the house and moved down here." He glances around the room again. "Back when *here* was a much less developed part of the world. You probably didn't have neighbors for two miles on either side of you when you first bought this house."

I don't say anything, but he's exactly right. We hadn't even been on the school-bus route at that time; Gwen or my father had to drive me to school until I got my license a year later.

"When Ann was old enough to go to kindergarten, she didn't. Your stepmother elected to homeschool her. That might have been considered a little odd in this neck of the woods, but your father put out the story that she had frail health, and people tended to accept that. Your dad let it be known that the damn doctors could never figure out exactly what was wrong with his little girl. People tried to be sympathetic without appearing to pry."

Well, that depended on the person, of course. Kurt Markham's mother used to grill me endlessly whenever he would bring me by his house or, in later years, when I'd run into her on some ill-fated shopping expedition. "So what exactly is it that's wrong with your sister, dear? My niece died of leukemia when she was four years old. The saddest thing. And George's nephew, he has lupus—although I never understand exactly what lupus is. But his doctor is at Barnes in St. Louis if you ever want his phone number. I do hope Ann's feeling better. And how about your father? He was always such an *interesting* man."

I never gave her any details. "They're fine, thank you."

Though, by the time I graduated from college, my father was in the dementia wing of a West County retirement center, and Ann was . . . Ann.

"Then your father got sick," Brody says, employing the most euphemistic term, "and your stepmother had already left town for good. You were a legal adult by this time. You kept the house, worked part-time, put yourself through school, got a job, and here you are." He leans forward over the table. "But Ann hasn't been seen around these parts much since she was about sixteen. You tell people she went to California to try to become an actress. People believe it because she was always such a pretty girl. But she's never gotten a job in any commercial or TV show they've ever heard of. Too bad. They'd like to brag about the local girl who made good."

About halfway through his recitation, I'd dropped my eyes again, but now I lift them to give him another unfriendly stare. "Sounds like you've learned a lot about my family," I say. "I'm just curious to know which of my friends and neighbors you've been talking to. And don't tell me you're *protecting your sources*. I'd like to know who gossips that much with total strangers."

"Well, my primary informant wanted me to tell you hello from her, so I know she won't mind," he says. "Ella Dartmouth—remember her?"

I nod. She'd worked as a secretary at Maryville for a hundred years, or thereabouts, and was one of the few people my father kept in touch with even after he left the university. She could have supplied virtually all the information Brody has just recited—and would have done so without having the slightest idea that her words had the potential to do any harm.

"Who else?" I ask.

"Your high-school principal."

I'm a little bewildered. "Mrs. McAvoy?" She'd been famous for knowing the name and family tree of every student at Dagmar High, but I wouldn't have said she was intimately acquainted with my situation.

"That's right. But we only talked about you in a general way. I told her I was doing an article about rural schools that turn out superstars—writers, actors, politicians, that sort of thing—and did she have any examples for me? I had a few yearbooks with me, to prompt her memory, and I'd point to a few random faces as we went through the pages. Yours was one of them." He shrugs, as if to say, *It was subterfuge, but it worked.* "I haven't had a chance to talk to anyone else in Dagmar. Thought I'd come to you next and see what you might tell me."

To myself, I'm thinking, *It could be worse.* Aloud I say, "It doesn't sound to me like anything they told you would have made you come to such a—such a preposterous conclusion. I can't imagine why you started looking for us in the first place."

He nods, as if he was expecting that response. "When your family was living in Kirkwood, there were—incidents," he says. "Neighbors would see Ann playing in the backyard. And then they'd look again, and there'd be a little white puppy racing around. A husky. And they'd look five minutes later, and the little girl would be back, but the dog was gone."

This is a little more damning, and I feel my heartbeat accelerate, but I keep my face impassive and only shrug.

"One of your next-door neighbors was a girl a year or two younger than you. Named Caitlyn. She was crazy about dogs, but her brother was allergic, so her parents wouldn't let her get one. She'd come over to your house and ask to play with the puppy, but your dad and your stepmother would always say no. They'd say it wasn't really their dog, it just came to their house sometimes, and they'd leave food out so it wouldn't starve.

"One day, Caitlyn sees the husky in the backyard, so she sneaks over and lets it out. The two of them take off for some park a few blocks away, where they play for a couple of hours. The puppy is really smart, Caitlyn says— understands every word she utters. Like, after they'd been running around for a while, Caitlyn announces, 'I'm really thirsty,' and the dog heads straight for the drinking fountain."

I roll my eyes, but under the table, where he can't see them, my hands are clenched together so tightly I think I might crack the bones. "Oh, that's impressive," I say.

He just keeps going. "Finally, Caitlyn and the puppy return home, to find the whole neighborhood in an uproar. Your family is searching everywhere for the dog—your stepmother is hysterical—your father has taken the car and is driving slowly up and down the surrounding streets, looking for a little white husky. Mind you, this is a dog they claim doesn't belong to them. When Caitlyn shows up with the puppy in tow, your stepmother falls to the ground and grabs the dog in her arms and just starts sobbing. Caitlyn's in trouble herself, her dad yelling at her for leaving the house without telling anyone where she was going, but she can't stop staring at the crazy neighbor lady making such a fuss over a dog that isn't hers. At one point, your stepmother looks up and demands, 'What happened to her foot?' There's a gash on the inside of the puppy's right foreleg, and it's bleeding a little though it doesn't seem to have slowed the dog down any. Caitlyn says she doesn't know.

"Her parents are hauling her into the house, but right before she's yanked inside the door, she sees your dad drive up. He's still cruising slowly down the street, calling out for the little dog. 'Ann! Ann! Come home, girl!'" Brody gives me a limpid look. "Ann? They've named the dog that isn't really theirs after their own little girl? But before she can think too much about it, she's hustled inside and has to deal with her own problems."

Brody takes a swallow of his Coke. I am attempting to sit there in stony silence, but the truth is I am remembering that terrible day in vivid detail. Caitlyn's recitation, via Brody, doesn't include the fact that I flung myself on my bicycle and pedaled as hard as I could to the places I happened to know were Ann's favorites. There was a farmer's market in downtown Kirkwood on Saturdays, and she loved to run between the stalls and snatch up fallen bits of fruit and baked goods. There was a jungle gym in a nearby schoolyard where she was especially fond of the rounded green climbing rock shaped like a turtle. Worse, there was a fountain outside one of the pizza shops on Kirkwood Road, and she was fascinated by the splash and play of water. She always wanted someone to pick her up and hold her so she could bat at the thin jets of water spraying out, until she and anyone in her vicinity were liberally drenched. The fountain's basin was curved and shallow, but deep enough for a child to drown in.

I raced to each location, one by one, but there was no sign of Ann.

I remember how my lungs had burned with the effort of those manic bike rides, how my legs felt simultaneously stretched and heavy, quivering with exhaustion. But those discomforts had been negligible compared to the sense of panic that had choked my throat, the feeling of dread that had cramped down on my stomach. My thoughts were desperate and circular. *Where could she be? Is she all right? Has something happened to Ann?*

Good thing I didn't know then how often I would lie awake over the next fifteen years, asking myself those same questions. No more frantic bike rides to likely hiding places, but equal amounts of worry and misery.

And these days, Ann is gone for longer than an afternoon.

Brody resumes his story. "Caitlyn is grounded for the next two weeks, and none of her friends can come over, and she can't watch TV. So she spends a lot of time in the backyard, playing by herself. One afternoon, little Ann Landon is out back, too, digging in her sandbox. There's nothing else to do, so, even though Caitlyn is eleven years old and not that interested in small children, she tosses a ball back and forth over the fence with Ann for a little while. Pretty soon she notices that Ann has a Band-Aid on her right wrist. A big one. 'Hey, what happened to you?' she asks. Ann says, 'I hurt myself when we were at the park.'"

Brody repeats that, as surely Caitlyn must have when she told him this overwrought tale. I don't remember our former neighbor all that clearly—I never paid much attention to her—but I think of her as a small, whiny girl who was always asking if she could borrow something. A toy, video, a black windbreaker that I wore everywhere because I thought it made me look sleek and mysterious.

"'When *we* were at the park,'" he says with heavy emphasis. "Caitlyn couldn't quite figure that out. Did Ann mean 'we' as in 'my family and me'—or did she mean 'we' as in 'Caitlyn and Ann'? But Caitlyn had never been to the park with the little girl named Ann. Only with the puppy that might have been named Ann, too. A puppy that had been injured in the exact same place that the little girl had a bandage."

I slap my hands to my cheeks in feigned astonishment. "What could this strange, mad coincidence possibly mean?"

"So Caitlyn gets the ball back from Ann and doesn't throw it over the fence again right away. 'Hey, Ann,' she says in a friendly voice, 'where's that little white puppy who lives at your house sometimes?' And Ann replies, clear as you please, 'I'm the dog. The dog is me.'"

He says these last words with the solemn portentousness you might reserve for announcing the location of the Holy Grail. There's a charged silence between us for a moment, though I've molded my face into an expression of slightly bored politeness, as if I'm waiting for the rest of a tale that has not fully engaged my attention. He just keeps watching me, his brown eyes steady, serious, unflinching.

Finally, I permit myself a little smile. "Oh—that's it? That's the whole story?"

"It's a pretty good one, don't you think?"

"Some woman tells you that, fifteen or eighteen years ago when she was eleven years old, my sister told *her* that she was a little white dog? And you *believed* her? I mean, what kind of evidence is that? What kind of reporter *are* you? If those are the best sources you can turn up as a general rule, I'm not surprised you gave up journalism."

His eyes narrow, and he sits back in his seat, regarding me with a measuring expression. "Interesting," he says. "I don't make you for the kind of person who's usually cruel, so the mockery must be a defensive maneuver. Am I getting too close to the truth?"

I take a deep breath, make an exaggerated expression that shows how hard I am trying to hold on to my patience. "Mr. Westerbrook—"

"Brody."

"I've had a long day. An emotional day. I'm tired. I'm in a bad mood. You're a stranger who's come to my door to make wild accusations about my family, and I think I've been pretty tolerant up to this point. But I find my civility is on the verge of giving way. I don't mean to be *cruel* when I say, could you just leave? Right now? Thank you."

He pushes his chair away from the table but doesn't stand up. "Sure. Fine. Thanks for talking to me. But just answer one more question for me. Will you?"

Again I make the God-give-me-strength face and say, in carefully neutral tones, "Of course. What is it?"

"Is your sister Ann a shape-shifter?"

I open my mouth but for a moment am unable to speak. I have lied about Ann for so long, to so many people, that you'd think it would be easy to lie now. *Oh, Ann's sick with the stomach flu. No, Ann's out of town visiting her mom's sister. Hey, sorry, Ann can't come over and play because Gwen took her into the city to go shopping.* Excuses roll off my tongue in such a facile manner that I'm scarcely aware of making them up anymore.

But I've never had to tell this particular lie. Never had to deal with the outright accusation, because no one had ever thought to level it before. Why would they? Why would it even occur to them to ask the question?

If I try to speak the lie, will my lips even form the words? Will that be like denying Ann's very essence? Will that, in some fashion, make her disappear? She has been gone so long—she is lost, perhaps, in danger, afraid—and maybe all that keeps her going, all that she has to hold on to, is the knowledge that I will never abandon or betray her. Will I cut off her sole hope of survival if I claim that she does not exist?

It's a bad time to become superstitious, but I find that I cannot give the answer I should. Instead, as if I am goaded beyond endurance, I snap out, "Don't be ridiculous."

He tilts his head to one side. "That's not exactly a no."

I come to my feet abruptly, almost angrily. "I can't take the question seriously enough to give you a yes-or-no answer."

More slowly, he stands up. I can't quite read his expression, but I think there's a certain amount of satisfaction in it. He believes that someone who can't say no is trying hard not to say yes. I think that's a bad rule to live by, but I suppose I can't blame a reporter for subscribing to it.

"Can I come back another time and talk about this some more?"

I allow my stupefaction to show. "Mr. Westerbrook—"

"Brody."

"I hardly think we have anything left to discuss. I'll wish you good luck on your—your book project, but I obviously don't have anything helpful to tell you—"

"Well, I think you do," he interrupts. "I'd like to come back in a couple of days and see if you have something else to share."

I'm shaking my head. "I just don't see the point. I think we're done here." I glance around, as if perhaps he's left a hat or umbrella somewhere, and I want to hand these items over to him before escorting him to the door. "So—"

"So then will you have dinner with me?" he asks.

This stops me cold. "What? No. Why would I?"

He grins. It's really criminal how attractive this man is, in a sort of friendly, unalarming, sure-I'll-invite-you-in way. "Because I've had a lousy day. I'm in a bad mood. The sink stopped up in my bathroom, the 'check engine' light is on in my car, and the person I drove two hours to see, getting lost three times on the way, won't give me the interview I need. I thought maybe having dinner with a pretty woman would rescue the day from being a total loss."

I laugh in disbelief. "So now you think that flattery—"

"And shared suffering. We've *both* had bad days," he interjects.

"Will be enough to make me forget my distrust of you—"

"Hey. I promise. No talk about shape-shifters over dinner. I won't ask questions—*any* questions. I'll just sit there and eat in silence, or make observations about the other people in the restaurant. You can talk or not talk as you like. We'll eat, I'll go home, that'll be the end of it. Whaddya say?"

I *should* say no, but it's a word I seem unable to muster in Brody Westerbrook's smiling presence. I feel so battered by the intense emotions of the day that I'm pretty sure I'll fall apart the minute Brody walks out the door and I can relax my hypervigilance. That's going to feel like hell, but there's no logical reason to think that extending my time in his company will ease me through the crash to come.

But the house will seem so small and still when I'm the only one inside it, my head constantly cocked toward the door, awaiting the sound of light footsteps. And I know if I don't go out with Brody, I won't have the energy to make a meal; I'll just dine on potato chips and yogurt and whatever else is closest to hand. If I don't just collapse on the sofa and dissolve into tears that leave me so limp and dispirited that I don't bother to eat at all.

I can't tell if I'm trying to find excuses to leave the house or excuses to spend another hour with Brody. Every rational sense I have is warning me to snarl at him, shove him out the door, and make sure every lock, both physical and imaginary, is secured against him. But my heart has set up a faint, exhausted mewling. My heart is craving kindness and conversation, and Brody has already demonstrated that he's adept at both.

He can tell I'm wavering. He smiles and holds out his hand. "C'mon," he coaxes. "It'll be fun."

"No questions?" I say. "You promise?"

His right hand still extended, he puts his left hand on his chest. "Cross my heart."

"There are only a few restaurants in Dagmar, and none of them are very gourmet," I warn.

"I'm not very picky."

"Then let me get a jacket, and we can go."

CHAPTER THREE

We take my Jeep because he wasn't kidding about the "check engine" light in his little Honda. It's just light enough outside that I can read the bumper sticker on his back fender. I'M PROUD OF MY CUB SCOUT. I give him a sideways look and decide to be blunt. "You've got kids? You're not wearing a wedding ring."

"Nieces and nephews," he says amiably. "I bought this one from my oldest sister last year. Didn't seem worth the trouble to try to scrape off the sticker and, anyway, I *am* proud of my little Scout."

"So you're not married?"

"No, are you?"

I can't help but laugh as I unlock the car door. "Oh, I have to believe you've already done your research on me, so you know the answer to that."

"Right again," he says, and climbs in beside me. He settles himself on the seat and looks around. "Huh. SUV."

I give him an annoyed look and start the engine. "What's that supposed to mean?"

"I don't know, it's just—you know. Gas guzzler. Oil crisis. Earth Day Every Day. You just seem like the type who'd be driving a hybrid and using cotton grocery bags."

"Yeah, well, I got stuck four times in the snow last year trying to come down that last hill, and I decided I needed a car that would get me through the winter. But I *do* use cotton grocery bags," I feel compelled to add. "And recycle."

"There you go. Knew I couldn't be wrong about you."

The parking lot at Corinna's is about half-full. Monday is the best night to come here if you don't like a crowd, which I usually don't, though the food selections are usually sparser. As everyone in Dagmar knows, Corinna does her shopping on Wednesday mornings, so when you drop by earlier in the week, you're likely to find that some of the more popular items have sold out.

We step inside, and Brody quickly takes stock of the décor. It's a quirky place, part diner, part bar, with dark wood paneling, low light, red vinyl booths lining three walls, and sturdy wooden tables in the center. The back wall features a mural painted by some long-since-graduated high-school student who'd won an art scholarship, and it depicts local landmarks and smiling faces in broad, cartoonish strokes. A small, low stage juts out below the mural, and here mediocre country bands are usually playing on weekends. There's a wooden dance floor butting up against the stage, big enough for eight or ten couples to do the two-step if they don't mind bumping into each other. On Thursday nights, when more people come to eat than to listen to music, Corinna sets up tables on the dance floor.

But those are the least desirable seats in the house. Everyone wants to be in one of the booths right against the front wall, pressed up against the windows, so they can sit there and watch anything interesting that happens to be going on in the street. It's rare, of course, that there *is* anything interesting happening in Dagmar—but you never know.

We're in luck. One of the waitresses is clearing a front booth just as we step in the door, and no one else is ahead of us. As everyone else does, I ignore the sign that says PLEASE WAIT FOR HOSTESS TO SEAT YOU and pull Brody directly over to the booth. The waitress, one of Corinna's daughters, gives the table a final wipe, and says, "Do you need menus?"

"I don't, but he does," I say, and she nods and departs.

Brody is still getting his bearings. "Cozy," he says. "In that land-that-time-forgot sort of way."

I grin. "I spent a lot of afternoons here when I was a teenager. Drinking root beer floats and eating French fries and talking about boys."

"Doesn't really seem like a teen hangout."

"It does when there's nowhere else to go." I tick off items on my fingers. "Teenagers come here in the afternoons between three and five. Families come between five and seven. Couples and groups of adults from seven to ten. I mean, those aren't strict rules, and anybody can show up whenever they like, but you feel out of place if you walk in and it's not the right time for you."

Brody looks around again. Sure enough, there's only one table featuring anyone under the age of twenty-five, a young couple with two squirmy boys, and they're already standing up and putting on coats and getting ready to leave.

Corinna's daughter drops off two laminated menus that are a bit the worse for wear. "We're out of pizza and sloppy joes," she says. "And there's only vanilla shakes left."

"What about the meat loaf?" I ask.

"Plenty."

"That's what I'll have," I say. I glance at Brody. "I recommend it."

He shakes his head. "I gotta see what my options are first."

"I'll be back in a minute," the waitress says, and disappears.

Brody studies his menu as if he's never been given a chance to order his own food before. "This is great," he says. "Look at these prices. A hamburger is three dollars and seventeen cents. Why *seventeen* cents? Why not twenty-five cents? And fish sticks. Four dollars and sixty-three cents. That's just silly. I love it."

I'm smiling. The precisely calculated prices are one of the things I have always found most endearing about Corinna's. The owner is a big woman with massive forearms and untidy brown hair, and I always picture her sitting in the kitchen, studying inventory lists and pricing sheets, and punching in numbers on a calculator as she determines to the penny how much she must make on every menu item to turn a profit.

"So what appeals to you?" I ask him.

"I'm a sucker for chicken pot pie. Is it any good?"

"Well. It's not very fancy. But going by down-home standards, and if you're in the mood for a hearty meal, it's great."

"Then that's what I'm getting."

The instant he lays his menu on the table, Corinna's daughter is back to take our orders. I ask for iced tea with my meat loaf, but Brody is seriously tempted by the vanilla shake.

"I'll save it for dessert," he decides. "Or maybe we can split a root beer float," he says after the waitress departs. "Then I can really feel like I've slipped back in time."

"I have a scünci in my purse, I think," I say. "I can put my hair in a ponytail."

"Too bad I left my letter sweater at home."

"Do you really have one?"

He nods. "I ran track in high school."

"Were you any good?"

"Won a few races but didn't qualify for State, so I'd say I was about average."

I slump against the worn vinyl of the booth and study him a moment. "So, okay," I say. "You know everything about me. What's there to know about you?"

He already looks as relaxed as a man can be, half-sprawling on his bench, one elbow up on the back of the seat, no tension that I can read in his body or his hands. He gives a little shrug as if to say, *Not much to tell*. "Grew up in Cape Girardeau. Pretty standard suburban Midwestern life. My dad worked for an insurance company, my mom had part-time jobs but spent most of her time running the family. I have three older sisters who don't think their days are complete unless they've called to boss me around about something."

"So you're the youngest and the only boy. Spoiled rotten, I suppose."

He grins. "Some people might say so. But I always kind of thought I was like the poor stupid dog that the crazy pet lady likes to dress up in Halloween costumes, you know? And you see the pictures of that dachshund or that beagle wearing the hat and the cape and the boots, and you think, 'That poor son of a bitch.' You know he's just got no say in his life at all. That's how I felt growing up. 'Brody, come here. Brody, go there. Brody, wear this. Brody, you can't do that.' And they always ganged up on me, so even if I didn't want to do whatever it was, I always had to."

I regard him through narrowed eyes as I consider this. "Yeah, okay, maybe, but somehow I'm not getting a meek-and-mild vibe off you. You don't seem worn down and docile. So I guess you figured out how to outsmart them."

He laughs. "I learned a couple of tricks that have served me well over the years. I learned to be compliant when I had to be—to give in with grace when it was clear I couldn't win. I also learned a certain—I hesitate to call it deviousness—"

"Oh, I think that's exactly the right word."

"I like to think of it more as a combination of charm and manipulation. A basic skill set that allowed me to get my own way on things that were really important to me without setting the whole household against me. And finally I learned—" He pauses a moment, trying to put it into words. Then he shrugs. "I learned to just walk away. I learned how to not care if I made people mad or hurt their feelings when I did something they didn't want me to do. I learned that I *could* ignore what they said, and the world wouldn't end, as long as I didn't mind if they were upset. My sisters call this my stubborn streak. I call it a survival skill."

"And how have these various survival skills carried over into the other areas of your life?"

He looks thoughtful. "Well, obviously, I chose a field where it's practically a job requirement to be good at getting along with people. People usually are willing to talk to you if you seem like you're attentive and accommodating. If you really seem like you're listening, if you really seem like you care."

Not me, I want to reply, but in fact I can already tell that's not true. He *is* easy to confide in. He *does* seem like he wants to hear what I have to say. It's seductive. Which is annoying. My voice is a little crisp as I say, "That's not what I meant. How do you treat your friends? Your girlfriends? Are you patient? Do you compromise? Or do you just shrug things off and walk away?"

It's a moment before he answers, and I think maybe it's because I've offended him. I don't really care. He's pushed a lot of my buttons in the short time since I met him; seems only fair that I push a few of his. But when he answers, he doesn't sound irritated, exactly.

"You keep asking me questions like this, I'm going to start asking a few of my own," he says.

"You don't get to ask me questions," I reply. "Those were the conditions under which I agreed to have dinner with you."

"I don't get to ask you questions on a certain topic," he agrees. "But all bets are off when we start delving into personal relationships and how we handle them."

Now I'm smiling. "So? How do you break up with a girl? Do you buy her roses and apologize and explain that it's all your fault, you just misunderstood your feelings? Or do you move all your stuff out one day while she's at work and send her a text message to let her know it's over?"

"So far I've been more dumpee than dumper, so I have a hard time answering that question."

I know my expression is incredulous. "Yeah, I don't believe that for a minute."

He looks genuinely surprised. "Don't believe what? That someone would break up with me?" Now he looks astonished. "And is that a *compliment*?"

I'm grinning widely. "Come on. You're a good-looking guy. You have to know that—you can't be ugly and be a TV reporter."

"Wait, so, are you insulting me now? Like the *only* reason

someone would stay with me is because I'm good-looking?"

"You're cute. You've got a great job, or at least you used to. You're fun to talk to. You don't seem—at least as far as I can tell after knowing you for two hours—like you have some dreadful social defect. I mean, on the surface, you'd seem like a great catch. Not the kind of guy women generally break up with. So either you're a real jerk when it comes to relationship stuff, or you're lying when you say girls break up with you."

He's laughing and shaking his head. "You're funny," he says. "I wasn't expecting that."

Our food arrives before I have a chance to decide how I feel about that assessment. The platters are massive—mounds of green beans and mashed potatoes almost obscuring my meat loaf, a humongous salad and three dinner rolls accompanying Brody's chicken pot pie. Sometimes I leave with half the meal in a to-go box, the sensible thing to do. Sometimes I eat every bite. Screw it.

We suspend conversation for a few moments while we both make serious inroads into our dinners. I hadn't realized how hungry I was, but then I remember that my flat tire ensured that I didn't make it out for lunch. I think I had breakfast, but it's a pretty distant memory. And I love Corinna's meat loaf platter. The beans come straight from a can, but the mashed potatoes are made from scratch, and the ground beef is smothered in ketchup and some unidentifiable sauce, maybe canned gravy. Who cares? It tastes wonderful.

"This is the best pot pie I've had in ten years," Brody says when he finally stops eating long enough to make an observation. "I'm coming back every night and ordering the same thing."

"Every night?" I repeat, looking up from my food. "How often do you plan to be in Dagmar?"

He smiles. "Hey, I haven't given up on getting you to talk to me sometime. Not tonight, of course, but maybe in a few days. Or a few weeks. You never know."

"Yeah, don't waste your time. After tonight, I'm not going to answer the door if you drop by or pick up the phone if you call. We're having a little truce right now over dinner, but once we've paid the check, that's over."

"Well, that seems harsh. So is that your style ending relationships? You make up your mind, and boom, it's all over? No room for explanations or apologies or renegotiation?"

"You and I are not *in* a relationship, so the question doesn't apply."

"Hey, you asked me questions on this topic, so I get to have my turn." He wipes his mouth with his napkin and studies me. "That *is* how you do it, isn't it? Come to a decision, then slam the door."

I shrug. Except for Kurt, I've only had two serious boyfriends, and neither of them lasted more than a couple of years. They were both nice guys but, I don't know. They weren't strong enough. That was how I explained it to Debbie. They couldn't have taken the weight of all the anger and worry and fear that constantly pull down my heart. So I could never be completely honest with them, could never share myself with them. I held back, and eventually I didn't feel like holding on.

"Once you know it's over, there's no point in dragging it out," I say.

"Remind me not to lose my heart to you," he says.

"I don't need to remind you," I reply in a voice of exaggerated patience. "Because we're not going to be hanging out together anymore. You're not going to be coming back to Dagmar to get to know me better."

"Maybe not, but there are plenty of other people here. Some of them might be willing to talk about Ann."

All the easy camaraderie I'd allowed myself to feel in the past half hour instantly drains away. Once again, I'm filled with tension, anxiety, and prickles of anger. "No. You can't. You can't keep coming back and asking people a bunch of questions about my sister. That would be—please don't. Promise me you won't."

He carefully lays his fork down and stares at me across the table, giving me his absolute attention. "I'm a reporter," he says in a gentle voice. "Reporters ask a lot of people a lot of questions and try to build a complete picture of a situation from multiple viewpoints."

"I don't care," I say tightly. "I want you to stop."

His voice is still soft. "Why? What do you think they'll tell me?"

"They won't tell you anything! They don't *know* anything! There's nothing *to* know!"

"Then why do you care if I talk to them?"

"Because if *you* keep asking questions, *they'll* start asking questions! Ann was always a little weird, I guess, but not crazy-weird. But if you start asking people if she's a shape-shifter—if you start putting ideas into their heads—I mean—what will they say? What will they think?"

"I think it's most likely they'll think I'm a lunatic," he says. He shrugs. "Unless they already think Ann's a shapeshifter. Either way, nothing's going to change just because I ask them a few questions."

"Brody, don't. Please." I have a sudden inspiration. "If you promise me you won't ask other people about Ann, I *will* see you again. I'll—I'll meet you up in St. Louis for dinner some night, and you can ask me whatever you like."

"Wow, and now you're really insulting me," he says quietly. "You think I'm the kind of guy who stoops to emotional blackmail."

"I didn't mean it as an insult," I say a little wildly. "I just—I want to protect my sister."

"So what would it hurt?" he wants to know. "If people found out. If they believed she was a shape-shifter. What would change?"

I'm taken wholly aback. Of course it would hurt her. Of course it would change her life. It's never even occurred to me that this is a secret that can be spoken aloud. "Well, they would—I don't know, they'd try to lock her up or something—tell the authorities about her—"

He makes a face that clearly conveys an opinion of *nah, they wouldn't bother*. "I just don't see that being a public safety issue that gets the cops and the public health officials all riled up," he says. "Hell, people keep *tigers* in their apartments in *New York City*, and no one even notices until someone gets bitten. Shape-shifters aren't problematic unless they go around killing people."

He stops abruptly, and I pounce on his words. "Exactly! Like the last shape-shifter who was identified in St. Louis! The one who murdered five people."

He gives me an innocent look. "What shape-shifter? Don't you know that footage was doctored?"

I'm so mad I want to stamp my foot, or throw something, or hit someone, preferably Brody Westerbrook. "My *point* is, if people think that's what Ann is, they'll do something to her. Something terrible."

"Well, how about this?" he says in a reasonable voice. "You tell me your story, you tell me the *truth*, and you let me talk to Ann. I—"

"Talk to *Ann*!"

"That's right. And then when I include her in my book, I'll conceal the details. I won't use her real name or location, just her story. No one will be able to find her. Nothing to worry about."

I stare at him for a long moment. I realize I've been subtly, relentlessly, herded into a perilous and indefensible position. I am at the edge of the cliff, and I can either leap off or make my way forward onto the narrow, treacherous path that has been left open for me. Whether that path leads to safety or the slaughterhouse is still undetermined. "I feel like I'm a field mouse," I say, trying for bravado, "and the big gray barn cat has just offered me a deal."

He smiles. "And it's a good one. Will you take it?"

I draw a long breath. "I might," I say, making my voice careless, "if Ann was actually a shape-shifter."

He laughs and leans back against his cushions. "You *are* a fighter," he says in an admiring voice.

I pick up my tea and take a sip, just to prove I'm relaxed enough to swallow. I hope he can't tell what an effort it is. "So I guess we've reached an impasse."

He doesn't answer; he glances up to see who's approached

our table while we've been so focused on each other. I'm
expecting it to be Corinna's daughter, so I'm caught completely off guard when the newcomer grabs a chair from one
of the nearby tables and pulls it over to the booth. He
reverses it and drops down in a straddle, resting his arms
along the back.

"Hey, darlin'," he says in the exaggerated Ozark accent
that Missouri politicians affect because they think it makes
them sound like common folk. "Good to see you out on a
weeknight."

Just when I'm thinking the day can't get any worse, Kurt
Markham has come to call. I make no attempt to keep the
hostility out of my voice. "Yeah—not so great to see you,"
I answer. "Go away."

Kurt turns his high-wattage smile Brody's way. "She's a
real friendly girl, as I'm guessing you've learned by now."

If Brody were a bug, I'd say his antennae have gone
straight up, but I can't tell what he's thinking as he assesses
our visitor. Kurt's bulked up since his high-school days, so
he's burly through his chest and shoulders, but he's still in
excellent shape. He still looks good in jeans and a leather
jacket, and the short military haircut suits his strong, even
features. He's big enough, and powerful enough, that he can
look menacing if he wants to, but people generally respond
so well to his particular brand of charm that he doesn't have
to get ugly. At any rate, Brody is returning Kurt's smile with
one of his own. I don't know him well enough to be sure,
but I think the expression is a fake one. My guess is that
Brody's default response to any new situation is a cau-
tious amiability that generally conceals what he's really
thinking.

"Friendly enough," Brody replies. "I guess we all have our
moods."

I don't know how this could be more awkward and
annoying, but it seems pointless not to introduce them. I
manage it without any grace at all. "Kurt, Brody Westerbrook. A guy I know. Brody, Kurt Markham. Guy who lives
here."

"Markham," Brody repeats. "Any connection to that subdivision I passed on my way down here? Markham Estates or something?"

"That's right," Kurt says, pleased. "I own three parcels of property that I'm developing around town. This is a small community, but growing fast."

"The houses I saw looked nice. What do they run, maybe twenty-five hundred square feet?"

Kurt hitches his chair even closer. "That's about average, but we've got some floor plans that are right at eighteen hundred—for the retired couple, you know, looking to downsize—and then a few that are over four thousand." I can see him trying to appraise Brody's financial status. "You looking to buy something in this area?"

"Oh, I don't know," Brody says casually. "Right now I rent in the city, but I've been thinking it's time to put down roots, so I might be looking at houses in the next six months or so."

Kurt reaches into an inner pocket of his jacket and pulls out a card. "Well, anytime you want to look at houses down around here, you call me. I'll personally give you the tour. The Markham Estates subdivision is almost all sold, but we're still breaking ground on Markham Gardens, and you can pick everything—layout, floor coverings, kitchen cabinets, you name it." He glances at me. "You're a friend of Melanie's, I'll give you a special deal."

I give him a fierce look. "Maybe I'll just sell him *my* house and save us all a lot of trouble."

Kurt's perennial smile modulates into a look of earnestness that I trust even less than his friendliness. "You know that was a good offer," he says. "I've always been fair in all my dealings."

I catch Brody's quick look between us, but he doesn't say anything. "Not good enough," I say. "I'm still not interested."

Kurt scoots his chair back and stands up. He's smiling again, and he hooks his thumbs in the pockets of his jeans. "I haven't given up on you, Melanie," he says. "You'll be hearing from me again."

I can't keep myself from scowling at his back as he saunters away, pausing to exchange hellos and hand slaps with a few other patrons. Everyone knows him, of course. Dagmar doesn't forget its sports heroes, especially if they never move away, and Kurt has parlayed a decent sense of business and a huge store of goodwill into a thriving operation. There are plenty of people here who have jobs because he's employed them to build houses—or because the growing population has caused a boom in the need for services. Hell, even Corinna has talked about opening a second location. It's no wonder you always see Kurt down at her restaurant. She feeds him for free, and even I can't blame her.

"Well, now, there's a nice rural Missouri boy with some old-fashioned charisma," Brody observes when Kurt's out of earshot.

"He's a prick," I say, and Brody laughs.

"You made it obvious you think so," he agrees.

I turn back to give him my full attention. "Well, at least I didn't *flirt* with him like you did. 'Oh, I'm thinking about putting down roots and buying a house.' Lying to his face for no good reason."

Brody shrugs. "I want people to like me. If I act like I'm interested in what they care about, they're more apt to like me. Pretty simple."

"Why do you care if Kurt Markham likes you?"

"Maybe he'll be a source for a story I write someday."

I lower my brows and give him a minatory stare. "Don't you even *think* of asking Kurt about Ann."

He's grinning. "I bet he'd tell me anything. He seems like a real genuine and up-front kind of guy."

I'm so irritated by Kurt's appearance that I lose track of the main issue for the moment. "You don't really think that, do you? I mean, you weren't sucking up to him because you actually liked him, were you?"

"I wasn't *sucking up* to him."

"But you didn't really fall for his good-ol'-boy act, did you? Everyone else does, and it's so depressing."

"After—what, five minutes' conversation?—I don't think

I'm qualified to provide an accurate personality assessment, but I'd say he's a big fish in a little pond and pretty proud of it. Smug, a little sleazy, but basically honest. He's broken the hearts of a few local girls, maybe made a couple of deals that weren't entirely aboveboard, but he's not an out-and-out villain. Most people like him. He could be a better man, but he could be a worse one."

"I hate him."

"Why? He trying to buy your house out from under you?"

I'm impressed that he figured it out, given the oblique clues during the brief conversation. "Yeah, but I'm not selling."

"Why not? Isn't the money good enough?"

Because I'm afraid Ann won't ever come home again if I do. "Because I won't give Kurt the satisfaction."

Brody's putting the rest of the pieces together. "So—what?—he needs your land to complete the rest of his Markham Empire? And you're his last real stumbling block? You could probably make almost any kind of counteroffer, and he'd agree to it. Could be worth a lot of money to him."

"I'm. Not. Selling."

Brody leans forward as if he's hatched a brilliant idea. "Hey, want me to start investigating? Checking out his tax returns and land deals? I could dig up some dirt on his company, go to the newspapers with an exposé. Hell, I could probably make some stuff up, stuff that's bad enough that the city inspectors would suspend his licenses until he got it all straightened out. That would sure slow him down for a while. Want me to do that? Will you give me an interview then?"

I stare at him for a long moment in which I wrestle with the implications of his offer. Is he really the kind of person who would stoop to those kinds of dirty tricks? Am I the kind of person who would want him to? Is he revealing his true nature? Is he testing me? Is he joking? I'd love to see Kurt Markham taken down a peg or two, and I admit I'd feel pretty gleeful if he ended up in trouble because someone found out he'd been engaged in shady misdeeds. And if I thought he had the power to hurt Ann in some fashion,

I'd promote whatever lie was necessary to thwart or annihilate him. But surely we haven't yet come to that desperate pass. And surely I am not bitter enough to want to harm Kurt just because I can.

"And you accused *me* of insulting *you* earlier," I finally respond. "I don't know what's more disturbing. That you've made the offer or that you think I might accept it."

"Is that a no?"

"It's a no."

He smiles. "That's what I figured. You drive an SUV, but you have a heart of gold."

I rub my temples. I am suddenly so tired I think I might disintegrate into dust on the vinyl of the booth. "You're exhausting me. Let's pay the check and go."

On the words, the waitress reappears and lays the bill on the table halfway between Brody and me. Dagmar is a pretty conservative place, but times are hard; lots of women are the breadwinners in local families, and waitresses no longer assume that men are going to be picking up the tab. I know Brody's on a limited budget, so I consider reaching for the check, but then I remember that I haven't had a particularly good time, and I didn't even want to be here in the first place. It's true that, despite these limitations and the fact that I really, really shouldn't, I sort of like Brody Westerbrook, but I harden my heart. Let him pay the damn bill. Serve him right.

He doesn't seem to be having the same internal dialogue; he just scoops up the paper, studies it, and says, "Bargain." He lays thirty dollars on the table for a total that I know cannot have exceeded twenty dollars. Add to the list of his positive attributes the fact that he's a generous tipper. So far, the only fault he seems to have is that he wants to destroy me.

"Maybe next time we can have that root beer float," he says as he scoots out of the booth and stands up.

"There isn't going to be a next time," I say, but I'm not sure my voice is convincing.

He shrugs and leads the way to the door. "I'll let you think it over a few days, then give you a buzz," he says. "Maybe you'll have changed your mind."

I'm still smiling as we settle into the Jeep. Maybe because I'm amused that he thinks I'll ever betray Ann. Maybe because I'm pleased at the thought that I'll actually hear from him again. It's full dark by now, and the parking lot is crowded, so I turn on the headlights and back carefully out of my parking spot. Not until I put the Jeep in drive do I notice the car that's parked two spaces over and spilling its four occupants onto the lot. The large man is occupied with keeping the two small boys from running into traffic, but the woman is standing next to her closed door, and she's staring at me right through my windshield.

It's Debbie, out for a dinner with the family, though it's awfully late by Corinna's standards. I roll down the window, and call, "I'll tell you all about it tomorrow." I'm almost laughing as I turn out of the parking lot, but there's an edge of hysteria to the sound. Seriously, this has been one of the strangest days I can ever remember.

"Is that one of the people you don't want me talking to?" Brody asks.

I snort. "Ha. She's one of the few people I'd trust not to tell you anything. If there was anything to tell. She's my best friend."

"Well, good. Maybe you can introduce me sometime."

I don't answer, and we don't speak again until we pull up in front of the house. I've left the lamp on in the main room but forgotten to turn on the porch light, so very little illumination reaches the front-yard-cum-gravel-parking-strip that borders the road. The sounds we make as we slam the doors and crunch across the rocks are very loud in the night-time stillness. I come around the Jeep to stand next to Brody at the driver's side of his Honda.

"I guess you don't want to invite me in," he says.

"Yeah, you know, I feel pretty battered. I just want to curl up and watch TV or maybe go straight to bed."

He nods. "Can I phone you later in the week?"

Now that I can't see his face, I'm struck again by the quality of his voice, a soothing tenor with a timbre of sincerity. I don't want to be seduced by vocal cords, so I try to peer at him through the darkness. "You already threatened to do it."

I think he's grinning. "Yeah, but it would be nicer if I didn't think you were dreading the call."

I make a helpless gesture with both hands. "I don't know what to say. I'm never going to talk to you about Ann."

He shrugs. "Okay. Maybe. Or maybe once you get to know me, you'll realize you can trust me, and you'll decide to tell me stuff. And if not—" He shrugs again. "Still doesn't seem like it would be a waste of my time to hang out with you."

I try to suffocate the treacherous little flare of warmth that curls around my heart at the words. God, when's the last time someone flirted with me? "Lotta great entrées you still need to try at Corinna's."

"Yeah. Just what I was thinking."

I can't come up with anything else to say, so I point at his car. "You think you'll make it safely back home before your car breaks down?"

He pats his chest in the general vicinity of his shirt pocket. "If not, I can always call my new friend Kurt. I bet he'd come get me."

I laugh. Not the worst way to end this long and tumultuous evening. "I bet he would." I step away, backing up toward the house and waving good-bye. "Drive carefully!" I want to add *Talk to you later!* but it just sounds *too* friendly and I can't have him thinking he's completely won me over. But I stand on the low slab of concrete that functions as my front porch, and I wave and watch until he's back on the road and out of sight.

Then I sigh and unlock the door and step inside. And Ann uncurls from the couch and throws herself at me across the room, and the dreary menacing everyday world, without any warning at all, spins into a glittering brightness that hurts my eyes so much I start to cry.

CHAPTER FOUR

JANET

I have decided I need to write it all down. In part, to make sense of everything for myself, as if chronicling the events of the last twenty years could ever do that. In part, to explain those events to anyone else who might be surprised or bewildered or horrified by what I have done. I do not plan to disguise my identity, but I will omit some details about times and places. I don't want anyone to be able to trace my footsteps and discover where I have gone.

Once I have gotten it all on paper, the trick will be figuring out who to send the story to. There are so few people who love me enough to worry about what I might have done. And yet I cannot stand to take these actions without leaving behind some kind of powerful record. Though the story itself is so powerful, so primal, I almost feel as if it would write itself in the soil and stones—speak itself aloud in the winter air. I almost feel that if another woman stood where I am standing right now, she would only have to grow still and look around, and she would know without being told exactly what had happened. If I gave away details, if I drew her a map to this spot, would she understand then? Would she nod, and put her hand against her heart, and say with conviction, "I would have done exactly the same"?

* * *

At times it seems to me that I didn't start to live until I met him. If I try, I can remember the earliest days, the trailer in Arizona, the apartment in Michigan, the farmhouse in Iowa where the straight rows of corn stretched out so far in one direction that you literally could not see the end of them. I can remember the fights, the screaming, the sound of my mother playing the piano, the smell of my father's cigar smoke, but only when I exert great effort. Most of my childhood is packed away in boxes that I have stored in the cellar of my mind, and that I never take out, and that I never want to sort through again.

But I remember every minute of my new life. My true life.

It was night the first time I saw him—past midnight, I'm sure. A half-moon was just rising to remind me that, dismal though the world was, it could still produce wondrous illuminations. I was sitting on the back deck, cross-legged on the wood itself, careful to avoid the three rotted planks and wearing jeans and socks against the possibility of chiggers. It was a warm Midwestern June, and the air-conditioning had broken the week before. The inside of the house was unbearable for so many reasons, only one of them being the heat. In another few moments, I planned to stand up and make my way to the sagging chaise-style lawn chair unfolded on the edge of the deck, where I hoped to fall asleep.

When I saw movement deep in the shadows of the yard, at first I thought a possum or a raccoon might be trotting across the lawn, headed toward the garbage cans snugged up against the house. But it was too big, and it moved too slowly, to be one of those common nighttime creatures. A dog, then, maybe. The neighbors' collie from up the street was always getting loose. She was a pretty dog, but old and untended. It was clear her owners didn't care if she died of heartworm or if she got hit by a car. More than once I had kept her in our own yard for a day or two, combing out her matted fur and making sure she got a few decent meals.

My father hated dogs, though, and he always chased her away when he realized she'd been hanging around too long. Once he shot at her with a BB gun, but he was drunk enough to miss. After that, I snuck food to the collie's house without trying to entice her to stay at mine. She hadn't come back on her own, either, unless she had returned tonight.

But no. The shaggy shape moved closer to the porch, into the faint fey light of the insufficient moon. I had given up on fear a few years ago since it never seemed to keep me safe, but a tingle of primeval warning set all my nerves to dancing. It was a wolf, lean and a little mangy; it moved in a graceless, jerky pattern as it approached the deck. I quickly realized why. It was holding its back right leg curled up toward its body, an indication of an injury or infection or some kind of pain. Its mouth was open, and its tongue lolled out; I saw the narrow ribs heave in a shallow, incessant panting.

It came to a halt about five feet from the porch and stared at me.

I stared back.

I'd never seen a live wolf before, though my mother collected drawings and figurines of them, claiming the wolf was her spirit animal. This one seemed smaller than most, which might have suggested it was female, but for some reason, even when it was too dark to tell by looking, I was convinced it was male. Maybe it was merely young. By dim moonlight, I couldn't pick out many white markings against its dark coat, but its eyes were a chatoyant amber, a peculiarly light color against the dense blackness of its face. If night had decided to take animal form and come visit me, this was what it would look like.

I waited for the wolf to gather his strength and bunch his muscles and leap for my throat and kill me. My nerves had quieted; I was at peace. I lifted my chin just enough to show him the long, smooth line of my neck. I kept my hands down at my sides. I didn't even bother looking around for a weapon. I would rather die this way, all at once, I thought, than the way my mother had been dying for years.

But the wolf didn't leap, didn't move, didn't even settle on his haunches. He merely stood there, waiting, watching me with his unreadable yellow eyes. He even stopped panting and closed his mouth, shutting away the display of sharp white teeth. All I could hear were the summer sounds of crickets and bullfrogs and voluptuous green leaves whispering on a light breeze.

The wolf gazed at me as if, with all his being, he was wishing he could speak.

If he was not going to kill and eat me, perhaps he wanted something else from me. I kept my gaze on him as I tilted my head, considering. "Are you thirsty?" I asked in a soft voice. "Hungry? If you're hurt, maybe you haven't been able to hunt. If I go in to get you some food, will you still be here when I come back out?"

Impossible that he could understand me, of course, but he made the smallest sound, almost a sigh, the sound a dog makes when it's about to settle at your feet after a long day of running. Moving cautiously, not wanting to startle him, I rose to my feet and glided across the deck, soundlessly opening the door into the kitchen. There was a pound of hamburger defrosting in the refrigerator and any number of big Tupperware bowls in the drawer next to the stove. But I went first to the bathroom just around the corner from the kitchen and rummaged in the cabinet. Could you treat a wild animal's wounds with the rubbing alcohol and Neosporin you'd use on a human? Would he even let me get close enough to try? I didn't know the answer to either question, but I gathered the supplies anyway, stuffing them in the pockets of my jeans. Then I grabbed a flashlight from the hall closet and tucked it under my arm before tiptoeing back through the kitchen to pick up food and water.

When I stepped back outside, the wolf was exactly where I had left him. I approached carefully, not certain if murmured words of reassurance would calm him, as they would a dog, or incite him to attack. But I spoke them anyway, a meaningless stream of nonsense uttered in my most soothing voice. *Hey there, my name's Janet, I want to be your friend . . . brought you something to eat . . . you know I would never hurt you . . .*

The first thing I set down was the container holding the water, and he limped over to lap it up in an eager, noisy way. He kept drinking even as I unwrapped the beef and laid it in the grass beside the Tupperware bowl, but his eyes cut over to verify what his nose must have told him had appeared. *Dinner, and no effort spent catching it, either.* A few more licks at the bowl, which was almost empty, and his head swung over to investigate the meat. Almost immediately, he tore into the soft red mass and consumed the whole package in a few efficient gulps.

Close-up, I could see that his fur was dingy and matted. There were brambles in the long hair and probably ticks, too, buried under the layers. He looked lean and exhausted, and I wondered how far he had wandered from his home territory. I didn't think wolves roamed far enough south to visit central Illinois—but I only based that opinion on the times my mother had begged my father to move the whole family to Minnesota, where she might spot a wolf in the wild.

At any rate, his torso was pitiably thin under the rough coat, and his forelegs looked downright stringy. Summer seemed like the time a wild animal would fatten up, not slim down. Maybe he just wasn't very good at hunting. Maybe his back leg had been permanently damaged some months ago, and he was on the very knife-edge of starvation.

Maybe he was rabid and as soon as he finished his meal he would bite me and infect me and I would die an agonized and writhing death.

In those days, I saw death around every corner.

But if the leg was the problem, maybe I could do something about it. I switched on the flashlight, which caused the wolf to flinch away as if I had swung at him with a golf club, but then he steadied. He lowered himself to his haunches and regarded me in the reflected light. I pointed the beam down toward his chest, then between his back legs. As I suspected, male.

"I'd like to look at your leg," I said, still in that soft voice. "So don't snap at me when I touch you, okay? Maybe I can help you heal. Okay?"

He didn't answer, of course, and his gaze never wavered from my face. I muttered, "It would be easier if you would lie down and turn on your side."

Practically on the words, he dropped his forepaws to the ground and rolled to his left, his injured back leg now fully exposed to my view.

I felt my nerves twitch to life again; my whole body cooled with spooked surprise. He could not possibly have understood me. He was just tired—and now, replete with a meal, sleepy. And he lay on his left side because he knew from experience that lying on his right side would cause more pain. That was all.

"Good," I murmured, still in that reassuring tone, and dropped to my knees. "Just stay like that. And don't move— don't pull away—and don't bite me. I'll try not to hurt you. And maybe I can do you some good."

I played the flashlight over the back leg, finding the foot a mess of clotted blood and strips of skin. I couldn't tell if it had been chewed or caught in a trap or even torn by a rifle shot, but it didn't surprise me at all that he couldn't walk on it.

I found a fallen branch and propped up the flashlight so the beam illuminated the injury. "Don't bite me," I said again as I soaked an old washcloth with alcohol. "But this will probably hurt."

The minute the wet cloth touched the ripped flesh, his leg drew away, and his whole body shuddered. But he didn't scramble to his feet, either to attack me or to flee. He did lift his head a couple of inches off the ground to give me one long, fierce look. For a moment, I froze and stared back at him. What message was he trying to convey? Was he warning me? Beseeching me? Assessing my speed and swiftness to determine how fast he would have to move to catch me if I ran?

Then he rested his head on the ground again and stared straight before him. On a man, that expression would mean gritted teeth, a girding of the gut against an expected onslaught of pain. I licked my lips and touched the alcohol to his foot again.

This time he did not move.

He did not resist at all, over the next few minutes, as I disinfected the wound as best I could, as gently as I could. In my household, it was a common thing to deal with injuries; I was completely inured to the sight of blood. Once I was done with the alcohol, I spread so much Neosporin on the wound that I emptied the tube, then I wrapped the whole thing in a cocoon of gauze. A couple of hours of contact with the rich soil of Illinois's farmlands would destroy the pristine white of the dressing, but even so I thought the antibiotic properties of the ointment might make a start at fighting off infection.

"Good. Done," I told him, my voice brisk as my task was completed. "Though it would probably be better if you had that bandage changed every couple of days."

As I spoke, he rolled back to an upright position and came to his feet, though he kept his back leg curled up behind him, several inches from the ground. I could not rid myself of the notion that he was actually listening to me.

"I've been spending a lot of nights outside lately," I told him. "Come back anytime after midnight, and everyone else will be in bed. I'm usually in the lawn chair." I actually pointed. "So if I'm already asleep, come over and wake me up."

I spared a moment to think about how unnerving *that* would be, startled from a dream by a black nose against my cheek, opening my eyes to find this dark face, these amber eyes, hovering over me.

"But don't show up before nightfall," I added. "My dad's got five guns in the house, and they're all loaded. And he likes to shoot things he doesn't understand."

The wolf swung his head as if looking at the house for a moment and considering its inhabitants, then turned it back to make eye contact with me again. The flashlight was still on; I could see his whole face clearly. It was fuller than a collie's but just as intelligent. The triangular ears were pointed straight up—again, as if he were *listening* to me. He was so close I could see the layered pattern in the yellow eyes. And they watched me, as if he was waiting for me to go on.

I moistened my mouth again. "I'll put out water every night," I said. "In case you come back. But farther back, toward the edge of the property. I'll put out food, too, but—" I shrugged. "There are a lot of squirrels and possums around here. It might be gone in half an hour. Of course, I guess you could eat the squirrels and the mice," I added with half-hearted humor. "So it wouldn't be a total waste."

I faltered to silence. What was I expecting? A reply? An acknowledgment? The longer I knelt there, face-to-face with the wildest creature I had ever encountered, the more surreal the whole evening felt.

"Well," I said, and switched off the flashlight. Instantly, the world seemed plunged into bitter blackness; you would not have thought such a small light could be so profoundly missed. I heard, or felt, the wolf shake himself, as if he, too, was feeling the strangeness of the night and trying to cast it off before trotting back into his dangerous life. *I cannot be the kind of soft creature who takes food from a human's hand or I will never be able to survive on my own.* I had recently learned the word *anthropomorphizing* in an English class, and now it rose unbidden to my mind. It was the first time I truly understood what it meant.

"Well," I said again—but realized I was speaking to an empty lawn. That stealthily, without my noticing it, the wolf had slipped away.

I expected there to be some repercussions in the morning when my mother couldn't find the hamburger in the refrigerator, but I was lucky. She'd been too drunk to remember she'd taken it out of the freezer to thaw, so she spent most of the breakfast hour slamming through the kitchen, swearing under her breath and demanding what she was going to make for dinner. She had the Crock-Pot out, and a few cans of tomatoes and beans, so I supposed she'd planned to have chili stewing all day.

"I'm going to get home late," she fumed, "and your father will be hungry."

"Don't worry about it," I said. "I'll stop at the store after school and pick up something to make. Just give me money."

You never had to persuade my mother to accept help. She always closed with you on the first offer. "That would be great. Here's a twenty, is that enough?"

"I guess. Unless you want me to get milk and cereal and other stuff, too."

"All right. Thirty bucks. But I'm not going to the store again until Saturday, so you better make it count."

"Okay."

I knew how to stretch a dollar—I'd learned *that* lesson during the lean days in Iowa. So I stopped at the discount supermarket instead of the upscale one, where my mother preferred to shop these days, now that she and my dad both had jobs, and there was a decent amount of money coming in. I bought two deluxe family packs of hamburger, five pounds each. I knew I could rewrap them and stuff them in the back of the freezer, and my parents would never realize they were there. I picked up a bag of dog food, too, though I used my own money to buy it since it would have eaten up a huge chunk of my limited budget. I reasoned that a starving wolf wouldn't be too picky, and if the meal was good enough for a dog, it probably wouldn't hurt a wolf. More Neosporin, more gauze, a few apples, some bread, and I had my supplies for the week.

Though half of me believed I would never see the wolf again.

And all of me hoped I would see him that very night.

* * *

Dinner was an utterly silent meal, an improvement over the shouting of the night before, but the air-conditioning still wasn't working, so the house was miserable. My father left with a muttered explanation about playing poker with the boys. My mother took a romance paperback and a bottle of Riesling to the upstairs bathroom, where I heard her draw water for a cool bath. I knew from experience she could soak in the water for more than an hour; sometimes she even fell asleep in the tub. I often worried that she would slip too low against the porcelain and drown, too wasted to fight her way clear of the water. I would check on her several times in the next sixty minutes to make sure she was still alive.

But while no one else was around, I had a chance to lug the twenty-pound bag of dog food out to the edge of the property. We lived in a small town that crouched on both sides of Highway 55 as it wound its long, monotonous way from Chicago to St. Louis. Most of this part of Illinois was filled with croplands, and the undomesticated areas were mainly given over to prairie grasses, scrubby trees, and the marshy lands that developed around meandering creeks that flooded every spring. But our neighborhood opened up onto a few acres of woods and underbrush that folded into short, rocky hills—not the best farmland, and not good for much else, either. "It's a fucking wildlife preserve out here," my father had snarled when the raccoons and possums and squirrels began parading through the yard during our first month in the house. But my mother and I liked to watch the animals hunt for food or chase each other through mating season. She bought a book about identifying birds, though I think she only opened it once or twice, when she was sitting on the back porch and sipping a glass of wine. I was the one who put out stale bread in the fall and birdseed in the winter—and now I was the one to put out wolf-feed in the summer. The thought made me smile.

I ripped a hole in the top of the bag and left it on the very back edge of the property, in the V of a couple of deadfalls.

Returning to the house, I washed the supper dishes and put them away. Then I made sure my mother traveled safely from the bathroom to the bedroom, where she flung herself facedown on the bed under the ceiling fan and asked me to make sure her alarm was set. It had to be ninety degrees upstairs, and just the effort of climbing the steps had made me break out in a sweat.

"Maybe you should come outside for a while, at least until it cools down," I said.

She just grunted into the pillow. "It never cools down."

"Well—you want me to get you an ice pack? Put it on the back of your neck."

Her laugh was muffled against the pillows. "Sure. That would be nice."

I went downstairs and came back up in five minutes, but she was already asleep. I pushed aside her long black hair to set the ice pack on the top knob of her spine. She didn't seem to notice.

Back downstairs, I poured myself a glass of iced tea and carried it outside, along with a book and a flashlight. Once I was sitting in the lawn chair, I spent more time holding the cool, sweaty glass against my cheek than I did drinking the tea, and even so I passed the evening on the worn, gritty edge of wretched.

Darkness fell a little after nine. My father returned at quarter to ten.

The wolf came at midnight.

I had fallen asleep at some point, but I woke up as I tried to shift positions and nearly fell out of the lawn chair. I turned on the flashlight to check my watch; the hands stood at 12:04. Then I swept the beam around the perimeter of the yard.

The wolf was standing about ten feet away.

I swallowed a squeak and scrambled out of the chair, which collapsed noisily behind me. It seemed rude to keep shining the light at my strange visitor, so I tilted it down, toward my feet, but then I couldn't tell exactly where he was. The waning half-moon had barely poked its head above the horizon, and it wasn't going to be much help anyway. I took a deep breath and stepped off the porch, surrendering to hope and faith.

A few paces into the grass, I came to my knees, propped the flashlight on a branch, and extended my right hand. "Did you come back so I could bind your foot again?" I asked in a soft voice. "Do you think the Neosporin helped at all?"

There was the faintest rustle of movement, and the wolf's lower body moved into the circle of light. Three thin, sinewy legs covered in black fur—one carefully retracted leg covered with dirty gauze. Anyone who had happened to spot him from a distance must have thought he bore an unusual marking, a single milky-white paw. If he had been careless enough to let anyone catch sight of him.

"Let me take a look at that," I said, still in a soft voice, and he obediently lowered himself to the ground and rolled to his side. I was beyond being astonished by my ability to communicate with him. I simply cut away the bandage and picked up the light to examine the wound.

It actually seemed as if it had improved in the past twenty-four hours; at any rate, it wasn't worse. As before, I wiped it with alcohol, smeared it with ointment, and wrapped it with gauze. The minute I was done, the wolf pushed himself to a seated position and watched me with an unwavering regard.

"Did you find the dog food?" I asked. "But, hey, as long as you're here, would you like more ground beef? Just stay where you are."

He was still waiting for me when I returned with food and water. He didn't fall on either with the same famished gratitude as he had the night before, but he still polished off a pound of hamburger and most of a bowl of water. Then he lifted his head, licked his lips, and turned that yellow gaze on me once again.

I couldn't help it. He seemed so intelligent, so tame, that I had lost most of my fear, and I had an almost uncontrollable urge to reach out and stroke that dense black fur. Slowly, so he could see what I was doing, so he wouldn't be startled, I extended my hand, palm up, showing no threat, only invitation. He lowered his head to sniff at my palm; I felt the cold black nose against my skin, the faintest exhalation of his breath.

Then the swift, unexpected flick of his tongue against my wrist.

I stifled a gasp and held my hand motionless. He lifted his head and met my eyes for so long that gold and black began to reverberate in my head. Then a sound or a movement behind him caught his attention. His whole body tensed and he whipped his head around to stare at the empty property in back. Without another glance in my direction, he whirled around and bounded off.

I was left kneeling in the dark, my hand outstretched, my face blank with wonder.

The wolf came back every night for the next week.

I had begun taking long naps in the afternoon since I was getting very little sleep at night; the air-conditioning hadn't been fixed, but a cold front had moved through, making the house habitable again. I was supposed to have a summer job working at the local McDonald's, but I conveniently forgot to sign up for any shifts for the week. My father was mad, but my mom just shrugged, and said, "Let her cook and do housework for a while. You'll see, she'll *want* to go back to her job."

And I did—I was always looking for excuses to get out of the house—but not right now. Not this week.

Every time the wolf returned, I checked his injury and rewrapped his wound. I could tell he was healing, and by the sixth night he was putting weight on his back leg again. "Pretty soon now, you won't need me," I told him as I tied the gauze that night. "Your foot will be fine—you'll be able to hunt—you can go back to Minnesota or Canada or wherever you came from, and you'll be able to take care of yourself."

He opened his mouth in a slight pant, but I didn't get the

impression he was trying to cool down. Rather, he looked like he was grinning. As if the notion of leaving the state was so impossible that it was actually amusing, if he could only explain it to me.

"But I'll be here anyway, if you want to come back," I said softly. "Even when you're healed—even when it gets cold—I'll still come outside two or three times a week, late, like this, and see if you're around. Feed you if you look hungry. So come back if you need me."

He still regarded me, still panting. Now I thought the expression on his face looked considering. What would he ask me for, if he could speak? *Can you offer me a place to sleep when the weather drops below zero?* Or maybe *My mate had a litter, but she can't keep them fed. Can you bring a few dozen pounds of beef to our den?*

Or maybe nothing.

"At any rate, you need to come back at least one more night," I told him. "I think I can take the bandage off for good tomorrow. And then—then you can do what you like."

A noise in the house caught his attention. I recognized the thud, the curse, and the clattering sound that meant my father had come downstairs for a late-night snack and bruised himself against a half-open kitchen drawer. I glanced over my shoulder to see if there was any reason I'd need to go inside, and when I looked back at the wolf, he was gone.

I sighed and came slowly to my feet, switching off the flashlight so I would be invisible from the house. My father had turned on the stove light in the kitchen, and in its eerie glow I could see him bumble from the refrigerator to the sink, eating a piece of leftover chicken without bothering to get out a plate. He also knocked back a shot of whiskey before turning out the light and, I presumed, heading up to bed.

I stood there a long moment, debating whether or not I should go inside and sleep in my own room. Once the wolf disappeared for the night, he never came back, and the air was cool enough now that I thought it might be sixty degrees by morning. A chilly temperature for sleeping outside.

I eventually went inside, moving stealthily in case someone was still awake. I had barely stepped out of the kitchen when I heard another heavy thud upstairs, and the sound of my father's voice raised in frustration. My mother responded with a rush of angry words, though I couldn't make out what either one of them said. I slipped into the living room, picked up an old quilt folded over the couch, and headed back outside to sleep in the lawn chair as best I could until dawn made its sullen appearance.

I felt dull and somehow disappointed from the moment I woke up, though at first I couldn't figure out why. It was a Monday, always the least congenial of days, and this one had a particularly prosaic, unglamorous feel to it. As if the parties and amusements of the weekend were over; now it was time to admit that the dull, undifferentiated days, unexciting as they were, constituted ordinary reality.

Time to return to McDonald's and ask to work a few shifts this week. Time to think about going back to school in the fall, when I would enter my senior year. Time to start behaving like an adult with responsibilities instead of a teenager with an exotic fantasy life.

Time to realize that the wolf might never come back.

My boss gave me a stern lecture about missing a whole week, then signed me up for twenty-five hours in the next seven days. I took a stroll through Walmart on the way home, looking at notebooks and pens and folders before tossing through a few of the sundresses and jeans on the sale racks. I'd need to work more than twenty-five hours if I was going to afford any upgrades to my wardrobe. I always dressed in the least memorable clothing I could find—neutral colors, nothing fashionable, nothing daring—as part of my campaign to be completely invisible in my classrooms. Even so, some of my jeans were so old I didn't think I could wear them for another year, and I only had two shirts I actually liked. I'd have to buy a few things just to get through fall semester.

Dinner was unexpectedly cheerful, as my mother had gotten a raise, and my father had received a big commission check. My mother hummed in the kitchen as I helped her clean up after dinner—"Ode to Joy," always a good sign.

"You know what, Janet? You and I should drive into St. Louis next weekend and go shopping," she said when I mentioned my visit to Walmart. "We could go to one of the fancy malls there and buy you some really pretty stuff. What do you think?"

"Sure," I said, since it seemed unlikely she would remember this plan by morning.

She lowered her voice to a theatrical whisper. "We won't take your father. It'll be a girls' day out."

"Sounds great."

After the meal I saw her go into the living room, where my father was sprawled on the couch watching TV. She snuggled up next to him and began kissing his cheek, murmuring something that made him burst out laughing. After a moment, he reached for the remote and turned the television off.

I picked up a magazine and headed outside.

Not intending to, I fell asleep before the sun had even gone down and woke up a few hours later, chilly and a little disoriented. Oh yes—outside, waiting on midnight, waiting on moonrise, waiting on a mysterious visitor who might never return. I slipped inside briefly to use the bathroom, grab a sweater, and gather my usual supplies, then I was back on the deck, shutting the door behind me. I'd left the kitchen light on, and its warm yellow glow spilled out onto the wood of the deck, picking out all the warped boards and the route of June bugs waddling by.

Stepping out into the grass, I stared toward the back of the property, where nighttime and braided shadows made it impossible to see. Yet there was movement there, some stirring of leaf or branch as a creature moved soundlessly through the dark, and I didn't think it was just my longing and my imagination that created the illusion. Deliberate motion—a shape taking on mass and substance—something approaching me from the back of the lawn.

He came just close enough for his silhouette to be visible in the reflected light from the house, then waited. I knew that hesitancy, I knew that limp, I recognized that soul.

But it was not a wolf who had materialized out of the darkness. It was a man.

CHAPTER FIVE

MELANIE

God help me, Ann is in love.

It's the second thing I learn as we sit cross-legged on the couch, eating ice cream and talking late into the night.

The first is that she's alive. And healthy, too, by her own account, though I think her face is drawn, and she's painfully thin. Other than that, she looks good. She must have arrived a few moments after Brody and I left because she's had time to shower and change into some old clothes I keep on hand for her. She's even applied a little makeup, borrowing my rouge and mascara, so she looks flushed and vibrant. And happy, oh my God, so happy. I feel myself fill up on that happiness, refuel in a way I wouldn't have thought possible even half an hour ago. I was weary and sad. Now I feel like I could run a marathon or dance through the night.

"In *love*," I repeat. "So tell me about him! What's his name? What's he like? Where did you meet him?"

"His name is William Romano. I met him out at Elephant Rocks a few months ago, and we've been together practically every minute since, except when I was visiting you."

Elephant Rocks is a state park some distance southwest of Dagmar. As you might expect, it features a tumble of humongous boulders that look like elephants if you're not too much of a stickler. "Met him in the park? Like, at a campsite? He borrowed matches or something?"

Her laugh trills out. "No—silly. We were in animal shape, and we recognized each other."

It takes me a moment to digest this. "You can recognize other shape-shifters just by looking at them?"

"Not when I'm human, but when I've changed, and they've changed, yeah, I can. It doesn't happen very often."

"So—" I'm not sure how to ask the question. I've just spent an evening with a dangerously attractive man, doing that careful dance of invitation and rebuff; even using the tools of language and visual interpretation, I couldn't swear I'd taken an accurate measure of his personality. How do you perform the courtship ritual with a man when you can't even speak to him or read his expressions? "How does that work exactly? How do you get to know each other when you're both dogs?" I feel my expression change. "Or— well—*is* he a dog?"

Surely no one else on the planet who's asked her sister about a new romantic interest has ever been forced to pose that question.

Ann laughs again, the sound so light and merry it echoes through the room like a wind chime. "Most of the time. A golden setter. Sometimes he's a wolf or some other creature."

Ann has never taken any shape other than that of a white husky. My first reaction is surprise that this William has multiple alter egos. My second reaction is that I don't know much about shape-changing in general, and there might be as many varieties of it as there are practitioners. "Really? He can be more than one kind of animal? Is that common?"

She shrugs, not interested. "I don't know. I've only met a few others."

Something to explore on another day. "So. William," I prompt her. "What's he like?"

"He's quiet, and he seems shy, but he's really not. He just doesn't like people very much. He stays in animal shape most of the time unless he's visiting his brother and his niece. He's so smart. He knows all the parks in the St. Louis area, he knows where you can always find food and where you can find a protected area to spend the winter and how to earn money doing odd jobs if you *need* money and—well, that doesn't explain it very well. He's just—I feel *safe* with him. I feel like nothing will go wrong when he's around."

I admit, the first items on her list of virtues don't impress me much, but those last few sentences win me over. I'm an enthusiastic supporter of anyone who can keep Ann safe. "Is he cute?"

She giggles. "*I* think so. You'd probably think he was raggedy. You know, his hair's long and he doesn't shave very often and he looks kind of—I mean, I don't think he's had an easy life. And it shows." She puts her hands to her chest in a mock swoon. "But I love his eyes. And I love his face. And I love his smile."

"You've got it bad," I say, shaking my head. "So tell me more about him—how you met and how you got to know him and all that."

She resettles herself on the couch to get more comfortable. "Well, I was in the park late last fall. And I got injured." She gives me a fleeting look and decides to gloss over this part. "It wasn't serious. But it slowed me down. And I was digging through trash one afternoon, trying to find something to eat, but I couldn't find much, and my ribs hurt, and I was hungry, and I was about to give up for the night. And then William showed up."

She pauses as if to remember the scene. "He's bigger than me, in animal shape, and you never know about wild dogs because they can be mean. So I backed away from the trash, in case he wanted it, but he just kind of watched me. After a moment, I realized he was human, and he wasn't going to fight me, so I let him come close enough to sniff me."

I make a strangled noise and her laughter peals out again. "It just sounds so ridiculous!" I exclaim. "And a little creepy! He *sniffed* you!"

"And he saw the wound in my side and he investigated that and then he let me know I should settle down and wait for him for a while—"

"How? How did he let you know that?"

She makes a helpless gesture. "I can't explain it. I just knew. So I curled up under one of the picnic tables and waited for him. And pretty soon he came back with a squirrel he'd caught, and we had a meal."

"So—your very first date and he takes you out to dinner," I say, though part of me wants to gag.

She smiles. "I guess so. And then over the next couple of days we hunted together—and played together—and explored the park—and—I don't know how to explain it. We just got along."

"Without words. Without faces."

"Well, we had faces. Just furry ones."

"My mistake."

"But my side was still bothering me, and it was getting really cold, so William wanted me to spend a few nights someplace more protected than the park. So he took me to Maria's house."

I'm bewildered. "Who's Maria?"

"His brother's girlfriend. Actually, they're married now."

"Is she a shape-shifter, too?"

"No, but his brother is."

I try to make the question sound casual. "Why didn't you just come here if you needed some R&R?"

Her smile is mischievous. "I wasn't sure I was ready to let you meet him yet. But I was *dying* to meet his family."

"What did William tell them about you?"

She shakes her head. "I don't think he told Maria anything. I just showed up at her door and she put out a blanket and some food, and I spent a few nights there until I felt stronger, then I left."

"So she just thought you were a stray dog she was taking in?"

"I guess so. But—" She makes a face. "She talked to me like I was a person. Like she knew I could understand her.

So I think she suspected. Well, she's been around William's family for ten or fifteen years, so she understands about shape-shifters."

"Gee, maybe I should meet her," I say, my voice dry. "I'd love to know an ordinary person who understands about shape-shifters."

Ann looks intrigued. "Maybe you could. William says she's really easy to talk to, and he doesn't usually find people easy to talk to."

"And of course I'd love to meet *William* one day. Even before I meet Maria," I say.

"Yeah, I want you to, but—I know you'll think he's odd."

I reach over to flick the tip of her nose. Small and cute and upturned and human. When she's in canine form, it's small and cute and black and inhuman. "I think *you're* odd, and I like you," I say.

"You have to like me," she says. "You're my sister."

"But back to William. When did you both decide the time was finally right to take human shape and get to know each other that way? And was that weird? Like, you seemed different than you thought you'd be?"

She thinks that over. "I guess we'd known each other two months before we took human shape together. He can change at will, like I can—which isn't the case all the time, apparently. He said his brother never had a choice about changing—just one day he could feel the pressure in him, and he'd have to shift. That'd be hard, I think."

"Yes, yes, but get to the good part. So you became human—"

Her face is wreathed in smiles. "And he was cute. And we talked. And we held hands. And we kissed. And—" She hesitates, but her smile grows wider. "And stuff. And it was like I'd already known him half my life."

"It didn't seem strange? No awkward moments? I'd think it would be like meeting a pen pal for the first time. You *think* you know him, but then it turns out you don't like the tone of his voice or the way he laughs or he's shorter than you thought he'd be. Or something."

"Yeah, I guess it might happen that way but—it didn't." She shrugs again. "We already knew each other."

I've tried not to let myself think about what she meant when she said they kissed *and stuff*, but the girl is twenty years old. An adult, and a most adventurous one at that. "So you've had sex with him," I say, keeping my voice composed. "I hope you remembered to use a condom."

She laughs so much that it's a minute before she can answer me. "Melanie, we had sex when we were animals, too, and we weren't using a condom then."

I put my hands over my face as if I can block out the images. "Ugh! No! Gross, don't tell me that, I don't want those pictures in my head—la-la-la, I can't hear you—"

She's laughing again, even harder. "Well, you're the one who brought it up!"

"I was just trying to be the responsible older sister—" A sudden thought stops me midjustification. "Wait. If you're having sex without protection—could you get pregnant? Oh God, if you're pregnant when you're a husky, will you have—will you have *puppies*? This is too weird. I can't get my mind around it. Of course, I'll help you, I'll do whatever I can but—I mean, if I have to raise a litter of half-human puppies, I don't think I can move far enough out into the country to keep people from wondering."

Now the tears are streaming down her face as she gives in to hysteria. Me, I'm so flummoxed at this new notion that I can't bother to be amused *or* horrified. I'm just stunned. What on Earth will I *do*?

"Shape-shifters obviously manage to get pregnant and have babies," she finally says when she has herself back under control, though she's hiccuping a little. "Or there'd never be any more shape-shifters. But I won't get pregnant."

"If you're having sex—"

"William had a vasectomy last summer after his sister had a little girl. He figured they didn't need any more kids in the family. So we don't have to worry about it."

"He *told* you he had a vasectomy," I correct her darkly.

Some men will say anything to convince a girl to sleep with them.

"I believe him."

But then my attention is caught by what she just said. "His sister had a baby? Is his sister a shape-shifter? Is the baby?"

"The baby—they don't know yet. The sister was, but she's dead."

"What happened to her?"

"William doesn't talk about it. I think she was killed in an accident or something."

"So who's raising the little girl? The dad? Is *he* a shape-shifter?"

"The dad doesn't seem to be in the picture. William's brother and sister-in-law—"

"Maria?"

"Right. They've got the baby. I haven't met her yet. I haven't met anyone but Maria—and it wasn't like she actually realized she was meeting me."

"So his family members don't know about you?"

"They know he's spending time with me. We just haven't bothered with formal introductions."

I take a deep breath. "Well. I would love to meet William anytime you want to bring him by the house. Or—whatever. I could meet you both at a park somewhere if he'd be more comfortable in that environment." I hear a certain doubt creep into my voice. "Of course, I'd prefer to meet him in human shape, since I don't have the ability to communicate with animals, but if that's too difficult for him—"

She giggles again. "Yes, I think it would be best if he was a man when I introduced you. I'll see what he says. I'd like you to get to know him."

"Good. Looking forward to it." And then I remember. "God—no—wait, it might not be safe for him to come to the house!"

Her eyes widen. "What? Why? What's wrong with the house?"

I rub my forehead and glance at the clock. Impossible, but it's just past 11 p.m. I feel like I have lived through a hundred lifetimes in this single day, and it's not even midnight yet. "There's this—guy. He showed up today. He's a reporter, he wants to write a book about shape-shifters. He's somehow gotten it into his head that they exist—and he thinks you're one of them."

"Cool!" she exclaims.

I can't have heard her right. "Cool? It's terrifying!"

She shrugs. "Why? So someone finds out I'm a shape-shifter. So what?"

Am I crazy? All these years have I poured every ounce of my energy into protecting Ann, concealing Ann, trying to keep the world from discovering her glorious, impossible secret—but for no reason? Is there really no danger? Is there really no worry? "I'm afraid of what people will do to you if they find out," I say quietly. "We live in a world where people are murdered simply for being gay, and I'm willing to bet there are a lot more homosexuals than shape-shifters. Even if you weren't rounded up by the government for being some kind of alien life-form, I think your friends and neighbors would make your life a living hell."

She shrugs again and stretches her legs out. She looks nonchalant, even sleepy. "I don't really have friends and neighbors. If people are mean to me, I'll just go away."

I feel a chill bloom around my heart and blow frost along the curved inner planes of my ribs. But maybe she doesn't mean what I think she means. "You haven't been human much lately," I say casually. "Are you finding it more comfortable to stay in animal shape?"

"Oh, yeah," she says drowsily. "Everything's easier when I'm a dog. I have more energy—I can get around more quickly—I don't really notice the heat or the cold. I don't know that I'd ever be human again if it wasn't for you."

And now my heart freezes so fast the next time it attempts to beat it cracks right in half. "Oh dear," I answer, still struggling to keep my voice light. "Now I'll feel selfish and whiny if I say, 'But pleeeeease remember to be human every few months, Ann, because I miss you so much!' I hate to be a bother."

She gives a sleepy chuckle and lifts one leg to prod me with her foot. "Silly. Of course I want to see you. I'll always come home to visit, no matter how long I'm gone. Don't you worry about that."

I'll always worry. No matter what you say. Whether you're gone a day or a decade, I will spend every minute of that time worrying. Worrying about you is exactly what makes me human. "All right, then," I say, trying to sound brisk and cheerful. "I'll keep that in mind. Now it looks to me like you're about to fall asleep right where you're sitting. Go to bed. I'll let Debbie know I won't be in the office tomorrow, and we can hang out together and talk about sister stuff."

She yawns and pushes herself to a more upright position. "Sounds good. See you in the morning."

She ambles off to the second bedroom, the one the two of us shared when Gwen and our father still lived in the house. I send a text message to Debbie, then lock up the house. I'm so tired I do believe I might dissolve into a pile of quivering atoms the minute I stop concentrating on my various tasks. Still, after I've brushed my teeth and changed into my pajamas, I can't resist creeping into Ann's room and proving to myself one more time that she's alive and she's here.

She's fallen asleep with the night-light on, and I can just make out her features. Without her sunny personality to animate her face, she looks even more gaunt; her body is a bag of bones under the thin cover. I try to use cold reason to argue away my new spike of fear. *She seemed perfectly healthy when you were talking. She didn't seem to be lethargic or in pain. She's been eating raw squirrels and other people's trash! No wonder she's thin. She's just fine.*

But I can't seem to get out of the habit of looking at Ann and imagining her surrounded by perils. She's a grown woman now—a woman with a lover who sounds far better equipped to watch over her than I've ever been—so I know it is time for me to resign my post as her chief caretaker and guardian. But still I stand there, another five minutes, another ten, trying to guess the content of her dreams by the fleeting expressions on her face, and wondering how in the world I'll get by if anything ever happens to Ann.

CHAPTER SIX

I'm making breakfast the next morning, still in my pajamas, when the phone rings. I'm not surprised to hear Debbie's voice.

"Oh no you will *not*," she says in her hopelessly bad approximation of ghetto speak. "You will not be sending me texts at midnight saying you'll talk to me in a few days when there is *so much* to talk about *right now*."

I cradle the phone between my ear and my shoulder so I can open the microwave and check on the bacon. Still not done. "Yeah, I thought that wouldn't appease you."

"So who was that guy? At Corinna's last night? Were you on a date that you didn't tell me about? How could there be *anything* in your life you don't tell me about? We have no secrets, remember? Since we were fifteen? So tell me."

"He's a reporter. He wants to write a book about shapeshifters. He thinks Ann's one."

Her voice instantly drops to a register of dread and awe. "Holy Mother of God." See? Maybe I'm not crazy. Maybe anyone with any sense would realize just how terrifying this development could be. "What did you tell him?"

"That he shouldn't be ridiculous, there's no such thing as shape-shifters."

"So why did you have dinner with him?"

Ann wanders into the kitchen just then, barefoot, her hair wet from the shower. She's wearing the nightgown I gave her for Christmas last year, and it hangs on her body as if she has the contours of a plank of lumber. The damp hair throws her jaw and cheekbones into sharp relief. She could model for an anatomy class that was too squeamish to examine actual skeletons.

I feel my throat close up with concern, but I try to focus on the conversation. "That's kind of a long story. Part of what I'll tell you next time I see you."

"Is part of the story the fact that he's really cute?"

That makes me laugh. "I guess so. Look, I'll talk to you later. Ann's eating pancake batter out of the bowl, and I need to take a shower and figure out how to spend the day."

"Are you coming to work tomorrow?"

"Depends. I'll let you know in the morning."

I hang up and swat Ann's hand away from the mixing bowl, though in truth I'm glad to see she has an appetite. "Here. I know you're used to eating your meals raw, but here's a whole *stack* of pancakes already cooked that I've kept warm in the oven."

"It smells wonderful. I can't remember the last time I've had bacon."

We eat breakfast and talk about what we want to do today. Well, mostly I make suggestions and she nods agreeably; clearly she doesn't have any preferences. I think if I'd been isolated from society and culture for two months, I'd have a whole list of activities I'd be eager to engage in, from seeing movies to shopping for clothes. But it's obviously pointless to upgrade a wardrobe she rarely uses—equally pointless to go out for a pedicure when she'll be running barefoot through the wild in a few days—and I can't imagine that a picnic in the park would hold much allure for someone who eats *all* her meals outdoors.

We're scraping off the plates and loading up the dishwasher when she has an inspiration. "Let's look through the photo boxes," she says. "We always say we're going to sort them and put them into albums. So let's do it."

"Ooooh, excellent idea," I reply, drying my hands on a dish towel. "They're all in three plastic bins in the closet in my room—the ones with red lids. You want to get them out while I take a shower? Just set them on the living-room floor so we can take up as much space as we need."

Within the hour, we've spread pictures and report cards and letters and other random mementos all over the central rug and the hardwood border of the living room, and we're trying to create piles of photos that represent a rough time line of our lives. In one stack go all the images of our father and me before Gwen and Ann showed up. In another are the photographs snapped after Ann had been born but we still had a house in Kirkwood. There are three groupings for our lives since we moved to Dagmar—early ones that include Gwen and our father, later ones in which she is mostly absent and he is clearly fading, and the most recent ones, in which both of them, for different reasons, are missing altogether.

Ann picks up a photo from that first Dagmar stack, a picture of the four of us in front of a Christmas tree when she was six and I was sixteen. Ann, as always, looks like she's just run inside after some joyful event that she can't wait to tell us about; she's bursting with health and excitement. Gwen has one hand on Ann's head, one arm wrapped around my shoulders. She's smiling, too, and she exudes a warmth and affectionate cheer that, by this time, I had come to realize was false—or, if not false, wholly unreliable. My father and I wear matching expressions of tension and desperate hope. We'd been in Dagmar about a year when this shot was taken (though I have no idea who operated the camera; so few outsiders ever set foot inside the house). We still believed that it might be possible to live a functional, if not entirely ordinary, existence in our new home—that we could control Gwen's increasingly erratic behavior, conceal Ann's bizarre condition, hold down jobs, finish school, carry on like normal people—but we were starting to fear that we could be wrong. Not that we ever discussed our situation out loud. We couldn't. We didn't have the words.

Ann is quiet for such a long time, as she studies our faces, that I finally have to prompt her. "What are you thinking?"

"Wondering about my mom. Do you think she's still alive?"

"I don't know. I think it's been nine years since we've seen her, hasn't it?"

Ann nods slowly, still staring at the photo. "You can't tell, just by looking at her face."

"Can't tell what? That she's a shape-shifter?"

"That she's the kind of person who'd leave. She looks like she'd hold on forever if she loved you."

"I think she did love you," I say softly. "I think she loved you, and Daddy, and even me."

Ann lays the picture down. Her face is stern. "Not enough, obviously."

"Not as much as we wanted," I correct her gently. "I think she gave us as much as she could, and when it was all gone—" I shrug. "So was she."

"When did you find out about her? When did you know she was a shape-shifter?"

"After you were born. After *you* changed for the first time. She used to sneak off for a week at a time, every few months—just be gone, not tell us where. It made Daddy crazy, at least the first couple of times. She never told him where she went or why. I think he must have just assumed she was going on benders or something. He stopped asking her about them, but he would get this—dark look every time she disappeared. Each time she came back, he was a little more remote. Like he'd realized he couldn't trust her anymore, but he still loved her, so he had to figure out how to accept her absences.

"Then you came along, and everyone in the household adored you, and at first we thought it would be okay. I mean, Gwen was *crazy* about you. Some days she carried you around, even when you were sleeping, because she just wanted to look at your face. And Daddy never said it out loud, but I'm sure he was thinking that, now that you were here, Gwen wouldn't abandon us again. You'd keep her home. But you were about three months old when we got up one morning and she was gone."

I'm quiet a moment, and Ann doesn't say a word. She's picked up another photo, this one showing the two of us in matching Christmas outfits. I think our grandmother had selected them and mailed them from Texas because *I* was too old to want to dress like my little sister, and neither my father nor Gwen managed that kind of organizational planning. I'm scowling, probably because I hate the dress; Ann, of course, is smiling.

"You were six months old the first time you changed shapes," I say. She's heard this part of the story a million times, but she doesn't stop me as I launch into it again. "I'd put you down for a nap and you fell right asleep. I went to the bathroom, and when I came out I checked to make sure you hadn't woken up. And there in the crib was a little white puppy, curled up asleep, right where you'd been."

"What did you *think*?"

"I spent a couple of minutes not thinking at all. Just staring. But, you know, I was only ten years old. I think kids tend to see the world as it is, not how they expect it to be—they're more open to magic. I knew I had put you in the bed. I knew that no one had had time to come in and steal you and leave a puppy in your place. So I knew it was you. I just didn't know what to do about it."

"So you ran downstairs to tell Daddy and my mom—"

"And Daddy said, 'What? Don't be ridiculous.' And Gwen started crying." Wailing and sobbing and carrying on in a way I had never seen a grown person behave. I was actually more afraid of Gwen's histrionics than I was of the transformed little sister sleeping peacefully in the upstairs bed. "She started moaning, 'It's all my fault, it's all my fault, I was afraid this would happen.'"

"And what did you think *then*?"

"I don't know what Daddy was thinking, but I remember very distinctly what was going through my head. I'd read too many fairy tales, maybe, with evil witches and jealous women trying to poison their stepdaughters. I thought Gwen had mixed up some kind of terrible potion, and she'd meant to give it to *me*, but somehow you had gotten it by mistake. It was so weird—I had that thought with such clarity—even though I really liked Gwen and she'd always been very good to me. It was just the old archetypes exerting their power, I guess."

"So then she finally calmed down enough to speak—"

"And she told us what she really was. Said that whenever she left the house for extended periods, she would go somewhere and become an animal—usually a bird, an eagle or a hawk. Said that she came from a whole family of shape-shifters, though she never saw her brothers or sisters anymore. That she knew she might pass on the genes if she ever had children of her own, but she'd taken the risk anyway because she loved us so much, she wanted to make a family with us."

"What did Daddy say?"

"He was watching her like he thought she should be committed to an asylum. I mean, it was obvious he thought she was either insane or she was making the whole thing up. He started talking in this calm, reasonable voice. 'Now, Guinevere, you know that transmutation of people into animals is physically impossible—'"

"Transmutation," Ann repeats, savoring the word like a piece of chocolate.

"That's what he said. You know the way he would talk. 'I'm afraid this must be some elaborate fantasy you've concocted. Maybe you've been under too much stress.' And she yelled, 'Stress! I'll tell you about stress! Living a lie like this for so long, afraid you'd find out, afraid you'd stop loving me—' And a lot more like that. I'd always hated being in the room when adults were arguing, so I just went back upstairs and sat on the floor in your room. I thought maybe you'd be a baby again but, no, still a dog. I got a book and sat there and read for the next half hour, while they kept fighting downstairs."

"Why didn't he just ask her to change shapes and prove she was telling the truth?"

"Oh, I think he did. But Gwen didn't have that ability—at least she said she didn't—at least, I never saw her change shapes. Neither of us did. I think the only reason Daddy ever came to believe her was because of you." I pause for a beat. "I believed her right away. I don't know why."

"So then what happened?"

"So finally they both came to your room. Gwen was still crying, but in a quieter way, and Daddy had developed this sort of stony calm. I could hear him talking as they came up the stairs. 'You'll see—Ann will be in her crib and she'll be perfectly normal, and then maybe you can stop spouting this nonsense.' And they walked in the room, and there was a puppy in the bed, and Daddy stopped as if he'd been shot by a bullet. Then he started shouting at me. 'Where's the baby? What happened to the baby?' And I said, 'I think that *is* the baby.' And he actually jerked me to my feet and slapped me. He'd never done that before. Never did it again. But he was so afraid—he really thought you'd been kidnapped or that I'd thrown you out the window or something. And he shook me and just started roaring at the top of his lungs. *'Where is the baby?'* And then—"

"Then my mom pointed at the crib, and said, 'Look! Look!'"

"And there you were, transforming right before our eyes."

Since then, I've seen Ann alter shapes a hundred times, maybe more. It's a strange, beautiful, unearthly sight that never fails to leave me both awestruck and greatly unnerved. But that first time . . . it was almost impossible for us to believe the evidence of our eyes. The husky's white fur seemed to glow, then take on the faintest pink tint, then smooth itself into skin. It was like watching a Saturday morning cartoon, or a really good CGI movie. You know someone's manipulating the special effects, but it looks pretty damn real to the naked eye. It took about a minute for the sleeping dog to become a sleeping baby, wholly oblivious to our shock and disbelief. She was naked; the diaper I'd put on her just an hour ago made a small, discarded shape beside her on the bed.

Gwen started crying even harder, and ran over to the crib to scoop Ann up in her arms. My father just stood there, shaking his head, and whispering "No" over and over. I do believe that's the moment his brain started misfiring as over-loaded circuits tried and failed to process what he had just witnessed. He was a man of science, but he had always considered science a rock, not a frontier; he could not believe it would present him with unexplored and impossible options.

I was young enough to accept miracles as commonplace. "I told you so," I said. "You should apologize for hitting me."

But he only gave me one long, agonized look and blundered from the room.

"How long did it take before Daddy just got over it and went on like everything was normal?" Ann asks.

"I'm not sure he ever really did get over it. I think part of him never entirely believed it was true—even though he saw the evidence, at least in you, over and over again. I think part of him had this thought at the back of his head that he was crazy, that this wasn't really happening. That he'd lost touch with reality." Which made it easier for him to slip into dementia, not even putting up a token fight. Why bother? He was already delirious.

"But he loved me."

I scoot over to drop a kiss on her sleek blond hair. "He *adored* you. He changed his life for you—moved down here, restructured his job, created a place where you could be safe. He didn't love Gwen quite so much after that, though. He felt she'd lied to him, maybe even betrayed him. They didn't fight anymore, and I think they still—you know—"

"Had sex," she says.

I brim with laughter. "Yes, but I meant—they still cared about each other. But it put a rift between them. And then she started disappearing for longer and longer intervals, and he stopped caring that she was gone—" I shrug. *And then he got sick and she went away and you grew up and here we are.*

"I think she's dead," Ann says.

"What? Gwen? Why do you say that?"

"Because I think she'd come back for me if she wasn't. Just to see me. I don't remember her that clearly, but when I think of her, she's always hugging me. Or laughing with me. Or singing to me. I remember her holding my hand and skipping with me down the middle of Bonhomme Highway." She gestures to the two-lane blacktop that runs outside the front door. "You were at school, and Daddy was at work. It was early afternoon. She said there wouldn't be any traffic, we'd be just fine. So we skipped down the road, running for the shoulder every time we heard a car coming. We almost got hit, like, three times."

"I'm glad you never told me this story before!"

"But it was fun. It's how I think of her. Happy. A little loopy. But—she loved me. So I don't think she would have left me behind for good unless she had to."

It's never been clear to me which would be worse—thinking your mother was dead or thinking she'd abandoned you. But it's obvious Ann has figured out the answer for herself, and I have no qualms about supporting her.

"I think you're probably right," I say softly. "Because nobody would ever abandon *you* of her own free will."

The moment is laced with such sadness and sweetness that it almost feels sticky. I cast about for something to say to change the mood, but I needn't bother; Ann's already been distracted by something else in the box. She makes an *oohing* sound as she carefully lifts out a hand-painted ceramic bank shaped like an A-frame house, maybe a five-inch cube with a pointy top. There's a slot in the roof to drop coins in, and a small, removable door on the front to provide access to the treasure inside. The door is held in place with a tiny padlock, just now snapped shut.

God knows why it has been stored in this box among photos and papers; I haven't even thought about it for at least five years. "I remember this!" Ann crows. She shakes it gently to make the coins inside chime against the china walls. "Our *special* bank where we only put valuable coins."

"Grandma used to send us real silver dimes and quarters, remember? The ones made before 1964. And we'd put them in here. I think there were a couple of silver dollars, too."

She rattles it again. "How much money do you think is in here? Let's open it up and see."

I shake my head. "I don't know where the key is."

She gazes at the bank. "I don't want to *smash* it to get the money out."

"Of course we're not going to break it! I think that bank was Grandma's mother's or something. I mean, it's really old. It's probably worth more than the coins inside."

Ann holds the ceramic house up to her ear and shakes it once more, listening intently, as if she will be able to determine its exact contents through sound alone. "There's something else in here," she says with conviction. "Paper? Did we drop in dollar bills, too?"

"I don't think so. Maybe Daddy did when we weren't looking."

She sets it down and stares at it thoughtfully. "I wonder if we could pick the lock. It doesn't look that complicated."

"Well, go ahead and try," I invite. "But I don't think *I'm* enough of a criminal mastermind to do it, even if it's simple."

"I bet there's fifty dollars in here, easy," she says. "Maybe more. And aren't silver coins worth more than their face value?"

"I have no idea. Anyway, why do you care? You don't even *spend* money."

"I just like the way it feels. When I was a kid, I had a big jar of pennies—remember?—and I'd dump them on my bed and just dribble them through my fingers. I could do that for hours."

She shakes the bank again and I pluck it from her hands, crossing the rug on my knees to set it on the coffee table next to the couch. "You *are* going to break it if you keep doing that. I'll take it to the hardware store sometime and see if I can find someone who can make a key for it."

She pouts ostentatiously. "I'll be gone before it's open."

I try not to be hurt by this hint that she's not planning to stick around very long. "Well, I'll make you a promise. I won't sell or spend any of the silver coins until you're back again."

"You better not."

The phone rings just then, startling me, and I jump up to answer it. Ann says, "Oh, I forgot."

"Forgot what?" I say over my shoulder.

"Someone called while you were in the shower."

I hold up a finger—*Tell me later*—as I pick up the receiver. "Hello?"

"Would you like an estimate on having your carpets cleaned? Our technicians will be in your area tomorrow—"

I hang up without answering. Rude, I know, but not as rude as intruding on my time with Ann. Still on my feet, I turn back to her, still sprawled on the floor. "Who called?"

"A guy? He said he had a package for you? He told me his name—" She searches her memory. "Brady Westinghouse?"

I feel every surface of my skin tighten with chill. "Brody Westerbrook?"

"That's it."

I come sit near her, perching on the edge of the couch, holding my body very still as if too much random movement will cause my limbs to detach and clatter to the floor. "He has a package for me? What package?"

"I don't know. He just asked if he could drop it off later today—"

"He *what*?"

She's startled at my frantic exclamation, and her big eyes open wide. "He asked if he could come by. I said I thought we'd be home. What's wrong?"

"Did he ask you who you were?" I say urgently.

"No—well, he knew who I was. He said, 'Are you Ann?' And of course I said yes."

"Jesus, Jesus, Jesus," I say, kneading my hands together. I don't know what to do. Run from the house right now, drive Ann somewhere safe? But where's safe? What if he shows up just as we're leaving and follows us wherever I go? What if we tear out of here before he arrives, and he parks on the gravel edge of the lawn and simply waits for us to return?

It's clear this isn't a guy who gives up easily. I don't know how long I will be able to evade him.

Ann's scrunched over to touch my hand with hers. "Melanie—what's wrong? Who is it?"

"That guy—that reporter I told you about. The one who wants to write a book about shape-shifters."

Astonishingly, she laughs. "Oh, for goodness' sake! You scared me! I thought it was, like, a doctor bringing you bad news or something. Or—you know—one of those bad guys in movies. Someone who was going to beat you up for not paying back the money you borrowed."

For a moment, I am so supremely irritated at her suppositions that I actually forget to be afraid of Brody. "*What?* You think I'd get mixed up with—forget it. Look, we have to get out of here. I don't want him talking to you."

She shrugs and seems to settle more comfortably on the floor. "I don't think it's such a big deal. Hey, maybe it's a good thing. He sees me, I act normal, he goes away."

"He doesn't seem like the type who just *goes away*," I say grimly. "And, anyway, you never in your life acted normal. I don't know why you think you can start now."

That makes her laugh. "You just watch."

"So—did he say when he'd get here?"

"Yeah, like, in two hours?"

She doesn't sound certain, but I glance at the wall clock anyway. When was I in the shower? It has to be almost two hours ago. "That means he'll be here pretty soon. Look, just—just don't say much. Smile a lot. Guys forget everything else when a pretty girl smiles at them."

"Maybe I should take my bra off," she suggests.

"Ann!"

"Well, maybe it'll distract him."

I lean over to put my hands on her cheeks and press hard enough to make her mouth purse into a fishlike O. "Just don't sit there and tell him what it's like to be a shape-shifter, okay? Just promise me you won't do that."

Her voice is distorted by the way I'm holding her face. "I promise."

From outside, through the front door, I hear the muffled sound of a car motor, then wheels crunching over gravel. I drop my hands and stand up, ready to run or rumble. Flight or fight.

"Company," Ann says, and flows to her feet.

I force myself to walk calmly to the door, but I've opened it before Brody's even made it up the lawn. The first thing I notice is that he's not driving his little Honda. What's parked next to my Jeep is a small blue pickup with a dent in the front fender and a sprinkle of rust across the hood. I'm able to summon a supercilious smile by the time Brody has stepped onto the small porch and greeted me with a smile of his own.

"New set of wheels?" I ask politely. "And so environmentally friendly, too! What happened to Earth Day Every Day?"

He looks rueful. "I had to take my car in to the shop. This is my neighbor's truck. It didn't seem like the time to be lecturing him on fuel efficiency."

We're on either side of the screen door, watching each other warily through the mesh. I'm not sure I'm going to invite him in. "I hear you have a package for me?" I say.

He has a small manila folder under his arm and now he extends it. "Yeah, I thought you might like to see a couple of stories that ran about Kurt Markham in the *St. Louis Business Journal*." He shrugs. "No real dirt, but he was fined a couple of times for missing a few inspection deadlines. Stuff like that."

I don't open the door. "You could have mailed them to me."

He shrugs. "Yeah . . . Actually, when I called this morning, I just planned to leave a message on your machine, 'cause I figured you'd be at work. And then someone answered, so I thought, well, if you were *home* and I was in the vicinity—"

He has no reason to be "in the vicinity" except to annoy me, and we both know it. But before I can say so, Ann skips up behind me. Even with my back to her, I can feel the radiant friendliness of her expression. "Hi," she chirps.

Brody smiles as he takes her in. I wonder how clearly he can make out her features through the screen. "Hey there," he replies. His eyes move back and forth between our faces. "The coloring's different, but it's easy to see you're sisters."

Ann laughs. "That's right. I'm Ann." She reaches past me and pushes the door open. "Come on in."

He catches the edge of the door with his left hand since he's still holding the folder in his right, but to my surprise he stays put. "I think Melanie would prefer that I didn't," he says.

"Ann's been gone awhile," I say in a frosty voice. He knows this from yesterday; he's not likely to have forgotten. "We have a lot to talk about."

"Sure. Have fun. We'll catch up later."

He turns to go, but Ann's voice stops him. "Oh, don't be silly. We were just planning to go out to lunch. Why don't you come with us?"

Brody and I both swing around to stare at her. His expression is speculative; mine is dumbfounded. Her own is both devilish and angelic, the look Ann has always worn when she's getting into trouble. "You want the reporter to come to lunch with us?" I ask, my voice ominously uninflected.

"Well, I'm sure he'll be bored," she says. "Since all we'll talk about is old friends and people he's never heard of."

Now Brody looks at me. "I won't ask any questions," he says, an interrogative lilt in his voice. "I'll just eat my meal and listen quietly. You won't even know I'm there."

"I suppose," I say, my tone still chilly. "You *are* awfully forgettable."

He laughs while Ann exclaims, "How rude!" I just shake my head. "Let me get a jacket," I say. "Ann, you, too."

"I'm not cold!"

"It's sunny out, but it's only about sixty degrees," Brody says, choosing this moment to support me. "Better bring a sweater or something."

"And put some shoes on," I add, glancing at her feet. I lift my eyes and briefly meet Brody's. "Five minutes," I say. He nods and releases the screen door so it settles back against the frame. He might notice that I never did invite him in.

Looks like I'm about to have my second meal in less than a day with a man I believe to be my nemesis. My life becomes less comprehensible by the hour.

CHAPTER SEVEN

I'm efficient, and Ann never did spend much time primping, so it is indeed no more than five minutes before we've combed our hair, applied the most rudimentary of cosmetics, and donned outerwear. But I can't bear to leave all the old photos strewn across the rug, so we take another three minutes to gather the piles and set them inside the bins and push the boxes against the wall. Then Ann trips blithely out of the house, and I follow, pausing just to lock the door.

Ann makes a little *oh!* sound of surprise and grabs my arm just as I've twisted the key. I turn to see what's caught her attention, but it's immediately obvious: a shaggy, skinny, gorgeously hued golden setter on its haunches about ten yards from the house. It looks healthy enough, but its fur is matted and it has that stringy appearance that often marks strays and feral dogs; if it were human, I'd say it looks grungy.

I'm guessing that it *is* human and that my opinion wouldn't change if I saw it in its alternate state.

Ann turns to me and speaks in a voice pitched to carry to Brody, who's leaning up against the truck. "Oh—look— it's the neighbor's dog. Can we leave him some food and water before we go? He looks hungry."

I unlock the door again. "Sure. Whatever you think he'd eat. I've got some leftover roast beef in the casserole dish on the bottom shelf of the fridge."

"That would be perfect."

I let her scoot back inside to fetch the appropriate menu items, resigned to the fact that she won't think to transfer the meat to an old dish that I don't mind sharing with a dog. I could go in and help her, but I feel like I need to stand guard and make sure Brody doesn't get it into his head to approach the newcomer and begin interviewing it about its life as a shape-shifter. I can't tell from Brody's expression if the appearance of the setter has tripped any alarm bells in his brain. He rests patiently against the truck, his arms folded, his face incurious, his posture relaxed. It's possible he hasn't even noticed the dog.

Quickly enough, Ann comes back outside, precariously managing the casserole dish and a big metal bowl full of water. I lock up behind her as she carries these items to the setter, who comes to his feet at her approach. I try to seem as though I am only casually interested in watching her greet him as she sets down the dishes. She ruffles the fur on his head, runs his ears through both hands, and then bends down to whisper something to him. His tongue flicks out and catches her across the nose and lips. She laughs, straightens up, and pats his head again before stepping away. We converge on the truck.

"You want to drive or should I?" Brody asks.

The truck only has one front seat; not ideal. "I will," I say.

"I'll get in the back," Ann offers, and pretty soon, we're on our way.

"We're not going to Corinna's?" Brody asks, as I turn left out of my drive instead of right.

"We have to get pie at Slices," Ann informs him. I can tell from the sound of her voice that she's perched on the very edge of the seat, which means she's not wearing her seat belt. "It's my favorite place in Dagmar. We *always* go there when I'm home."

"I'm sticking with you two," Brody says. "Pretty soon, I'll know *all* the cool hangouts."

Slices is located in a small strip mall about five hundred yards from the interstate. We're a little late for the lunch crowd, so I know we'll get a good parking spot and a booth near the front window, not that the view is inspiring. The neighboring businesses are a bank, a nail salon, a mortgage company, and an empty storefront. The surrounding landscape is nothing but parking lot, feeder roads, highway, and wide, empty stretches of dun-colored land waiting with great passivity for spring to turn it green, thereby improving it by only a fraction. But you don't come to Slices for the surroundings.

Brody almost gasps as he steps inside. The first sight that greets any visitor is the long glass-fronted counter filled with about thirty different varieties of pie. The "mile-high apple pie" is the most impressive, but the cherry, blueberry, black currant, French silk, lemon meringue, and other choices look equally luscious. The rest of the place is fairly bland, a brightly lit white-and-chrome space that gives an impression of airiness. I'm sure the intended effect is to make diners believe there's plenty of room for dessert.

"I think I'm in heaven," Brody says.

Ann smiles at him, then at me. "I knew I liked him," she says.

I just shake my head and follow the hostess to our booth. I sit first, and Ann, just to be contrary, takes the opposite side, making Brody choose which sister he will sit beside and which sister he will watch. She probably thinks he plops down next to me because he likes me; I'm sure it's because he wants to study her.

"I already know what I want," he says, when the waitress tries to hand him a menu. That causes another ripple of laughter from Ann.

"So do I," she says.

I had glanced at the menu board when we walked in, so I know the soup of the day is chicken noodle. "And so do I," I finish up. "The soup and salad special and a slice of cherry pie."

"Pecan pie and turtle cheesecake," Ann says.

I frown at her. "You have to eat a meal first. I have to fatten you up."

"I had breakfast. That's a meal. Anyway, I bet there are more calories in a piece of cheesecake than there are in a bowl of soup."

The waitress nods. "There are."

"Bring her a cup of soup anyway. And the pie," I say.

"I'm getting *three* pieces of pie," Brody says. "Maybe four, but I'll let you know later. And don't even bother trying to bring *me* soup."

Ann glances at me. "He's perfect."

"Because he eats badly? You have a fine set of criteria."

"Because he's capable of whimsy."

This has Brody laughing. He still seems utterly relaxed; he's leaning back against the cushions, one arm along the back of the bench, not quite close enough to touch my shoulder. "My sisters would call it irresponsibility, but it's the same general personality trait that's been with me since I was a kid," he agrees. "I'm glad somebody appreciates it."

"Melanie's so serious all the time," Ann says.

"I can be fun," I defend myself. "I can be spontaneous. I just can't survive on sugar and carbs."

I've been wondering how we are possibly going to manage a conversation where most topics, from *What do you do for a living?* to *Tell me about your childhood*, are off-limits. But I have underestimated my companions. Ann is already beaming at me, reminded of some memory.

"Yes, you *can* be fun," she says. "Remember the first winter we lived here? And it snowed, like, two feet right before Christmas? You built a fort for us on the front lawn. And you had me make a mound of snowballs. And we crouched in the fort and threw snowballs at all the cars going past until Daddy came home and made us stop."

"Seems a little lawless for Melanie," Brody observes.

"I had anger issues even back then," I say. "I wasn't displaying criminal tendencies, just relieving some of my frustrations."

"Did any of the passing motorists take exception to being pelted with snow?"

"They might have, if we'd actually *hit* any of them. I have dreadful aim, and Ann was only five or six. No arm power."

"I'm better now," she assures me.

"I always loved winter," Brody says. "My two older sisters usually wouldn't come outside if there was more than a couple of inches of snow on the ground or the temperature was below twenty. So I had the yard and the swingset and all the toys to myself."

"What about your youngest sister?" I ask.

"Yeah, Bethany wasn't so prissy, so she'd be out there sometimes, but it's a lot easier to share with two than four."

"Bethany and Brody?" I repeat. "Are they all B names?"

He rolls his eyes. "Bailey, Brandy, Bethany, and Brody."

"And they all end in a Y!" I exclaim. "I bet you all just hated that growing up."

"Particularly Brandy," he says. "The rest of us would sort of like our names, if they weren't all matchy-matchy, but Brandy always says, 'They might as well have named me Tequila and *totally* destroyed my life.' Professionally, she goes by her middle name, which is Amanda, but none of us call her anything but Brandy."

"Brandy Amanda?" Ann asks in delight. "Do you ever slip and call her Brandy Amandy?"

He cracks up. "We do it on purpose. She *hates* it."

"I don't even know her, and yet I find myself filled with sympathy for the wretched life she must have led," I say.

He makes a rude sound. "Don't waste your pity on her. She's tough. She'd eat you for breakfast if you stood in her way."

"What's she do?" I ask, and then wish I hadn't. He now has the right to ask the same question about *my* sister.

By his half-smile, I guess he's realized the same thing, but he just answers the question. "She's a corporate lawyer. Travels all over the world making deals. Making money. She's our success story."

I'm intrigued. "Huh. Usually the middle children lead the calm, stable, traditional lives. The older children are the overachievers, and the younger ones are the clowns and entertainers."

Brody and Ann exchange glances. "I think we were just insulted," he says. *"Clowns?"*

"Oops, forgot my audience."

"I don't know about you," Ann tells him, "but I'm *very* entertaining."

Brody half turns to give me an appraising look. "I guess the jury's still out on whether or not I am."

Fortunately, our food arrives before I have to answer that. Brody arranges his three plates in front of him and debates aloud whether to eat them one at a time, or take bites out of each one in sequence. Ann reaches for her cheesecake, but I lean across the table and swat at her hand.

"Soup first," I say sternly.

She sighs but obeys, spooning up a mouthful and slurping it noisily just to get on my nerves. "So what about your other sisters?" she asks. "What do they do?"

"Bailey's a psychiatrist and Bethany's a teacher. God, this is the best blackberry pie *ever.*"

"And you're a reporter for a TV station?"

"Used to be," he says around a mouthful of food. "Now I mostly do freelance writing and editing."

Ann's gaze is absolutely limpid, her voice innocent as a child's. "And I understand you're writing a book? What's it about?"

For a moment, the silence at the table is absolute. My stomach has clenched so hard and so fast that I've momentarily lost the ability to breathe. I can't even summon the will to glare at Ann as she deserves. God, for a girl as fresh-faced, as happy as she is, to be so bent on self-destruction. She would run headlong to disaster and be laughing the entire way.

Brody swallows, sets down his fork, and takes a drink of water. Then he smiles at both of us. "Ah, let's not talk about boring work stuff," he says. "Tell me some more fun stories about when you were kids."

It's a moment before I realize that, given Ann's wayward

sense of humor, this topic could be just as dangerous. That's because all my brain cells are coping with my sense of shock that he would so kindly and deftly turn the subject away from the one I dread above all others. It's deliberate, too; he's made me a promise, and by this action, he is demonstrating that he'll keep it. He is trying, without much fuss or flourish, to prove to me he is someone I can trust.

I am staring at him, but he still appears to be giving most of his attention to Ann. Even so, I catch his quick, sideways glance in my direction, his faint smile. "Man of my word," he says, so softly my sister might not have heard him. "Always."

Ann has flopped back against her seat cushions, still highly entertained. So maybe she has caught the byplay after all and correctly interpreted it. At any rate, she finally decides to behave. "Well, the most fun we had—at least as *I* remember it—was the time we took a family vacation out to Yosemite Park," she begins.

The dangerous moment is past. Egged on by Brody, Ann and I alternate the narration of that disastrous trip out to California. Ann got carsick and threw up all over the backseat; we were stranded on the roadside when the alternator went out; the motel refused Daddy's credit card because Gwen had forgotten to pay the bills for three months running; and I had to be rushed to a local emergency room when I fell on the parking lot and broke my arm. By the time we get to the dinner where the busboy spilled an entire pot of hot coffee in Daddy's lap, she and I are laughing so hard that we can barely complete our sentences. Brody is roaring right along with us—even the waitress chuckles as she brings Brody a fourth piece of pie, just because our laughter is so infectious.

I suppose there's a lesson here somewhere, a moral about how even the most appalling events of your life will, at some point when you reexamine them, turn into treasured memories. How pain and bitterness will fade and even transform, alchemize into something that is both sweet and comforting. Perhaps I am supposed to be discovering that even the things I fear might one day become the things I embrace.

But all I really take away, all I really learn from the afternoon, is how happy I am when I can spend an entire day with my sister.

We linger long enough over lunch that I feel we need to leave an awfully generous tip for the waitress. Brody doesn't protest when I announce that I'm buying the meal, which I rather like; he's not much of one for macho posturing. Then again, a boy with three older sisters probably never got much chance to try it. It's close to three by the time we're back at my house, and the day has gotten grayer and chillier.

"Looks like it's going to rain," I observe as I pull up next to the borrowed truck. "You probably ought to get going before the storm."

He nods as we all clamber out. "You're probably right. Ann, it was great to meet you. Maybe we can talk more someday. Melanie—" He narrows his eyes, then smiles. "I'll be in touch."

Ann insists on standing there and waving good-bye until he's backed out and pulled away. Then she turns to me, and exclaims, "He's *cuuuuute*!"

"He's obnoxious," I say, though silently I admit that he's also cute. I make shooing motions to get her started toward the door. Then I think to look around, but there's no golden setter in sight. I spot the dishes still in the grass and head over to collect them.

Ann trails behind. "He isn't! Not at all! And he really likes you."

"Oh yeah? How could you tell?"

"The way he looked at you whenever you were talking. Even when your stories were boring, he was fascinated."

"My stories aren't boring!"

"Some of them are."

By this time, we're at the door. "Well, I just want to thank you for being circumspect in the stories *you* chose to tell—but first I want to yell at you for asking him about his book. What were you *thinking*?"

She bubbles over. "I was thinking how much fun it would be to ask him questions about shape-shifters, and find out what he's learned, and act like I was trying to believe him but secretly thought he was crazy."

I unlock the door and push it open, balancing the empty dog bowls in my free hand. "You're the most troublesome girl," I inform her. "I don't know why I miss you so much when you're gone."

She doesn't bother to answer. She gives a little squeak of pleasure and pushes past me to run into the living room. I manage not to drop the dishes as I realize, with a start of fright, that there's a strange man standing in my house. Strange to me, anyway, not to Ann, and I try to quiet my pounding heart by telling myself this must be William. The shape-changer that Ann has fallen in love with.

He's taken her into an embrace, so at first I can't collect many details about his physical appearance, but he's definitely as thin and rangy-looking as the underfed setter. His coloring is different, though—he's got brown hair, just now pulled back into a ponytail, and the permanent-tan skin that I associate with a Mediterranean heritage. Spanish, maybe, or Italian. He's wearing baggy nondescript clothes that he might have scrounged from a Goodwill office's throwaway pile, and he's not wearing any shoes.

He gives Ann a final squeeze, then they fall away from each other and she urges him over to me. My first thought is that he's too old for her. His face is attractive in a sort of starved-Christian-Bale manner, but it's weathered enough to make him appear forty years old or more. A bad match for twenty, I think.

And then I wonder. A shape-shifter's life is a hard one; even Ann is starting to look older than her age. I promise myself I will make no assumptions, and I manage to smile at him as they halt in front of me.

"Melanie, this is William. William, my sister. Mel, I told him where he could find the spare key. I hope it's okay that he just let himself in?"

"Of course. It's your house as much as it's mine." I'm not

sure if I should offer to shake hands—William just doesn't seem like the traditional sort—but then I think it would be rude if I don't. I extend my hand and he instantly takes it; I can't help but notice how rough and callused his palms are. "I'm happy to meet you."

"Yeah, Ann talks about you all the time." He lets me go and looks around. "And the house. Growing up here. I wanted to see it."

Ann still has her arm looped through his, and she's leaning against his shoulder. You'd think she was a high-school girl with her prom date, she looks so happy to be with this guy. "I wasn't expecting him," she says. "I was going to stay with you a few days, then meet him again, but—" She squeezes his arm. "He missed me."

"Well, I'm delighted to have a chance to get to know him," I say, though in truth I'm a bit unnerved. And a tiny bit put out. This William gets to spend weeks—months—with Ann, while I only have a few days, and now he's intruding on the brief time we have? It seems so unfair.

One time Debbie told me that whenever Charles's mother comes to visit, Debbie can feel the old woman's resentment emanating from every bone and hair follicle. If mother and son happen to be having a quiet conversation in the kitchen, and Debbie walks in, the older woman gives her a look of such burning reproach that Debbie quickly mumbles an apology and backs out of the room. *She hates me because I get to spend all this time with him, and she doesn't. But if Charles isn't around, she actually likes me a lot. It's so weird.*

I have turned into Charles's bitter, possessive mother. It is, indeed, so weird.

I gesture toward the kitchen. "Are you hungry? We just had lunch, but I could make you a sandwich or something."

The arrangement of his features doesn't change much, but I can tell he's amused. "No, thanks. Ann fed me right before you left."

Which is when I remember why I'm holding the empty dishes. "Oh! Right! Well, take a seat, let me put my things away, and we can hang out and chat for a while."

A few minutes later, we're all sitting in the living room, making what feels to me like awkward conversation. I might be the only one who notices. William's settled onto the couch in a position so deliberate that he might be posing for an 1880s-era photograph—one where he would have to sit absolutely still for the eternity it would take for the image to form in the plate. He doesn't seem nervous; I don't think he's worried about making a good impression on me. I think he's just not used to sitting on furniture so he doesn't know how to relax into the cushions. Ann is curled up next to him, shoulder to shoulder, her hand laced with his. She's still beaming. In a more fanciful mood, I might say her blond hair is glowing.

"So! Tell me about yourself," I invite him.

He shrugs so minimally he might not have moved his shoulders at all. "Not much to tell. Born down near Rolla. Have a brother and sister, but my sister's dead. My brother and his wife are raising my niece."

"Yes, Ann mentioned that. I'm sorry to hear about your sister."

He shrugs again and doesn't answer.

Small talk is clearly pointless, so I go straight for the big stuff. What the hell. "So tell me about your shape-shifting. I don't know how it works for anyone except Ann."

Now he nods infinitesimally, as if this is a question he was expecting. "I'm usually not human more than three or four days a month. If that. Used to be I'd go months without shifting, but I like to check in with Lizzie often enough so she won't forget me."

"Lizzie?"

"My niece. So I head on over to Maria's about once a month."

Maria? Oh, I remember. The brother's wife. "Ann told me you don't know yet if the baby is a shape-shifter."

That almost invisible smile again. "Right. But probably. The rest of us all are."

"When do you—is there a typical time for someone to first display signs—I mean—"

"Usually by the time you're three you'll have changed. Sometimes the first week of your life. It varies."

This is surely the oddest conversation I've ever had with anyone. "And Ann said you're usually the shape we saw earlier today? The setter?"

He nods. "Sometimes a wolf. Sometimes other things. I can usually direct it—I can say what and when. Dante's never been good at that, though he's learning."

"Dante?"

"My brother. He can't control what shape he'll become or when he'll turn. He just feels it coming over him, and he can't stave it off." William glances down at Ann. "But I've showed him some techniques I use to control it, and he's been able to shift between shapes a little more easily. It's helped a lot."

"Ann can control it," I say, feeling absurdly proud. Hey, it sounds like that's a hard thing to do, and yet she mastered the skill when she was just a child.

Ann stirs and sits more upright though she still doesn't release William's hand. "So why aren't you at Maria's right now?" she asks. "I thought that's where you were going to spend the week."

"They were headed over to Illinois to spend some time with Maria's mom, so no one was going to be at the house. Figured I might as well come here."

"How'd you find the place?" she asks. She looks over at me with a grimace. "Everything's changed so much! All that new construction! I swear, Mel, I wandered around for an hour in dog shape before I could figure out where I was."

I try not to show how much this alarms me. This has always been my greatest fear, of course—that Ann will forget the way home. I force myself to take a casual, even irritated tone. "That damn Kurt Markham," I say, shaking my head. "He's buying up every tract of land between here and Highway 55 and turning it into some megasuburb. I'm surprised *anyone* can find their way. All the developments look the same, and they all have practically the same name— Markham Manors, Markham Estates, Markham Big-Dick Bungalows—"

Ann giggles and William laughs out loud. I continue on, even more aggrieved. "He keeps offering to buy this place, but I tell him I won't sell."

"That's right," Ann says with zest. "Anything to thwart his plans of world domination."

"So I think he's just going to keep building stuff around me," I end with a sigh. "Next time you come here, there will be Markham Mansions on both sides of the house and across the street."

Ann has lost interest; she's turned back to William. "So how *did* you find our house? I never brought you here."

He offers that faint smile again. "Looked it up online when I was at Maria's. Google will draw you a map to any address in the country."

"Terrific," I say. "Nice to know there's no such thing as privacy anymore."

His grin widens. "Shows you a satellite map, too. Picture of your house, right there on the computer screen. Great stuff."

I don't know why I find it odd, incongruous, that William is adept at online data retrieval. It's not like shape-shifting is an old-fashioned, courtly pastime incompatible with twenty-first-century technology. And yet I find it natural to picture him bemused by televisions and cell phones, maybe even afraid of horseless carriages when they rattle by. "Well, I'm glad you were able to locate the place," I say. "How long were you planning to stay?" I glance at Ann to include her in the question.

They exchange looks, communicating silently. "A few days," William answers. "Unless you'd rather not have me underfoot."

"Not at all. I'm glad you're here," I say. "Just let me know if there's anything you need, and I'll be happy to get it."

Ann is smothering a yawn. "I think what I need is a nap," she says. "Humans stay awake too long. I always forget that until I'm back in this body."

She comes to her feet, pulling William up beside her, and they head to her room. I stand up, too, just for something to do, then move indecisively around the house for a few minutes. I rinse the breakfast dishes and load the dishwasher and think about moving the photo boxes back to my room and think about calling Debbie and try to decide if I like William and try not to think about Brody Westerbrook and how attractive he is even though he wants to write that terrible book. I decide that I really ought to go to work tomorrow, even though Ann's only going to be home for a few days, since William's presence changes the dynamic, and I'm not sure I can get through too many more conversations with him; best, perhaps, to limit the attempts to dinner. And that makes me start wondering what I should prepare for dinner tonight since I assume everyone eventually will be hungry again, despite our various lunchtime meals of leftovers and pie. I don't know what William likes to eat, but he doesn't strike me as being too particular. Maybe I'll just order a pizza. The biggest benefit I've been able to identify in the construction of Markham Manors is that the Papa John's folks are now willing to deliver in my neighborhood, something that was unheard of five years ago.

I hear the soft sound of a door closing and even softer footsteps coming up behind me. Ann always runs through the house, so even before I turn around, I know it's William. I summon a smile as I face him.

"What can I get you?" I ask. "Something to read? Something to drink? I can turn on the laptop if you want to find a map to someone else's house."

He doesn't bother to smile at this sally. "I'll take a beer if you've got one."

"A beer sounds really good."

We stand in the kitchen for the next few moments, sipping a couple of Schlafly Pale Ales in what I am able to persuade myself is companionable silence. Then William sets his bottle on the counter and gives me a look that's so serious I feel a shiver slalom down my spine.

"Maria and Dante aren't out of town," he says. "I just wanted to come here because I'm worried about Ann."

CHAPTER EIGHT

JANET

His name was Cooper, and he was sixteen. And he was like no boy I'd ever met before. Soft-voiced and preternaturally calm, he was imbued with an inexplicable gentleness that sat oddly against the wildness that marked his face and loaded his every gesture. He was ungainly and thin, too tall for his weight, with ragged black hair that he'd clearly cut himself, probably using a knife and not having access to a mirror. He had a poet's face, the lips too full, the nose too bony, the cheekbones famished. His eyes were huge and striking, a complex brown instead of the wolf's distinctive amber, but it was clear they remembered everything the wolf had seen.

He was wearing a pair of jeans so ragged they were scarcely better than scraps, and a Cardinals T-shirt that looked brand-new. The shirt, he confessed, was stolen; the jeans were part of a cache he kept in a hideaway about ten miles up the road. Sometimes the items were still there when he came back to his human shape, and sometimes they weren't. He'd learned to adapt.

We sat side by side on the edge of the deck, our feet in the grass, and talked the whole night through.

"What do you want to know?" he asked.

"Everything. I guess you should start at the beginning."

He spread his hands in a gesture of uncertainty. His fingers were extraordinarily long, eerily graceful. They looked as if they should belong to a concert pianist. "I don't remember the beginning anymore. It seems like I was always living with my mom, and always turning into a wolf. I don't remember the first time it happened."

"Have you always changed into a wolf?"

He nodded.

"And how long do you stay in that shape?"

"It varies a little bit, but it's usually a couple of weeks as an animal, a couple of weeks as a human."

"And—does it happen all at once? What does it feel like? Does it hurt?"

His eyebrows drew together as he tried to figure out how to reply. "It's not painful," he said at last. "But it feels like—stretching too far. Like one person is pulling on my shoulders and someone else is pulling on my feet, and my ribs are splitting open, and at the same time I'm yawning so wide my jaw's about to crack. And then everything snaps into place, and I'm the wolf again." He glanced at me. The kitchen's yellow light painted squares and other patterns on his cheek. "It's the other way around when I'm becoming human again. Like someone's squishing me together into one big ball, making my bones fit into places that are too small. So there's all this pressure, then—suddenly—it's fine."

"Do you get any warning? Can you tell you're about to change?"

"I can now. When I was a kid, it was harder. But these days I can feel—something. My hands start tingling, and it's like my blood starts itching. Usually about a day before it happens, one direction or the other. So I know to be someplace where people aren't likely to see me."

"Do you go to school?"

"Not anymore."

"Can you read and write and do math and all that stuff?"

"Sure. I'm not very good at it, though."

"How'd you get hurt?"

"A fight with a wild dog. I had a bite on my shoulder, too, but it healed faster."

"Why didn't you go to your mom's place so she could take care of you?"

He turned his head away and was silent for a long moment.

"Cooper?" I asked. "Why didn't you go to your mom's? Does she live in a big city, somewhere you can't get to her when you're in animal shape?"

"She doesn't see me anymore," he said at last.

I'd touched him every night when he was in wolf shape, and far more danger to me than he was now, but I hesitated before laying my hand gently on his forearm. "Why doesn't she see you?" I asked in a soft voice.

"A few years ago, she met a guy. Davey," he said. "She didn't want him to know about me, so she told him she and my dad shared custody. Every time I was turning into a wolf, she'd get me out of the house and tell Davey I was with my dad. So she'd drive me somewhere—like Boy Scout campgrounds or a state park—and set me free. Then she'd come get me in a couple of weeks. She always left behind a backpack of food and clothes, so I would be all right if I changed shapes before she came back."

"What happened?"

"Davey followed her once. Thought maybe she was seeing my dad on the side or something, I don't know." He made another one of those uncertain gestures with his expressive hands. "They had a big fight, they broke up, he came back. Told her I was a freak, I should be turned over to a zoo. Stuff like that."

I was filled with indignation. "So she kicked you out? For a *guy*?"

"Not at first. Not until the baby was born."

"Oh," I said. I could instantly see how that would change the whole situation. "Uh-oh."

"Yeah. The minute Davey found out she was pregnant, he was after her to turn me out of the house. And she kept saying, 'No, no, no, Cooper's a good boy, he'd never hurt me or you or a baby or anyone.' But once the baby came home—"

He shook his head. "I don't know what happened. I don't know if *he* looked at me or *she* looked at me or if *I* looked at the baby, but something changed. One night she came into my room and gave me five hundred dollars and told me I had to leave by morning. Said Davey would kill me if he ever found me at the house again. So I took the money and left."

"How old were you?"

"Thirteen."

I just stared at him. I was seventeen and fully human, and I couldn't imagine trying to feed myself, clothe myself, take care of myself all on my own—with only five hundred dollars in hand. "What did you *do*? I mean, the wolf could survive on his own, I guess, but the boy—"

"I had a rough few months," he admitted. "I already knew how to live in the wild—I could build a fire, and catch fish, and you'd be surprised at how much food and other stuff campers leave behind in the parks. But it was February when she made me leave, and winter was hard. I think I almost froze to death a couple of times. I found myself wishing I could just be a wolf all the time. At least I'd be warm." He shrugged. "But I made it through, and summer was easier. And then I made some friends."

"Wolf friends or people friends?"

His smile was like a glimpse of moonlight on a cloudy night, brief and breathtaking. "People friends. There was a church group that brought poor kids to the parks to go to camp in the summer. They'd set up a couple of folding tables and cover them with food and yell for everyone to come and get it. So I'd run up with all the other kids and stuff my face. Most of the kids didn't know each other, so it didn't matter that they didn't know me. I just ate as much as I could and ran off before they started playing volleyball or whatever. It was great."

"And no one ever questioned you?"

"Well, eventually. Every week, there'd be different kids at the camp, but some of the same grown-ups were there all the time, and after a while a few of them noticed me." He gave me a sideways glance and that quick smile again. "But, like I said. Church group. Trying to do good things and take care of people. So one day a couple of them came up to me and said they'd noticed I'd been hanging around, and they wanted me to feel welcome to stay for the whole experience. They even had an extra sleeping bag so I could camp out overnight with everyone else. A sleeping bag! It was the closest thing I'd had to a bed for six months."

I wanted to cry; I wanted to cover my mouth to hold back my horror. But Cooper spoke so casually that I felt I had to show the same serene acceptance of his fate that he did. "How much did you tell them about yourself?"

"Not much," he said. "I told them I was living on my own. Told them I didn't want to move to town and go live in the boys' home like they said I could. One of them, James, he told me he would let me spend the summer 'running free,' as he put it, but as a concerned and responsible citizen he was duty-bound to inform the police that there was a minor living on his own in the woods behind the Boy Scout camp, and that he was pretty sure someone would come looking for me."

"That was actually a nice thing for him to do. The *right* thing to do."

"Sure, maybe, but I couldn't go to a juvie center any more than I could go to a boys' home."

"Did anybody ever come out to the park looking for you?"

"Yeah, a couple of times, but they didn't look too hard and they weren't very smart and it was easy to stay out of their way."

"So what did you do once summer was over and the church didn't bring kids out anymore?"

"Well, by then I had a sort of permanent place set up. James had given me one of the old tents that he said was so beat-up they were just going to throw it away. And he let me keep the sleeping bag and some other things—a plate and a cup and soap and matches and some T-shirts. So I had, you know, my own campsite pretty deep in the woods. I was by water. I still knew how to hunt. I was in a lot better shape by the time winter came back."

"And nobody from the church ever figured out what you really were?"

"Didn't seem like it."

"Does *anybody* else know the truth about you?"

"I don't think so. I don't think my mom even told her parents or her sisters."

"So—your mom. All this time, you've never seen her again?"

He shook his head. "I used to go by the house now and then at night. Try to see in the windows, watch over them, make sure everyone was still okay. But they moved about a year ago, and I don't know where. There's a new family living there now."

I was quiet a moment, turning all this information over in my head. I didn't love my own family, but at least they provided a place where I could sleep, a more or less steady supply of food and other essential items. I was used to believing I was self-sufficient, but compared to Cooper, I was woefully dependent and unprepared for adversity. His story made the world seem like a much bigger and scarier place than it ever had before—and I'd considered it intimidating enough as it was.

"Did she ever tell you—before she kicked you out—did she ever tell you how you got to be this way?" I asked presently. "Were you born under a full moon or something like that? Did she get bitten by a radioactive spider when she was pregnant with you?"

He grinned briefly, and I was somehow heartened to realize that, despite his odd circumstances, he was a teen boy who understood a comic-book reference. "My dad was a shape-shifter."

"What was *he* like?"

"She never talked about him much, but when she did, she sounded like she really hated him. I remember this one time when I was about eight, and I almost changed when we were at the Laundromat. She had to shove all our wet clothes into a couple of laundry baskets and run me out to the car so no one would see me turn into a wolf. And I remember her crying and swearing the whole drive home. 'That lousy bastard! He never told me what kind of kid he was leaving me with!

He said there were things I should know about him—he said he had a *disease*, except he called it a *condition*. He didn't tell me it would ruin my life!' Stuff like that."

"She said that? Right in front of you? You'd ruined her life?"

"Well, I was a wolf."

"But you can understand people even when you're a wolf, can't you?" He nodded. "And she knew that, didn't she?" He nodded again. "Then that was awfully mean."

"She was upset."

"Did she ever tell you any more about your dad? Like, where you might look for him if you wanted to find him?"

"I don't think she knew where to look for him. I don't think it occurred to her I might want to find him."

I tilted my head and surveyed him by the faint yellow light from the house. "And do you want to find him?"

He shrugged. "I don't know. Maybe. Might be interesting to get some answers."

"What would you ask him?"

He thought a moment. "If there's a way to control it."

"What do you mean?"

He knotted his hands into fists, and for the first time I saw a darker emotion course through him—fear, maybe, or a kind of tired, hopeless anger. Not so accepting of his fate after all. "Maybe there's a way to stop the changing from happening—or from happening so often. Maybe there are drugs I could take or exercises I could do or food I shouldn't eat. Maybe I could hold it off for a few days, at least—be human for longer periods of time. And then figure out how to lead a more normal life."

"If you could control it completely, would you ever choose to be a wolf again?"

He looked at me gravely for a long moment. Even in the uncertain light, I was struck by the wild beauty of his face—the full lips, the enormous eyes, the dark halo of his tousled hair. "No," he said.

I didn't know him well enough to be surprised, and yet I was. Maybe because what he was seemed to be so exotic and, therefore, something to prize. Maybe because I was still young enough to be intoxicated by mystery, and he was the most mysterious creature I had ever encountered. "You'd be ordinary?" I said, my voice half-teasing, half-curious. "Instead of extraordinary, which is what you are?"

"I think anyone who isn't ordinary wishes he was," he said quietly. "No matter what makes him different, he wants to be the same as everyone else."

"But all of us who *are* ordinary—and boring and predictable and just like everyone else in the world—all of us want to be unique. We wish we *were* different. Or at least interesting."

That swift smile again, quickly fading. "I have to think you *are* a little different," he said. "I can't imagine anyone else I've ever met just sitting down and having this conversation with me."

"Well, you haven't met that many other people, so you aren't really qualified to judge."

"Maybe not, but I think most people would be afraid," he replied.

I considered that for a moment. "I don't think I was ever afraid," I said at last. "Even when you first showed up as the wolf."

"I could tell you weren't. That's why I got close enough for you to see me. But I don't know why you aren't more—" He made a slight gesture, searching for a word. "Freaked-out by my story. I don't even know why you believe me."

"I used to hear about shape-shifters all the time," I told him. "My grandmother was part Navajo, and when she lived with us in Arizona, she'd tell me stories about the skinwalkers. Of course, they were pretty scary! They'd steal your soul if they could. So I always believed that people could take the shapes of animals." Now I was the one to shrug. "I don't know why I wasn't frightened, though. Maybe because I always wished *I* was the one who could change shapes."

He lifted his heavy eyebrows. "What animal would you want to be?"

"Any animal. A bird, maybe, so I could fly away, anywhere I wanted to go."

He glanced over his shoulder at the house, shadowed and sleepy except for the gold light in the kitchen windows. "You'd leave your family?"

I made a rude noise. "In a heartbeat."

"Why?"

"My dad's crazy, and my mom's a loser." It was more complicated than that, of course, but I figured that was what it all boiled down to.

"Still, if they love you—" he protested.

"I don't know that they do," I interrupted. "Your parents don't have to kick you out of the house to be terrible people."

"I suppose not," he said. He gave a little laugh. "I used to prowl past houses at night—not just my mom's, but homes in the neighborhood where I used to live, and other little towns I happened to be in. And I would look in the windows, and I'd see moms in the kitchen making dinner, and dads outside mowing the lawns, and kids running up and down the stairs or watching television or playing some game. And I'd think, '*I* want that house. *I* want that life.' From the outside, they always looked so perfect."

"And from the inside, a lot of them probably sucked," I answered. "You can never tell from looking how good or how bad someone else has it."

"I'll try to remember that."

A short silence fell between us. I knew there were hundreds more questions I ought to ask, but my mind had gone completely blank, and I was, all of a sudden, so tired I could hardly keep my eyes open. Too many late hours and nights of little sleep. I found myself unable to stifle a yawn.

"I should go," Cooper said, coming abruptly to his feet.

I jumped up beside him. "Wait. Not yet. Tell me—you'll come back, won't you?"

He gazed gravely down at me. When we stood side by side, he was so much taller than I was that I had to tilt my head way back to meet his eyes. "I will if you want me to."

"I do! Isn't that obvious? I want to be your friend."

"It would be good to have a friend."

"And you'll have to let me know what I can do for you. Like—should I buy you clothes? Is there anything you need?"

That swift smile, just as swiftly disappearing. "I can always use food."

"Anything in particular?"

"Meat's pretty easy to come by, at least in the summer," he said. "I miss fruit the most. And bread. And potato chips. And cookies."

"But you probably don't have anywhere to keep perishables for long," I said, thinking out loud. "What about—do you have a can opener?"

He looked surprised. "No."

"I mean, obviously the wolf can't use a can opener, but if you've got some soup and chili and peaches on hand, you could eat all that as soon as you turned human."

"That would be great," he said. "But you've done so much for me already—"

I smiled up at him. "I'm just getting started."

O ver the next two weeks, Cooper came to my house every night. I had developed a rhythm for my days that allowed me to accommodate these strange nocturnal assignations and still manage to do everything else I was committed to. I slept late in the mornings, ran errands before my shift at McDonald's, took a nap in the afternoon before my parents came home, and made sure they saw me diligently doing my chores before they went upstairs to bed.

Then I waited outside for Cooper to come.

I spent every cent I earned over those two weeks on stuff for Cooper. Not only did I buy him the junk food he craved, and the canned goods that would sustain him during lean times, but I picked up camping gear that would improve his life: an insulated cooler, an LED lantern, a radio and batteries, matches, a Swiss Army knife, and a first-aid kit. That made me think of other toiletries that might come in handy, so I bought him soap, shampoo, and toothpaste. And a toothbrush. He didn't look like he needed to shave yet, but I made a mental note to think about razors in the future. I even secured a bicycle for Cooper when the teenage boy down the street got his driver's license and hung a sign saying FREE from the handlebars of his old road racer.

"Tell me what size jeans you wear, and I'll pick up some new clothes for you when I get my next paycheck," I told him at the end of that second week.

"I don't know what size jeans I wear," he said.

"Hmmm. I guess I should take your measurements."

"You shouldn't," he said. "Janet, you should stop buying me things. You can't spend all your money on me."

"Why not? I don't need any more clothes. I have as much food as I want. I'm not making a car payment. Why can't I spend my money on you?"

"Because it doesn't seem right."

I patted him on the arm. Usually, at least once every evening, I found a reason to touch him, briefly, just in passing. Just to reassure myself that he was real. "You're not used to generosity," I said. "But I never knew how to be generous before. I like it. It makes me happy. You have to let me give you things, so I can keep on being happy."

He made a small sound of helplessness and frustration. It had become obvious during the past two weeks that I could argue circles around him even when I was wrong. He hadn't figured out yet that the only way he could win a quarrel with me was to simply fail to show up one night. He didn't have a clue about the power dynamics between two people.

"I just don't want to take more than you have to give," he said finally.

"Don't worry about it," I said. "I'm surprised to find out I know how to give anybody anything at all."

He nodded, glanced away, looked back at me. "This is the last day," said in a quiet voice. "I can feel the change coming over me."

Something made a sharp stab in my chest—excitement or disappointment or both. "So you'll be a wolf tomorrow," I said. "Come back anyway."

"It's more dangerous."

"For you or for me?"

"For me."

Maybe he did know how to win an argument, after all. I couldn't possibly beg him to put himself at risk for my sake. "I'll worry about you," I said. "The whole time you're gone."

"I'll be fine."

"And you'll come back? The first night you're human?"

He nodded. "If you want me to."

"Of course I want you to! Two weeks from now. Here. In this very spot. I'll be waiting for you."

"It might not be two weeks exactly."

"Well, I'll be here anyway."

He nodded again, and, after a moment of silence, we both came to our feet. And then we stood there a moment, awkward and indecisive. Good-byes were hard even for people with well-rehearsed social skills, and neither one of us qualified. "Let me give you a hug," I said softly, "then you can go."

He stepped forward willingly enough, but put his arms around me uncertainly, as if he couldn't tell how close to pull me, how much pressure to exert. I wrapped my own arms around his waist and hugged him hard, laying my cheek against his lean chest. He smelled like sweat and dirty boy and grass and woods and summer. His heartbeat was stronger and wilder than my own.

"Be careful," I said, letting him go with reluctance.

"I will."

"Don't forget me."

"I won't."

Another moment of silence so full of unspoken thoughts that it did not seem silent at all, then he was gone.

I went to bed and cried for half an hour before exhaustion shoved me down the crooked stairwell into sleep. Over breakfast I was monosyllabic, at work I was sullen, and in the afternoon, I was too inconsolable to nap. Instead, I wandered out to the deck to flop down on the lawn chair and stare moodily over the yard to the border of trees that marked the beginning of public land. Somewhere past that boundary, Cooper had slipped into his alternate existence. I was beyond curious to know what the other half of his life looked like. I wanted to jump off the deck, break through the tree line, track him to his lair, and gaze around. I wanted to know what the wolf saw. I wanted to know how the wolf lived. Someday, perhaps, I could convince him to take me to his camp in the woods.

But part of me was afraid that, despite his promise, he might never come back at all.

I had been sitting there maybe half an hour when my eyes fell on a white plastic bag that had blown onto the lawn and come to rest against the lower edge of the deck. It was the kind of bag you'd use to line a kitchen trash can, and after a moment's inspection, I realized it had not drifted into the yard by accident. For one thing, it appeared to have been wrapped around some short, cylindrical object; for another, it had been carefully weighted down with a couple of ornamental rocks from my mother's garden. This was something someone had deliberately left behind.

I jumped up and knelt in the grass to unwrap the package. Out slipped a stiff piece of paper, maybe twelve by fourteen inches, that had been rolled into a tube. I flattened it over my thighs, then simply stared.

It was a pencil sketch on the back of an advertising flyer, an intricately rendered woodland scene as viewed from about the height of a toddler. Every inch was crammed with detail—summer bushes dense with leaves; fat tree trunks alive with squirrels and birds and butterflies; fallen logs covered with lichen and mushrooms and busy ants. The perspective was imperfect, and the artist's hand had smudged the graphite in more than one place, and there were a number of places where dirt had marred the purity of the paper. But the drawing was exquisite.

A gift from Cooper. A glimpse into the wolf's world. A thank-you. And a promise of a return.

CHAPTER NINE
MELANIE

I'm at PRZ about an hour early Wednesday morning so I can clear out the e-mail, voice mail, and snail mail that's accumulated in the past thirty-six hours. I know most people hate spam, but there's something about it that I find calming. A few clicks of the mouse, *delete forever*, and you never have to think about it again. A single problem, a quick solution, move on. If only all of life's challenges could be dealt with so cleanly.

I hear high-heeled shoes clicking across the tiled squares of the reception area, so I know Debbie's on the premises long before I see her. The other women in the office wear clogs or slides or soft-soled loafers, but Debbie is incapable of dressing down in a professional environment; she hates the very notion of "business casual." I admire her standards even as I make no effort to adhere to them myself.

She doesn't even bother stopping at her office before she comes to mine. She's still wearing her trench coat and carrying her briefcase as she steps in, closes the door, and drops to the comfortable chair pulled up close to my desk. "Okay, tell me everything about this guy, and I mean everything," she says.

I swivel in my chair and just look at her. Instantly, her demeanor changes. "What's wrong?"

"I think something's the matter with Ann."

"What? She's sick? She's hurt?"

I shake my head. "I don't know. She's—tired. Maybe that's all it is. But after she went to bed last night, her boyfriend wanted to tell me—"

"Wait—she has a boyfriend? Start from the beginning."

I take a deep breath. "She got here Monday night, told me she's fallen in love with a guy named William—"

"Does he know about her? About what she is?"

"Yeah. He's one, too. And so is everyone in his family."

"Wow, that'll be interesting."

"I'm sure. Anyway, Ann and I went to lunch and when we came back, there he was. She'd told him where I hide the key and so he was sitting inside the house. We all talked awhile, then she went to bed."

"Did you like him?"

I shrug. "I thought he was odd. I mean, he kind of looks like a homeless person—of course, he kind of *is* a homeless person—he's scruffy, and his hair's long and scraggly, and he was wearing these beat-up old clothes. You know. Not quite the upstanding citizen that you would want your sister to end up with."

Something I've said has diverted her. She scrunches up her pretty features as she pursues a new thought. "Huh. Wouldn't it be interesting if—maybe homeless people are *all* shape-shifters. And one of the reasons they don't want houses or cars is because they don't *need* stuff like that most of the time."

"I think we as a society would be lucky if that were the case, but unfortunately I think they only represent a small minority," I say in a tired voice.

She snaps back to attention. "But we digress. So William's this weirdo—"

"No, no, I didn't say that. He's just odd. And almost—ill at ease. Like this isn't a shape he's very comfortable in. Like he hasn't been human very long or very often."

"So I guess that most of the time when they're together, they're not."

"That's what I gather. Anyway, everyone tried hard to be polite and get along, and as I say, Ann went to bed. And then William came to find me and told me he was worried about her."

"Worried in what sense? What's bothering him?"

"That's the thing. He couldn't be very specific. He just said she seemed to tire easily, her energy level was low, and she seemed to be forgetting things."

"What sorts of things?"

I'm silent for a moment. "Well, she almost forgot how to find her way home, apparently."

Debbie just stares at me.

I shrug. "She said she got lost because of all the new construction."

"A valid point."

"And she *did* find the house eventually. But William seemed to consider that another bad sign."

"What does he suggest you do about it? Can you take her to a doctor?"

I give her an *are-you-crazy* look. "I'm not sure she's ever been to a doctor. I mean, I guess when she was a baby she got all her vaccinations. And last time she was home, I took her to an urgent-care center to get a tetanus shot because I just shudder to think of all the rusty nails and bad water she's exposed to. But I honestly don't remember a time she's seen a doctor for the flu, or an ear infection, or a broken bone, or anything."

She's surprised. "I never realized that. She must be incredibly healthy."

I sigh. "Or she *used* to be incredibly healthy. Now—I don't know."

"Maybe William is just being overprotective. Maybe he's creating a crisis out of nothing."

"Maybe. Although he doesn't seem like the type who panics easily."

"Well, what did *you* think? Does she look sick to you?"

I consider. "I thought she looked thin. And like she's aging faster than she should. You know, she was always so radiant. And now her skin looks a little dull, and there are more lines around her eyes than there should be on a twenty-year-old. But I attributed that to—well, it must be a hard life. It would age anyone."

Debbie nods. "So maybe she's just exhibiting normal wear and tear for someone of her type, and William is simply concerned because he loves her. And if she doesn't appear to be in imminent danger and you're not going to take her to a doctor for a physical in any case, I'm not sure there's anything you can do."

"Except worry."

"Except worry," she echoes. "And you'd do that regardless." She wriggles in the chair to resettle herself and unbuttons her coat. It's a dark purple microfiber that most people wouldn't have the nerve to wear, but of course it looks fabulous on Debbie. Everything does. "So now that we've settled *that*, let's get to the good stuff. Tell me about this guy! This reporter. He's writing a book about—"

She doesn't finish the sentence. Both of us have caught the sounds of voices in the anteroom as the other two employees drift in more or less on time. In fact, a second later Chloe knocks on the door and sticks her head in. She's braided her brown hair and wrapped it around her head so she somewhat resembles a homesteading farmwife, but the look sits well with her general air of competence and serenity.

"Hey, Mel. Everything all right?"

"Sure. Did I miss anything important yesterday?"

"Just a couple of phone calls. I left messages on your desk."

"Go away," Debbie says. "I'm trying to worm top secret information out of her, and she's being difficult."

Chloe grins and withdraws, shutting the door with a deliberate *click*. Debbie faces me again. "So? This guy?"

"Used to be a reporter. Now writing a book. Yes, on that topic. He had a lot of information on my family from when we used to live in Kirkwood. He had stories from some of our neighbors at the time, talking about how they would see a little white dog in our yard." I glance at the door. Chloe is not the type to listen at keyholes—Em is, but she usually spends the first hour of the day on the phone with her mother—but even so, I speak in code. Debbie knows how to translate. "And he had some basic information on our lives once we moved down here. He knows, for instance, that Ann was homeschooled and generally considered sickly. I'm not too worried about the people he's already talked to—they'd only have the most general information about us—but I think he's going to keep talking to people. Keep digging. And then—I don't know what he'll learn."

Debbie lets out her breath in a long, gusty puff. "Well, I can totally see why you'd be alarmed, but I'm not sure you have anything to worry about. I mean, no one knows the truth, do they? Except me. And you know *I'm* not going to say a word."

"I keep going over it in my head. Who would know anything? Who would suspect anything? She had friends, but as far as I know, none of them ever saw her—" I glance at the door again. "Like that. Kurt's mom was always curious, but I don't think she was smart enough to figure it out. I mean, she probably thought Ann had a mental disorder and we were keeping her at home so no one saw her throwing fits or foaming at the mouth."

"You never told Kurt, did you?"

I give her a look of scorn. "We barely *talked*, let alone about important things."

She giggles, momentarily the high-school girl again. "You didn't talk because you were too busy making out."

"Oh, like you were sitting there with your legs crossed like a good little virgin."

She laughs even harder but returns to the main point quickly enough. "So no one knows. So you're safe. And you didn't tell him anything—"

"And I'm not *going* to tell him anything. I don't trust him."

"So why did you have dinner with him the other night?"

I give her a lopsided grin. "And lunch with him yesterday."

"*What?* How'd *that* happen? Wait—was Ann there? Did he actually meet her?"

"Oh, yeah. She invited him."

"Seriously. You are so bad at telling stories. Start from the beginning."

I fill her in on every detail of my two encounters with Brody Westerbrook. It seems to take a long time; I seem to have spent more hours in his company, or filled those hours with more meaningful conversation, than you would normally expect from a new acquaintance. She listens intently, asking for clarification now and then, but at the end it's clear that, not intending to, I've drawn a portrait of someone that she is prepared to endorse wholeheartedly.

"The more you say, the more I like him," she decides after I recount the conversation at Slices when he passes up the opportunity to talk about his book.

"Ann thinks he likes me."

She laughs in disbelief. "Well, duh!"

I make an exasperated sound and sink back against my chair. "He doesn't like me. He's being nice to me so he can trick me and trip me up and make me tell him stuff about my sister."

"Maybe," she says. "But he sounds more genuine than that. And let's just look at all the things we've learned about him." She enumerates on her fingers. "He's cute. He's curious. He's comfortable. He's kind. Change *kind* to *caring*, and they're all C words. Good ones. The combination just doesn't get better than that, *chica*."

I sigh again. I didn't get much sleep, and I am, this early in the morning, already exhausted. Maybe William should start worrying about me, too. I say, "You've forgotten one C word. He's catastrophic."

She ignores that, as if it's not the most important of all Brody Westerbrook's attributes. "So are you going to see him again?"

"I'm guessing it's going to be impossible to avoid it, since I'm guessing he's pretty tenacious when he's working on a story and one of his sources is recalcitrant."

She taps her lip with her index finger. Her lipstick and her nail polish are a perfect match. "I'd like to meet him. Can we arrange that?"

"Sure, he'll ask me which of my friends he can interview, and I'll point him right in your direction."

"I thought maybe a more lighthearted, fun, social occasion? We could have the two of you over for dinner one night."

"Debbie, we're not in *high school*. Brody and I are not *double-dating* with you."

She grins, unrepentant. "Well, it was fun then. It ought to be even more fun now if Kurt's not the fourth person in the car."

"*Everything's* more fun if Kurt's not around."

"I think you should bring him to our house for dinner one night. That has the added advantage of letting you see how well he interacts with my sons so you can decide whether or not you'd want to have children with him."

"*Debbie!*" I wail, but she's gone off in peals of laughter. I start pelting her with all the unfortunately not-very-deadly objects on my desk—a windup plastic cow, a stress ball, a mostly empty box of Kleenex. Still laughing, she fends them off with one hand and pushes herself to her feet.

"I've got to make some calls," she says when she's able to speak again. "Think about dinner."

"I'm not making plans with anybody while Ann's in town."

"Bring her along," Debbie invites. "Bring the boyfriend— what's his name? William. I'm dying to meet him, too."

I am momentarily diverted by the image of *that* dinner table. "Yeah, I don't think so," I say. "Let me get some work done. See you at lunch."

I slog through the day without much enthusiasm, resisting the impulse, every half hour or so, to call the house and check on Ann. I don't want to wake her if she's repairing bones or tissue with restorative sleep; I don't want to disturb her if she's talking or—whatever—with William. Just in case she's forgotten them, I've left my office and cell-phone numbers on a piece of paper in the kitchen. She'll call me when she has time.

But she doesn't call.

I'm fighting back a sense of unease when I leave work about fifteen minutes early and speed down Bonhomme Highway toward home. Clouds are threatening to turn the chilly March air into disagreeably cold March rain, but the streets are still dry as I take the hilly road to my house a little too fast for optimum visibility around blind curves. There's one scary moment when I top a rise from one direction as an eighteen-wheeler barrels over it from the other. He blares his horn and I wrench the Jeep to the shoulder as we charge past each other, my tires churning up rocks at the edge of the road. *Okay, okay, slow down,* I tell myself. I won't be much use to Ann if I'm dead.

Still, I'm traveling way too fast and have to stomp on the brakes as I skid onto my front lawn. Against the dreary pewter of the sky, any light from the house would make a bright contrast, but I can tell before I'm even out of the car that no lamps are on. "Ann?" I call as soon as I've unlocked the door and stepped inside. "Ann? Are you here?"

The house is silent in that eerie, echoing way that a building only has when it's been unexpectedly abandoned. It's as if the bricks and the flooring and the furniture and the walls are still waiting to be stepped on and leaned against. They haven't quite accustomed themselves to solitude yet; they're holding themselves in readiness.

"Ann?" I call again, but the hopefulness has evaporated from my voice. I hit the wall switch at the door and quickly take in the fact that there is no one in the kitchen or living room, then I check Ann's room. The bed is unmade and there are shoes on the floor—signs of recent occupation, but no guarantee that the last tenant plans to come back anytime soon. Ann usually leaves a mess behind whenever she goes.

I retrace my steps, looking for evidence that she plans to

return. She's only been here a day. Surely she can't have left already, without a word of good-bye. I find it in the kitchen, on the counter, next to the note that holds my phone numbers. She has had so little need to write throughout her lifetime that her handwriting is still girlish and round; you'd think the note had been penned by a child.

> *Mel—don't worry. William and I decided to try to find the nearest park and spend the afternoon. We'll be back tonight or maybe tomorrow. Don't hide the key someplace new! See you when we get back.*
>
> *A*

The emotions that flood me are half relief, half resentment, and in both cases they are intense enough that I know I'm overreacting. She has her own life; she cannot be bound to me so tightly by my affection that she strangles. Even if she were my daughter, not my sister, I should not experience this extreme level of painful loss. I can't explain it—I'm a little embarrassed that I feel it—and I don't know what to do with all the grief and anxiety and anger that are percolating just under my skin. I slap my open hand against the plaster of the kitchen wall, so hard that I bruise my palm. Then I plunge through the house and fall to my knees on the couch, punching the back cushions with all the force I can muster.

The whole goal is to stave off the tears, but it's no use. As soon as my arm tires, I cover my face with both hands, as if, here in the empty house, I'm afraid someone will see me. I'm already crying.

CHAPTER TEN

That's the way it goes for the next three weeks.

Ann and William come and go like eccentric ghosts who make appearances based on some opaque algorithm of their own. They might be sleeping in her room when I go to bed at night, but gone when I wake in the morning. They might have breakfast with me in the morning, then disappear before I return from work. Sometimes they're home for only a few hours before vanishing for two days. During one forty-eight-hour period, they never leave the house.

I'm starting to get used to William though I still don't find him easy or comfortable to be around. He is obviously attempting to be a thoughtful guest, rinsing out any dish he touches and never leaving clutter in the main areas of the house. He hauls the garbage out on trash night and fixes a leaky faucet in the bathroom—which surprises me no end, as I hadn't expected him to possess stereotypical masculine skills. But I don't quite know how to interact with him when Ann's not around. He doesn't make idle conversation. He doesn't watch television. He'll play games if we drag out the Chinese checkers board or the Monopoly box, and he's unexpectedly adept at putting together the old thousand-piece puzzle of Neuschwanstein Castle that Ann unearths one evening. But he has no social graces. He makes no attempt to be entertaining. He can sit for hours in a silence so absolute I would swear he was sleeping except that I can see his eyes move to track my progress across the room. I'm working on learning to like him, but I have to confess I find him spooky.

Ann, by contrast, is her usual delightful self, though a somewhat more sedate version. After William's alarming announcement, I am watching her even more closely than I ordinarily would, and what I mostly notice is how much she's slowed down. She doesn't *fling* herself across the room with her usual manic energy; now she strolls, or even saunters. As best I can tell from her frequent absences and my own hours at work, she sleeps about half of every day. Even so, she never seems entirely rested. She yawns a lot, or drowsily curls up against William on the couch. But she doesn't seem unhappy; she doesn't seem sick. She doesn't complain of fever or pain. I can't tell from observation if there's anything wrong, and when, one afternoon, I ask her outright, she merely laughs.

"Nothing," she says. "Is there anything wrong with you? Except that you're a big ol' worrywart?"

No. No, that's my main affliction.

During this three-week period, I hear from Brody seven times.

Twice he sends brief, cheery e-mails with attachments he thinks will amuse me. One is an article about his sister Brandy's winning a humorous internal company award for "most likely to stare down a tiger in the wild." What did I tell you? he writes on his accompanying message. One is an article about two Oregon hunters who claim to have photographed a half-man-half-beast creature in some cave off the rocky coast. The creature is so obviously fake that you can actually see the store price tag hanging off the actor's left elbow. This is what I'm competing with. This is what the vast American public believes is the true nature of shape-shifters, his message says this time. And you wonder why I've made no progress on my book.

I've wondered no such thing. But I cannot keep myself

from replying though I know it will only encourage him to stay in touch. Maybe you need a new topic. Maybe it's time to expose the atrocities of kitten hoarders. He answers with a message box that holds only a smiley face.

Three times he phones. Like the e-mails, the calls are short and amusing. Once he wants to know if Slices will deliver a whole pie to his downtown address. Once he opens with, "I know it's a long shot, but would you have any interest in going to a hockey game tonight?" And once he calls to see if I'll have dinner with him if he drives down from the city.

I turned down the hockey game, so I can't believe it when my response to the dinner invitation is, "I'd love to."

But Ann and William have disappeared again, and the house has taken on that echoing sound, and it's the weekend, and I've remembered the kind of soul-stealing loneliness that you only feel when you aren't expecting to be alone. I brace myself for a series of questions and subtle attempts to draw me out, but in fact Brody spends most of the evening talking. He's just finished writing an article about a college professor who's taken his whole undergraduate accounting class down to Mexico to help a group of village women organize a profitable business around their traditional crafts of pottery and weaving.

"I love this kind of stuff," he says, still buzzing with enthusiasm. "You know—'one man can make a difference' acts of faith and inspiration. Putting good into the world in tangible ways. Makes me feel like a piker. Makes me feel like I should find someone and donate a kidney. Do something to make my life worthwhile."

"You don't think you've done anything worthwhile up to this point?" I ask.

"Nothing big," he says. "Nothing that has changed someone else's life in a material way for the better."

If you write your book, you'll change mine in a material way for the worse, I think. "There's still time," I say. "Maybe you'll save a drowning kid or win the lottery and give all the money to charity."

He's regarding me quizzically. "You don't think about

these things?" he asks. "Making the world a better place? Leaving your mark?"

"If I say no," I reply, "will you think less of me?"

"I would think less of you if you were a serial killer," he answers. "Anything other than that, I think I'd just find intriguing. Still trying to figure you out."

"I never really felt like I had that much time or energy left over to try to save the world," I say. "Mostly I'm just trying to keep things together. Get through the day."

He tilts his head, still watching me, as if sifting my words for more meaning, so I elaborate. "You know a little bit about my life growing up. Gwen was—odd. Unreliable. My father started getting sick when I was a teenager, and he was pretty much out of it by the time I was in college. I've been taking care of Ann since I was ten years old—I was practically her only parent by the time I was eighteen. I never had much time for idealism. I was just trying to get dinner on the table." I shrug. "Maybe it sounds selfish. Maybe someday I'll start volunteering at soup kitchens. Probably not anytime soon, though."

He nods, as if something in my answer has satisfied him, and asks, "How's Ann?"

I tense up a little, but it's the first time he's posed a direct query about her since he met her, and this question could be viewed as innocuous. "Good. Tired. I think she's run herself pretty ragged, so she spends a lot of time lolling around the house when she and William aren't off—" I'm not sure how to complete the sentence. "Hiking or something," I end lamely.

"William?"

I nod glumly. "Her boyfriend."

"Sounds like you're not a fan."

"I don't dislike him. He's a little old for her, maybe, and kind of a strange guy, but I don't think he's abusive or anything. Just—odd."

He nods. "Like Gwen was odd."

It's a split second before I remember I'd used the same word to describe my stepmother, and another moment before I realize what I've revealed to him. He knows—or at least suspects—that Gwen was a shape-shifter; and now he suspects the same of William. But because he made me a promise, he won't ask outright.

I tilt my chin defiantly. "Now that you mention it," I say, "they're a little bit alike."

He grins. "Just what I'd have expected. Maybe he'll turn out to be a good choice for her, then."

My voice is icy. "I don't have any say in the matter one way or the other. So I'm doing my best to like him."

"I'm sure you are. I'd love to meet him."

"I can't imagine you will."

But of course, the seventh time I hear from Brody during that three-week period, that's exactly what happens.

It's around noon on Saturday, I'm clearing away the lunch dishes, and Ann and William are trying to decide where they want to spend the next couple of days. The weather forecast is sublime—sunny days predicted to hit sixty degrees, dry nights no colder than forty—and she wants to take him down to Johnson Shut-ins State Park. He seems to think it's too far, so he's been offering alternate venues. I try not to wonder why he's so bothered by the distance, which isn't that extreme. Maybe he's feeling lazy. Maybe he's worried that the rain will move in sooner than the weatherman says. Surely he's not concerned that Ann doesn't have the strength to make it that far.

"You don't have to go at all," I say as I load the plates into the dishwasher. "I told you, Debbie's having me over tonight for Charles's birthday. She'd be glad to have you guys, too. I'm sure there's plenty of food—Debbie always makes enough to feed the whole neighborhood."

William shows me the expression I like best, a curiously sweet smile laced with humor and self-knowledge. "Dinner parties are not my natural habitat," he says.

"Well, you wouldn't have to worry about Charles and Debbie, who like *all* kinds of weird people," Ann says. "But I don't feel like I can sit still at someone's house and behave. I'm all—" Her whole body twitches in a simulated spasm. "On edge. I need to run. I need to see the world a different way. I need to shift."

That's when the doorbell rings.

For a moment I'm frozen—*Who's there? Did they hear Ann's last remark?*—even though common sense says the door's too thick, and her voice is too soft too carry. My pulse is already at double time when I hurry across the room to open the door, and it kicks into a frantic beat when I see Brody on the other side.

"I swear I'm not stalking you, I swear I really did have a reason to be in Dagmar," he says, talking fast. "Had an interview this morning with a guy who runs a business right across the street from Corinna's, and I thought, what the hell, it's ten minutes out of my way, I'll see if Melanie's home."

Ann has come dancing up behind me, her smile so bright that I can *feel* it even with my back to her. "Brody! Come on in! Are you hungry? We just finished lunch, but there's plenty left."

His eyes cut sideways to acknowledge her, but then he looks right back at me. "Not if Melanie doesn't want me to come in."

"Don't be silly." She pushes past me to unlatch the door and swing it open in an inviting way. "You can meet William."

Brody remains unmoving on the porch, his eyes locked on mine. I haven't said a word. I'm furious, I'm frightened, I'm trying to figure out how to play this. Did he hear Ann's careless declaration? *I need to shift.* Will he take one look at William and instantly know what he is? *He's odd—like Gwen was odd.* Will it make things better or worse if I lock him out of the house and refuse to speak to him again and force myself, though it seems impossible, to henceforth remain unmoved by his careless charm?

It almost seems as if he can hear what I'm thinking. "Just let me know what you want," he says in a soft voice. "I won't do anything that makes you uncomfortable."

"Sure," I say finally, my own voice rusty. "Come on in."

I turn away and let Ann act as his hostess, chattering as she leads him toward the old oak table. "I've had lunch," he says.

"You could have a soda," she suggests.

"That sounds great. Something without caffeine if that's an option."

I head to the kitchen to fetch a chilled Sprite, so I don't witness the introductions Ann makes between Brody and William. I assume they shake hands—I hear William mumble something—but it's Brody's response that gets my attention and makes me whirl around so fast I almost drop the can.

"Have I met you before?" Brody says. He sounds puzzled, or maybe just thoughtful, dredging through old memories.

William is wearing a half-smile that clearly indicates Brody has asked a stupid question. "I don't think so. I've never been to Dagmar till recently."

"No, it wasn't here. You just look so familiar."

William hunches a shoulder and doesn't answer. By this time, I've made it over to the table, and I hand Brody the can, belatedly thinking to ask, "Did you want a glass? And ice?"

"No, this is fine. Thanks."

"Sit down, sit down," Ann says, still acting as hostess. "Brody, would you like some cookies? They're just store-bought, but they're pretty good."

"No, no dessert, thanks. Unless you have pie," Brody says, sinking to a seat. The rest of us arrange ourselves around the table though no one actually relaxes. I have the notion that William has gone into some kind of feral high alert, like a hare trying to outsmart a wolf. Brody, who is leaning casually against his chair back, is clearly still sorting through his memories, looking for a match. Ann is bouncing around like a child who's eaten too much candy, and I'm as tense as a violin string. If you ran a finger across my forearm, you'd wake a low G.

"Sorry, no pie," Ann says. "But you and Mel could drive over to Slices if you'd like."

He glances her way. "You'd come, too, wouldn't you?"

She shakes her blond head. "William and I were just leaving. We're going to spend the weekend—" She pauses, then smiles luminously. "Camping."

"Tents and amenities, or roughing it?" Brody asks.

Now she laughs. "Roughing it."

"I need a tent and a sleeping bag," Brody says, "but I scorn these modern-day campers who set up their RVs in the state park and get electricity and water and cable TV, for God's sake."

"Mel hates to camp," Ann says.

Everyone looks at me, so I figure I have to speak. "That's putting it too mildly," I say, making some effort to sound humorous. "Absent the apocalypse, I'm never going camping again."

William unexpectedly enters the conversation again. "You should do it the way we do," he says. "Then you'd change your mind."

There is a brief silence while everyone at the table considers what exactly he might mean by that.

Then Brody looks over at me with a smile that is both understanding and amused. "So if they're going to be gone all weekend," he says, "are you free? We could go to dinner tonight. Or see a movie. Or something."

"Darn," I say in a voice of exaggerated regret. "I can't. I have plans this evening. Too bad."

Ann sits up. "Hey, take him with you to Debbie's. She won't mind." In fact, Ann knows that Debbie would more than *not mind*. I've told her Debbie's completely inappropriate response to Brody's appearance in my life. Debbie would *love* to have him at her house tonight.

But I just say, "Oh, I couldn't. How rude."

By this time, Brody and I have had enough conversations that he can name the major players in my life. "Debbie—that's your best friend from high school, right?"

I nod. "Her husband's birthday is today, and she's having me over for dinner."

Ann jumps up. "I'll ask her if Brody can come."

She's racing off to find the phone before I've quite registered what she's planning. "What? Wait—*Ann*—"

I'm on my feet and about to run after her when William suddenly says, in a voice that nails me to the spot, "*I* know where I met you before."

I glance over at Ann, who's punching numbers into the phone, then down at William, who's leaning slightly forward in his chair. I had that wrong before. Not prey—predator.

Brody is still lounging in his own seat. "Really? I can't place it. Where?"

"At Maria's house."

At first Brody looks bewildered. "Maria—?" But I can see the exact moment he puts the pieces together. "Maria Devane. When I went there to interview her. You're right. That was you."

Now William's grin widens to lupine proportions. He looks like he's just eaten a meal raw, and liked it. "Sorry if I hurt you."

Brody shrugs. He appears to be wholly at ease, but I'm wondering if he's just very good at hiding stress or animosity. "Hazard of the profession. Sometimes people don't like it when you come knocking on their doors, asking questions."

I insert myself into the conversation. "What questions?"

Brody gestures in William's direction. Neither man bothers to look up at me. They just continue watching each other across the table. "Last year. I was trying to get reaction interviews from people who worked with a murder victim's wife. I went to the house of a woman named Maria Devane, and William was there, and—let's just say he made it forcefully clear he didn't think I should be bothering her."

"It's Maria Romano now," William says, as if this one detail is the most important part of Brody's speech.

"Maria?" I repeat, aiming the question at William. "*Your* Maria? Your sister-in-law?"

I'm finding it a little difficult to accept the magnitude of these particular coincidences. Maria took care of Ann a few months ago when Ann needed shelter; Brody showed up at Maria's door and happened to encounter William at her side. How odd that Brody's life has already intersected, even so tangentially, with Ann's, with William's. He has dedicated his recent life to finding shape-shifters, and yet, before he even knew they existed, he practically stumbled across two of them at one woman's house.

Unless meeting William was one of the things that sent Brody on this quest to begin with. Unless Brody also encountered Ann while he was interrogating Maria. Unless that's the reason he first showed up at my door.

I find that I can't speak. I can scarcely breathe or swallow. Not that anyone is expecting me to contribute another comment. The men are still eying each other, measuring each other. William still looks poised to pounce, but Brody, though he keeps his face perfectly amiable, doesn't look ready to back down. Distantly, as if the sound is coming from an alternate universe, I hear Ann's laughter. She's across the room, on the phone with Debbie, oblivious to the undercurrents of our conversation.

"Sister-in-law," Brody repeats. "That explains why you were so protective."

"My brother was out of town. I was watching out for her. You made her nervous."

"Didn't mean to," Brody says. "Just trying to get information. Part of my job."

"There are some things people don't need to know," William says.

Into the silence that falls between them then, Ann's laughter sounds again, closer this time. She's heading back toward the table, the cordless phone pressed against her ear. "You tell her," she says, and offers me the handset. "Debbie wants to talk to you."

I shake my head. "Tell her I'll call her back."

That's when Ann senses the hostility at the table. She quirks her eyebrows but doesn't look too alarmed. Speaking into the phone again, she says, "She'll call you in a few minutes . . . Sure . . . Okay, tell Charles happy birthday from me!" She makes a kissing sound and disconnects. "Debbie says you should bring Brody to dinner tonight."

"What a surprise," I say.

Brody finally looks away from William to glance up at

me. "I'd love to go," he says, "but I'm not feeling any great sense of welcome from *you*."

"You're *kidding*," I say in exaggerated shock.

He grins; Ann laughs again. But her restlessness permeates the air, blows through and dissipates the tension that holds the rest of us in place. "William. Let's go," she says, her voice half command and half supplication. "We want to get there before sunset."

Unexpectedly, William swings his gaze in my direction. His eyes are dark and serious. "Do you mind if we leave?" he asks.

I realize, with a mild sense of shock, that he's asking if I'm afraid to be left alone with Brody. He's offering me his protection—which, I'm pretty sure, would be damn close to boundless. What wouldn't he do to keep his lover's family safe?

"No—not at all—go on, have a good time," I reply, my words a little more disjointed than I'd like. "How long do you plan to be gone?"

Ann comes over to put her arm around my shoulder and kiss me on the cheek. "A few days," she says. "Or until the weather turns."

"Have fun," I say.

Giving me an impish look, she skips over and kisses Brody on the cheek, too. "William's bark is worse than his bite," she whispers, then she laughs so hard she can hardly stand up straight.

William's already at the door. Another hug for me, a wave of her thin hands, then she joins him, and they both slip outside. I hear a few words in her high, excited voice, then they're gone.

Brody has slewed around in his chair to watch me, but I don't meet his gaze. I pull out the chair across from his and collapse in it, feeling like I've gone a few rounds with William myself. I might need several hours to recover.

"Interesting guy," Brody comments.

I nod. I'm thirsty but too stressed to stand up again and go back to the kitchen, so I reach for his Sprite and down a few swallows. "I'm still figuring him out."

"I imagine that might take a while."

Now I gather the strength to look at him. "So what did he do to you? Beat you up?"

Brody's smile is faint. "Not that bad. Punched me a few times and told me to get the fuck away from Maria. My cameraman got the whole thing on tape if you want to see it."

"Not particularly." I take another drink. "So what did you think of him when you first met him?"

"I thought he was the kind of guy who overreacted. Kind of guy who'd bring a nuclear weapon when he only needed a handgun. I'm not sure I've changed my mind."

I'm still holding the can up around mouth level, and I eye him over the rim. "When you met him at Maria's house," I say slowly, "were you looking for shape-shifters?"

His eyes narrow, but all he says is, "Nope. Just friends and family members who wanted to emote on camera, full of sympathy for the murder victim." He takes the can away from me and finishes off the contents. "Though it turns out the victim had been killed by the shape-shifter we caught on camera a few weeks later. So maybe there was a connection after all."

"Ann's spent some time at Maria's," I say.

"Really? I guess that makes sense." His voice is wholly neutral.

"Did you ever see her there?"

He looks at me a long moment as he analyzes the pattern the way I have. "I was at Maria Devane's house for about five minutes one time," he says, his voice deliberate. "I had a few civilized words with her, and a few uncivilized words with William. I didn't see anyone or anything else. I didn't come *here* thinking I'd meet anyone I'd met *there*. I've never lied to you, Melanie."

"It's just so hard to trust you," I say. "When I don't really know what you want."

"You know exactly what I want," he says. "I want to write a book about shape-shifters. And I want to be your friend. And I don't want the one thing to interfere with the other thing."

I'm listening closely. "You don't want friendship with me to screw up your book?"

He smiles. "I don't want my book to make you afraid to be my friend."

"You realize there's no such thing as shape-shifters."

"Then I guess I won't be writing that book after all. Might make it easier to be your friend."

I shrug pettishly; I am both unnerved and excited by this byplay and afraid to continue it any longer. "Do you want another soda?" I ask abruptly.

He doesn't quite laugh. "Sure."

I fetch another can of soda, and glasses for both of us. He accepts his portion with a word of thanks, then says casually, "So Ann and William are going camping this weekend?"

"That's right."

"No sleeping bags, no tents, no gear at all? Not even food?"

"I guess."

He sips his drink. "They gonna hitchhike wherever they're going? 'Cause I didn't see a car."

I almost choke on my soda, but I manage to swallow a mouthful. It burns all the way down my throat. "I didn't ask," I say. "Makes me too nervous to know all the details of the way Ann lives."

He nods. "I can see that."

"I just hope it doesn't rain on them."

He nods again, and for a moment there is silence between us. I'm wondering if I should offer him lunch again, or at least some pretzels. Actually, I'm thinking I should let him know, kindly, of course, that it's time for him to leave, but I don't really want him to go. A dilemma.

He sets his glass down with a *snap*. "So are you going to invite me to Debbie's tonight or not?"

Startled, I meet his eyes. "Do you want to go? Celebrate someone's birthday with total strangers?"

"You bet I do."

I spread my hands in a helpless gesture. "Okay, then. You can come."

CHAPTER ELEVEN

Five hours later, Brody and I are in his Honda, heading for Debbie and Charles's house. We have not spent all the intervening time together. He has notes he needs to transcribe from his morning interview, and God knows I have enough laundry and housework to keep me occupied until the end of the world itself. So I draw him a map to the nearest library and tell him when to return, then I spend the day trying to put my home—and my mental state—back in order. I don't know how successful Brody is at completing his tasks; I haven't gotten too far on mine. I'm starting to think I should accustom myself to the notion that chaos is going to be my natural state from now on.

"So the car's all fixed now? No more engine trouble?" I ask, as we pull away from my house. It's not quite full dark; the world appears to be halfway through a complete cycle of dissolution, just now at the stage of crumbling gray. The car's headlights throw a brave circle of illumination ahead of us, providing reassurance that the road, at least, is still solid, though the trees and bushes and houses on either side are fading into nothingness. I'm noting all this as I gaze out the window, thinking how much I like being driven down Bonhomme by someone else. It's a rare treat.

"Well, the service light came on once this morning when I was getting on the highway, but everything seemed fine on the trip down."

"That's not as reassuring as it could be."

"Time to live dangerously."

Debbie and Charles live on the other side of town from me, so the trip usually takes twenty to twenty-five minutes. Brody seems equally willing to drive in silence or engage in banter, but I start fooling with the radio before we've been in the car five minutes.

"Let's see what you've got on your CD player," I say, then practically slam back against my seat as power chords played at a very high volume come muscling out of the speakers. Brody laughs and spins the dial way down.

"What the hell is that?" I demand.

He gives me a look of scorn, so withering I can discern it even in the fading light. "Def Leppard, of course. *Adrenalize.*"

"Seriously? An eighties hair band? That's embarrassing."

"Oh, man, if you don't like Def Leppard, I don't know if I can work on this friendship thing anymore."

"This is the kind of music teenage boys play when they think they're cool," I say in disparaging tones. "Yes, and when they want to blast women out of the car."

He glances at me again. "So what do you listen to? Let me guess, country music."

He's right, but I don't want to give him the satisfaction of knowing it. "Maybe."

"And when you were eighteen, your favorite singer was Madonna. Or Celine Dion. Or the Spice Girls!"

Three for three, though my Spice Girls phase was short. "Let's not talk about music," I say.

"Let's not even listen to it," he answers. He punches a button, and the silver disc slides out of the dashboard slot. The radio station that comes on in the wake of the ejected album is some talk program, but he switches it off before I can figure out if it's brainy NPR or sports-mad KMOX. He asks, "What should I know about Debbie and Charles?"

"They were high-school sweethearts. She was a cheerleader, he was a smart, nerdy guy. Valedictorian. When he asked her out the first time, she only said yes because she felt sorry for him. She figured he was such a dork that he'd never even kissed a girl, and here he was, seventeen years old. They got married three years later."

"So did you think she married the right guy?"

"Oh yeah. He's one of my favorite people on the planet."

"She owns the company where you work, right? PRZ? What's he do?"

"He's a lawyer."

"They have kids?"

"Two boys."

"Sounds like the perfect life."

I lean back against the seat but turn my head a little to survey him. Mindful of Debbie's comments a few weeks ago, I say, "So you want kids?"

He glances over at me, a wicked grin barely visible in the dashboard light. "I want to date a cheerleader." When I'm silent, he bursts out laughing. "Yeah, I know you were one, too. Ann told me. Hey, it's every teenage boy's fantasy come true."

"I guess all you need is to play Def Leppard on your Walkman while you make out with her under the bleachers, then you'll have achieved every single one of the life goals you set out when you were seventeen."

"That does sound like an awfully good afternoon."

I manage to ignore this comment because we've gotten to the point where I need to start giving him turn-by-turn directions. In another five minutes, we've arrived on Debbie's street. She and Charles live in a big, modern, three-story brick house in a development only a few years older than Kurt Markham's projects. To me, the neighborhood feels featureless enough to be a suburban subdivision, but Debbie loves it. On her street alone, there are ten kids close to the ages of her own boys, and all the parents share in carpooling and after-school responsibilities.

"I never did buy into all that clean-country-living crap,"

she's told me more than once. "I'm a city girl trapped in a rural lifestyle. Bring in every big-box store you can think of! Build up the whole corridor! Give me an outlet mall! I'll be happy."

We pull into the driveway, and Brody reaches into the backseat to retrieve a brown paper bag whose contents clink together. "What's that?" I demand.

"A couple of bottles of wine. Thought I should bring something. They drink, don't they?"

I smile. "Sort of. You'll hear Charles's opinion on the topic soon enough."

"Should I leave them in the car?"

"Nah. Come on in."

Debbie's already at the door waiting for us. She's dressed in pressed black pants, a silver sweater, and black patent-leather pumps—casual attire for her. "Hello, hello, you're right on time!" She greets me with a hug, then holds her hand out to Brody. "I'm Debbie Zimmer. Don't believe anything Melanie has told you about me."

He's grinning as he shakes her hand. "Funny, that was going to be my line."

We've barely crossed the threshold into the immaculately kept living room when Stevie and Simon come charging up from the basement. They're eight and seven, almost carbon copies of each other, with Debbie's rich black hair and Charles's round moon face; they have a puppy-dog energy that always makes me happy.

"Melanie, can you come play Mario Party with us?" Simon demands. He's the older one, the more talkative of the two, but Stevie's the fearless one who's always in trouble. He's already broken three bones in three separate incidents and will undoubtedly break a dozen more before he's of legal age.

I bend down to give each of them a hug, which they endure for about two seconds before wriggling away. "Maybe later," I say.

"No," Debbie contradicts. "She's *my* guest, and *I* get all her attention tonight. This is her friend Brody," she adds.

"I'll play with you later, if your mom will let me," he tells them. "I'm pretty good at video games."

Debbie slants me a look that says, *I like that answer*, but only says, "Into the dining room, everyone. Everything's ready to eat."

E specially as compared to the little interlude at my house after lunch, dinner is a delight. The boys are mostly well-behaved, and hilarious when they're not. Charles is his usual well-spoken, humorous self; he tends to dominate the conversation, but it's hard to mind when he's so entertaining. Despite his obvious intelligence, and his somewhat intimidating size, there's something about him that just puts people at ease. He's a big guy, both tall and hefty, always a little disheveled but never deteriorating all the way to sloppy. A little too goofy-looking to be handsome, he has a round face, owlish green eyes, and a growing bald spot in his thin, dark hair. But he's appealing. You meet him, and you instantly want him for a friend.

Debbie's a lot more sharp-edged, except she knows how to conceal that fact, and the impression she always gives is one of warmth and welcome. And those are genuine parts of her personality, but underneath them she's always watching and weighing; it's the rare individual who fools Debbie or catches her off guard.

It's surely on purpose that she's seated Brody next to her, at the foot of the table, and me next to Charles, at the head; the boys are separated, one on each side to keep them out of trouble. Conversation is mostly general, but now and then Charles and I fall into a private discussion, which leaves Debbie and Brody free to try to figure out the other person without giving too much away. I get the feeling each has found in the other his or her perfect foil. They're both skilled at conducting charming interrogations while leaving their subjects glowing with pride that *someone*, finally, has found their stories interesting. I wonder which one will manage to learn the most from the other.

The food is relatively simple, pasta and salad and bread. Charles is the cook in the household, but Debbie no doubt insisted she make his birthday meal, and this is her fallback menu. We all have seconds and thirds, complimenting the chef, then Debbie brings out the German chocolate cake she's made for the occasion. It bristles with thirty-one small candles in a rainbow of colors. The kids watch, rapt, as Debbie and I try to light them all without scorching our fingers or having the first ones burn down all the way to the icing before we're done.

I'm pretty good at this particular task. I strike a match and get three wicks to light before the flame begins to lick at my fingertips, then I drop that match and light another one. Debbie, by contrast, burns herself three times before the whole cake is aflame, and she is scowling and sucking on her index finger as everyone else applauds and whistles when the job is finally done.

"Happy birthday, Daddy!" Stevie calls out, and I take the opportunity to pitch the traditional melody in a reasonable key. There's more clapping, then Charles blows out the candles, needing three breaths and Stevie's assistance before every flame is extinguished. Debbie cuts the cake, and I serve the ice cream, but the boys are restless, so Debbie shoos them into the other room to watch TV and eat their dessert. The rest of us linger around the table, exclaiming over how good the cake is and having second pieces.

"Anyone want more wine?" Debbie asks, getting to her feet. "Brody, thanks for bringing it. It's really good."

Charles divides a look between me and Brody. "Who's driving?"

Brody lifts his eyebrows. "I am."

"Then Melanie can have wine. You'll have coffee. Or tea, if you'd rather."

Brody's interest is piqued, but all he says is, "Coffee's fine."

I explain. "Charles's dad was killed by a drunk driver when he was ten. So he's pretty fierce on the topic. If you're out with him somewhere, and you're the driver, you get one drink. Maybe."

"He takes keys away from strangers," Debbie says as she refills my glass. "In bars and restaurants. He calls cops to tell them drunk drivers are leaving such-and-such location."

"I haven't done that in years," Charles defends himself.

"It's mortifying," Debbie adds.

"I think it's kind of cool," Brody says. "Most people aren't brave enough to live by their principles."

"Most people don't *have* principles," Charles says.

"Well, people *have* them," Brody replies. "But sometimes they're pretty sketchy. Or flexible. People like to say they're honest, but leave them alone in a room with a million dollars on the table, and they're likely to sneak a few twenties into their pockets."

"*I* wouldn't," Charles says.

"He wouldn't," Debbie agrees, sinking into the chair that Simon has vacated so she can be closer to Charles. "And if he saw other people trying to steal the money, he'd report them."

"You make me sound like—what's that word they use on cop shows? A snitch."

The word sounds funny pronounced in Charles's earnest voice, and Brody and I both laugh. Debbie smiles and reaches up to smooth back his hair. "It's why I married you," she says. "For your sterling heart."

Just then, the telephone rings, a musical jangle of three different bells on three different units, in the kitchen, the dining room, and maybe the living room. The sound cuts off abruptly in the middle of the second ring, so I assume Stevie or Simon has raced to answer. Debbie tilts her head and gives Charles an inquiring look. He seems to engage in a moment of internal debate, then shrugs. "Someone for one of the boys," he decides.

"Oh, good," she says. "Maybe someone wants to rent them for the weekend."

Five seconds later, Simon tears into the room, the cordless handset still in his grip. "Mom, can I go over to Marty's?"

Marty is a kid across the street who, according to Debbie, owns every electronic and digital device ever invented to lure a child into ignoring his homework. He has his own laptop. His family was the first to buy a Wii. He was born with a Game Boy in his hand.

"It's your father's birthday," she says.

Simon is aggrieved. "I sang 'Happy Birthday'! What more do you want?"

"Blood," Charles says. "I want your blood. And maybe a little respect directed at your mother."

Simon rolls his eyes. "Can I go?"

Charles makes sweeping motions with his hand. "Go. Leave. Take your sleeping bag and spend the night."

Simon's eyes light up, but Debbie puts her foot down. "You're not spending the night, but yes, you can go. Be back by ten, okay?"

"Okay. Bye. Happy birthday, Dad."

"Thank you, ungrateful child."

He dashes out of the kitchen, talking excitedly on the phone, and a few moments later, we hear the slam of the front door. "Never have children," Debbie says to Brody.

He grins. "Jury's still out on that one," he replies. He nods at Charles. "So, do you always play that little game? Guess who's on the phone before you answer it?"

"He's better than Caller ID," Debbie says.

"He doesn't guess," I inform Brody. "He *knows*. It's his superpower."

Charles is nodding serenely. "It's true. Ninety percent of the time, I know who's calling as soon as the phone rings."

Brody leans his elbows on the table and appears both intrigued and skeptical. "*Really*. How do you do that?"

Charles makes an indeterminate gesture. "Some of it's process of elimination. My mother and my sister have already called to wish me a happy birthday. Debbie and the boys are all home. I'm not expecting a crisis at work. We're on the do-not-call list, so we don't get many junk calls.

Marty tends to call right at seven o'clock, because that's when his family finishes dinner." He shrugs. "My brain snaps through all the possibilities and lands on the most likely one."

"It's his superpower," I repeat. "It can't be explained away rationally."

Now Brody is grinning at me. "Superpower," he echoes. "Really."

"Everyone has one," Debbie says. "Even you."

"What's yours?" he challenges her.

"I can make people talk to me."

"All people," Charles confirms. "The mean-looking lady at the DMV who won't make eye contact or give you a civil answer? She talks to Debbie. Shows her pictures of her grandkids. *Smiles*, for God's sake."

"And don't go shopping with her," I say. "Every salesclerk will tell you his or her life story. I mean, one day we were buying shoes. The salesman is kneeling there at her feet, and I make some joke, I don't remember what, and he says, 'Are you two sisters?' I say, 'No, we've just known each other fifteen years.' And he says—swear to God, like it was the most natural segue in the world—'I've been married to my wife for fifteen years. But we're not very happy. I'd leave her, but we have five children together.' And before you know it, we learn about how he was born in Jamaica, but he grew up in France, and his father was a doctor until he lost his leg in a car accident—"

"And his mother won some international lottery, which is how they got the money to move to America—" Debbie chimes in.

"So he went to college in Little Rock, which is where he met the wife that he now wishes he could get rid of," I finish up. "I thought we would *never* get away from him."

"That one was a little extreme," she says.

"*All* your conversations with strangers are like that."

"I can't help it," she says. "People confide in me."

I am living proof of that. Until I met Debbie, I had told no one, *no one*, the truth about Ann. In fact, I had gone to elaborate lengths to conceal, from relatives and friends and neighbors down the street, what exactly she was. I had evaded questions, lied outright, constructed detailed scenarios that explained where Ann had been or why she had behaved a certain way. I had assumed I would go to my grave sharing this secret with only my father, Gwen, and Ann herself.

But I had told Debbie before I had known her a month. "That explains a lot," she'd said. That was it. No exclamations of horror or astonishment, no accusations of lying or hysteria. Just calm acceptance. And the burden I had carried for so long, that I had thought would bow me to the ground, became in an instant something manageable, something ordinary, something that I could bear as long as I had to and still not break.

"So what's your superpower?" Charles asks Brody. "Everybody has one. It's not *super*, obviously, it's just— something you can always do. That other people can't."

Brody is looking thoughtful. "Well, going by those rules—I can find keys."

"Oohh, that's a good one," Debbie says.

I'm not convinced. "What, like your car keys? Your house keys?"

Brody nods. "I never lose them."

"That's not the same as *finding* them."

"Right, but I can do that, too. My sister Bethany loses her keys about once a month. She'll call and have me drive down to Cape just to look for them. And I've found them in the weirdest places. Under the refrigerator. In the washing machine. In a pair of shoes at the back of her closet. I've never not been able to track them down."

"Can you find other stuff, too?" Charles asks. "Like gloves and math books and jackets? Because we've lost a lot of those."

"Nope, just keys."

"Well, I suppose that's useful," I concede grudgingly.

"The first time it happened, I was maybe eight or nine," Brody says. His face has gotten that faraway expression that settles over people as they're revisiting a memory. "And the whole family was locked out of the house. We were on our way back from church or something, maybe there was a turkey cooking in the oven. I don't remember, but I do know that my mom and dad were really upset, and Bethany was crying, and everyone was really agitated. And I remembered that, like, two years before, my sister Bailey had dropped her house key in the garden and she'd never found it. So I started poking through the weeds and scratching in the dirt, trying to see if I could find that old key now that we needed it. And sure enough, about five minutes later, I dug it up out of the mud at the base of a rosebush. Opened the door like a charm. Everybody was happy. And *I*," he concluded, "had discovered my superpower."

Charles nods approvingly. "That's a good origin story," he says before glancing in my direction. "So what's *your* special ability?"

It's been clear for the past five minutes that someone is going to ask this question, but I don't have a good answer. So I say, "Dating the wrong men."

Brody looks affronted. *"Hey."*

"That's not having a superpower, that's just being a woman," Debbie says.

"Hey," Charles says, using Brody's exact inflection.

She scoots her chair over so she's close enough to kiss him on the cheek. "But I married you, darling, so the description doesn't apply to you," she says in a sugary voice.

I glance at Brody. "It doesn't apply to you either, since we're not dating."

The look he gives me then is hard to read—half-smiling, half-speculative—as if he's trying to figure out how and when to prove me wrong. But he doesn't say anything.

"So?" Charles says. "What's your power?"

I shrug. "I don't have one."

"Yes, you do," Debbie says. She's still pressed up next to Charles, and his arm has draped itself over her shoulder. What I've always liked, and envied, about them is that they're comfortable showing affection for each other in public, but they don't overdo it. A kiss, a touch, a hand laid on a forearm, a pat on the back. If there's a group of people crowded into a room, they don't have to sit side by side to be happy, but if they're in a movie theater in the dark, they're always holding hands. "You know when to let go."

I turn a frown in her direction. "Say what?"

She waves at the remains of the cake. "Like when we were lighting candles. You always dropped the match before it burned you. *I* wasn't smart enough to do that."

"That's a pretty pathetic superpower," I say.

She sits up so she can speak more energetically. "No, but it manifests in a lot of different forms. Remember Girl Scouts? The roller-skating badge?"

Charles directs his question at Brody. "Who gets a badge in *roller-skating*? Seriously?"

Brody shakes his head in sorrow. "We had to build fires and put up tents and rescue old ladies from submerged cars if *we* wanted to earn badges in Boy Scouts."

Debbie ignores this byplay. "And they had us do that stupid routine where you'd line up and hold on to the waist of the person in front of you, and then you'd skate around the rink all connected together until someone tripped or something and everyone would fall down—"

"Crack the whip. That's what it's called," Brody says. "It's supposed to be fun, the person at the end goes really fast—"

"Well, it wasn't fun. Everyone ended up bruised and scraped up—"

"Katie Malone broke her arm," I remember.

"Right! But you never got hurt. You always let go before the pileup."

"That's not a superpower, that's a highly developed sense of self-preservation," I tell her.

"And in high school. When you were going out with Kurt—"

Brody straightens up so fast he almost knocks his chair over. "Kurt Markham? You went *out* with him?"

"Oh, God, he was so cute back then," Debbie says.

"He was always an asshole," Charles informs the table. "Even when he was seventeen."

"You went out with him?" Brody repeats.

Debbie points at me. "Homecoming King and Queen. Melanie and Kurt."

"This really changes how I think of you," Brody tells me.

"Well, since I don't *care* how you think of me—"

"But here's my point," Debbie says. "Everyone thought you were the luckiest girl in the school. And you broke up with him, and no one could understand why."

"Because he was an asshole," Charles mutters.

"And then a month later he had that horrible car accident when his new girlfriend was in the car, and she almost got killed. Remember? You let go of him just in time."

I roll my eyes. "I think you're stretching an unlikely premise a little too far."

Debbie shrugs. "It's your superpower. You don't get to ask for it. You just take what you get."

Stevie has slunk into the dining room, gloom hanging on him so heavily his little head is bent toward the floor. "What's wrong, devil child?" Debbie asks cheerfully.

"We didn't get to finish our game," he says. "And now Simon's at Marty's and I'll have to go to bed before he gets back and it'll be *tomorrow* before we get to finish it."

"Oh my God, the world will end," Charles says.

Stevie fixes Brody with an accusing stare. "You *said* you'd come play with us later."

Debbie snaps her fingers and points toward the door. "No harassing the guests! Out! Downstairs. Read a book or something. Improve your mind. You can play games tomorrow."

But I'm not surprised to see Brody smile and come to his feet. "I said it, and I meant it," he agrees. "Let's go."

The three of us watch in silence as Brody and Stevie head back toward the basement, Stevie already chattering. As soon as it seems likely they're out of earshot, Debbie turns to me with her eyes big and her mouth widening in a smile.

"He. Is. *Adorable!*" she exclaims in an excited undervoice. "Good-looking and funny and scrumptious! How are you resisting him?"

"He does seem like a nice fellow," Charles says in a more

temperate voice. "Why are you resisting him? Is he a felon or something?"

Debbie waves a hand. "Long story," she says. She swears she's never told Charles the truth about Ann, and I believe her, but I have to think she's dropped some kind of hints. Enough to let him know he shouldn't question me about her, in any case. Because Charles will ask thoughtful and detailed questions about every other area of my life, but all he ever says about my sister is, "How's Ann?"

"Yeah, he's been pretty nice the past few weeks," I admit. "I like him more than I should. But he's still—" I glance at Charles. "Dangerous to my peace of mind."

He lifts his hands in a gesture of surrender. "Tell secrets if you must. I'll clear the table."

So for the next ten minutes Charles putters in the kitchen while Debbie and I huddle together so I can whisper a transcript of the afternoon's edgy conversations. She responds with the appropriate gasps and sounds of dismay at the right places, but it's clear she's still wholly in the Brody's-a-good-guy camp.

"Okay, so he saw Ann and William dash out the door without so much as a flashlight between them, but he still didn't learn anything absolutely damning," she says when I'm done. "He just thinks they're quirky."

"He thinks they are exactly what they are, and the more *they* hang around while *he's* hanging around, the sooner he's going to know for sure."

"Well, then, you have only two choices," Debbie says. "Tell him to go away. Or tell Ann to go away. Nothing else you can do."

I stare at her because, put in those stark terms, I realize I am not prepared to do either. Well, obviously, I would choose Ann over Brody if I had to choose one person I was going to keep in my life. But I am far more reluctant than I realized to say out loud that I want Brody gone from my life forever.

Debbie sits back in her chair, a look of satisfaction on her face. "Thought so," she says.

Now I'm annoyed. "Thought what?"

But she doesn't get a chance to answer because Brody's climbed back up from the basement and come to join us at the table again. Like Debbie, he's decided to change seats; he lowers himself into the one next to me.

"That kid has the hands of a brain surgeon," he says. "A ten for dexterity."

"Did he beat you?" I inquire.

He nods, but defends himself. "I inherited Simon's score. I could have won if I'd played the game from the beginning."

"Yeah, you lost to a seven-year-old," I razz him. "Maybe if you're really nice, he'll offer you a rematch."

He opens his mouth to answer, but the phone shrills again with its many voices. Automatically, we all look toward Charles, who strolls over from the kitchen.

"Who is it?" Debbie asks.

He points at Brody. "Someone calling for him."

Debbie and I both show him expressions of bewilderment, but Brody has started laughing. "Who even knows you're here?" I ask him.

Stevie comes racing into the room with the cordless in his hand. "Mom, it's some woman and she wants to talk to some guy who doesn't live here." Apparently, despite bonding with Brody over Mario Party, he's forgotten his guest's identity.

Brody takes the phone from him. "It's my sister," he says, and then speaks into the receiver. "Hey, Beth. Good job . . . Yep. He didn't know your name, of course, but he knew you were calling for me. Weird, huh?" He listens for a moment. "That's kind of a lame superpower," he says. "I'd work on that if I were you. Okay, thanks. Bye."

He hits the OFF button and grins at the rest of us. "I did *not* think Charles would get that one."

"You told Bethany you were coming to Debbie's house?" I ask. I'm still confused.

But Charles, obviously, is not. "He was testing me," he explains. "He must have called his sister from his cell phone when he was in the basement with Stevie and given her this number. He thought he could trick me, but I—I am gifted enough to see beyond his feeble machinations."

"I never would have thought of that," Debbie says. Her voice is admiring.

I poke Brody in the shoulder. "So what's Bethany's superpower?"

He looks pained. "She can disentangle jewelry. What the hell?"

But Debbie and I are instantly covetous. "Oh, man, I want *that* magic!" Debbie exclaims. "I've got a necklace I haven't been able to wear for three years because I can't get the knot out of the chain. Does she take commissions?"

"Knowing Bethany," he says, "she probably does."

Debbie turns to me with an expression so sincere it has to be fake. "Don't mess this up," she says. "You have to keep this guy around for a while. At least until I get that necklace fixed."

If she were close enough, I'd hit her. I can't even figure out how to answer, but fortunately Charles says, "You know, I think I want just another little sliver of cake. Anyone else?"

And between the cake and the coffee and the conversation, the next hour goes by in about five minutes. I don't even realize how late it is until Simon tramps through the front door, calling out a good-bye to someone who has accompanied him home.

"Crap, is it ten o'clock already?" Debbie exclaims, jumping out of her chair. "Stevie should have been in bed a half hour ago. No, no, you guys don't have to leave," she adds, as Brody and I instantly come to our feet. "I'll just throw him in the shower for a few minutes and run back downstairs."

"Clearly, it's time for us to go," I say firmly. "But thanks for having us over. It was a wonderful meal. A fun time."

Charles has stood up, too, and he and Brody shake hands. "Good to meet you, sir," he says to Brody. "We look forward to more chances to get to know you."

"I had a great time," he says. "I'll come back anytime you invite me."

There's more along these lines as we all move in an untidy group toward the door. Once I've got my coat on, Debbie gives me a long hug. In my ear she whispers, "Kiss him good night for me," then pulls back, laughing. She embraces Brody, too, but I can't tell if she passes on any instructions.

Finally, we're outside in night air that has grown sharply cool, and I'm rubbing my hands and saying *brrrrr!* as we climb into the Honda. There's a bad moment or two when the car won't start. Brody's cursing under his breath and gently pumping the accelerator, leaning over the steering wheel as if he can *will* the ignition to catch. I've already imagined borrowing the boys' sleeping bags and bunking down in the basement when the motor turns over, and Brody leans back with a sigh of relief.

"Well, that would be a total bummer of a way to end an utterly delightful evening," he says as he backs out. I wait for him to ask me for directions, but he seems to have remembered the way back to the highway. It's sort of annoying; I got lost in Debbie's labyrinth of a neighborhood for the first year she lived here.

"You seemed to be having a good time. Or was that just good manners?"

"No, I thought they were great. All of them."

"Did you let Stevie win?"

"I would have, but I didn't need to. He beat me all on his own."

"What did Debbie tell you about me when I was busy talking to Charles?"

He glances over at me, amused. "What makes you think we were talking about you? Narcissistic, are we?"

"Fine," I say, and reach out to turn on the radio. Sports talk, unutterably boring. Not asking permission, I start punching buttons until I find a station playing music. It's soft rock, so I'm sure Brody hates it, but he makes no comment, and we finish the rest of the drive without speaking.

The tires crunch on the gravel as he pulls onto my lawn. I've grown a little tense during the last quarter mile. This nighttime outing bears so many trappings of a *date* that I can't picture how it's going to end, and the possibilities are making me nervous. Brody's probably been thinking along the same lines. At any rate, without cutting the motor or turning off the headlights, he looks over with a smile.

"Walk you to the door?" he offers.

My laugh sounds shaky. "I could make you some coffee if you like."

"That'd be great, but I don't want to push you."

"Too late for that," I say, and step out of the car. I hear him chuckle as he catches up and steps inside the house just a beat behind me.

I've left on only one light, the stained-glass lamp in the living room, so the main part of the house is shrouded in a semidarkness that seems weighted with romance. Even so, I can't bear to hit the wall switches and send brightness arcing through the rooms. I make coffee by the dim cooking light over the stove while Brody drops to the couch and relaxes so completely he appears to be sprawling. When I approach with the two steaming mugs, he only sits up enough to be able to drink without spilling hot liquid all over his shirt.

I sit cross-legged and sideways on the couch, so I'm facing him. Partly to see him better, partly to keep him from putting his arm around me. If he was so inclined. "I have a commission for you," I say.

"Really?" he murmurs, slurping at his coffee. "Ow, that's hot. What kind of commission?"

"I want you to find a key for me."

His eyes are alight with deviltry. "The key to your heart?"

I make a face at him. "No. The key to this—" I lean back and reach behind me, because the little ceramic bank is on the end table next to the couch. The coins rattle as I settle it on the cushions between us. "This cute little artifact. Something Ann and I had when we were kids."

He rests his coffee cup on his stomach and picks up the house with his free hand. "Oooh, you'll be rich."

"Hey, there are a lot of silver coins in there. Some of them might be worth something. And there might be other stuff in there. Stuff with sentimental value. So I want you to find the key."

"All right." He picks up his coffee again and takes a few

meditative sips. Maybe he's imagining the nooks and crannies of my house where small keys might have gotten lost. Maybe he's just savoring his coffee. "As long as we're talking about superpowers, I have a question about yours."

"All right," I echo, but I'm wary.

"Debbie says you know when to let go. Do you also know when to hold on?"

I meet his eyes. I know my expression is a little fierce. "When something's worth keeping," I say, "I hold on forever."

"I guess that's the trick," he says. "Knowing what's worth it and what isn't."

"I guess that's something we all have to figure out for ourselves."

He blows on his coffee. "While we're on the subject," he says, "how can you really believe we're not dating?"

There's absolute silence for a moment. "That's not the same subject," I reply at last.

He gives me that teasing half-smile. "Yeah, kind of it is."

I lean forward so that my posture underscores the intensity of my expression. "We're. Not. Dating," I say.

He pulls himself to a more upright position, bends over to set his mug on the floor, then half turns to face me more directly. "Then what do you think we're doing? I'm hanging out at your house, I'm meeting your friends and family, we have lunch, we have dinner, we have coffee—"

"We're just—" I flounder. "I mean, you're working on that book and I'm just—I guess we're getting to know each other—"

He leans over and kisses me. He doesn't pull me into his arms, he doesn't scoot closer, he just lays his mouth against mine with a warm and definite pressure. For a moment I'm flushed with such complex emotions that I can't even sort them out—shock, pleasure, dread, longing, worry, hope, elation—and then I jerk back and stare at him.

He smiles. "We're dating," he says, and hops up from the couch. I gaze after him as he heads to the kitchen and flips on the overhead light. I can hear him as he begins tossing through the mortifyingly messy junk drawer right next to the passably well organized silverware drawer.

"I saw an old key ring in here the other day when I was looking for a pen," he calls. "Five or six keys on it, one of them really small, like a luggage key. But I'm wondering—"

I shake my head, as if to shake away the kiss, but I don't rub it off my mouth. I don't say anything, but he doesn't expect me to. Anyway, not more than another minute elapses before he mutters *ha!* and I hear the tiny jangle of metal. He saunters back into the living room, whistling, brandishing something in his hand. As he said, it's an old key ring, a round loop hung with an insurance company's plastic logo and an assortment of keys. I've seen them any number of times these past ten years as I've gone rooting through the junk drawer, looking for something, and I've always thought, *I should really figure out if any of them still work.* But I've never bothered to take them out and try to fit them into any locks in the house.

He drops down next to me, flicking through the options. "This one might go to the front door—this one's a key to an old Buick, and you can probably throw it away—and this one is so rusty I can't imagine it goes to anything that's still functional. But here. This little one. I bet it's the one you want—"

He inserts the tiny key into the miniature lock, and I hear it snap open. He grins at me, absurdly proud. "Is that a great superpower or what?"

I make a crooning sound and take the bank from his hands, gently slipping the padlock free and removing the ceramic door that guards the treasure. I stick a couple of fingers through the narrow opening, but that doesn't dislodge more than a coin or two, so I flip the bank over and start shaking it until items come bouncing onto the couch.

"Hey—hey—you're going to lose half of them between the cushions," Brody admonishes. He fetches a dish towel from the kitchen, and I start shaking the bank again, a little more carefully. Dimes and quarters and half-dollars drop like silver manna onto the unfolded linen.

"Oh, these are cool—look at these old Mercury Head dimes," he says, picking up some of the smallest pieces and squinting at them in the semidarkness. "This one's pretty worn, but this one's practically mint condition. Wonder if it's worth anything?"

"I think there's at least one silver dollar that was a collectible back in the day," I tell him. "I mean, it probably wasn't worth more than ten dollars at the time, but maybe that's gone up a little."

"And look at these old Liberty half-dollars. I'd forgotten about them."

The bank's almost empty, but I can hear a few pieces still rolling around inside, stubbornly resisting my efforts to shake them loose. At least one coin appears to be trapped in the folds of a piece of paper that's also still stuck inside. I poke my fingers awkwardly through the door again, trying to pry free the last items.

A penny falls to the dish towel with a copper clatter as I scrape the paper through the door. "What's *that* doing in here?" Brody asks, picking it up. "Oh, wow. It's from 1934. Look, it's got the old wheat sheaves and everything."

I've found myself with two sheets of paper, both folded as small as they will go. Mystified, I drop one and smooth out the other. "I have no idea what these could . . . be . . ."

My voice trails off when I see what I'm holding.

It's a pencil sketch of two girls standing side by side, badly done by my sixteen-year-old self. You can tell one figure is supposed to be older than the other because she's significantly taller, but not much else distinguishes them. I've clearly spent a lot of effort drawing unrealistically lush, cascading hair and long-lashed eyes that are way too big for the wobbly oval faces. Not so much time on arms and legs and torsos, though there's so much detail in the necklace of the taller girl that I can instantly call to mind which piece of jewelry it's supposed to represent. And I've obviously given up completely before I even attempted to portray our shoes, so our feet are hidden by a convenient patch of grass.

"What is it?" Brody says, craning his neck to see.

"One summer. I was babysitting and Ann was bored. I got out paper and pencils so we could draw, but she was crabby and said that didn't sound like fun. So I said we'd make *special* pictures. We'd each draw a picture of the two of us together, but we wouldn't show them to each other. We'd put them in the bank and not take them out for ten years. And then, before we even *looked* at the first ones, we'd draw another set of pictures and see how much we'd changed."

"That was creative," he says. "Did she go for it?"

"Yeah. We spent the next hour, each of us in our own corner, working on our drawings. Then we folded them small and put them in the bank."

"I'm guessing you didn't do the anniversary set, though."

I shake my head. "Forgot the whole thing until this very moment."

As I've been speaking, he's picked up the second piece of paper and started to unfold it. "So that's yours? And this one's Ann's?"

I nod. I'm still studying my sketch, thinking that I probably wouldn't have done a much better job at twenty-six even if I'd remembered the plan. I notice that I've given Ann a prominent piece of jewelry, too—a fake-gold bangle bracelet that she used to love beyond reason. There had been a stretch of time when she wouldn't leave the house unless she had it on. I smile, wondering if she'll remember that detail when I show her the pictures.

I flip the page so Brody can get a better look. "See this?" I start to say, but then I realize he's staring at Ann's drawing, the expression on his face halfway between astonishment and triumph. My stomach balls into a hard knot and I snatch the paper from his hand.

Oh, but I know before I look at it what the image will be.

Six-year-old Ann has drawn me with great looping balloon arms, stick legs, and a tiny head covered with dandelion-puff hair. Clown shoes and a triangle-shaped skirt represent my ensemble. But that's not what Brody's been staring at.

Next to me, the only other figure on the page, is a small dog with huge pointed ears and a long whippy tail. The significance of the creature is impossible to overlook. It's a self-portrait. This is how Ann sees herself.

CHAPTER TWELVE

JANET

The last fight I ever had with my parents happened the day after I graduated from high school. I'd already been accepted at the University of Illinois in Urbana-Champaign and offered a decent scholarship package. I hadn't decided what my major would be, but I was attracted to careers like marine biology and archeology, so I was planning to load up my schedule with science classes. I'd been assigned a dorm and a roommate. It says a lot about me when I admit that the part of the college experience I was most worried about was living with another person. I had always been good at my classes and never any good at making friends. I had no reason to expect that college would be any different.

My dad waited until the Sunday after graduation to tell me that he'd accepted a transfer to Los Angeles. I stared at him in disbelief.

"How long have you known this?" I demanded.

"Couple of months."

"We didn't want you to be distracted from school during finals," my mother added. "So we waited to tell you."

"But it's time to start packing," my father said. "We're moving at the end of June."

I crossed my arms. "*I'm* not. I'm going to college."

"Plenty of good schools in California," my dad said. "If you're a resident of the state, education is practically free."

"I'm not *going* to California," I said. "I have a perfectly good scholarship to go to school in Illinois. You'll just have to go to Los Angeles without me."

Maybe if I'd taken a more reasonable tone, my father would have been reasonable in turn. He would have agreed that it would make sense for me to attend the school to which I already had the scholarship; he would have conceded that telephones and interstates and airlines made it simple for far-flung family members to stay in touch. He would not have ignited into a rage and screamed that I had always been contrary and difficult, impossible to please, and that if I would not move with them to California, I could consider myself officially on my own for the rest of my life. *Don't bother calling, don't bother coming to visit. If you don't want to live with us as our daughter now, then we don't want you as our daughter ever.* My mother alternated between begging him to make sense and pleading with me not to be stupid, until she, too, grew angry and began berating me for my stubbornness and my hatefulness and my disastrously willful nature.

"No wonder you never have any friends!" she screamed. "You're a sociopath, that's what you are! You don't have any human emotions!"

We'd been standing in the kitchen—well, that makes it sound too calm. We'd been pacing through the kitchen, each of us pausing now and then to slam a hand against the countertop or shake a fist in someone's face; my father had already swept his arm across the cluttered table and sent half a dozen dishes crashing to the floor. Now I pivoted on my heel and stalked through the door, heading to the living room, where I'd left my purse on the sofa. My father followed me, still yelling. When he saw that I was planning to dash out the front door, he grabbed my arm and jerked me back.

"Don't you walk away from me, you little bitch!" he

roared. "Don't you dare leave this house unless you never want to be allowed back in!"

I swung my purse so hard at his face that it knocked him backward. He stumbled and released me, cursing. I knew the minute he caught his balance, he'd grab me again, and that's when the hitting would start. "What makes you think I'd ever want to come back?" I snarled, and I ran out the door.

Probably everything would have been okay eventually. It wasn't the first time I'd had a screaming match with my parents, not the first time I'd walked out, or been kicked out, or been told I should never come back. I wouldn't even have to say I was sorry—no one in my family ever did. I could just reappear at the dinner table the following night, and no one would mention the threats and the insults from the day before. The argument would have continued, but in calmer tones, maybe; it's possible we could have worked something out.

But I didn't go back. I didn't want to be forgiven. I didn't want to be their daughter anymore.

And I certainly wasn't moving to California.

I suppose it's a lie to say I didn't go back. After spending the night uneasily moving between the parking lot of the train station and a booth at an all-night Denny's, I returned to the house around noon the next day when my parents were both at work. They hadn't bothered to change the locks—though that was a promise my father had made more than once during such fights in the past—so it was easy enough for me to get inside and gather what I needed. Clothes, mostly, plus some towels and toiletries, enough to fill two big wheeled suitcases. I only had a couple of pieces of jewelry worth any money—a pearl necklace my parents had given me when I turned sixteen, and diamond earrings they'd given me two years later—and I picked these up, too. Not because they had any sentimental value but because I thought I might be able to pawn them if I ever needed the money. I was tempted to toss through my mother's jewelry box and pick out the few pieces she owned that might net me a few hundred bucks, but I decided against it. I didn't want to give them any reason to come looking for me.

I made a quick detour out back to leave a message for Cooper. A red ribbon tied to one of the patio posts meant I had dropped a note in the rusted old coffee can I'd placed at the back of the property line. For the past year, anytime I knew he would be in human shape and looking for me, but I'd be unavailable, I'd communicated with him in this way. From time to time, he'd also left messages—or drawings— behind in the same manner. I had seen him just two nights ago, and I knew he'd only been human for five days. He would find the note soon enough. In the past year, during the weeks he was in a man's shape, we had never gone more than three nights without seeing each other. Sometimes we would even meet in daylight at a shop or a restaurant so I could buy him food or an item he needed. I had to admit, those outings—the ones that to most girls would seem like the most relaxed and normal interactions with a guy—to me seemed the most surreal.

But it would be useful now to have Cooper take a young man's shape and come find me where I waited.

I stepped back inside through the patio entrance, called a cab, dragged my suitcases to the front porch, closed and locked the door, and dropped the key through the mail slot. Ten minutes later, the taxi arrived. I had the driver take me to the McDonald's closest to the highway exit for the state park where Cooper had his base.

"Somebody's really meeting you here?" he asked doubt- fully as he pulled up in the semideserted parking lot.

"Someone really is," I assured him. "I'll be fine."

And I knew I would be.

I had a new job before Cooper even arrived. I asked to speak to the manager, told him how long I'd been work- ing at the McDonald's in town, explained that I was moving out this way and might not have a car so I was hoping to effect a transfer. He called my boss, who apparently said, "Yeah, she's a pretty good worker, but she doesn't pick up enough shifts," and hired me on the spot.

"When can you start?" he asked.

"Tomorrow."

"Be here at ten. Unless you want to put in a few hours right now. I'm short in the kitchen."

"I would, but I'm not sure when my friends are going to get here."

In fact, it was close to nightfall before Cooper stepped through the glass door, looking tense and worried and, as he always did in small, crowded spaces, edgy as a hawk. His face smoothed out as soon as he saw me, though, and he slid into the booth across from me.

"What happened?" he asked.

"Had a fight with my family. I'm not going back there." I gestured at the two suitcases I'd leaned against the wall. "I took all my stuff and walked out."

His eyes narrowed and he considered me. "I wouldn't recommend leaving your family behind," he said quietly. "If you have any choice about it."

"I don't have a choice," I replied. "They're moving to California at the end of the month. And I'm not leaving you behind."

Again, he thought it over before he answered. I'd cut his hair for him a couple of weeks ago, but it still tangled into big sloppy curls that made a dark halo around his face. He said he looked like a girl; I said he looked like a poet. But then, I'd always thought so. Just now he looked like a poet struggling to find a word or work out a rhyme.

"I don't think *I* should be the reason you make any decision as huge as this," he said at last.

His hands were folded before him on the table. I covered them with my own, leaning forward to give my words more intensity. "You're the reason I make *every* decision," I said.

He shook his head slightly. "You might be sorry about that someday."

"Well, I'm not sorry about it today."

He nodded slightly. "So what do you plan to do? Where are you going to stay?"

"I'm going to live with you."

His big eyes widened. "Live with me? In the park?"

"Sure, why not? It'll be like an extended camping trip."

He looked doubtful. "You might find it pretty miserable."

"No I won't. You've got a tent. A sleeping bag. There are public showers by the RV lots." I jerked my head toward the front counter. "I've already talked to the manager. He'll let me work here for the summer." I grinned. "And you and I can eat lots of burgers and fries over the next few months."

"What about school?"

"I'll take the bus up to Champaign in August. Nothing's changed except that I don't live with my parents anymore."

He was quiet a moment, still thinking it over. I felt a momentary unwelcome swirl of doubt churn through my stomach. Slowly, I released his hands and laid my own in my lap. "Unless you don't want me to live with you," I said.

Now his smile came—as always, so sweet that it sugared my heart. He turned his palms up, an invitation for me to return my hands to his. I did, and his fingers closed around them reassuringly.

"I'd love to have you," he said. "I'm just not sure it will be the easy life you seem to think."

"I don't think it will be *easy*," I allowed. "But it will be with *you*. So it will be just fine."

It was a damn long hike from the restaurant to the park, wheeling two suitcases behind us, as well as Cooper's bike, since he refused to ride on ahead of me. And, again, it was no simple chore to maneuver the suitcases down the progressively narrower tracks to the remote site where Cooper had set up his camp. I had been here twice in the past nine months, so I knew what to expect: literally nothing but a small tent, a packed-down clearing of dirt in front of it, and a small cache of goods and utensils. And then the trees spreading out in all directions. Here in early summer, they were so thick with leaves the sunlight barely filtered through. The ground below them was covered with an eternally renewed carpet of dead leaves, fallen branches, climbing vines, and low bushes that choked off any easy access through the woods.

"Home," I panted, dropping my suitcases to the ground. It was scarcely eighty degrees, but the exertion had left me hot and sweaty. "I love it already."

We made dinner from a couple of Extra Value Meals and the items Cooper had on hand, and we talked about our options. He said I should use his bike to get to work until he found another one—he had become very good at scavenging for items left behind in the park—and he would mark the trails from his campsite to the exit and the nearest bathrooms. We inventoried his possessions and glanced over my checkbook, trying to figure out what we needed and what we could afford to buy.

"I'll have to call the school," I said. "Tell them that my circumstances have changed. Maybe they'll help me emancipate myself."

"Maybe you can go up to Champaign over the summer and talk to a counselor or somebody," he suggested.

"Maybe I can. But you have to come with me."

"You're afraid to go a hundred miles by yourself?"

"No. I want you to come so you can look around. See where you can live while I'm in school."

He watched me a long time with those big eyes. "Maybe it's not such a good idea," he said at last.

"What's not?"

"Me coming to college with you."

I tilted up my chin in a mutinous fashion. We'd had this conversation more than once already—in fact, before I even applied to school, we'd talked about where I could go that he could come along. I'd offered to stay in central or southern Illinois, closer to his familiar haunts, but he'd been distressed at the idea I would restrict my life so much to accommodate him. So then I'd started looking at schools in Minnesota and northern Wisconsin, close to the Canadian border—places where a wolf might be expected to thrive. But each of us, it turned out, felt more comfortable staying in state. The Champaign campus had seemed ideal for us both.

"If you don't come with me, I don't go," I said.

"It just seems that—Janet, I don't want to hold you back. If you're tied to me, you won't do all the other things you should be doing."

"I don't want to do those other things, whatever they are."

"Maybe you'll feel differently, once you're in school. Once you're around new people and trying new things."

"I don't like other people," I said. "I never have."

He looked sad. Or maybe it was that artist's face; it always looked just a little haunted. "Maybe you would if I didn't take up so much of your time."

I leaned forward and put my hands on his cheeks. He had started shaving regularly the past few months; his stubble felt bristly as pine needles against my palms. "Until you were in my life, I didn't want anything badly enough to fight for it," I told him. "I didn't care about anything enough to miss it. I didn't love anybody, I didn't love anything. I just existed. I just endured. You're the first thing in my life that ever made sense. I think you're the last thing that's ever going to make sense. It's not just that I don't *want* to leave you behind. It's that I don't know how to arrange my life if it's not arranged around you."

Ever so slight against my fingertips, I felt the motion of his nod. We were sitting face-to-face, knee to knee, in that cramped clearing right in front of the tent. Keeping my hands cupped against his cheekbones, I leaned in and pressed my mouth against his. Closing my eyes, I fell into that kiss as if falling into oblivion.

We had not made love yet, Cooper and I, but it was something that was always on my mind. I was a virgin, of course—blundering antisocial girl that I was—and I assumed that Cooper was though I had not asked. Whenever he was human, we touched with increasing frequency; we held hands as we walked, we kissed in the dark. Those last two times I had spent the night at his campgrounds, we had lain side by side in the small tent, body pressed to body, hands wandering. But we had done no more than explore. I wasn't sure he was ready—I wasn't sure I was—all I knew about sex was that it could leave broken hearts and pregnant girls in its disastrous wake.

But everything was changed now. I had thrown off my other ties; I had unequivocally chosen Cooper over everything else in my life. It had not been a hard choice, but it was still radical. Loving Cooper closed off so many other options—a normal life of friends and family, a suburban house, barbecues with the neighbors, Sunday drives on autumn afternoons, family vacations at Disney World. I could snatch moments of that ordinary life, I supposed, during the weeks that Cooper was human, but he would never be the traditional wage earner who worked in the factory or the office five days a week, came home to pot roasts and the evening news, and mowed his grass on Saturday mornings. He would be passionate and unreliable and struck dumb, now and then, by a wordless poetry he struggled to express.

If I was going to love him, I would have to build a life that was broad enough to include him but rich enough to survive his absences, that made room for him without depending on him. I would have to be strong enough to be solitary, open enough to be joyful, and immune to surprise.

If I was going to sleep with him, I would have to practice diligent birth control—or be prepared to end up with a child as exotic and preternatural as Cooper himself.

I was the one to pull away from the kiss, scrambling to my knees so I could peer down at his face. His expression was as sober and stricken as if I had just informed him that the world was ending. I rested my hands on his shoulders and touched my forehead to his.

"I'm not sure if you're sure," I whispered. I could see his

eyes, so huge and unfathomable, so close to mine. "I'm always the one who makes decisions, but I don't want to push you into this if you're not ready."

"I'm not afraid," he said instantly. "Are you?"

I shook my head, slightly, just rocking my forehead against his. "No."

"Do you want to stop?"

"No. But I don't have—I didn't think to bring—with everything else that happened—"

"I have condoms," he said unexpectedly.

That made me giggle. "You do? When did you buy those?"

A smile broke through his somberness; he looked boyish and eager. "About three months ago. Just in case."

I lifted a hand to stroke his cheek and marvel at the roughness of his whiskers. "I've never done this before."

"Me either."

"But I've seen movies. I mean, not *porn*, but sexy movies."

"I've read books."

"Me, too. I know how it's *supposed* to go."

"I'm ready," he said. "I want to."

"I love you," I whispered.

For an answer, he rose to his knees before me and enfolded me in another embrace. His long arms wrapped around me and drew me close, and closer still. We kissed each other greedily, making one long deliberate feast of the banquet we had only tasted before. The more we kissed, the wilder we became, the less courteous. I tugged at his clothes and he pulled at mine and I heard my mouth make small sounds, gasps or grunts or quick furious moans of frustration. We were both fully human and yet there were moments I felt as if purely animal instincts had come over me, instinctive, incautious, insatiable.

We did not bother crawling into the tent, though as soon as we were naked, Cooper snaked out a tattered blanket to cover the hard earth, and we wriggled on top of that. He was so long and lean, a thin supple plank of a man, but his pale, smooth skin covered powerful muscles. I had never thought of myself as particularly soft, especially feminine, but I was struck by the contrast between our bodies as my full round curves eased against his taut planes. I could not press myself close enough to him, I could not stroke enough of his surfaces to satisfy my need for touch. I kissed him again and drew him down on top of me and felt his body enter mine.

Oh, God, that joining with another soul.

I cried out, half in pain and half in discovery. This was the reason. This was what drove the days forward, kept the world whirling on its axis. This closeness with another being. This mingled breath, mingled effort, straining bodies, slippery skin, touch, heat, kiss, thrust, *shock*, and satisfaction.

I knew at that moment, though I had known it before, that I could never love anybody else, or even try.

You can't spend every minute having sex, though there were days that summer that we tried, and in the weeks that followed, we had to work out all sorts of logistical and personal-space issues. But more quickly than I might have expected, we had come up with a routine of sorts. Cooper scrounged up another bike, so I rode it to my job almost every day. I worked as many hours as I could, saved every penny that we didn't absolutely require for food and clothing and other essentials, and learned just how well I could tolerate a fairly primitive mode of camping. If it hadn't been for the public showers and bathrooms, I don't think I would have survived so well; I have always been able to endure most situations if I can ultimately manage to get clean.

I'd also contacted the university, made arrangements for my mail to be sent to the local post office, and marked off key dates on a calendar so I would be sure to move to Champaign in time for freshman orientation. I wasn't ready to leave my strange but semimagical existence quite yet—I was enjoying it too much for that—but by fall I thought I would be.

Cooper worked all summer, too. He had taken employment doing janitorial work for a nighttime cleaning service, though of course he could only accept shifts two weeks out of the month. His incurious boss paid him in cash and didn't ask questions. We assumed he thought Cooper was an illegal immigrant, or possibly a convict out on parole; it was also possible his boss's own life didn't bear close examination, so he liked to surround himself with other people from the fringes of society. At any rate, the arrangement worked in our favor, and Cooper brought in a reasonable amount of money during the weeks that he was human.

Of course, half of the time he was not.

I had been living with him nearly ten days when we lay together one night after making love. It was absolutely pitch-black inside the tent—even if there had been moonlight, it could not have penetrated the tree canopy, let alone the canvas.

"I won't be here tomorrow night," Cooper whispered.

I had been bracing myself for this announcement. I had known him long enough now to be almost as attuned to the rhythms of his body as he was. "That's what I thought," I whispered back.

"Will you be afraid to be here without me?"

"I don't know. Maybe."

He was silent a moment. "I can stay nearby," he offered. "I can watch over the campground. If you need me, just call out, and I'll be here in a few seconds."

I stroked the curls away from his face. Strange to think that, before twenty-four hours were up, the dark hair would turn to black fur, the smooth skin would disappear beneath a rough coat. "I have another idea," I murmured. "Come back here anyway. Sleep just outside the tent—or inside, next to me. I won't be afraid."

"You might be," he said. "You might find it stranger than you like."

"I won't. I've been around the wolf before."

I had—though not often since those first two weeks, when he had come to me, injured and in need of tending. I had never been certain if he stayed away because he thought I would fear him, or because he didn't trust himself not to hurt me, or because he didn't want to run the risk of being shot or captured. But I wasn't afraid, and I wasn't worried, and the last reason could not apply when we were so deep in the forest.

"Yes, but you know me better now," Cooper said. "You'll be looking for more of *me* in the animal, and I'm not sure how much of *me* you'll see."

"Only one way to find out," I replied.

"Well," he said, "we'll see."

In the morning, I kissed him good-bye as if it were any other day, and I biked down to the highway and to the McDonald's. And I worked my shift, and took my paycheck, and rode back to the campsite, pushing the bicycle alongside me as I walked the last yards to the tent. Cooper was nowhere in sight.

And even though I had expected his absence, even though he had told me he would be gone, I felt myself overcome with the most unendurable sense of loss. I looked frantically around the campsite, I struck off into the surrounding undergrowth, calling out his name and hoping to come across him watching me from some nearby hideaway. I was crying—hard enough and stupidly enough that, once I had tramped around for about ten minutes, I couldn't see well enough to find my way back to the campsite. For a moment, I was really afraid. Lost and alone in an untracked mile of woodland with no sense of where even the smallest haven lay. Would anyone, even Cooper, ever be able to find me again?

I forced back my tears, made myself stand still enough to get reoriented, and finally discerned the shape of the tent about fifty yards away. Only once I had arrived safely back at the clearing did I allow the tears to well up again, and I flung myself to the ground, sobbing without restraint. I didn't usually give in to self-pity, but at the moment I felt utterly abandoned. I had nothing in the world, no one, except Cooper, and Cooper was gone.

It was probably an hour or so before I pulled myself together, and even then I was limp and woeful. I wasn't hungry, but I made a light meal before sunset arrived since I knew food preparation was difficult in the dark. And when night did fall, much more swiftly and inexorably than I'd expected, it was as if I was alone on the Earth on the very first day of creation. The woods rustled and whispered around me, never entirely silent or still, but that just added to my utter and uneasy sense of solitude. When Cooper was here, talk or laughter or lovemaking shut out the noises of the night; there was always something to say and someone to say it to. Now every minute seemed fat and slow, climbing reluctantly toward dawn on the huddled backs of all the heavy minutes that had piled up before it. It didn't seem possible enough of them could accumulate to reach daybreak.

Our batteries were low, so I didn't want to use a flashlight to read or a radio to listen to music. There was nothing to do at all. I lay on my back in the tent and stared up at impenetrable darkness and waited for night to crawl by.

I had expected the first day without Cooper to be the worst one, but in fact, the next three were just as bad. I seriously considered striking the tent and moving it closer in to the public campgrounds, just to combat my desperate isolation with the knowledge that other human beings were nearby. I even thought about renting cheap lodgings for a couple of days—there was a Motel 6 down the road from McDonald's, and it cost less than forty dollars a night—but we were both so used to hoarding our money that I couldn't bring myself to be so wasteful. Maybe toward the end of the week, if things didn't get better. If I didn't get used to living without Cooper.

That third night, I made myself stay busy while it was still light. I took a pillowcase full of dirty clothes down to the public bathrooms and washed them out in the none-too-clean sinks, ignoring the sidelong glances of the other campers, then carried them back and hung them from the branches to dry. I swapped out the batteries in all our appliances since I'd remembered to buy some that afternoon when I was on break. I read a few chapters of *The Metamorphosis*, since an information packet from the university had let me know this would be required reading in my freshman lit course. I listened to a baseball game, the broadcast floating mysteriously through the air more than a hundred miles to emanate, spectral and unreal, from my radio speakers. And I waited for the onset of night with a mounting sense of dread.

We were deep into June now—in fact, I realized with a jolt, today was the summer solstice. There would never be a day so long for the rest of the year, never a night so brief. But instead of consoling me, the thought only added to my terror. If I could not endure this relatively short span of darkness without Cooper at my side, how would I manage for the next six months, each day progressively shorter than the last as the moon bit off the minutes one by one? Night would come sooner tomorrow, and even sooner the following day, and before long all daylight would fail before five o'clock. I told myself it wouldn't matter then. By the equinox, I would have moved to Champaign and established myself in my dorm room, where there would be other people always within call; by the winter solstice, I would be familiar with the campus even at night, unafraid of its outlandish shadows. Things would get better, not worse, as the year progressed.

But I didn't believe my own words.

I withdrew to the tent as night collected itself outside, coiling around the campsite like a malevolent dragon. But I didn't feel safe. I didn't feel settled. Panic filled my lungs so densely that there was no room left for air.

I could not sit still. Leaping to my feet, I stumbled through the flap, tripped over a discarded shoe and came to my knees on the hard ground outside the tent. He had said he would stay nearby; he had said he would watch over me. He had not responded to my tears that first night, but maybe he had been hunting at that particular moment. Maybe he only returned to the campsite once deep night had fallen.

"Cooper," I called, my arms outstretched in supplication,

a gesture he might be able to see, even in the dark, with his predator's eyes. "Cooper, please. I need you. I'm so afraid without you. I can't do this alone. Please don't stay away. Please, if you're out there, come to me—stay with me. Cooper, I love you."

My voice broke on the last few phrases; my words were so choked with tears that I wasn't sure he would have been able to understand them even if he had only been a few yards away. For a moment, when all that answered me was the incomplete silence of the whispering forest, I was swamped with blackest despair. I dropped my hands to my folded knees, laid my face against my forearms, and wept uncontrollably.

Then there was motion on the edge of my senses—no sound, only the sudden sharp awareness of another presence. I jerked my head up, wiping my cheeks with my hands, momentarily flooded with fear. Cooper wasn't the only wild animal roaming these woods. There could be anything from a bobcat to a fox rustling through the undergrowth, and I couldn't see well enough to tell what kind of visitor was creeping into my campsite.

"Cooper?" I whispered.

The shape drew nearer, black even against the blackness, a form and weight and silhouette I knew as well as my own. I felt his cold nose press against my wet cheek, and I let out a little cry of relief and gladness. I flung my arms around his neck and buried my face in his brushy fur. His head turned inward and he nuzzled my throat. One of his forefeet came up, callused and clawed, and rested on my leg. It was as if he had spoken aloud words of comfort and reassurance. *Don't be afraid. I'm with you. I'm always with you.*

I sighed and turned my head so that my wide, flat face for a moment rested against his narrow, pointed one. Then, without another word, I pushed myself to my feet and felt my way back into the tent. The wolf padded in behind me. I lay on my side on top of the sleeping bag, and he stretched out next to me. Side by side we slept peacefully through that brief and glorious night.

CHAPTER THIRTEEN

MELANIE

❦

It's a week before I speak to either Ann or Brody again. I'm actively avoiding Brody, refusing to pick up his phone calls and not answering his e-mails, but I don't talk to Ann because she hasn't been around. Since she and William left to go camping, they haven't been back, and I'm so worried that I think my skull might split from tension.

I'm not much use at work, but I continue to go into PRZ every day because I need the distraction. Debbie—whose true superpower is friendship—seems to know exactly when to sit with me so I can rant and rave, and when to leave me entirely alone. She runs interference with Em and Chloe, makes me go out to lunch every day, and tells me at least once an hour that everything will be all right. I don't believe it, and I'm not sure she does either, but it's still desperately important for me to hear the words.

I can't forget that the last thing I said to Brody was *Get the fuck out of my life.*

Seconds after I'd snatched the paper from his hand, I'd leapt to my feet, and said, "Go home. Now. Just go."

He'd stood up in a more leisurely fashion. "All right, you're obviously upset, but can we—"

"No! We can't *talk about it*. We can't *be reasonable people*. We can't do whatever you're going to say! Just go!"

"Do you really think—"

"How could I have been such an *idiot*! All along, this is what you've wanted—you've wanted me to trust you, to let my guard down, so you could sneak in and destroy my life—"

"How can you possibly believe that? Don't you know me any better than that by now? I'm not—"

I had charged across the room and flung the door open. My body temperature, cooled by dread, had dropped to zero, so I hardly noticed the chilliness of the air that swirled in. "I don't care! Just go."

His face was entirely sober as he joined me at the door. "Do you really think I would do anything to hurt you?" he said, raising his voice to be heard over my continuing commands for him to leave. "Do you really think I would hurt Ann? I just want to write a book."

"I don't care," I said. "You're too dangerous."

"Melanie—"

"Get the fuck out of my life!" I grabbed his arm and *shoved* him out the door, accidentally banging his wrist against the glass, punching his shoulder to hurry him along when he stopped on the threshold as if to try one last argument. He probably outweighs me by thirty pounds, and he's clearly stronger; I could tell that I only pushed him out because he let me. But I was too angry to be grateful, too terrified to be relieved. As soon as he was clear of the frame, I slammed the door shut and threw the locks, then sagged against it, panting as if I'd been running. I didn't move until I heard the rattle of his feet on the gravel, the coughing sound of his motor reluctantly grumbling to life, the whine of his tires as they hit the pavement and pulled away.

Oh God oh God oh God oh God.

I crumpled to the floor, right there at the doorway, shaking all over with nerves or despair. Stupid—so stupid—how could I have let this happen? From the minute I met him, I had known what Brody wanted, and I had known it was a treasure I could not yield up. And yet I allowed him to charm me, entertain me, wear away my sharp defenses. And now he had it, the truth about Ann, and he had run away with it, a smiling thief with a prize so astonishing it could only be described in whispers.

This was the man who had bragged he could find any key, open any lock. I'd spent so much time guarding my own heart that I'd lost track of the other items, priceless and exquisite, that were also in my care.

I couldn't even bring myself to hope he wouldn't spend all that bounty in one profligate spree. I couldn't hope that he would care for it with the reverence and affection something so rare deserved.

I drew my knees up and dropped my head, shivering uncontrollably. All I could think was, *What have I done? How soon is the world going to end?*

In fact, the world blunders on for that entire week, and I stumble along with it, like a water-skier dragged behind an inexpertly guided motorboat. The one incident that sends a spike of clarity through my general fog of misery is receiving another offer on the house from Kurt. He sends it by registered mail, so I have to go to the post office to retrieve it. It gives me great satisfaction to stand there in the small dingy lobby, rip the paper to shreds, then buy an envelope and stamps so I can return the scraps to him that very afternoon.

"How much did he offer this time?" Debbie asks when I tell her the story.

"I didn't even look."

By Friday, I'm a little calmer, though I still feel like my skin is just a degree away from igniting. I've gained a small measure of peace, though I can hardly admit it, from the last e-mail Brody sent me, on Thursday morning. I don't open it, of course, but I can't help noting the subject line, which reads: I'm not writing anything about Ann. I decide I have to believe him, if only to keep from going crazy. Even if he really means *I'm not writing anything about Ann this month*, it's still enough to get me through the weekend.

Oh, but there are even more joys to light me through these dark days. Because when I make it home from work that night, Ann is waiting.

"I can't believe you were so mean to Brody," she says. We're sitting on the couch, eating gelato out of two pint containers. One's raspberry, one's chocolate, and after every few spoonfuls, we swap. Dinner was a little sketchy, egg-salad sandwiches and a couple of sad apples, so I figure it won't hurt us to consume as many gelato calories as we want. Especially since Ann looks like she's lost five pounds in the past week.

"I can't believe I was ever nice to him," I reply. "I should never have let him get that close."

"I'm going to e-mail him," she says. "Pretend I'm you. Tell him you're sorry."

"Oh, no, you're not!"

"All right, then I'll call him. I'll tell him I'm me and that *I'm* sorry and would he like to meet me for pie at Slices?"

I stare at her helplessly. "You can't do that. Why would you do that?"

"And you'll be so worried about what I'll say that you'll come along, too, then you'll see him again and forget why you were ever mad."

"Ann—" I set the carton down so I can press my fingers to my temples. I'd like to think it's the cold gelato that's given me a headache, but I know better. "It's to protect *you* that I need to stay clear of Brody."

She leans over and touches a finger to my nose, leaving behind a chilly smear of chocolate. "I don't need protecting," she says. "I'm not afraid of him."

"You're not afraid of anything," I say. It's an accusation.

"Plenty of stuff," she says. "Just different things." She offers me her container, and we swap flavors again. "New topic."

I sigh to indicate I'm only humoring her. "What?"

"Wanna go meet somebody?"

"Sure. Who is it?" I say, though I'm pretty sure I can guess.

"William's family."

"I thought *you* hadn't even met them, at least officially."

"Well, I did. This week. I really liked them, and I thought you would, too."

A family of shape-shifters, all of them as strange as Ann's strange boyfriend. And she thinks I'll like them? But there's only one way to respond to this particular invitation. "I would love to get to know them," I say, then I pause. "Wait—is this a subtle message? Is this like asking your mom to meet your boyfriend's parents so you can announce you're getting married?"

She laughs. "Yeah, I don't see us as the types to rent tuxedos and buy wedding gowns and go marching down the aisle."

"Plenty of other ways to get married." I wait, but she's silent. "So? Is that what this is?"

She shrugs. She appears to be studying her hand as she digs her spoon into the raspberry gelato, making curved patterns in the creamy surface. "I can't imagine being with anyone but William. I can't imagine finding someone else who understands me and likes me and interests me and— and just *fits* me this well. He seems to feel the same." She lifts her eyes to give me a brief, shy glance. How odd to see laughing, confident Ann this uncertain. "I mean, that's what love is, isn't it? That's what commitment is?"

Not that I'm an expert on the topic, I say only in my head. "Yeah. I think it is. Lucky you."

Now she's smiling again. "I know. Lucky me."

We have an early dinner with William's family the very next day. From what I can gather, Ann and William had a heart-to-heart at the park, laying out their feelings and their plans for the future, then went directly to Maria's house. (Even though Maria has been married to William's brother Dante for three months, everyone still refers to their place as *Maria's house*.) So Dante and Maria have had a few more days than I've had to grow accustomed to the thought that their family member has found a permanent full-time lover.

I don't know how they reacted; I'm still trying to absorb the implications. Will they set up a household together for those days that they're human? Will they regret William's decision to have a vasectomy, find themselves longing for children? Will they open bank accounts, register to vote, become more *normal*?

Will I see Ann more often? Or less?

We buy a couple of fresh containers of gelato as a hostess gift before we drive up on Saturday afternoon. The meal has been set for five o'clock to accommodate the baby's schedule. Maria's place is in the partially developed countryside off Highway 44, in a sparsely populated neighborhood that practically backs up to woodland. The perfect setting for a woman married to a shape-shifter. Her house is a little two-bedroom bungalow, not much bigger than mine, and even before we've knocked on the door, I've decided I'm going to like the owner. The yard is tidy enough, and the house is in reasonably good repair, but it's clear Maria doesn't spend much time landscaping or repainting the shutters. What she cares about is all on the inside.

The woman who answers the door is tall, well built, and looks to be my age or a little older. She has a mass of curly dark hair, shadow-blue eyes, and a baby on her hip. Though she's smiling, I read a history of worry in the shape of her mouth, the faint tension around her eyes. This is someone who has spent much of her life loving someone with a perilous and unmentionable secret.

"Hi, come on in," she says, pushing the door wide with her free hand. "I'm Maria, this is Lizzie, and dinner is almost ready."

She manages to hug Ann without jostling the baby, then shakes hands with me, appraising me with eyes that are searching and sober, despite the continued smile. "Great to meet you. I have to say, I never thought William would be bringing a girl home to meet the family, but I'm glad it's one as delightful as Ann."

So I was right. I do like Maria the minute I meet her.

Dante's another story. He's in the kitchen slicing meat loaf, but he doesn't need a weapon to look dangerous as hell. He's lean and sinewy, with long, dark hair caught in a pony-tail and a face both beautiful and unnerving. Like William, he exudes a certain indefinable air of *wildness* that you'd probably notice even if you couldn't interpret what it meant. If I met him on the street, I'd cross to the other side, and I'd continually be looking over my shoulder to make sure he hadn't decided to follow me and murder me in the dark.

"Dante, it's Ann's sister, Melanie," Maria tells him.

He nods. "Hey."

Probably not the easiest guy in the world to make con-versation with. All I can think to say is, "We brought gelato. Is there room in the freezer?"

William sidles out from some interior room. I'm glad to see that he moves as soundlessly here as he does in my house. That means he doesn't consider my house hostile territory; stealth is just his standard mode of operation. I'm surprised when he takes the baby from Maria because he doesn't seem like the type to fawn over children, but he seems perfectly at ease with her in his arms. For her part, Lizzie chortles and grabs at his hair. If she's not afraid of her scary uncles, this little girl isn't going to be afraid of anything.

"Is she ready for a nap?" he asks Maria.

"I wish. No, she wants to stay awake and visit with our guests during the meal and throw food on the floor and scream if I don't give her more applesauce and otherwise make Melanie pray she never has a baby."

"How old is she?" I ask, because I can never tell.

"Almost ten months. Just about to start walking. Life will never be the same."

Ann has gone over to stand by William and flirt with

Lizzie, tapping her on the nose, the chin, her left ear, making the little girl scream with laughter. Something about the baby's expression, and the shape of her eyes, reminds me of William; I'm guessing her dead mother shared a family resemblance with her brothers.

I vaguely remember Ann's telling me that the baby hasn't shifted shapes yet, so I don't make the inquiry. I'm curious, but it seems like a rude question to ask of people you hardly know. So I say, "She's beautiful."

"I think so, too," Maria replies. "And since she's not mine by blood, I can say that without sounding conceited."

Dante speaks up from the kitchen. "We're all ready here, once everyone knows what they want to drink," he says. "Let's eat."

The meal isn't quite as uncomfortable as it could have been, though neither William nor Dante says much, and I still find Dante unnerving. But Ann has always been a talker, and Maria is clearly aware of how bizarre the whole situation is, how unusual her menfolk appear to be, so she makes a great effort to engage me in conversation. We mostly discuss trivialities, our jobs, funny things Lizzie has done, how cold and wet March has been, but maybe April will be better. So it's no worse than your average conversation with a total stranger on an airplane, but it's not exactly relaxed, either.

As predicted, Lizzie is restless and vocal, and three times she starts to cry, then cheers up again when Dante or Maria gives her a morsel of food from one of their plates.

"She ought to fall asleep pretty soon, but I think she'll start screaming if I just try to put her to bed," Maria says. "Melanie, are you up for a walk in the park? We'll make the guys clean up the mess."

I notice that Ann isn't included in the invitation, and I figure this is no accident. "That sounds great," I say. "It's been such a beautiful day."

Fifteen minutes later, Maria is pushing a stroller around

a small oval sidewalk that encloses a deserted playground not far from her house. I'm walking beside her at a meandering pace. The sun's still up, but not for long, and it's no warmer than sixty degrees, so all three of us are wearing a couple of layers of sweaters and jackets. Lizzie is kicking her legs with great energy and expressing herself in meaningless words that she utters with conviction. I suspect she will be much more outgoing than either of her uncles.

"Ann tells me this is William's sister's child," I say. "But she didn't tell me what happened to her mom."

"Christina," Maria says on a sigh, then gives me a quick sideways glance. "Don't take this the wrong way, but I'll have to know you a lot better before I tell that story."

I put my hands up in a brief no-problem gesture. "Hey, I'm not particularly good at confiding secrets, either."

"So we'll just have a policy where we aren't offended at the questions that are asked—or the questions that aren't answered."

I laugh. "We probably have a lot in common, though. Might be nice to have someone to confide in now and then."

"I just want to make sure I have this right. You and Ann are half sisters, correct? And you're not—she's the only—"

"I'm not a shape-shifter," I say, putting the words right out there. "Her mom was, and Ann is. But my father and me—no." I pause for a beat, then go on. "I've always believed that learning the truth about Ann and Gwen is what made my father basically lose his mind. But for some reason I never found it hard to accept. Maybe because I was pretty young when Ann first started changing shapes. Maybe because there was nothing Ann could have done or been that would have made me give her up."

She glances at me again. "She tells me you're essentially the one who raised her."

"Not for the first five years, but after that—yeah."

"Then maybe you have advice for me. Lizzie hasn't changed shapes yet, but everyone expects that she will. And it's something I have to be *prepared* for, in case it happens. But—what do I do? Never take her out in public? Never leave her with a babysitter? Never let her leave the house? That seems like a pretty hard life."

I think it over. "When Ann was little, she didn't change shapes that often. Mostly at night, mostly when she was sleeping. I think she was about two and a half when she started turning into a dog during waking hours."

"A beautiful white husky with blue eyes," Maria murmurs. "That's what she looked like the first time I met her. She was so unearthly. I wondered if she wasn't one of *them*. But I wasn't sure until William brought her over this week."

"She's beautiful now, but you should have seen that puppy," I say. "Cutest creature ever. She just *romped* through the yard."

"And she could control her changing? Even that young?" Maria asks, getting back to the main point. "William's always been able to shift at will, but Dante still has trouble with it—he says this irresistible *pressure* comes over him, and he can't stop it."

"I guess everyone's different," I reply. "Ann has always seemed to have some control over it. At any rate, if we were going to some public place, like the grocery store or the library, I would just say to her, 'You have to be good. You have to hold tight.' Those were my code words, I guess, *hold tight*. Even when she was really little, she knew what they meant, and she never shifted when she shouldn't have." I give Maria a helpless look. "Maybe it's like toilet training. You have to find the key that works for that kid."

"I keep trying to figure out what to do about the babysitter. I mean, I have a job, and it's not like William and Dante can stay home with her all the time. But what if she changes shapes when she's with the nanny? Do I warn her ahead of time—and make her think I'm a lunatic? She'll call child services on me!"

I think this over. "Gwen stayed home with Ann, so I never thought about it. Do you have a relative you can trust with the truth? Can you ask that person to be the nanny?"

She gives the ghost of a laugh. "I haven't told anyone in my family the truth yet. I mean, I'm sure they'll freak out.

Who wouldn't?" She's silent a moment. "But I've been thinking I should tell my mom. She's not easily flustered or rocked off balance—she might be able to handle the news just fine. She lives over in Illinois, and I don't know that she'd want to move down here just to watch the baby—but maybe. She's crazy about Lizzie."

"Well, here's my thought. You can keep a secret from your friends, you can keep a secret from your neighbors, you can keep it from your family, but you always need *someone* to confide in. At some point, it's just going to be too heavy, you know? When I was fifteen, and everything was going to hell at our house, I told my best friend about Ann and Gwen and all of it. Best decision I ever made. There were times I couldn't have made it through the day without knowing Debbie would understand."

She gives me a quick, worried smile. "It's not just knowing who to trust, knowing who won't betray you. It's knowing who's strong enough to bear up under the knowledge of something so—so impossible."

"That *is* the trick," I agree.

"I have told one person—just one—*my* best friend, and you're right, it saved my life. But I feel so responsible for Lizzie. She's this—this perfect entity, this absolutely blank slate. Anything I do could be the wrong thing, could twist her or hurt or even destroy her. Sometimes, I'm paralyzed by that knowledge."

"Well, I was too young to think that way when I was taking care of Ann," I say. "I *did* know she was precious, and rare, and had to be protected at all costs. I knew I couldn't let people find out about her. I knew I had to stand between her and the rest of the world."

Maria gives me another small, sympathetic smile. "That's a hard way to live, though," she says. "Sacrificing everything for someone else. I chose to love Dante, and I chose to adopt Lizzie, and I've built my world around them. But a sister— she's a tangent. She's a powerful connection, but she's never going to be the core of your life." She lifts one hand from the stroller to make a gesture of farewell. "I mean, one day she falls in love and moves away and starts her own life. One day Ann meets William and everything changes. If she's all you care about, that leaves you pretty lonely."

I'm sure she doesn't mean her words to be poisoned knives cutting patterns in my skin, but that's certainly the effect they have. Maybe Ann has told her about Brody, maybe she's just guessing that a woman my age might want to get married and have a family and lead a traditional life. In the past year, Ann has already slipped farther and farther away from me; it's clear her relationship with William will not bring her any closer. On the one hand, I will need to find ways to fill my heart when she decamps from it; on the other hand, she will always remain a part of my life, and whoever shares it with me cannot be shocked and horrified at the great mystery that is my sister. All our previous words hover around my head, swirl in my memory. *Who do you trust, who will not betray you, who can bear up under knowledge so impossible?*

I'm silent for so long that I'm afraid she'll ask me one of those questions I cannot answer, but she's distracted by leaning over the top of the stroller and trying to see the baby's face. "I think Lizzie's asleep," she murmurs. "Life is good."

I manage to answer. "And when it's not good, it's certainly interesting."

CHAPTER FOURTEEN

Ann falls asleep on the drive home and I almost can't wake her up and get her in the house. I actually consider bringing out a blanket and pillow and leaving her in the car—no doubt she's slept in worse places—but finally I manage to rouse her enough to support her into the house and back to her room. She collapses on the bed without a word and is instantly deep in slumber again.

I stand in the doorway for a few minutes, watching her in the faint illumination from the night-light. What could be making her so tired? What have she and William been doing with their time? Is he, perhaps, a bad influence on her, leading her down destructive paths that sap her strength and put her at risk? And if he is, can I do anything about it?

I putter around the house for the next two hours before seeking my own bed, but the questions circle in my mind so long and so insistently that it's past two before I fall asleep. No surprise, then, that the clock says 10:15 when I finally open my eyes to find morning sunshine pouring in over the windowsill like floodwaters over a dam. With a stretch and a groan, I pull myself out of bed and note the quality of the stillness in the house. I figure Ann must have snuck out early; I hope she's left a note to tell me when she'll be back.

But when I peer in her room, I find she's still lying in the bed.

For a moment, fear transmutes every bone in my body to ice. Sleeping? Comatose? *Dead?* I hurry to her side, see her chest faintly rise and fall even before my hand goes to her cheek, which is warm and flushed. At my touch, her eyelids flutter, and she murmurs something, then turns over on the mattress.

Just sleeping then. My heart, which has stopped, stampedes back into action. I try to control my trembling as I tiptoe out of the room.

Don't panic. She's just tired. Don't worry. She'll be fine.

I find it hard to convince myself I'm telling the truth, but I take a shower and get dressed and make breakfast as if everything is normal.

It's close to noon before Ann stumbles out of her bedroom, yawning widely and still wearing her pajamas. "Wow, how long was I out?" she asks as she takes in the angle of the sun, then glances toward the clock in the kitchen. "What, like *fifteen hours*? That has to be a record."

"I was starting to get worried," I say lightly.

She waves a careless hand. "Just catching up. I love sleeping in a nice soft bed. Did you make breakfast? I'm starving."

O ver the meal—which is actually lunch—she remembers that she disapproves of my recent treatment of Brody. "You should call him and apologize," she says.

"I have nothing to apologize for."

"Well, sometimes you can be sorry even if you didn't do anything wrong."

I change the subject, telling her about some disaster at work, and I think she's been sufficiently diverted. But while I'm loading the dishwasher, she lifts the cordless phone from the cradle and leans against the kitchen cabinet.

"Which one of these recent calls is from Brody?" she asks.

"What? Ann, put that down! Don't call him!"

She ignores me. "Debbie—Debbie—work—Debbie—eight hundred number, probably a junk call—oooh, and *unknown caller* in a 314 area code. Is that Brody?"

"I have no idea."

"Let's try it." I hear the beeps of the individual numbers being pressed, then the purr of the phone ringing at the other end, so I realize she's put the call on speaker.

"Hello?"

"Brody!" Ann could not sound more delighted. "It's Ann Landon! How've you been?"

"Hey, Ann. Nice to hear your voice," he says. "What's going on?"

"I was just standing here talking to Melanie and I wondered if you were busy. We could get pie or something. Just the two of us."

There's a moment of silence. "Am I on speakerphone?" he says.

She laughs. "How could you tell?"

"Is Melanie in the room? Is she okay with you calling me?"

"Who cares? I can make friends with anybody I want."

"Good in theory, but it doesn't always work in practice," he says.

"So you don't want to go get pie? It's Sunday—that's usually the blackberry special."

"I'd love to. But only if Melanie comes, and only if she *wants* to."

"Oh, if you and I go somewhere, you can bet Melanie will want to come along."

"Yeah, that's not good enough," he says. "I'm not blackmailing anybody into doing anything."

"Give me the phone," I say to Ann, but she turns her back on me.

"See, here's the trick with Melanie," she says. "You have to find out what she cares about, then you have to care about it, too."

"That's the trick with anybody," Brody tells her.

"I mean, you can't just *pretend* to care."

"Yeah. Right. Pretending never works. Authenticity all the way."

"Give me the phone," I say again.

"And you know, there's only one thing Melanie really cares about."

"I know," he says. "I knew that the day I met her."

"So that's why you and I have to be friends."

"Works for me," he says, "but I'm still not doing it behind her back."

I grab Ann's wrist, hard enough to make her yelp, and force the phone out of her fingers. I switch out of speaker mode before I put the handset to my ear.

"Actually, you're wrong. I'm ready to sell my sister to the highest bidder just to get her out of the house," I say. "So you'd better think of something else that matters to me if you want to be friends."

"Well, hell, doesn't that go both ways?" he says, as casually as if we've been speaking every day for the past week. "Don't you have to find out what *I'm* interested in and figure out how to love it?"

Only if I like you, only if I care about you, only if I want you in my life. I'm still not sure any of those things are true, but I'm beginning to suspect they are. "Yeah, I suppose so," I say.

"Then we've got a lot to talk about," he says. "I can taste that blackberry special already. See you in about an hour."

You'd think this little outing would be as tense and uncomfortable as dinner at Maria's house the night before, but, strangely, it's not. None of the credit goes to me. I'm not exactly sulking, but I'm not exactly playing talk-show hostess, either, trying to engage my guests in conversation and making sure everyone has a chance to speak.

Ann and Brody don't seem to need my assistance, though; they're chatting with the ease of old friends. Maybe it has something to do with birth order, that youngest-child insouciance. They've never thought the world was so scary; there's always been someone else around to take care of them, to keep them safe. I don't know whether I should feel envious or resentful.

"So Debbie told me something interesting the other day," Brody says to Ann.

"Really? What? Didn't you just love Debbie and Charles?"

"And the boys. They seemed like a great family."

"So what did Debbie tell you?"

He gestures in my direction with his fork, which is covered with a thin film of purple pie filling. "Melanie used to date Kurt Markham."

Ann rolls her eyes. "Yes. He drove a red Camaro."

"That's why she went out with him?"

"Well, I don't know if that's *why*, but everybody in town knew that car. It had a horn that made this funny sound— *ah-ooooo-ga*—and every time he'd drive by the house, even if he wasn't picking her up to go somewhere, he'd blow the horn."

"Show-off," Brody says.

"I always thought it was kind of sweet," I say. My first foray into the conversation in ten minutes. "It meant he was thinking about me."

"Did she date lots of football players?" Brody asks.

"Two," she says. "But Ian only lasted for about three weeks."

"What did he do wrong?"

"He wasn't Kurt," I say. "I ditched him when Kurt asked me out."

"That's kind of mean," Brody says.

"He was the captain of the football team. I was a shallow girl."

He regards me through narrowed eyes, clearly not believing me. Well, he knows I bore heavy responsibilities at home; maybe he thinks those cares and duties weighed me down in all aspects of my life. But they were exactly what made me want to be heedless and superficial whenever I had a chance. The world had seemed so heavy to me when I was seventeen. Sometimes, I rebelled.

The world seems even heavier now. And I have no idea how to make it seem lighter for even an hour.

"So how long did you stay with Kurt? And why did you break up with him?"

I lie. "I can't remember."

"He almost hit me," Ann says.

Brody's eyes grow comically wide. "Hit you? With his fist?"

"With his car," I say shortly.

"He didn't see me," Ann says in exculpation.

"He was driving too fast. He always drove too fast."

And she was almost impossible to see. Little white husky, scampering out from the bushes on the edge of the lawn, running headlong into the path of the car. It was night, and Kurt had no reason to expect a dog on our property. Give him credit for slamming on the brakes when I screamed—*I* was always on the lookout for that tumbling, frisking creature, and I'd seen her the instant she poked her nose out. But oh my God, the terror in my heart when I saw how close his bumper came to her face.

Jeez, you nearly gave me a heart attack, he'd said when Ann scrambled whimpering to the porch. *I thought I was gonna hit a kid or something. But it's only a dog.*

I broke up with him the next day. It would have been that night except I was unable to speak.

"Yeah, and then he had that accident a couple of months later," Ann says.

"Well, I think it's always a good idea to break up with bad drivers," says Brody. "I used to go out with a woman who couldn't spend five minutes in the car without using every cussword you ever heard. This guy's an asshole, that guy's a shithead, didn't you see the fucking light turn green? She tailgated people on the highway, flipped people off if they cut in front of her. Very tense to be a passenger in her car."

Ann and I look at each other and burst out laughing.

"What? What's so funny?" he says.

"Melanie's sort of an irate driver."

"But I never tailgate," I add. "I just yell."

"Wow," he says. "You're full of surprises."

Ann gives him a sunny smile. "Aren't we all."

The waitress returns to refill water glasses and coffee cups, and Brody decides to have another piece of pie.

"How is it you don't weigh three hundred pounds?" I ask him. "Every time I see you, you're downing food like you're afraid you'll never get another meal."

He laughs. "I've always had a lot of energy, bounced around the room a lot—burned through calories so fast I couldn't gain weight if I tried. It's starting to catch up with me, though, and once I started freelancing, my whole life-style slowed down. Sitting down and writing is about as sedentary as it gets."

"So tell us about your book," Ann invites. "What's it about?"

There's a charged silence for a moment. Brody looks at me; I shrug, nod, and look away. He settles his elbows on the table and leans forward to address Ann.

"I want to write about shape-shifters. People who can transform into animals. I think they're living all around us, most people just don't know it."

She puts an expression of fascination on her face. "And have you actually met any people who can do this? Change shapes?"

"Yeah," he says. "Three of them."

That wrenches my attention back to him. "You never said that before! I asked you, the very first day we met, and you just sort of"—I move my head in an indeterminate fashion—"didn't answer."

"I didn't know you very well then. I didn't know if it was safe to tell you anything."

Now Ann's rapt expression is more genuine. "You've seen them? Truly? You've watched them transform?"

He nods slowly. "Spookiest thing I've ever seen in my life."

She flutters her hands in the air. "So? Tell us, tell us! What was it like? What kinds of animals were they?"

"One was a guy who was maybe thirty or thirty-five years old. Skinny, quiet. A little odd. Not somebody you'd be afraid of, exactly, but you'd think there was something weird about him. He turned into a wolf right before my eyes. His body started growing hair, his face roughed up—five minutes, it was all over. If I hadn't been looking for this very phenomenon, if I hadn't been hunting for shape-shifters, I'm not sure I'd have believed I was really seeing it. But he let me touch him. I could feel his fur. It wasn't a trick or an optical illusion. It was real."

"Wow," Ann says. She glances at me.

But I'm not ready to let down all the barriers just yet. I'm not ready to give him Ann. "You said you saw a couple of different ones?"

"Yeah. There was a girl, maybe ten years old. She could become a bird. She just—shrank down and started growing these black feathers, so fast you couldn't follow the motion. Flapped her wings and took to the air, then came down and landed on my wrist. It was astonishing."

"What about the last one?" Ann asks.

"That one I saw from a distance. I might have thought that one was some kind of illusion, except I'd already witnessed the first two. This was a guy turning into a deer. He was running at the time, so it was almost like a cartoon show—you know, the figure gets all blurry as it moves across the screen, and then it's something else entirely. Still pretty amazing to watch."

"So where did you see these incredible things happen?" I ask. My voice is cool enough that you could suspect me of mockery if you didn't have reason to believe I had firsthand knowledge of these incredible things.

He smiles at me. "Someplace in the Midwest. I was only admitted onto the property because I swore not to divulge any details."

My eyebrows arch in polite surprise. "Oh—so when you write your book, it's going to be full of 'anonymous sources' and 'undisclosed locations.' You realize that people are going to think you're making it all up."

"They thought I was making it up when I had live footage of an actual transformation, so, yeah, I realize that."

"Then why bother? Why even try to tell the story?"

He cants his head and considers for a moment, as if struggling to articulate the reason. "When I started doing the research," he says at last, "it was just because I was curious. I was fascinated. I wanted to find out as much as I could. But once I met a few shape-shifters, when I saw how difficult their lives could be—most of them just existing on the edge of civilization, without access to medical care or social services—I thought maybe the book could do some good. Raise awareness, raise empathy, maybe even raise money." He shrugs. "I don't know. Maybe not."

"I don't think *empathy* is what you'll get if you write about shape-shifters," I say, my voice a little dry. "I think you'll get hysteria. Lynch mobs. Talk of werewolves and full moons and crazy folks wailing, 'Oh, my God, what if one *bites* me?' And cops and public health officials showing up at people's doors to crate up the abominations and haul them off for testing. *That's* what you'll get."

"You might," Ann says ruefully. "Especially if you draw maps to the houses of all the shape-shifters you've interviewed, and say, 'Here's where you can find this little girl who can change into a crow.'"

He glances at me briefly, but answers her. "I was never planning to do that. I'm not a complete idiot. I do realize there are risks that come with this kind of exposure, and I was never going to put my sources in danger. But I did think the whole lot of them could benefit if we started the public dialogue. 'Did you know that these beautiful, amazing creatures live among us—and some of them could use your help?' That's all."

There's silence for a moment as everyone waits for someone else to speak. As the two of them wait for me to speak. Ann, who's sitting next to me in our booth, pokes me in the ribs. "So?" she says. "Do you have anything to tell Brody?"

I fold my hands before me on the table and take on my most solemn expression. "I do," I say in a low voice. "I'm a shape-shifter. I'm a Doberman pinscher in my other form."

Ann bursts out laughing, and Brody shows me a crooked smile. The waitress brings Brody's fresh piece of pie and smiles, but you can tell she's wondering what's so funny.

William is waiting for us when we get home from Slices, and Brody doesn't linger long enough to do more than nod in his direction. "I'll call you," he says to me, and takes off.

Ann grabs my hands and starts a ring-around-the-rosie-style dance in my front yard. "Mel and Brody sitting in a tree," she chants. "K-i-s-s-i-n-g. First comes love—"

I yank free and stride for the door. "You're so childish."

She hurries after me, and William falls in step behind us. "I like him. I think you should go out with him."

He already thinks we're dating. Or he did. "We'll see. William, how long have you been waiting out here? I thought Ann showed you where I hide the key."

"I was fine," he says.

We all go inside, but neither of them can settle; it's clear they're eager to go off someplace together. I make them eat one last meal before they leave even though Ann says she's too full of pie to cram down another bite. But I can't bear to think of her foraging in the wilderness for the next week—or two—devouring whatever raw meat or abandoned leftovers she can find. I have to feed her now while I can.

"We'll be back in a few days," she says vaguely, as they head toward the door. It's closing in on four o'clock, so they'll have a few hours of daylight to travel wherever it is they're going. "Don't worry."

"I always worry," I say, and kiss her on the cheek. William endures a kiss from me, too, then they're gone.

I stand in the middle of the empty house and wish it were already time for them to come home.

CHAPTER FIFTEEN

B rody calls Monday night as I'm curled up on the couch, eating the last of the chocolate gelato and watching TV shows I don't care about for whatever distraction value they can provide.

"Just checking in," he says. "Seeing how you're doing."

"I'm okay."

"You sound a little down."

"Yeah. Ann and William left yesterday, and I don't know when they'll be back, so—" I assume he can imagine my shrug.

"So you're lonely."

"A little, I guess."

"Well, if you're up for a drive into the big city, *Wicked* is playing at the Fox Theater. I could get us tickets."

I don't go into St. Louis that often. It's not a particularly big downtown area, so it's not like I'm a rural girl afraid of urban menace, and the drive usually takes less than an hour, so it's not like the effort is too immense. It's just that I don't seem to feel the need for much more than I have right at my fingertips.

"Debbie saw it a couple of years ago when she was in New York, and she loved it. Sounds like fun."

There's a beat. "Is that a yes?"

I find myself giggling. "Yeah. It's a yes."

"Cool! I'll buy tickets. What night? Wait, I'm looking at an ad in the paper right now . . . Looks like it's sold out Friday and Saturday, but there are seats still available for Thursday night or Sunday afternoon."

"I'd prefer Thursday night, I think."

"Me, too. Want to come to my place or meet at the theater?"

"Your place? The scummy little apartment that you pay someone to clean?"

"Wow. Is that how I described it to you at some point?"

"First day we met. Inspired me with raging curiosity to see it."

"Yeah, that's sarcasm, isn't it?"

"Kind of. Tell you what. I know how to find the Fox, so let's just meet there. What time?"

"Do you want dinner first? There are a couple places around Grand Avenue we could try."

"Sure."

"Then meet me at six. Oh, and Melanie?"

"Yes?"

"This is actually a date. In case you were wondering."

I bite my lip, but the laugh comes anyway. "Glad you cleared that up for me."

"I always like to be on the same page. Saves trouble."

"Oh," I say, "I think you kind of like trouble. See you in a couple of days."

But he finds reasons to call Tuesday and Wednesday. Once to let me know he has the tickets in hand. Once to see if I'd prefer to eat Italian cuisine or American bar food. I mean, those are the excuses he gives. I know he's just calling because he wants to hear my voice.

I know because that's why I'm glad when I answer the phone to find him on the other end.

Our Thursday night outing is a complete success. Even

the things that go wrong seem so hilarious that they contribute to the rightness of the evening. The strap on one of my black-leather heels breaks as I'm getting out of the Cherokee, so I'm forced to put on the beat-up old white walking shoes I always leave in the back. They clash horribly with the semislinky red dress I thought would be appropriate for the gaudy opulence that's the Fox, but Brody says he admires a girl who makes bold sartorial choices. At the restaurant, he casually slips his credit card into the leather portfolio to pay our bill, but the waitress brings it back almost immediately. I can tell he's mortified as she starts to say, *I'm sorry, sir*, and he appears to be mentally reviewing his banking balance to figure out which checks might have bounced.

What she actually says is, "I'm sorry, sir, you gave me your driver's license instead of your credit card. Unless you wanted me to bill the DMV?"

We're still laughing when we arrive at the theater and find our places behind the world's tallest couple, but at intermission we slip to some unoccupied seats farther back in our section and we can finally see the whole stage. The musical is magical, or maybe it's the mood. At any rate, I'm humming as we exit with the crowd, and I didn't know a note from the play before I went in.

"Time for a drink before you drive back?" Brody asks.

I glance at my watch. Already past eleven, and it'll be midnight or better before I'm in bed. "Better not. Workday tomorrow."

"Best part of being a freelancer," he says. "I can set my own schedule."

"Sure. Harp on that. Make me resent you even more."

I'm parked in a small lot a couple of blocks from the theater, and we walk slowly so we don't get to my car too soon.

"So what are you doing this weekend? Can we make plans?"

I spread my hands. "I think all I need to do is pay a few bills and scrub the bathroom."

"So how about dinner tomorrow night?" He smiles down at me. "And maybe dinner Saturday night, too?"

"You might find I don't wear that well when you're around me so often."

"Yeah, maybe. You might find the same thing about me."

"So? You want to risk it?"

"Better to find it out now. Before we've wasted any more time on each other."

I'm choking back more laughter. By now we've courted death crossing the parking lot as all the other theatergoers are backing out of spaces and edging past us toward the exit. We pause at my car, and I slip my hand in my purse, hunting for my keys.

"Well, that's a romantic way to put it," I say.

"Doberman pinschers aren't known for their love of romance."

"Yeah, but you're not the Doberman type. You're more of—" I pull the keys out and pause, studying his face for a moment by the incomplete illumination of the streetlights. "I don't know my dog breeds that well. Something playful and energetic. Particularly exhausting as a puppy."

"Border collie, maybe," he says with a grin. "Always busy. Always getting into trouble. But friendly and reliable."

"Sounds about right."

"So? Friday and Saturday night?"

"Yes to Friday. We'll see about Saturday."

"Sounds fair," he says. Without any fanfare, he leans over and presses his lips to mine. I bend into the kiss just enough to let him know I like it, but I don't linger too long. It's not the right setting for melting embraces. "What time?"

"Anytime after six. I'll be home."

"I'll be there."

Brody hasn't specified that he wants to go *out* for dinner, and I figure it's time I showed a little generosity of my own to repay his kindness and patience. So I take off work early and stop to buy ingredients for a meal, complete with wine. I'm not a particularly inventive cook, but I have a few specialties that always turn out well enough to serve, and

Brody doesn't seem especially picky, anyway. I'm halfway through meal prep before I realize I'm humming again—either a melody from *Wicked* or some tune that I've made up on the spot. It surprises me to further realize that I'm actually happy.

When's the last time *that* happened when Ann was out of sight?

When Brody steps through the front door, he's delighted. "Two great minds!" he exclaims. "I was going to suggest we stay in and cook! I almost stopped at the store as I was coming through town, but I thought, 'No, what if Melanie's already all dressed up? Wouldn't want to disappoint her.' This is *great*."

"It's pretty simple," I warn him. "Shepherd's pie and a salad. And store-bought cake because I didn't feel like baking, too."

"Perfect. I'll love it all."

He does, too, taking third helpings of everything, even the mediocre cake. "I think you have a tapeworm," I tell him. "Otherwise, you couldn't possibly eat this much all the time and stay so slender."

"That's it. You've discovered my secret. I hope you're not repulsed."

"Ew. Is it contagious? *Transferrable?*"

"Studies are inconclusive," he says. "In fact, I'm part of a research group trying to determine if tapeworms can be passed on through activities like kissing. I was hoping you'd be willing to be my research partner."

"Now that's original," I say in an approving voice. "That's not a line any guy has ever used on me before."

"And that is my goal," he says, standing up and starting to clear the table. "Introducing you to joys you have never yet experienced."

After the meal, we settle in to watch television. I have about five DVDs and no cable service, so our options are limited, but he claims he's always wanted to see the new version of *Sense and Sensibility*, and we pop the disk in the player. Truth is, the movie is just an excuse to get comfortable on the couch, both of us slouching down, shoulders touching, then hands entwined, the occasional kiss exchanged.

Truth is, soon enough the movie becomes nothing but background noise. Like high schoolers at a drive-in, we start making out, kissing madly, slipping our hands inside each other's clothing. But unlike those hormone-crazed teens experimenting with sex for the first time, we're not driven and desperate. We're leisurely, amused, relaxed, and tender. And talkative.

"Very pretty," Brody says when he peels back my shirt to find a daisy-patterned bra beneath it. "Do the panties match?"

"No, I needed black underwear with my black skirt. But my blouse was white, so no black bra."

"But please tell me you *have* a black bra."

"Oh, is that your particular fetish?"

"I would say it's a universally flattering look for women."

"You're easy."

"You have no idea."

Pretty soon we're down to three items of clothing between us, though my bra is hanging from my shoulders so loosely you could hardly say I'm wearing it. We're stretched out side by side on the couch, wrapped together so tightly I'm not at all worried about slipping over the edge, and I'm starting to get a little high on the pure unadulterated opium of physical touch.

"This is where we have to start making decisions about boundaries and intent," Brody says.

"We do?" My voice is breathless.

"Yeah, 'cause if we aren't careful, there are gonna be some messy fluids pretty soon, and while that doesn't bother *me* any, it's your couch, and—"

I'm laughing so hard that my body is shaking his where it presses against mine. "Messy fluids! You're killing me with romance!"

He kisses my cheek and nibbles his way to my earlobe. "It was a magician's trick," he whispers. "Deflecting you from the real issue at hand."

His breath tickles, and I pull my head back. I'm trying to get a good look at his face, hard to do when it's so close to mine. "Are we gonna have sex?"

"That's the real question."

"Well, yeah. Aren't we?"

He kisses my mouth. "Well, yeah. Here or somewhere else?"

"Well, I wasn't feeling too particular, but since you brought up the fluid thing—"

Without another word, he sits up, leaving me briefly chilled. Then he scoops me into his arms and jogs into the bedroom with me bouncing against his chest, laughing again. It seems pointless to keep any underwear on at this juncture, so we're both naked as we slide under the deliciously cool sheets and instantly seek each other's heat again.

"And then the next question—" he begins.

"Oh, my *God*!" I exclaim. "Do you always talk this much?"

"You've known me for six weeks now. You know the answer to that."

"I mean, during sex?"

"But this is an important question."

"Yes, I'm on the pill. No, I don't have any diseases."

"Same here. I mean, I'm not on the pill, of course, though I understand they're working on birth control for men—"

I make a sound of exasperation deep in my throat and pounce on him, covering his body with mine, kissing his mouth as hard as I can. His arms wrap around my back, suddenly drawing me in so tightly that my skin burns and my bones ache. And it feels so good, so good. I cannot remember the last time I have rested on someone else, relied on someone else, given myself completely to someone else, holding nothing back. For a brief time we are as frenzied and focused as those teenagers in the backseat of a car, as seduced by sensation, as bent on a single exquisite goal, and even Brody, for those pleasurably laboring minutes, abandons conversation. And yet we communicate all the same.

It's not more than five minutes that we have been lying there, languorous and entwined, before Brody begins talking again. We're spooning in the bed, his right arm resting on my waist, our hands clasped and snugged up against my heart. I feel spent but triumphant, utterly at ease, as if I have come to rest in a palatial resort after months of arduous travel.

"When I was eight years old," he says without preamble, "I fell into a frozen pond and almost drowned."

"Oh, no," I say through a yawn. It's hard to get too worked up by a story that clearly has a happy ending.

"My whole family had gone to visit some friends of my dad's. They lived way out in the country somewhere, and they had a pond in the backyard and a collection of ice skates they'd amassed over the years. There were two kids who lived there, boys about my age, and they took my sisters and me out to go skating. It was, like, ten degrees out, and I remember being really cold before the whole adventure even started."

"I'll bet."

"Plus I wasn't a very good skater—and neither were those boys—and people kept falling down and it wasn't as much fun as I'd thought it would be. And then someone tripped and someone else crashed into me, and two things happened at once. Someone's skate ripped across my leg and cut my thigh right open. And too many of us hit the ice at once, and it cracked, and I fell in."

The story is starting to get more exciting. "Wow, you must have been scared."

"So scared and so cold that I think I went into shock. These days it's hard for me to sort out what I *remember* and what I *think* I remember because I've heard the story so often. But somehow they dragged me out of the water and back to shore, where I was bleeding profusely and shaking so hard I couldn't talk.

"And Bailey. God love her. She was so calm. She just took charge. She told the boys to run back to the house to get help. She told Brandy and Bethany to start pulling off all my wet clothes, starting with my trousers. The blood was gushing out of my femoral artery and Bailey, cool as you please, takes off her belt and makes a tourniquet on my leg."

I've now turned over in his arms as if to hear the story better. "How old was she?"

"Fourteen."

"And she knew to make a *tourniquet*?"

He nods. The bedroom is dark, but we left a hall light on, and it's just bright enough that I can see the outline of his face. "She did it right, too, or so the paramedics said later. Anyway, so once Brandy and Beth have taken off my clothes, she takes off *her* coat and has them move me onto it—so I'm not lying on the cold ground—and then she tells them to lie down on either side of me and try to keep me warm with their own body heat. Bailey takes off her sweater and wraps it around my legs and feet to keep them from freezing. The whole time, she's talking to me, telling me everything's going to be fine, the ambulance will be there in a minute. Beth's crying, and Brandy keeps telling her to shut up, which means Brandy's terrified, but everybody does what Bailey says. And pretty soon the ambulance comes and they take me to the hospital and I have frostbite and a big-ass wound, which is now a big-ass scar, but otherwise everything's just fine."

"Wow," I say again, snuggling closer. "I hope Bailey got recognized by the hometown paper or something for saving your life."

"Yeah, you know, there was an item about it on the local news the next day, and I think her Girl Scout troop actually did a recognition ceremony for her, but that's not the point of the story."

"There's a point to this story? Because, you know, a lot of times, with your stories, there isn't."

He puts a hand under my chin and tilts my face up, leaning back enough that he can look me in the eyes. For someone who can be so silly, he looks deadly serious. "To me, that's what love looks like," he says. "Most of the time it's just in the background, but in extraordinary circumstances, it's extraordinary. Creative, unstinting, tenacious, and drastic. The day I met you, I knew you would have reacted just like Bailey did—you would have done whatever you had to do to save Ann."

"Oh, God, please don't tell me I remind you of your sisters."

He doesn't quite smile. "Not in the way you look or talk. In the way you love whatever you have chosen to adopt as your own. I realized that's what I've been looking for my whole life. I realized nothing else would ever be good enough for me."

I'm silent a long moment, but I don't squirm free, and I don't look away. "*Love.* That's a pretty big word for people who've only known each other a few weeks."

"It's what I want for the long term," he says—adding, as if he can't quite help himself, "though I'll take sex for now."

I poke him in the ribs hard enough to make him yelp. "Lucky for you, the sex is good enough to carry us through for a while."

"I'll say." His fervent voice makes me giggle, but I quickly sober up.

"It's too soon to know anything for sure," I say, and now I lean my head forward again to rest it on his chest. "I have a hard time letting my guard down enough to love someone."

He strokes my hair with one hand. "What do you think my chances are?"

"I'm thinking you like love so much that you make it easy for people to give it to you."

"So my chances are good."

"That's what I'm thinking."

"If it helps any," he says, "I think I fell in love with you that first day. When you cried in my arms and then—suited back up in all your armor and pretended it didn't happen. So strong. So defiant. And so wounded, all at once. I wanted to kiss you then." As if to make up for this omission, he kisses the top of my head. "Everything I've seen since has just intensified the feeling."

"That's sweet," I say. "But I think you just know how to deal with women."

He laughs, then tugs on a fistful of my hair. "So tell me a story. I told you one."

"What kind of story?"

"Anything you want me to know."

I lie there a few moments in silence, while he continues to brush his hand across my hair and down my back. I hardly want to tell any heroic-older-sister tale after the one he's just recited; I can't think of anything I've done that's quite so dramatic, anyway. And that's not the point of this little exercise, I think. The stories are stand-ins for emotions. His gift to me was love. I think what he needs from me is trust.

I have never yet admitted to him in so many words that Ann is the creature he believes her to be. But if I trust him, that's exactly what I'll do now.

"When I was sixteen or so, and we'd been living here for about a year, Debbie and I went on a hike with our Girl Scout troop. Ann wanted to come along, and the Scout leader didn't mind, so I brought her. I can't even remember where we went—Pere Marquette, maybe, over in Illinois. There were probably thirty girls along that day, a whole busload of us, and a handful of parents. Naturally, people got separated on the trails, and eventually Ann and I got lost. We'd even lost track of Debbie along the way."

I wriggle closer to him to absorb heat from his skin; I still get chills thinking about that day. "I had no idea where we were. I couldn't hear voices from the other girls. I didn't have a compass. I knew you were supposed to be able to tell north by which side of the trees the moss was growing on, but since I didn't know which direction I was supposed to go, north didn't help me much. This was in the days before everyone on the planet had a cell phone, so I couldn't call for help. And we had about two hours of daylight left."

"What did you do?"

"I didn't want to panic Ann, but I vaguely remembered hearing somewhere that if you were lost, you should stay put, so search parties had a better chance of finding you. So when we came to a sort of clearing where I thought we might be visible from overhead—in case someone sent a helicopter for us—I said, 'Let's sit here for a while and play a game.' So we counted the different kinds of trees we could see and the birds we could identify and the bugs we saw—plenty of bugs. And after about twenty minutes, Ann said she was hungry and wanted to go back. And I said, trying to sound cheerful, 'Well, honey, I think we should wait here till someone comes to get us.' Of course she asked why, and I said, 'I'm not sure I can find the way back.' And she said, 'Oh, I can.' Cool as you please."

I'm silent a moment, but he, for a wonder, doesn't speak, just waits. "So I said, 'Really? You're just a little girl. How can you know the way back?' And she said, 'When I'm a puppy, I can always find my way home.'"

I resettle myself in Brody's arms, but he's still quiet, letting me tell the story at my own pace. "Well, it was a dilemma for me," I say slowly. "I was the big sister. I was the one who was supposed to do the rescuing. And Ann was six years old. Could I possibly believe a child of that age could lead us out of the woods? Wasn't she likely to get us more lost? But it was true—she'd always found her way home before. And I really didn't want to spend the night in the park, cold and hungry. So I said, still casual, 'That would be great if you think you won't get lost. But as soon as we catch sight of the rest of the troop, you'll have to turn back into a little girl. They don't know your secret.' And she just said, 'Okay,' and she turned herself into her other shape."

I detour from the main story for a moment. "She takes the form of a white husky with pale blue eyes. Most beautiful creature you ever saw. At this stage, still a puppy, all big paws and playful energy. But with an expression—I can't describe it. You could have lined up a dozen white huskies in front of me, and I'd have been able to pick Ann out in a heartbeat. This dog just *looked* like her. Still does."

Brody risks a comment. "I'd like to see her that way sometime."

"Stick around. You will."

He kisses my head. "Another incentive."

I resume the tale. "So Ann starts sniffing at the ground—picking up our scent, I suppose. Of course, whenever she changes shape, she sheds her clothes, so *that* presents me a bit of a problem. I take her little sundress and knot it real loosely around her neck, so she can slip into it when she changes back. I carry her sandals, and I just leave her underwear behind.

"Pretty soon she takes off, still sniffing the ground, and I follow her as fast as I can. I actually have to call her back a couple of times because she gets so far ahead of me. I was lost, so I don't know for sure, but she never seems to lose the trail even for a moment. And about fifteen minutes later, I hear voices ahead of us, calling for us. The Scout leaders had realized we were missing, and a hunt was already on.

"On the one hand, I'm hugely relieved, but on the other— where's Ann? I don't want us to make it safely out of the wilderness just to have her exposed as a shape-shifter. I can't call for her without everyone else hearing me, so I stay back where I am and start whistling. And then whispering. 'Ann. Ann. Where are you? It's time for you to come back to yourself.' That's what I always used to say whenever I wanted her to take her human shape again. 'Come back to yourself.' But she doesn't hear me or she's off in the woods playing or—I don't know. So I stand there, a few yards away from the rest of the troop, hearing people calling our names, and I don't know what to do."

"Pretty scary."

"And then I hear one of the Scout leaders cry out, 'There she is! Ann, we've been looking all over for you! Where's your sister?' And I hear Ann's voice, totally human, totally calm, saying, 'She was right behind me. Look—there she is.' And I step out of the woods and everyone runs up to hug me, and then the Scout leader starts yelling at me that I have to be more careful, don't I realize how dangerous the woods are? What was I thinking, going off alone like that? And how could I have let my little sister walk *barefoot* along the trails? And I tell everyone I'm sorry, and Debbie brings me some water, and pretty soon we're all back on the bus again going home.

"And never, not for a minute, did Ann act like it was a big deal. Then, or later, when I tried to get her to talk about it. She wasn't lost, she wasn't afraid, it didn't bother her to switch between shapes. It was just as easy to be a dog as to be a human—and more useful, at least some of the time. To her it was like—like choosing to stand up or sit down. Whatever felt right at the moment. It was the first time I truly understood that shape-shifting wasn't something that just happened to Ann. It wasn't like getting the flu or the measles. It was part of her. Like hair. Like hands and feet." I shrug. "Or like paws and a tail."

"Although from what I've seen of Ann," Brody says, "that's how she would have accepted anything in her life that could be considered outside the norm. If she'd been born deaf, or with only one arm. She wouldn't have been fazed at all."

I manage the ghost of a laugh. "Maybe. I'd like to think so. She has a happy nature and a peculiar blindness to the existence of obstacles. I envy her. And I admire her. And I worry about her every single minute. I can't think of anything I wouldn't do to keep her safe."

Brody draws me closer again, snuggling into the pillows. "Oh yes," he murmurs. "That's the kind of love I want."

Well, of course Brody stays for the whole weekend. We don't even get out of bed until almost noon on Saturday, and the rest of the day unfolds at a gloriously leisurely pace. I do the most minimal cleaning imaginable. Brody heads to the grocery store and comes back with meat and barbecue sauce and potatoes to roast in the fire.

"Fabulous, but I don't actually have a barbecue pit," I inform him.

"I know, so I picked up a cheap little charcoal grill at the store. It was, like, thirty bucks. Also some briquettes and some lighter fluid."

"My manly man," I say, pretending to swoon. "My hunter-gatherer. Are you going to do the cooking, too?"

"You betcha."

It's a beautiful day, bumping up against seventy degrees, and the sun is a brassy blond as she dips toward late afternoon, so we're perfectly content to spend the next few hours outdoors. Brody hasn't seen my "backyard" till now, and he pauses to take it in once he lugs the grill around the side of the house. I own twelve acres and most of them spread out in three directions from the back patio as if it were the tassel on the base of a fan. The yard itself is small, maybe thirty feet by forty feet, with delineated patches where I sometimes bother to put in a vegetable garden but more often do not. It's dotted with a couple of random shrubs, a line of butterfly bushes on the north edge, and patches of violets and lilies of the valley that I make no attempt to nurture or control. But just outside this relatively clear space, the woodland starts closing in.

Like most Missouri foliage, it's a tangled mess—oaks and hickories and black locusts and sycamores and cedars roped together with aerial vines, and rendered nearly impassable at ground level by whippy shrubbery in varieties I cannot begin to identify. In winter it all just looks like one big maze of thin brown limbs, dry and dead, but in spring it's a study in green. You would not have believed there could be so many variations on the same basic color, from the regal emerald of the firs to the shy lime of the willows. And when the flowering trees are in bloom, as they are now, it's like a Seurat painting, pointillist clusters of brilliant color stretching across the woven canvas of branch and sky.

"Oh, this is amazing," Brody says. "I wouldn't sell this place even if I *didn't* have a sister who was a shape-shifter."

"Yeah, I love it," I say. "The house isn't much, but the property is stellar."

He sets up the grill on the patio while I sweep off six months' worth of brown leaves and dead bugs. I don't really have outdoor furniture, so while Brody starts the fire, I wrestle a couple of kitchen chairs out the side door and around to the back, then bring out the beat-up folding card table. It's April, which you'd like to think would be too early for mosquitoes, but apparently not. So I also fetch the buckets of citronella candles and a few tiki-style torches Debbie gave me a couple of years ago which I'd never bothered to use. I'll save them for nightfall, but I light the citronella right away, and its smoky, smudgy scent immediately clogs the air.

"This is the *life*," Brody exclaims, as the flames writhe in the grill for a few moments before dying down. "I don't care if we start fighting and eventually can't stand each other. I'm not leaving this place."

"Buy yourself a Markham Manor," I suggest. "You can barbecue in your backyard every night."

"Wouldn't be the same. Not without the view."

We sit outside long after sunset, long after the meal is finished and we've taken the dishes inside and we've made and eaten s'mores, because it turns out Brody bought the ingredients for those as well. I'm chilly once the sun goes down, so I bring out a couple of old afghans and we wrap ourselves in those, then fold up the card table so we can scoot our chairs close together while we watch the moon rise. We talk—this is Brody; of course we talk—mostly telling more childhood stories, the majority of them funny, a few of them laced with pain or sadness.

He wants me to tell him about Gwen's disappearance and my father's death, but those are the tales I like least, so I abbreviate them. "She started being gone more and more often, for longer and longer periods of time. When she got back, she'd be quiet and remorseful and very affectionate, especially with Ann. By the time I was twenty, she was gone almost all the time. I think that's the year we saw her twice, for about a week each time. And then we saw her once the year after that—the year Ann was eleven. And that was it. She's never come back."

"What do you think happened to her?"

"I think her animal side became so powerful that she was almost never human anymore. I think she *would* have come back if she could have. I was so angry with her at the time, but I've thought about it a lot since then. I think she couldn't do any better. I think she was at the mercy of her nature."

"Do you think she's still alive?"

I remember the conversation I had with Ann on this very topic, and I shake my head. "If she was," I say, "she'd come back to see Ann. So she has to be dead."

"And your father died, when? Five years ago?"

"Six. But he'd been pretty much out of it for two years before he died. Stopped recognizing us. Didn't know who he was or where he was." I make a fatalistic gesture. "Like Gwen, I think he held on for as long as he could. He'd been having these bouts for years. We didn't know at first if he was just losing his memory or maybe getting Alzheimer's, but he could tell he was slowly sliding down into madness. He used those exact words to me one time. But he was so afraid for Ann. By this time, it was clear Gwen was a lost cause, and I was just a teenager when he had the first episodes. He was afraid if something happened to him, Ann would be taken away and put in foster care, which would have been disastrous for so many reasons. So he fought it. He figured out ways to work from home, to get more time to finish his research, to *pretend* to be a functioning head of household. But shortly after I turned twenty-one, he just let go.

"About a month later I was able to get him in a nursing home out in West County. Ann and I went to visit him every few days until he stopped recognizing us. And then we still went once a week. I have to be honest, it was a relief when he finally died. He wasn't anybody I knew anymore. He had changed more than Ann ever could have."

"Pretty tough on you," he comments.

"Everybody has it tough one way or another," I reply. "And as I say, things got easier once he was gone. I'd been going to school part-time at Maryville, and after he died, I had more time and energy to finish my degree. There was life-insurance money, which helped a *lot*, so I paid off the house and got a new car. Then Debbie opened her company and hired me. Life actually got better there for a while."

"You make it sound like it's bad again."

I hesitate long enough to make him straighten up in his

chair and try to get a good look at my face by the wavering light of the tiki torch. "Melanie? Is something wrong? You're not still worried that *I'm* going to do something to hurt Ann, are you?"

"You're a complication," I tell him honestly, "but no, I'm not afraid of that. Exactly."

"Then what's bothering you?"

"Just—as always. I'm anxious about Ann."

"Is it that you don't like William? For which I could not really say I blame you."

"I'm starting to get on board with William. I think he loves her, and I think he watches out for her. It's just—she seems frail to me lately. A little sickly, maybe. Maybe not. Maybe I'm just borrowing trouble."

He doesn't make some patronizing comment like, *You worry too much, you know?* He doesn't offer hearty reassurances that he has no way of knowing are true. He just squeezes my hand, and says, "I guess if something's wrong, you'll find out eventually. And deal with it then."

"Yeah," I say. "I guess you're right."

The chill finally chases us back inside. Brody lifts his blanket above his shoulders and throws it over my head, then draws me closer, so we're embracing inside the world's smallest tent. And that leads to kissing and that leads to lovemaking and that leads to another night of whispering in bed until we each fall into an exhausted but blissful slumber.

I am sleeping so heavily, in fact, and dreaming so vividly, that I can hardly claw my way back to wakefulness when I hear and finally decode the sound that means someone is knocking furiously on the door. I struggle to open my eyes, to sit up and orient myself. I'm in my own bed in my own house. Brody is beside me, also fighting to wake up. By the faint color limning the square of the bedroom curtain, it's daylight, but barely.

"What's going on?" he says, rubbing his eyes.

Adrenaline is quickly clearing the fog from my mind, or

maybe it's fear; an urgent early-morning summons cannot be good. "Someone's at the door," I say briefly, and hop out of bed. I smell like smoke and sweat and sex, and of course I'm nude. I grab a robe and stuff my feet into slippers as I run for the living room. Brody's right behind me, barefoot but wrapping a blanket around his waist like a sarong.

When I fling the door open, all my terrors come to life on one sharp and alarming tableau. William is standing there, pale and disheveled, holding an unconscious white husky in his arms. He's gripping her so tightly to his chest that I cannot make out anything of her face except that her eyes are closed; her paws are folded before her as if she is merely sleeping. But from William's expression, I know that is not the case.

I push the door wider, and he brushes past me, carrying his precious burden across the room to the sofa. Brody and I trail behind him, Brody silent and me uttering frantic questions. *What happened? What's wrong with her? Is she hurt?* William doesn't answer, and I think it's because he doesn't know, which frightens me even more.

The three of us kneel on the floor in front of her, and I take hold of one of the slim white paws, feeling the bone and tendon through the fur. "Ann," I say, pitching my voice in the tone I have always used to catch her wayward attention. "Ann. You're home. You're safe now. Come back to yourself. Come back to me. Come back."

And then it is as if she shimmers, or wavers, or pulses between dimensions at a rate too rapid to be visible to the human eye. The white fur ruffles, then smooths out, then darkens to ivory, to sand, to the rosy-pink beige of flesh. The pointed black nose shrinks down, tilts up, melts back into the re-formed face, and matted blond hair spills untidily across her cheek, down her back, over one slim shoulder.

She is naked, she is still unconscious, and she is bleeding at the mouth.

CHAPTER SIXTEEN

JANET

Unexpectedly, I loved college.

I had let all the logistical challenges of relocation distract me from my real and growing fear about how badly the undergraduate experience would go. What if I hated my roommate, my courses, my teachers, the university environment? What if I wasn't as smart as I believed I was, unable to maintain the grade point average I needed to keep my scholarship? What if here, as everywhere else, I had trouble making friends?

What if Cooper could not adjust to a new routine, a new state park? What if neither of us could bear the days we would have to live apart, while he was in wolf shape and I was attending school? Except for those few miserable days we had stayed apart at the campgrounds, we had slept beside each other every day of the summer, no matter what form Cooper was in. How would both of us adjust to a life in which I had to follow a more normal routine?

Only one way to find out.

He was human for two weeks in the middle of August, so we packed our scant belongings and made our way to U of I about a week before classes were scheduled to start. Before my roommate had even showed up, we settled my stuff into my room and familiarized ourselves with the campus, then spent a couple of days trying to figure out where Cooper would spend his time. It was almost fifty miles to the nearest state park big enough for him to hide in, but about half the distance away was a private-estate-turned-nature-preserve that featured some prairie, some woodland, some statuary, and a whole lot of human activity like conferences and weddings. It seemed unlikely a true wild animal would be able to keep out of sight in such a place, but Cooper had a thinking man's ability to exercise caution, and we both believed he could stay there safely, at least for short periods of time. A tent was out of the question, but a wolf wouldn't need a tent.

When he was human—well, we weren't sure yet how that would go. Depending on my roommate's attitude about overnight guests, he might be able to stay with me most of those nights. Just in case, we investigated local homeless shelters and other options, like the bus station that stayed open all night.

"I'll manage," Cooper assured me. "I always do."

He was in town, attending a free church breakfast on the Sunday morning before classes started, when I first met my roommate.

She came banging through the door, loaded down with four pieces of luggage in matching red leather, followed by two people I took to be her parents. They were all fair-haired and exceptionally good-looking in an almost offensively healthy way. The father was over six feet tall, broad-shouldered, and bespectacled, like an athlete who had decided to turn accountant. The mother was petite, precise, wearing heels and nylons and pearls even on this sticky late-summer day, and she talked incessantly.

"Oh dear, the rooms aren't very big, are they? Is that the closet? Is that the *only* closet? And where's the bathroom? Down the *hall*? Are you sure? You're going to have to do something about those curtains, they'll look horrible with your new bedspread. I thought they said there would be a refrigerator in the room. *That's* a refrigerator? I thought it was a safe. You won't be able to keep much food in there, will you? Well, at least you won't gain any weight."

Her daughter and husband ignored her with what seemed to be the ease of long practice. The tall man carefully dropped a heavy box at the foot of the bed I hadn't claimed, and said, "I'll be back in a minute." The girl let all the straps and handles slide from her arms and took one long, critical look around.

I took a long, critical look at her. She was neither as petite as her mother nor as strapping as her father, but she was built like the girls who'd been cheerleaders and tennis players back at my high school. Her wheat-colored hair hung straight to her shoulders, then made a slight upward flip; her eyes were a guileless blue. No doubt she had been cast as Cinderella and her direct descendants in every school play from kindergarten on. If I'd had to bet, I'd have said she was the high-school homecoming queen and she'd come to college to major in fashion merchandising and find a frat boy to marry.

God knows what she thought when she first laid eyes on *me*, but I very much doubted she could have come anywhere close to guessing the truth.

She gave me a careless, easy smile, and said, "Hey. What's your name?"

"Janet."

"I'm Crystal."

Crystal turned out to be the best roommate in the world. First, she was hardly ever home. She had a boyfriend of her own, a junior who shared a rambling old house with three other guys, and she practically lived there with him. It was clear she had only taken up space in the dorm so her parents believed that was where she stayed. One of my primary tasks was to take calls from her mother, claim that Crystal was in class or in the shower or downstairs in the cafeteria, then phone the boyfriend's house to tell her to call home. This was easy to do and an exceedingly small price to pay for the astonishing privilege of almost total privacy.

Second, she was nice. Despite her gorgeous looks and her well-to-do background—and the fact that she had, indeed, been homecoming queen—she was nothing like the bitch I was expecting. She wasn't particularly effusive or extraordinarily warm, but she was friendly to everyone, never bad-tempered, and casually thoughtful. For instance, on the mornings she came back to the room to pick up new clothes or swap out some textbooks, she would always stop for coffee and donuts at a little stand down the street, and she'd invariably pick up a pastry for me. It was a small gesture, maybe, but I was not used to small kindnesses, and I appreciated them immensely.

Third, she liked Cooper. Their very different schedules ensured that they almost never ran into each other, but when they did, she'd always sit and talk to him for a few minutes. It turned out she was majoring, not in fashion merchandising, but graphic design, and she was interested in all kinds of art. She and her boyfriend even took a weekend trip up to Chicago that fall so she could see some exhibit at the Art Institute.

We had been living together for three weeks, and I'd seen her for all of five hours, when she happened to be home on a Friday afternoon. I was sitting at my desk, trying to get all my homework done before the weekend, since I was pretty sure Cooper would be human again by the following morning. I'd done a little decorating since she'd been here last, and she wandered over to examine one of Cooper's drawings that I had thumbtacked to the wall. It was larger than his typical work—maybe sixteen inches by twenty inches—carefully done on real artist's paper instead of his usual discarded scraps. It was a view of one of my favorite scenes from the park where we'd lived all summer, a wooden bridge over a little stream that was so smooth throughout most of its run that you would swear it had no measurable current at all. But here under the bridge, it flowed over a tumble of rocks, and suddenly its surface went from glassy and still to ruffled and wrinkled. It was as if only the presence of those stones could force the water to show its true nature.

The centerpiece of the image was me. I was leaning with my spine against the handrail of the bridge, my elbows resting on top of it; my head was flung back, my eyes were closed, and I was obviously glorying in the feel of sunlight on my face. My hair was so long that it trailed over the railing. We'd just come back from an afternoon in town, so I was dressed a bit more nicely than usual, in a sundress and sandals. I probably even had makeup on though you couldn't tell it from the sketch.

I hadn't really been posing. I'd simply paused there on the bridge to rest after the walk from the bus stop through the park. Cooper had said, "Stay like that for a moment," and pulled out a slip of paper and a pencil. He'd worked on the bigger image for a couple of weeks, never letting me look at it until it was done. I loved it.

After Crystal had studied the piece for a few minutes, she said, "I like that. The detail is incredible. That's you, isn't it?"

"Yeah. Cooper drew it."

"He did? He's really good. Is he taking classes?"

To this point, I hadn't given her much information about Cooper except his name. It didn't seem like it would be hard to conceal the truth from her. She wasn't a very curious girl. I shook my head. "No. He's working, trying to save money." This was true as far as it went. He'd found another part-time job, this time with a landscaping company that was also willing to pay its workers in cash. I thought there was probably a vast network of people in this country who were existing under the radar, paying no taxes, registered in no census, ghosts that made no mark on the official system at all.

"Does he work in other media?"

It had been hard enough to keep paper dry and find a place to store the soft-leaded pencils in the tent. Working in oil or watercolor had been out of the question. "Not so far, but I think he'd like to someday."

"He ought to learn how to make an etching. Looks like a style that would suit him."

"I'll tell him that."

Actually, Crystal was the one to make that observation to him a couple of weeks later when their paths intersected. She even lent him a battered copy of an old art book that described various printmaking processes and how they'd been modified through the centuries. "There's a studio downtown. You can rent time on the press," she told him. "Let me know if you ever want to go talk to the owner, and I'll take you in and introduce you."

"Thanks. I'd like that," Cooper said.

So the roommate whom I'd dreaded so much turned out to be the easiest and luckiest part of this unfamiliar new life.

Although, as I said, I loved the whole college experience. I didn't make friends in all my classes, but on the whole I found my fellow students more congenial—more like me—than I'd ever found my high-school classmates. Certainly there were plenty who seemed to have come to college for no reason except to party. But there were others who were smart, serious, awkward, and odd, and those were the ones I sat by in the lecture halls and ate with at dinner. Sometimes, we studied together; we picked each other when we needed lab partners; and we chose our spring classes specifically so we would have a few courses in common. For someone like me, who had had nothing resembling a social group in high school, this was a whole new world of human interaction.

Cooper worried a little that I would be so intoxicated by the possibility of fresh friendships—*normal* friendships—that I would slip away from him, find him an encumbrance, an embarrassment, a mistake. Well, that had been at the back of his mind before we even made the move to Champaign. But it didn't happen. I had known it wouldn't. I had attached myself to him, formed myself around him; like the little stream running under the bridge, I only showed any depth or complexity when he was in my path. I was not about to seek out a new channel. Without the texture and the beauty he brought out in me, I would be nothing at all.

It was during the spring semester, when I was taking three intro-to-science classes, that I first stumbled on the idea that would become my obsession for the next fifteen years. I still wasn't positive what I wanted to major in, but I was pretty sure it would have a scientific bent, and I had filled my schedule with anatomy, biology, and chemistry classes. The chemistry professor was a real character, with wild gray hair and an untrimmed beard and the general air of someone who had scrambled out of bed, with a hangover, only ten minutes before the start of class. But he was charismatic and entertaining, with an effortless way of making his subject come alive.

"It all seems pointless now," he reassured us one day as we struggled through a lab experiment that, by the end of class, no one had managed to get right. "But one day it will all make sense. One day the breathless synergy of math and science and the human body will make your blood tingle and your mouth fall open in wonder."

We all laughed and groaned and continued with our lab work. My mind wasn't really on the exercise, though; it had been two weeks since I'd seen Cooper, and all I could think about was that he might be waiting for me in my room when I got out of class. I was never so grateful to see an hour draw to a close.

"See you next week," said my lab partner, as we left class.

I was almost running already; I waved over my shoulder. "See you then!"

Cooper indeed was in my room, freshly shaved and showered and wearing a set of clothes I'd laundered for him while he'd been gone. He'd picked up a pizza and a liter of soda, because neither of us liked to go out on the first couple of nights he was human, and Crystal had already let me know she wouldn't be around this weekend. We had the room to ourselves; we could burrow in with almost as much isolation and privacy as we'd had at the campsite.

But Cooper was in an unexpectedly down mood. It took me a while to tease the reason out of him, but eventually he told me he'd had a near miss at the nature preserve. A boy who was maybe ten or twelve years old had spotted Cooper and started pelting him with rocks. This drew the attention of the kid's father, who called the groundskeepers, who called some animal-control people, who spent a couple of days looking for tracks and spoor.

"I was able to stay out of their way, but it scared me," he said. By this time, it was full dark and we were lying face-to-face on my bed. We'd lit a few candles, but they did little more than make it barely possible to read the expressions on each other's faces. We hadn't made love yet; we were too busy talking. "I'm not sure how much longer I'll be able to stay there, not if people are looking for me."

"Maybe you should go to Walnut Park for the next couple of months," I said, resting my hand on his shoulder and drawing him close enough for a kiss. "I know, it's a lot farther away, but it's a lot bigger. It's less likely that anyone will find you."

He turned on his back to stare up at the ceiling. My hand came to rest on his chest, just over his heart. "Maybe I just shouldn't turn into a wolf at all," he burst out. "God! If only I could walk away from it! If I could—cou!—find a pill or get a blood transfusion or change the cells in my body. If only I could be normal!"

For a moment I was frozen beside him, then I scrambled up to a sitting position. "What if you could?" I said, speaking slowly, though my mind was seething with excitement. "What if there *was* a pill? I mean, people use drugs to control diabetes and blood clots and—and—well, other diseases. Maybe there's a chemical way to control *your* changes."

At first he looked hopeful, but then his expression clouded over again. "Maybe, but how would I ever find out?" he asked. "It's not like I can go to a doctor and say, 'Hey. I'm

a shape-shifter, but I don't want to be. Got a cure for that?'
He'd call the zoo—or the cops—so fast I'd never be able to
run away in time."

"Maybe," I repeated. "But I'm taking all these chemistry
and biology classes. Maybe I can be some kind of researcher.
Maybe *I'll* be able to study your blood. *I* can do experiments.
Maybe *I'll* find the cure for you."

He gazed up at me. In the wide eyes, the full lips, the
dark hair, I saw the poet, the lover, the artist, the man I
adored; but I also saw the wolf, the wild creature, who would
do anything he had to in order to survive. "Yes," he whispered. "Oh, I hope you do."

I bent down to kiss him. "I will," I said, and kissed him
again. I thought about the chemistry professor's words about
synergy. I didn't have to wait until I found a position in a
lab, I thought. I could take what I was learning in all my
science classes and start conducting tests right now. "I
promise."

His hands came up, and he pulled me down on top of
him, and for a long time the only words between us were
spoken in breathless whispers. But I had my cause now; I
had my *raison d'être*. I would study and learn and experiment, over and over again, until I found the cure for Cooper.
I would change his life, I would give him what he wanted.
Because he was *my* life, because he was what *I* wanted. I
could hardly wait for dawn to come, so I could begin.

CHAPTER SEVENTEEN

MELANIE

I don't know what to do.

For the next two hours, I simply hover anxiously, watching over Ann. I rest my hand on her forehead, checking for fever, but her body temperature seems close to mine. I press my fingers to her wrist, feeling for her pulse, but I don't know if the heartbeat I find is too rapid, too slow, too weak, too urgent. Once I have wiped the smear of red from her face, there is no more blood. Her breathing seems a little labored but no worse than you might expect from someone with a bad cold.

And she has woken once, long enough to smile and say my name, before falling back asleep.

So I don't know if I need to take her to a doctor. I don't know if the risk of *not* taking her to the ER outweighs the risk of *taking* her. Will she die if I don't? Will she expose her terrible secret if I do? How can I possibly know?

William is as alarmed as I am though he shows it differently. Mostly he sits, very still, in a chair he has pulled over next to the sofa, and does nothing but watch over Ann. He hasn't had much information to give me about what has driven her to this state. No, she hasn't been injured. Yes, he would know. Yes, he's been concerned lately. She hasn't had much energy or appetite, but she hasn't seemed any worse than she did when he first told me he was worried. Until this morning. When he woke up—in a ditch or under a bridge, I'm sure, though he's not specific—and she did not.

"Do *you* think she'd want me to take her to a doctor?" I ask him.

He shakes his head. "We've never talked about it. But I don't think so."

"Would you want her to take you if *you* were the one lying on the couch?"

His brooding eyes don't leave her still form. "No," he says. "Unless there's a broken bone or a wound that's been ripped open—something that can be fixed—I don't think doctors can help people like us." He makes a slow, broad gesture that seems to indicate his heart, or his chest, or maybe his whole body. "I think we're too different inside. They could hurt one of us instead of helping us."

But I'm still not sure.

"Let's keep watching her," I say at last. "If she seems to get worse, if she can't breathe, if she starts bleeding again, then I'll take her to the ER. If she's not better by—" I hesitate. I have no idea what deadline would be reasonable. "By tomorrow morning. I'll take her in. And then—whatever happens, happens."

William glances at me with those hooded, unreadable eyes and makes no comment. I don't know if he agrees or disagrees. I don't know if I'm right or wrong. I don't know, I don't know.

It's clear Brody has tried to stay out of the way while William and I hash through the dilemma. After taking a quick shower, he's been working in the kitchen, making coffee and cooking a light breakfast. I've already gulped down some coffee, but my stomach has been too knotted up for me to tolerate the idea of food. Once I arrive at my nebulous decision, I feel a little better. Almost hungry. I leave William to keep vigil and slip inside the kitchen to find Brody.

He turns from the stove, where he appears to be making pancakes, and draws me into a long hug. "Any change?" he asks.

"Not really."

"Do you think we should try to get her to eat or drink something?"

"Maybe later. William said they ate a pretty solid meal last night, so I don't think she's in immediate danger."

"Could you eat something? I can make toast if you can't face pancakes. Or scrambled eggs."

"Actually, the pancakes are starting to smell really good."

William declines to join us, so Brody and I settle around the oak table, me choosing the seat that allows me to view the sofa where Ann is sleeping. The pancakes are delicious; he must have added something to the basic Bisquick recipe. I feel better instead of worse once I've eaten, which isn't always the case.

"So are you going to take her to a doctor?" Brody asks.

"Only if her condition deteriorates or isn't better by tomorrow morning."

He nods, as if he approves, but I have the sense he would try to support any decision I made at this juncture just because he realizes how close I am to disintegrating into a wild, rotating frenzy of panicked atoms. "If you're open to suggestions," he says, "I may have one."

I tense up, because additional input can only undercut the fragile state of balance I've achieved, but I say, "What's that?"

"I met this woman in central Illinois a few months back. She's a vet. A vet who specializes in shape-shifters. Maybe you could take Ann to see her."

I stare at him for a moment because it takes me that long to absorb what he's said. Somewhere in the world is a medical professional who knows about people with Ann's condition and is actually qualified to treat them? Someone to whom I can tell the truth—someone I can trust with Ann's secret and Ann's life? "Are you sure?" I ask, a not very cogent question, but he seems to know what I mean.

"I was at her place the day I saw those three people turn into animals. She takes care of all of them. She's not about to betray anybody."

I lean my elbows on the table because suddenly my body

feels so heavy that my spine won't hold me upright. "That would be—I can't even tell you—such a relief. Such a gift. If you think she'd be willing to see us. If she takes strangers as patients."

"I think she'd want from you what you'd want from her. Discretion and silence."

"Then yes. Sign us up. How do we get hold of her? Where exactly in Illinois?"

"She's got a place a little east of Decatur, but I think she keeps offices in Springfield, too. Might take us three hours to get there. And I don't know if you want to wait until Ann's in better shape for travel—"

I shake my head. "I want to go the minute she's willing to see us."

"Then I'll give her a call."

From Dr. Kassebaum's name, I am expecting someone ample, fair, and pale, but in fact she's almost the exact opposite: a small-boned woman, not very tall, with olive skin and glossy black hair. She's wearing big silver hoop earrings, a crinkly ankle-length skirt in bright red and orange, and a denim vest. Although she's friendly enough, she's a little remote. This is not a warm, empathetic counselor; this is a survivor who's willing to share her hard-won knowledge to help you pull through as well.

It is close to sunset Sunday evening when I meet her, and my head is still spinning at how quickly events have unfolded on what is looking like it will be a very long day. The minute Brody calls her and explains the situation, she agrees to join us in Springfield that evening. If she does, in fact, have an office in that city, she doesn't want us to come to it. Instead, she gives us directions to a motel that she says is on the outer edges of town. A place, I gather, where nobody asks questions and nobody pays much attention to the guests. Perfect for our purposes.

It takes me a little time to organize my life to make even this short a journey. I have to call Debbie to warn her that I won't be at work in the morning (to which she replies, "Are you *kidding*? Go, go!") I have to pack clothes and close up the house and assemble food to take us at least part of the way to our destination. William and Brody outfit the Jeep with enough blankets and pillows to allow Ann to travel comfortably in whichever shape suits her best. I am certain that William would prefer to be in animal form and that he remains human because he feels he can be more useful in this incarnation, at least for the moment.

All of this takes time, so it is past three before we all climb in the Cherokee and hit the road. Brody drives because I am too distracted to focus. We find the motel with no trouble, and drive around to the back of the long, narrow building where the less desirable rooms look out over the desolate parking lot. Dr. Kassebaum has told us she's in room 105; it's the only one on this side of the building where there appears to be a light in the window.

Ann has regained consciousness, though she's drowsy and disinclined for conversation. When William lifts her out of the Jeep so he can carry her inside, she snuggles against him, her hair half obscuring her face. The motel door opens before we even have a chance to knock. And there's Dr. Kassebaum, with her unsmiling face and her sober professionalism. Almost on the instant, I feel myself subtly relaxing. I am certain, for the first time in my life, that I've found someone who understands exactly who and what it is I love. I feel like I can transfer some of my burdens to her, and she will know how to dismantle them. She will turn them light as air.

The room is small, most of the space taken up by two queen-size beds, and she motions for William to carry Ann to the one farthest from the door. Brody and I perch on the edge of the other bed, while Dr. Kassebaum pulls up a round-backed chair that looks like it was manufactured in the sixties and uncomfortable even then.

"Can you give me a quick family history?" she asks, opening a notebook and picking up a pen. I like that; my own primary-care physician has begun typing all her notes into a computer, and she never looks up at my face while I'm speaking.

I strive to be concise. "Ann's twenty years old. Her mother was a shape-shifter, her father was fully human. I haven't seen her mother for about nine years and believe she's dead. Our father died six years ago from complications of dementia and pneumonia. There's no history of heart disease in my family, that I know of, or diabetes or anything like that. Our father's mother died of breast cancer, but no one else in our family has had cancer of any kind."

"I assume she's sexually active?"

God, could all this lethargy have a simple, almost joyful root cause—could Ann be merely pregnant? But then I remember. "Yes, but her boyfriend has had a vasectomy."

Dr. Kassebaum nods and makes a note. I can almost hear what she's thinking. *She could have had sex with someone besides her boyfriend.* That would suck for William, but if it means Ann doesn't have any terrifying fatal disease, I'll welcome the news.

But do I really have the strength and courage and sheer tenacious bloody-mindedness to raise another shape-shifter child—?

"Can you describe her exact symptoms and when you first noticed them?"

I think back. It was about six weeks ago that William first confided his concern, and about the same time that I'd started to notice her loss of energy, her tendency to sleep away half the day. Well, if I'm being honest with myself, I'll admit that I started getting anxious about Ann last summer, and none of my fears had been assuaged when I saw her over Christmas. She'd been her usual happy self, but a little vague, a little scatterbrained. Once or twice I'd found myself wondering if she was falling prey—far, far too soon—to the carelessly destructive disease that had claimed my father's memory.

But now I'm afraid it's not her mind that's failing her. It's her body.

"There have been—inklings—faint suggestions of things

that could be wrong—for about a year," I tell Dr. Kassebaum in a halting voice. "A sort of forgetfulness. A deep exhaustion. Small things that by themselves don't seem to mean much. But lately. The past couple of months. They all seem to be magnified."

"Has she complained about pain or weakness? Has she exhibited any typical signs of illness, such as fever or coughing?"

"No—not around me." I glance toward the other bed. Despite the fact that Ann and William are in the same room with us, neither one seems to be paying attention to a word of this conversation. "You could ask William. He's been spending more time with her than I have."

She nods. "I'll interview him, too. Have you noticed any correlations between her level of exhaustion and her transformations between animal and human state? That is, is she most likely to be tired on the first day or two after she's turned human again, then she seems to recover her strength?"

I frown, thinking it over. "I'm not sure. I didn't notice."

"Have there been any changes in her typical cycle?"

Does she still think Ann might be pregnant? "Her menstrual cycle?"

"Her shape-shifting cycle." She glances up from her notebook. "Most shape-shifters have a pattern. Some are human twenty-five days of the month and animal five days. In others, it's reversed. Some alternate between shapes every three or four days. Some always become the same animal, while others might be anything from a rabbit to a buffalo."

I shake my head but, again, I'm not sure. "I don't think that's changed, but you might ask William. Ann has always turned into the shape of a white dog—a husky—ever since she was a little girl. And she's always been able to transform more or less at will."

"That's unusual," Dr. Kassebaum comments.

"William can control it, too. But his brother can't."

"That's unusual, too. Siblings."

"Really? Why?"

Dr. Kassebaum lifts her dark eyes to mine again. It strikes me that what I first took as professional gravity on her part is really sadness. I wonder if she, too, loves a shape-shifter; heartache guaranteed. "When humans learn their partners have burdened them with a shape-shifter child, they tend to terminate the relationship—so, no second babies. And few of the shape-shifters I've met have been eager to bring more of their kind into the world. Their own lives have been hard enough. They don't want children of their own to face the same challenges."

"So maybe one day all the shape-shifters will be gone from the world."

"Maybe," Dr. Kassebaum says. "But if folklore is any guide, they've been around a long time, and I expect they'll be with us to the end of the world."

"I can't decide if that's comforting or not."

"No," she says, "neither can I." She closes her notebook. "Now I'm going to talk to William and examine Ann. Perhaps it would be best if you and Brody were out of the room. There's a vending machine in the lobby if you wanted to get a soda or a snack."

Brody takes my hand as we step outside, and the slanting rays of the setting sun hit me squarely in the eyes. I'm surprised to learn it's still daylight and that the day itself is rather fine. I would have said I was living in perpetual night, perpetual chill, a gray, drab corridor of hell.

"What do you want to do about tonight?" Brody asks as he shuts the door behind us.

"Can you be more specific?"

"We could book a room here and spend the night. A couple of rooms, if we get one for us and one for Ann and William. Or we can drive back to your place. If we leave by seven or eight, we'll be back by midnight. I'm up for it either way."

"I don't know," I answer at last. "I guess it all depends on what Dr. Kassebaum says about Ann."

He leans over to kiss the top of my head, but doesn't say *Everything will be all right* or *Stop worrying so much*. For a man who talks as much as Brody does, he has an uncanny gift for knowing when to be silent. There's really nowhere else to sit, so we climb back into the front seat of the Jeep and wait there, holding hands, and bracing ourselves for whatever dread news the day might bring.

CHAPTER EIGHTEEN

D r. Kassebaum has a few tests she wants to conduct on Ann, and these include drawing blood and letting it ferment overnight, or something, so there's no question of returning home right away. Brody and I have already decided to take a room for the night, and Dr. Kassebaum turns her key over to Ann and William. She needs to return to her office to perform the tests, she tells us, but she'll be back before noon to tell us what she's discovered.

In her absence, the four of us head out to a nearby Pizza Hut for a mostly silent meal. Ann's sleepy, William is never talkative, I'm too tense to make conversation, and even Brody can't overcome all those obstacles. Back at our rooms, we separate for the night. Brody and I watch mindless sitcoms until we fall asleep by ten.

I wake in the morning with a sense of doom. Maybe it's because I'm in strange surroundings—maybe it's because I'm alone in the bed—maybe it's because the situation that brought me here will shortly be explained, and chances are slim that I will hear good news.

I take a quick shower, and by the time I'm out, Brody has returned with orange juice and bagels that he's found at some nearby QuikTrip. "The bagels are stale," he says, "but I figured they were better than starvation."

I'm finishing mine off when I see Dr. Kassebaum step out of a car that's just pulled into the parking lot. I knock back the last of the juice and hurry out the door. "What have you found out?" I ask.

She gestures at the door of room 105. "Let's all talk about it together."

As it did the night before, the motel room seems like an incongruous place to discuss medical mysteries and receive news that will change your life. Dr. Kassebaum places the round-backed chair halfway between the two beds; William and Ann sit on one, backs against the headboard, legs extended before them, and Brody and I take similar poses on the other. It seems like we should be having a slumber party, not girding ourselves for battle, which is what I feel like I'm doing. "So," I ask, "have you come to any conclusions? Do you think you know what's wrong with Ann?"

Dr. Kassebaum nods, her face in its usual grave lines. "I have a theory. At this point, it's all just guesswork, because there is so little we know for sure about shape-shifters and their physiology."

"But you think—?"

"I think the stress of frequent and lifelong transformation between states has worn Ann's body out to a dangerous degree," she says. "I think, as she goes forward, she'll find that the more often she moves between shapes, the weaker she'll become. Furthermore—although this is not usually the case—her body seems to degrade more sharply when she's in her human shape. In her canine form, she seems healthier and stronger. I'm guessing it's because the animal's organs are smaller than the human's, and when she shifts to the larger shape, the organs don't enlarge correspondingly as they should. But as I say, that's just a theory."

"Huh," Ann says. "It makes sense, though."

Dr. Kassebaum goes on. "I've written up a suggested nutritional plan and identified various supplements she might take when she's human, and I'd like to give her some inoculations that will help her fight off disease no matter which form she takes. Unfortunately, there's not much else I can do for her. My advice—and I cannot say it strongly enough—is that Ann should greatly curtail how often she shifts between shapes and drastically limit how much time she spends in human form. If she doesn't, I'm afraid she doesn't have too many years left to her."

The words strike me with the force of boulders, burn me like firebrands held against my skin. "She doesn't have— what do you mean? Are you saying she could *die*?" Of course that's what she's saying. She's tried to phrase it as gracefully as possible, but there's no graceful way to pronounce a death sentence.

She fixes me with her dark eyes. "Shape-shifters in general tend not to live long lives," she says. The compassionate tone does nothing to soften the brutality of the words. "I've rarely known one to live past fifty."

"But Ann's only twenty! She should have—if she lives to fifty, she should have at *least* thirty more years!"

Her voice gentles even more. "None of us are guaranteed a particular life span," she says. "Bodies wear out at different rates, and Ann's, unfortunately, is a fast one. She can't reverse the damage she has absorbed so far, but she can be careful about how much new damage she inflicts."

Ann speaks again, sounding incredulous. "So you're telling me I should take husky form and stay that way? Not become human *ever*? I don't think I can live like that."

Now Dr. Kassebaum rests her gaze on Ann. "I'm afraid it's the best of two bad choices."

Ann shrugs, her usual insouciant nature partially reasserting itself. "And if I just do what I've always done? Change shapes when I feel like it?"

"Then I doubt you'll live out the year."

The sudden silence is so startled, it's as if someone has slapped the room itself. Then I jump from my bed and scramble over to Ann's, grabbing her hands with both of mine.

"Do it," I say frantically. "Take your husky shape now, before we even leave for home, and stay that way. I don't care. Take off with William as soon as we get back and go hang out in the parks and woodlands for six months. Or come to the house and stay there as long as you want—just don't shift back. Just don't become human."

She leans forward until her forehead is touching mine. "You'd miss me," she says.

"I'd still get to hang out with you, just like I used to," I reply. "Don't you remember? When you were a kid, you'd be a puppy for weeks at a time. We'd go running in the yard or playing in the creek. I'd tell you all about what I did at school or what Debbie said or what the cheerleading coach made us do. You'd sleep at the foot of my bed. It's not the *same*, it's not like having a conversation with you—me telling you something and you saying something back—but it's still you. I know what you're thinking. I can see *you* in your eyes. I'd miss you, but you'd still be there."

She makes the smallest motion with her head, a negative shake that I can feel more than I can see. "I'd miss you," she says softly.

"You wouldn't. Most of the time you'd be off having adventures with William—" I glance at him for corroboration, and he nods. "But when you came back to the house, we'd watch TV together. Go for walks. Whatever. You'd just be in your other shape. You'd get to be with me as much as you wanted."

Her eyes, so close to mine, flick to one side. "Would Brody be there some of the time?"

I catch my breath, but he answers before I can. "I'll be there a *lot*," he says. "I'll take you for rides in the car. That'll be fun."

I add, "But we'll make him leave the house when we just want to have girl time."

She repeats my own words. "It's not the same."

"It's not," I agree. "But it's better than nothing."

She straightens up, pulls away from me, moves restlessly

on the lumpy bed. "I don't know," she says. "It seems so extreme." She gives Dr. Kassebaum a look that's just a shade less than accusatory. "What if you're wrong?"

"I don't think I am," Dr. Kassebaum says. "But of course you have to make your own choices."

Brody's the one to break the brief silence that follows. "So what now?" he asks, directing his question at Dr. Kassebaum.

"I'll give Ann some immunizations and other boosters. Make a list of recommended nutritional supplements. But there's really nothing else I can do." She glances at me, where I'm still kneeling beside Ann on the bed. "You're welcome to call anytime you have questions or anytime there's a change in Ann's condition. And I imagine there will be some changes."

"So. If we do this. If she stays in her other shape all the time—will she live out the normal span of her life?" I ask. Fifty years is too short; I will only be sixty, with the potential for another twenty or thirty years ahead of me. I can't imagine navigating all those long, dreary decades without Ann's sunny presence in my life.

Dr. Kassebaum hesitates. "It's hard to predict," she says at last. "But I doubt it."

A bony skeleton hand has wrapped itself around my gut, and now it squeezes hard. I feel its desiccated nails pierce tissue and slit arteries. "How long, then?" I manage to choke out.

"Nothing is certain in medicine."

"I realize that. Give me an estimate."

"Probably not more than two or three years."

I gasp. The cramped hotel room is suddenly airless, or my lungs have ceased to function. In any case, I can't get a breath. "That can't be true," I whisper.

"I'll do what I can to extend the time," Dr. Kassebaum answers. "But she has to change her lifestyle, or nothing I do will matter." She gives Ann a straight and level look. "It's up to you. You have to decide how long you want to live."

* * *

Imake William ride in the front seat next to Brody, an arrangement that clearly thrills neither of them. They don't complain, but Brody immediately tunes the radio to some unobtrusive jazz station to obviate the need for conversation.

I ride in back with Ann and argue for three and a half hours.

"I don't like it. This is stupid," is her primary form of rebuttal to every point I make. "What does she know, anyway? She's just guessing."

"She might be guessing, but she knows more than any of us do. Ann, admit it, you haven't felt well for weeks."

"I've been *tired*, but I haven't been *dying*."

"But you feel better when you're in your other shape."

"I suppose, but—"

"Let's just try it for a while. A few months. Promise me you'll go three months without being human. See how you feel."

"I don't want to go three months without talking to you!"

I try to speak lightly. "You've done it before. Disappeared for *longer* than three months. Making me worry about you every day."

"See? You'd be worried this time, too!"

"Yes, but you wouldn't be gone that whole time. You'd come visit me. You'd just be a dog."

"Woof," she says bitterly. "That's a great conversation."

I reach over to tug on a lock of the yellow hair. "Hey, I've had worse. I've had worse conversations with *you*."

"Very funny."

"So do you promise? Three months?"

She tosses her hair. Under the aggrieved petulance, I sense a real fear; she is responding childishly because she cannot bear to face the news head-on like an adult. I don't blame her, but I can't let her get away with it. I can't let her pretend this isn't happening and blithely refuse to moderate her behavior. I can't let her die one day before she has to.

"I can't tell time when I'm a dog," she says. "How will I know when three months are up?"

"I'll make signs and put them in the backyard. A count-down of days. You can read numbers, can't you, when you're a husky? And words?"

"Simple words."

"So if I make a sign that says 'NOW!' you'll understand that the three months are up?"

"I suppose." She gives me a darkling look. "But don't cheat. Don't pretend it's only been three months if it's really been four."

I'm surprised into a guilty laugh. I was already planning to do just that, except I was considering six months instead of three. "All right, I won't. So is it a deal? Do you promise?"

She's silent a moment, looking out the window. "I'll think about it," she says at last.

"Ann!"

And then we start all over again.

By the time we make it back to my place, I'm exhausted, Ann is still being stubborn, and William has reached his limit. He's barely out of the car before he transforms into the golden setter and goes bounding up the road. Ann glances after him, but not as if she's annoyed. More than the rest of us, she understands his inability to endure con-finement or prolonged human contact.

Brody circles the Jeep and puts an arm around each of us. "Let's just have a nice quiet afternoon followed by a nice quiet dinner," he says. "I can barbecue again, or maybe make tacos. Unless this is one of those nights you just want sister time. And then I can head on home."

"No," Ann and I say in unison.

"We might need a distraction," she says.

"Or a referee," I add.

"Happy to be either," he says. "Let's go on in."

The next few days are tense, emotional, and wearing, and it's hard to look ahead and anticipate things getting much better. It's actually a relief to go into PRZ in the mornings and bury myself in work. Debbie has pried the entire story out of me in five minutes, but its sheer irreversible horribleness leaves her with almost nothing to say.

"Fuck" is all she has to offer.

"Yeah," I reply. "That about sums it up."

Through it all, Brody is a rock. When my constant pleading has left Ann ruffled or angry, he's able to tease her back into a good mood. When I find myself at the oddest moments—putting away dishes, washing my face, going through laundry—succumbing to inconsolable tears, he finds me, he puts his arms around me, he lets me cry against his shoulder. If he has a life of his own, he's subjugated it to our crisis. I figure, once the immediate danger is past, he'll make a dramatic decision; he'll either tender his regrets and light out for good or pack up his stuff and move in.

I hope it's the latter. I have leaned against him so much this past week that I've begun to think I can no longer stand up straight on my own.

"Tired of me yet?" he asks Thursday night as I come home from work to find cookies cooling on the kitchen counter and a chicken casserole in the oven.

"Are you kidding? This is every woman's fantasy come true. A man who's good in the kitchen *and* the bedroom. If only you'd do the ironing, too."

"Yeah, Brandy tried to teach me to iron once. Well, it was really punishment for something I'd done, I can't remember what. Broke her music box or ran over her Barbie with my bike, something like that. But after I burned two of her favorite shirts, she said I could never touch an iron again. And honestly, I never have."

I put my arms around him and rest my head against his chest. Just for a moment. Just long enough to feel a little of my strength come back. Then I'll stand on my own again without assistance. "Anyway. No. Not tired of you. Kind of afraid it's going to go the other way."

"What, that I'll become bored with you?"

"Or just get sick of all the angst and drama."

"Not even close," he says. "Just can't picture that day ever coming."

"Still. There must be things you need to do. Appointments to keep. Deadlines to make."

"I've been making those deadlines. Conducting interviews by cell phone, filing articles by e-mail. I have the world's most portable job."

"I mean, I'd understand. If you needed to leave for a while. Or longer."

He sets his hands on my shoulders and pushes me far enough away so he can see my face. "Do you *want* me to leave?"

I move my head from side to side in slow motion, like a windup doll that's almost entirely run down. "No. Not ever."

He draws me back into his embrace. "Well, then, that's settled," he says.

I'm sure it's not. Clearly you need more words to ratify major life decisions—and Brody needs more words in almost any situation you can imagine. But I think it's settled for *now*. I think he won't be leaving anytime soon. And once I have pulled myself together again, once I have figured out how to concentrate on something in my life other than Ann, I think I can convince him not to leave at all.

On Friday, William returns, but he keeps his setter shape. He's a better-natured dog than he is a human, more playful, easier to have around. He rarely leaves Ann's side, sleeping on her bed at night and sitting at her feet whenever we're in the house. She doesn't say anything, but I can feel her yearning toward him on a primitive level; I can feel her desire to join him as he races around the newly green yard, chasing after birds and squirrels. She resists because she does not want to abandon *me*. Because, although she has not promised it in so many words, it is clear she is going to try to maintain her canine state for a sustained period the next time she shifts between bodies. Because, if she is not going to speak to me for a very long time, she wants to make sure she has left nothing important unsaid.

"It's supposed to be a beautiful weekend," I say to her that night as she helps me dry and put away the dinner dishes. Brody is sprawled on the couch, watching a baseball game, and the noise from the stadium covers the sound of our conversation.

"Yeah, I heard that on the radio. Almost eighty degrees."

"Good time to be outside. Gardening. Playing softball. Camping." She hands me a glass, and I set it in the cabinet. "Good time to be living in the park."

"It's too soon," she says.

I shake my head. "It's not. You're ready to go. I can tell."

"I'm not ready to leave you."

I lay my dish towel over my shoulder and turn to face her, putting my hands on her cheeks. I'm smiling and crying at the same time. "You're ready to go with William. You're ready to get on with your life. It's okay. That's what you're supposed to do. You're supposed to grow up and leave home."

She summons fake indignation. "You're kicking me out? You want me to leave?"

"I want you to be happy."

"I'm happy."

I shake my head, then hug her. Now my tears have started in earnest, and I think she's crying, too. "You're not," I whisper. "You're supposed to be some glorious magical creature running free through the world, not a sad girl chained by love in a small dark house. Go. Go with him. Leave tonight. Come back and visit from time to time, but do not, do *not*, take human shape until I tell you that you can."

"I love you," she says, her voice muffled against my neck. "How many more times am I going to have a chance to say it? I love you. Best sister ever."

"It doesn't matter if you never say it again," I reply. "I'll remember this one time forever."

We cling for another minute, for five, then she tears herself away. She's sobbing so hard she won't look at me, and she falls to her knees in a small ball of misery. But I know what she's doing. She did it all the time when she was a little girl, when she was hurt or sad or angry, when complex emotions were too much for her to bear. She pulls herself in, she tucks her head down, and she lets go of everything that makes her human. Still crying, I drop down beside her, my hand on her blond hair, so I can feel it change textures as I watch her rapid transformation. The hair under my palm grows thicker, rougher, springier as it wavers from yellow to silver to white. Her hunched shoulders grow pointier and more powerful; the curved back straightens and rises as a furred tail unrolls like a coiled belt.

She scrambles up on all four feet, her nails scratching the ceramic tile, and utters a short bark. It's a happy sound; it always has been. I cannot keep from flinging my arms around that brushy white neck, hugging her one last time, and her paws scrabble against my jeans as she licks my nose and barks once more, right in my face. The sound makes me giggle, as it's meant to, and that's the last thing she sees before she scampers out the kitchen and through the open front door. Me laughing.

CHAPTER NINETEEN
JANET

The four years of undergraduate school sped by like a missile on a constantly accelerating trajectory. By the time I was a junior, I'd learned enough about getting loans and scholarships that I could afford the move off campus into a small apartment that I didn't have to share with anybody but Cooper. Just in time, too—winter that year was bone-chillingly cold. Cows were freezing in fields, families were dying in cars that had run out of gas on the interstate. Maybe a wolf could withstand those subzero temperatures, but this one didn't have to. He could curl up in our bedroom and sleep away his animal weeks, warm, safe, and well fed.

I had turned our second bedroom into a laboratory of sorts though I hadn't made much progress in devising a serum that would keep Cooper from shape-shifting. I was sure it would take me years to find the cure, if there was one. But the fact that I was thinking about it, working on it, gave Cooper a level of peace he had never experienced before. From the moment he had met me, he had known he was not alone, but now he grew familiar with hope as well as love. It changed him almost as much as his own internal imperatives did.

By the middle of my senior year, I'd been admitted into

grad school, and I'd believed that receiving that acceptance letter was the single event that would most shape my next few years. But two other events had just as much impact on my life, if not more.

The first one was meeting Cooper's mother.

It had occurred to me that I might have more success with my scientific experiments if I could study the blood of another shape-shifter—preferably one related to Cooper. Since he almost never talked about his family, I wasn't sure how he would feel about me trying to locate any of them, and I broached the subject hesitantly one night as we sat watching old movies in the apartment. He listened carefully as I explained my thesis, then shrugged.

"You can talk to them if you want, if you can find them," he said. "But I don't think either of us is ever going to get much satisfaction from our parents."

I nodded. My mother had actually gone to the trouble of tracking me down through the university system, and we'd exchanged a few letters. But I didn't feel any fugitive affection for her, any bittersweet fondness. And I never thought about my father at all.

Cooper's family was a different story; Cooper's family held a key I was desperately eager to discover. So I spent the next two months looking for his mother. During the days before the Internet had changed the whole process, the very verb of searching, the hunt was a frustrating and difficult exercise. She'd moved from the house he grew up in, and he couldn't remember her second husband's last name, though I found one of his old neighbors, who filled in some of the blanks. Nonetheless, when I reached too many dead ends, I hired a private investigator, and he was luckier than I was: He came up with an address a week later.

"And I think it's good," he told me. "I called the house, pretended to be a salesperson, asked for Cassandra Blair. She said, 'This is Cassandra *Alvarez*, what do you want?' so I think it's her."

I didn't tell Cooper I'd found her. I waited until a week

he was in wolf shape, then I rented a car and drove to a little town in southern Illinois to look for a woman who had thrown a child away.

I found the house with no trouble, a small, slightly battered clapboard bungalow with a cracked front porch, a neglected front yard, and a big backyard delineated by a chain-link fence. A boy and a dog chased each other across the back lawn, playing keep-away with an old stuffed animal that was no longer very stuffed. The boy must be Cooper's half brother, I thought; he looked about the right age. He was scrawny and dark-haired, but from this distance I couldn't see if he resembled the man I knew. The dog was a beagle, a much less alarming pet for a child than a wolf.

When I knocked on the door, it was answered by a woman whom I would have recognized anywhere as Cooper's mother. She had the same full lips and poet's cheekbones, the same dramatic coloring. She was smaller and more heavyset, but the curves and angles of her face were just as arresting as Cooper's.

As soon as she saw a stranger at the door, she said, "I'm not buying."

"I'm not selling," I replied. "Are you Cassandra Alvarez?"

The fact that I knew her name scared her just a bit. This was someone who'd had some experience with cops or debt collectors showing up at her door, I thought. "Yeah? So?"

"I want to talk to you about your son."

Involuntarily, she glanced over her shoulder, though I didn't think she could see through the entire house to make sure the boy was still playing in the back. "Carter? What about him?"

"Your other son," I said. "Cooper."

She took one swift, hard breath, her hand clutching the doorframe as if she needed some support. I saw her scanning my face, trying to figure out if I could be a social worker, someone with the child-protection agencies, and deciding I was too young. "What about him?"

"I want you to tell me about his father."

* * *

In the end, she allowed me inside, but only because I wouldn't go away, and she couldn't quite bring herself to slam the door in my face. She didn't offer me anything to drink, just gestured at a worn country-print love seat, and said, "I'll be right back." I listened to her footsteps hurry into the other room and pause before she strode back. My guess was that she'd gone to check on Carter before returning to confront me. While she was gone, I glanced around the room. A little untidy from daily living, a little too crammed with secondhand furniture that didn't all go together, but a perfectly respectable working-class house. Better than some of the ones I'd grown up in.

The wall that seemed to separate the living room from the kitchen had been decorated with about a dozen small and inexpensively framed family photographs. There were three of Cassandra with two women about her age—sisters, probably—and two of Cassandra with a good-looking dark-skinned man that I supposed was Davey Alvarez. By his last name, I had expected him to be Hispanic, but in the photos he appeared to be part African-American as well. The rest of the pictures all showed Carter at various stages. He had his father's rich skin and his mother's wide features, and in a few smiles and surprised expressions, I caught a strong resemblance to his half brother.

There were no pictures of Cooper on the wall.

Cassandra came back and dropped onto a nearby chair, gazing at me with definite animosity. "Who are you, and what do you know about Cooper?" she asked.

"I'm a student at U of I and I met your son"—I stressed the words—"about five years ago. He told me his story. Recently, we decided it might be useful for him to know a little about his heritage, so we thought we'd try to find his dad. Which meant first we had to find you."

Cassandra shook her head. She had laid her wrists along the armrests in what was clearly meant to be a relaxed pose, but I could see her fingers spasming against the wood. "I don't know where he is if that's what you're asking."

"Maybe not, but you could tell me what you do know about him. His name. What he looked like. Where he came from."

She snorted in disgust. "Well, I know what he *told* me, but I don't know if it's *true*," she answered. "His name was Loren DeAngelo. Most of his family lived in Michigan, but he and his mom had moved south—first Chicago, then St. Louis, then Memphis, and back up to St. Louis. Following Highway 55, he said. I always figured he'd probably ended up in New Orleans."

My heart grew tighter and smaller as she spoke. It would be hard enough to find a shape-shifter who lurked around the same general vicinity for ten or twenty years, but one who was always on the move would be almost impossible to track down.

"What did he look like?" I asked.

This time her response was almost a laugh. "He was fucking gorgeous, what do you think? I'm not the type to sleep with guys a day or two after I meet them, but he was— I mean, this long dark hair, these eyes so black you honestly couldn't see the iris. These muscles on his arms—" She shook her head. "I couldn't keep my hands off him."

"How long were you together?"

"Two months, maybe three."

"Did he ever shape-shift while he was with you?"

"Uh, *no*, because beautiful as he was, I think something like that would have sent me screaming from the room. He'd be gone for a while—like a week at a time. Told me he was traveling for work." She turned her head to one side as if to look away from the bitterness. "Fucking liar. Fucking lying prick."

"So then, what did he tell you about—"

She suddenly leaned forward on the edge of the chair, intense and furious. "He didn't tell me anything. When he found out I was pregnant, he acted like it was the worst thing ever, like no girl had ever gotten herself knocked up before.

He tried to convince me to get an abortion, and I said, 'Are you *kidding* me? You can be an asshole and walk away from this child, but I am *not* killing an unborn baby.' So then he said, well, he had this condition, he'd need to tell me about it, because the baby would probably be born with it, too."

She laughed again, still incredulous. "He said he turned into an animal a few days every month. And I said, 'Is that right? Then show me.' And he said, no, he couldn't do it on command, and anyway, he wouldn't bother because he could tell I didn't believe him. And I said, 'Damn right I don't believe you, you ignorant lying bastard!' And pretty soon he slammed out of the door, and I never saw him again."

"And then you had Cooper, and he started turning into a wolf—"

She nodded slowly. Her eyes had lost a little focus, as if she was looking backward at a memory. "Yeah. He wasn't even a year old the first time it happened. By that time I'd almost forgotten what a weird-ass thing Loren had claimed he could do, and Cooper, he was the sweetest little baby—" Her voice trailed off. For a moment longer, her eyes gazed at that misty memory, then her expression hardened, and she gave me another cold stare. "He was a baby who could turn into a *beast*. You have no idea how hard I had to work to make sure no one ever saw him do it. I had to live in these crappy little towns, and take crappy little jobs, and never leave him alone with babysitters on certain days, and keep him home from school so much that one principal thought I had some disease where I'd make my kid sick on purpose. It was horrible. It was impossible. But I did it."

"Well—until you stopped doing it," I said. I could be just as chilly as she was. "Until you kicked him out.

Her chin came up, and her expression became even more unfriendly. "I had a *baby*," she said. "I couldn't leave the baby alone in the house with a *wolf*. A wild animal."

"Had you ever seen Cooper offer harm to anyone before—to you, a neighbor kid, a dog, *anything*?"

"Well, he was eating *something* when he was foraging out in the woods, and I don't think it was cupcakes and peanut butter sandwiches," Cassandra shot back at me. "I think it was squirrels and rabbits and other little critters that couldn't get away fast enough, and you're damn right I thought he might hurt Carter. I couldn't take a chance, don't you see that? Carter was a *baby*. He couldn't protect himself."

I was on my feet, unable to sit still a moment longer. "And Cooper was thirteen!" I cried. "He could hardly protect himself *either*! And you *dumped* him on the side of the road like a bag of trash—"

She had jumped up, too, and now she grabbed my arm with one hand. The other one was balled up like she was ready to punch me. "Don't you dare judge me!" she exclaimed. "I did what I had to do to take care of the people who depended on me! I made some hard choices—I'm a good mother."

I wrenched away from her. "You're a terrible mother," I whispered. "You're a terrible person." I turned toward the door, finding it difficult to see because my eyes had suddenly filled with tears.

She clutched my arm again and I swung back to face her, absolutely ready to slap her if she made one more protestation of her virtue. But her face had changed; her grip had changed. She looked, suddenly, like a woman haunted by even more mistakes than the ones I knew about. "How is he?" she asked in a soft voice. "I've wondered so often—is he all right? Does he remember me? Does he hate me?"

I was tempted to be as cruel as she'd been, simply to walk out the door and not allow her the smallest balm of reassurance. What stopped me was knowing that Cooper would never have been so vindictive. "He's good. Tall—over six feet now. Skinny." I nodded at her. "He looks like you. He doesn't read too well, so he doesn't really like books, but he's an artist. He draws and sketches, and he's really talented."

An expression that was almost a smile crossed her face. She loosed her fingers and slowly dropped her hand. "He used to love to draw, when he was little. I was always buying him paper and crayons and paints." She looked down at the floor, but I'd seen the look her face showed—a devastating sadness that, for a moment, almost made me feel sorry for her. "Does he hate me?" she asked again.

"It would make more sense to me if he did, but he doesn't," I said. "I don't think Cooper knows how to hate."

She nodded and did not answer. For a moment, I expected her to ask if she could see him, if I would set up a meeting for her, and I already knew what I would say. *No. Never. I will never give you another chance to break his heart.* But she didn't ask. "So did you learn what you came here to find out?"

"Yeah," I said. "You can't help me find Cooper's dad. That's all I wanted to know."

She looked up again, her face once again a hostile mask. "He's probably dead," she said flatly. "That's something else Loren told me. Shape-shifters don't live that long. If they live to be fifty, it's like a miracle."

Now I was the one to be swamped by devastation and despair; I was the one to sustain a near-mortal blow. Dead? Cooper could be dead soon? He was in his early twenties now, but did that mean half his life was over—*more* than half his life, if he did not attain the normal span for a creature of his kind? Oh, no, no, no, no. I was not going to live years and years, decades and decades, centuries and eons, without Cooper beside me. There would be no enduring the emptiness of those days. I would kill myself if Cooper died; melodramatic though it sounded, as soon as I had the thought, I knew it was a true one.

"Guess you didn't know that," Cassandra said, reading the look on my face. "Sorry."

"You can't be sure," I said. It was hard to speak, my mouth was so dry and my lips so stiff.

"He wasn't lying about the rest of it, even though I thought he was. I don't know why he'd lie about that." She watched me curiously a moment. I must have been absolutely drained of color, I must have appeared to be on the verge of fainting, because she actually spoke with compassion. "Do you need to sit down? Do you need a glass of water?"

"No," I said, barely breathing the words. "I'll be fine."

"I guess you love him, huh?" she said. She sounded a little wistful, a little relieved, a little pleased. "I guess you'll be sorry to see him go."

I put a hand to my heart. I wasn't sure I'd be able to answer, but I managed a few words. "He's everything. He's my life."

"You can't ever make somebody else your life," she said. "Anybody."

I found the strength to draw myself up straight and head with an assumed steadiness toward the door. "That's only one way you and I are different," I said as I brushed past her. "And the reason my life is better than yours is that I still have Cooper. And you don't."

I never told Cooper I had found his mother, and he never asked. I wasn't sure what he'd deduced—that I had nothing to report, or that I couldn't bear to repeat what I'd discovered. But he had learned a long time ago that knowledge could hurt him, so he was willing for me to keep my silence.

I did spend some effort trying to track down Loren DeAngelo, though I didn't have much hope of finding him. My private investigator forwarded me information about other DeAngelos, including a family from Detroit, where a Loren DeAngelo dangled in solitary state off the genealogical chart, credited with no heirs. His birth date would have made him about the right age to be Cooper's dad—but, according to this record, he'd died five years ago. I sent out letters to a few of his relatives, but no one ever answered, and two of the envelopes came back unopened, stamped UNABLE TO FORWARD. I promised myself that one day I would drive to Michigan and see if I could convince some of Loren's relatives to talk to me if I simply showed up at their doors.

Maybe I'd make that journey when I was out of grad school. When I could afford a trip to Michigan. When I could bring myself to tell Cooper that I had found his mother, and she didn't deserve to have him as a son.

I was haunted by the one detail she had tossed off so casually. *If they live to be fifty, it's like a miracle.* As soon as I thought about it, it made perfect sense. The strain on their bodies undoubtedly ate up their physical resources at a phenomenal rate, and Cooper, at least, was always transforming into an animal that had a general life expectancy of less than twenty years. Average that with the typical human life span, and the outlook was not good. The outlook was horrifying.

I honestly did not believe I could live without him. I absolutely did not intend to.

But it took a supreme effort of will for me not to start hovering around him, fussing over him, checking him constantly for signs of aging or ill health, treating him like someone on the near edge of death. Nothing had changed, except my perspective. No wonder Cooper was sometimes afraid to seek out new knowledge. It reordered the universe.

I had expected the visit to his mother to change Cooper's life, but it hadn't. It had changed mine.

Crystal was the one who was directly responsible for the second event that would have such a major impact on our lives. Against all odds, she and I had stayed friends after graduation, exchanging birthday cards and, now and then, meeting for lunch or coffee. During the summer between our junior and senior years, she had taken a job at an art gallery just to earn some extra income, and she'd been hired on full-time once we graduated. So much for the graphic-art degree, though she did use some of her design skills to create ads, posters, and signage for the gallery.

"We're having a show next month at Gallerie Adele," she told me one afternoon as we had tea and scones at a struggling little teahouse that probably wouldn't be in business another month. "All local artists. I wondered if Cooper would like to exhibit."

I was so surprised I practically spit out my half-chewed scone. "*Really?* Are you sure he's good enough?"

"He's at least as good as two of the artists my boss has already lined up—better, I think, than the woman who does watercolors of cats." Crystal rolled her eyes.

"What would it entail? How many pieces would you want? Is there a size requirement? Do you want etchings or monoprints?" True to her word, a few years ago Crystal had introduced Cooper to the mad artist/master printer who owned an atelier in a run-down building in the business district. They had developed an instant affinity for each other, and Cooper spent virtually all his time at the atelier when I was in class. He still fooled around with pencil sketches when he was just sitting around the apartment, but most of his recent work consisted of small editions of exquisitely detailed hand-colored graphics. My apartment was full of them, and I'd given a dozen as gifts. Crystal herself owned five or six.

"We're taking five to seven pieces from each artist. They have to be professionally framed, but we'll split those costs with him. And he has to be willing to sell them at a fifty percent commission. Size—nothing bigger than twenty-four by thirty-six, but I don't think he's got anything that large, does he?"

I shook my head. "I don't think he's done any prints over ten by twelve. Crystal, this would be awesome, but are you sure? I don't want you to get in trouble with your boss."

She smiled. She was just as pretty as ever, even more sophisticated than she'd been at eighteen. Her blond hair was pulled back in a severe style, but it only served to make her facial structure more elegant, her blue eyes more striking. I often found it hard to believe that she was still with the ex-jock-turned-business-major she'd been dating since we met. Maybe he reminded her of her father. Maybe he had charms that were not visible to the rest of the world. Certainly the same could be said about my own boyfriend.

"I won't get in trouble. My boss wants me to start build-

ing up my own stable of artists. If any of Cooper's pieces
sell, I'll get the commission check. So, really, Cooper would
be doing me a favor if he agreed to exhibit. Everybody
wins."

"And how often does *that* happen?" I said.

Cooper was, predictably, excited and nervous about the
opportunity to display his work, but neither of us had any
idea how to pick the most commercial pieces from dozens
of images. We spent a couple of exceedingly pleasant days
laying out all our top choices on the floor in the living room
and studying them and debating out loud which ones we
liked best and why.

His favorite was a full-figure portrait of me standing in
a doorway, a long, narrow etching in a sepia-brown ink. He
had spent hours working on the cross-hatching of the shadows behind me, the intricate floral design on my dress, the
splintery texture of the wood around the doorjamb. My hand
rested against the frame, and I gazed in profile at something
on the other side of the door, out of the range of the picture.
As I was in so many of Cooper's portraits, I was barefoot.

"I love it," I agreed. "It's my very favorite picture of me
ever. But is anybody else going to be interested in it? I mean,
anybody who doesn't know me? Why would they want a
portrait of me on their wall?"

"It's a picture of a pretty girl lost in thought," Cooper
said. "Who doesn't like to look at something like that?"

"We'll ask Crystal," I said. "She'll know."

The images I liked best formed a diptych, two views of
a densely detailed autumn landscape. One was a straight-on
shot of a small boy, six or seven years old, staring at the
viewer in surprise and wonder. His hand was lifted as if he
was reaching for something—maybe a soap bubble or a butterfly. Cooper had not said so, but I was pretty sure this was
meant to be a portrait of himself at that age.

The matching image was of a wolf, also staring directly
out of the paper. It was modeled directly after photographs
of Cooper I had taken last summer, so the wolf had midnight-
black fur and amber eyes and a rather unsettling look of

human comprehension. Behind him, a slightly different version of the autumn landscape unfolded in the same subtle greens and reds and golds. It was clear that these two creatures had accidentally stumbled across each other on one lazy October day; each was fascinated, unable to look away. There was no aura of menace in the images, no sense that the wolf was about to spring for the child's throat. All either face exhibited was amazement and curiosity and delight.

I knew the diptych showed Cooper staring at himself across the divide of transmogrification, but surely no one else would see anything but a boy peering into the face of the wild as the unblinking wild stared back.

"These have to go in," I said. "They're the most striking things you've done."

In the end, we needed Crystal's input. She came to the apartment four days later and, in her three-inch heels, stepped delicately down the rows of artwork we had left on my living-room floor. The first three she picked were my favorites and Cooper's, and after about half an hour, she settled on four others.

"Will you come to the opening?" she asked after she had carefully packaged the paper between protective sheets of tissue and acid-free matboard. "Or will you be traveling then?"

"I'm not sure yet," he told her. "I have a trip planned right around then. I'm not positive I'll be able to make it." *If my body holds to its usual schedule, I'll be a wolf that weekend.*

She nodded and turned to me. "But you'll come, won't you, Janet? And then if anyone wants to know more about Cooper, they can talk to you."

"Sure," I said. "Can I wear a name tag? 'I'm the artist's girlfriend.'"

"Maybe we could call you the artist's agent," she said with a smile. "Sounds more businesslike."

Cooper was, in fact, in his alternate state when the night of the opening rolled around, so I headed downtown to the gallery to represent him. I arrived a little late because my last class had run long, and the gallery was already crowded. I estimated there were about seventy people milling around in a space that was not particularly large. I had to maneuver carefully between brightly dressed people standing before brightly painted canvases and holding bubbling drinks and plates of fanciful hors d'oeuvres. Amid the colorful landscapes and bold abstract serigraphs hanging on either side of his display, Cooper's etchings looked almost stark, but I thought that might be a good thing. They offered an oasis of calm and quiet in a setting that might otherwise seem brash and clamoring. Some people would find them restful; I know I did.

Not five minutes after I took up my post, a fiftysomething woman stepped over to speak to me. "Are you the artist? I love your work."

"No, he couldn't be here tonight. I'm his agent."

"His work is so understated but so beautiful. I've toured the whole exhibit, and I've come back here three times already."

I was delighted. "Cooper will be thrilled to hear that."

She took a sip of her wine and studied the hanging pieces as if she had not seen them before. "I like them all, but the ones that really pull my attention are these two." She pointed to the diptych, which had been minimally framed in a thin wooden moulding stamped with a leafy pattern that mimicked the foliage in the art. "How big is the edition, do you know?"

"He rarely prints more than fifteen or twenty of anything."

"Are there any left?"

I was momentarily confused. "Do you want one? These two are for sale."

She gave me a sideways glance. "Not anymore. I already asked, and apparently they sold almost the minute the doors opened."

Now I was stunned. "*Really?* That's wonderful! This is Cooper's first exhibit, you know, and he wasn't sure there'd be any interest."

"Oh, I'd guess he has a promising career ahead of him."

"I'll check back at the apart—the studio," I stammered. "I'll see what's still left in stock. If you leave your contact information with Crystal, I think we can get you another set."

"I'm counting on it."

Before the evening was over, three more of Cooper's pieces had sold, and two more customers inquired into the availability of the diptych. I was so jazzed with adrenaline and triumph that I was afraid to take a sip of wine because I thought it might make me spin into euphoria. My only regret for the evening was that Cooper couldn't be there to enjoy his success, but I was convinced this wouldn't be his only chance. Surely Gallerie Adele would want to take him on as a client. Surely he could eventually mount one-man shows—perhaps sell posters and reproductions—design a line of gift cards—who knew what else? If he started selling regularly, and once I got launched in my own practice, we could afford to buy a house out in the country and build a studio in the back. Cooper could safely roam the property when he was in wolf shape, work on his art when he was human. Not only did it seem to be the perfect setup for a shape-shifter, it offered me the first glimpse I'd ever had of a life that would both fulfill him and keep him safe.

Late in the evening, when exhaustion had begun to trample my elation, Crystal brought a man over to meet me. He was of medium height, stocky, probably in his mid-thirties, though his brown hair and neat goatee had almost completely yielded to gray already. I didn't know much about men's clothing, but his suit looked expensive, and on his left hand he wore a thick gold ring set with a line of diamonds. I didn't need Crystal's quick glance and nod to alert me that this was someone important to the gallery—and, probably, to Cooper.

"Finally! You've been surrounded by people all evening," she said lightly. "I wanted to introduce you to Evan Baylor. He owns an art gallery in Chicago and specializes in Illinois artists. He's so impressed by Cooper's work, he wants to see more."

"That's excellent news!" I said, shaking the dealer's hand.

His grip was firm and his intense green eyes were hard to look away from. He wasn't that much taller than I was, so I had the feeling that he was looking straight into my own eyes and all the way into my soul. A peculiar sensation. "Although I think we're committed to Gallerie Adele for the moment." I didn't know how this art business worked, but I did know I was going to be loyal to Crystal.

Evan Baylor looked amused. "We work with Gallerie Adele to make sure everyone receives an appropriate commission," he said. "Including, of course, the artist himself."

"Evan isn't just a dealer," Crystal said. "He's a collector."

He gestured at the wall—at the images of the boy and the wolf. "I bought these two for myself the minute I saw them this evening," he said. "Quite beautiful."

"So you're the one," I said with a smile. "I met a couple of people tonight who were very disappointed that they hadn't gotten here first."

"I've got to get back to the front," Crystal said. "But Evan, ask her anything you want about the artist. She's his manager, but she's also his girlfriend."

"I thought we were going to try to be more professional than that," I said with a mock frown.

She smiled. "Evan likes the personal angle," she told me. "He says that's how customers develop a sense of connection to artists, and that's what keeps them buying." Someone on the other side of the room waved to her, and she nodded briskly. "I'll talk to you later," she said, and hurried off.

I turned my attention back to the disconcerting but intriguing Evan Baylor. "So!" I said. "What would you like to know about Cooper?"

"Only one thing, really," he said. "Am I right in thinking this is a self-portrait?"

"The boy?" I said.

"The wolf. Am I right in believing he's a shape-shifter?"

CHAPTER TWENTY

MELANIE

The summer is a disaster.

At first I think it will be all right. The first month goes more or less as planned. Ann and William stay away for four full weeks, long enough for me to start worrying, even though I tell myself every single day that this is what I wanted for her, this is normal, she has been gone for far longer stretches, and everything has been just fine. Then one night they show up just as I'm getting home from work, loping down the two-lane road just ahead of the Cherokee. I honk in excitement and race them to the house. I'm barely out of the car before Ann's jumping up to put her forepaws on my chest and trying to lick my face. William sits on his haunches nearby, panting slightly, his mouth agape in a canine grin.

"Come in, come in!" I exclaim, waving them toward the door. "Are you hungry? I've got some good leftover roast. And I bought special dog food, the *expensive* kind, because nothing's too good for my sister. And her boyfriend."

I give them food and water, call Brody to tell him they've arrived, and he can come down tonight anyway as we'd planned. "Maybe tomorrow or the next day," he says. "You guys could use a little time together."

William wanders off before nightfall, but Ann sticks close beside me all evening. At dinner, I sit cross-legged on the couch, a TV tray on my lap, and tell her everything that's happened in the past couple of weeks. Brody's excited about a new series assignment he's picked up, interviewing ten regional philanthropists about what they expect to be the most important charitable causes worldwide over the next decade.

"He loves all that do-goody stuff," I tell her. "And I have to say, I'm starting to get more interested. They're doing all these cool experiments with energy, did you know that? Like, if cars go across a bridge, they make it shake, and you can—can capture that motion and turn it into electricity. Or something."

I tell her Debbie's big news. "She's pregnant. She and Charles had decided two was enough—he was going to get his vasectomy *the next week*. Debbie's still kind of stunned, but the boys are delighted. And I think Charles is, too, or he will be once he gets over the shock."

I fill her in on all the details of my life. "Another offer from Kurt! Three hundred thousand dollars this time. Can you imagine? I think Daddy paid ten thousand for the whole thing. Let's see, work is fine—a little boring, but there are days boring is not a bad thing. Brody is great—he's so upbeat all the time. You know me, I can be irritable and tense and just—just not a lot of fun. He makes me happy. I like to have him around." I spread my hands in an I-can't-explain-it manner. "We're good."

We watch TV together, me stretched out on the couch, Ann lying across my feet, her nose resting on her paws. I'm not sure how much she's actually taking in of the dialogue or story lines but, hell, I'm not really absorbing much either. I'm just feeling peaceful, relaxed, content. I'm just thinking, *This is good enough. I can do this for the next ten years.*

But it's not good enough for Ann. She's still sleeping when I leave for work, but she's awake and restless when I get home that night. She follows every step I take from the front door to my bedroom, where I kick off my pumps and change my dress pants for sweats, and back to the kitchen. I offer her the uneaten half of my lunchtime sandwich, but she doesn't want it. She presses against my calves and begins an anxious whining.

I bend down to cup her muzzle in my hand. "What's wrong, girl? Timmy fall down the well?" She barks, an indignant sound, but then she whines again, meeting my eyes straight on with her icy-blue ones.

Oh, I can read the thought in her head.

I drop to my knees, my hand still under her chin, my eyes now fierce as they gaze into hers. "Don't do it," I warn. "You promised. It hasn't been three months yet—it's only been a month! Don't do it. Don't you dare."

She reaches out one paw and scratches at my thigh, a pleading gesture. I shake my head, implacable. "No. It's not okay. No." I lean closer, speak directly into that alert white ear. "Hold tight, baby. Hold tight. Stay the way you are."

Clearly disappointed, a little sulky, she drops her head to my knee and rests it there. I bend down far enough to keep speaking in her ear. "And if the temptation is too much for you, then leave. Go find William and run wild again. Don't stay very long if you're just going to want to be human."

Now she utters a heavy sigh. I read it as acquiescence. I pat the top of her head and push myself to my feet. "Come on. Let's go for a walk. You'll feel more cheerful after you've chased a few rabbits."

We pass another quiet evening, but it doesn't feel as contented. I can tell she's feeling strain, and that raises my own level of stress. In the morning, she trots out the door beside me when I leave for work, and I bend down to ruffle the fur around her face.

"I can tell what you're thinking," I inform her. "You're leaving. You won't be here when I get back. Good. Have fun. Come back when you can."

And she has, indeed, vanished by the time I return from work. I'm a little sad, and Brody's disappointed when he arrives an hour later, but I know it's for the best. Apparently, we're going to have to restrict ourselves to short visits, or she will not be able to resist becoming human. And much as I miss her, I cannot have her take that risk. I would sacrifice anything to keep her alive.

It's another three weeks before she reappears. I manage my worry by reminding myself how dangerous it is when she's actually at the house; I tell myself that she's keeping away to avoid giving in to temptation. I even, finally, put up the countdown sign in the backyard, and change it every day before I leave for work. Seven weeks down, five to go, before the first three months are up. Before, even though it's still risky, she can take her alternate form. Before she's my sister again.

But I'm still at the office one Wednesday afternoon when Brody, who's been working from my house, calls my cell phone.

"Ann and William are here," he tells me.

"Great! Did you feed them? How are they?"

"Human."

"*What?* Both of them? Ann, too?"

"Ann, too."

I close my eyes and lay my head on my desk, the phone still pressed against my ear. Ann must take the cordless from Brody's hand, because the next voice I hear is hers. "Don't go all tragic on me," she says, her voice brimming with laughter. "We arrived this morning, and it just felt right to change."

"Ann, you *know* you aren't strong enough to—"

"Oh, pooh. I feel fine. Don't be so negative all the time."

"Don't be so—how can you *say* that to me? When you know—"

"Listen, Brody and I are going to make you a big ol' scrumptious dinner. Anything you're in the mood for, or should we just surprise you?"

"Oh, you've already surprised me."

She laughs again. "All right. We'll come up with something fabulous. See you later. Kisses!"

I'm so anxious about Ann that it's impossible for me to

enjoy the meal that night—though it actually *is* very good, roast pork, twice-baked potatoes, asparagus, strawberries, homemade chocolate cake. I don't want to poison the time we *do* have together by fighting with her, but I cannot simply let this transgression slide.

"You're killing yourself, and I want you to stop," I say to her bluntly as we sit on the patio while the men clear the dishes. "If you were smoking cigarettes or drinking too much alcohol, I'd tell you the same thing. I love you too much to let you keep indulging in self-destructive behavior. And I'm telling you. Don't. Be. Human."

It's past eight o'clock, and the approaching sunset is laying a golden sheen on every leaf in the nearby woods, every blade of grass in the half-wild yard. Ann herself looks like a study in gold and gray, partially obscured by shadows, partly lit by the sun. I'm sitting tense and upright in my newly purchased patio furniture, but she's sprawled back on her chair, relaxed and drowsy. She makes a lazy gesture.

"I can't do it," she says. "I can't be here and not want to slip into this part of my life. The minute I see the house, I want to change."

"That's not even true! You've spent *thousands* of hours in this house shaped like a dog, and you were perfectly happy! In fact, when you were growing up, there were plenty of times I wanted you to be human, and you refused, and we were right here. In this very house. So don't give me that crap."

She laughs, but it's a sleepy sound. She looks like she could drift off right here if I would be courteous enough to stop talking. "What can I say? It's different now. I don't think I can come home and see you and not change shapes."

"Then don't come home," I say, though the words have so many razor-sharp edges that they slash my lips to ribbons as they come out.

She shakes her head. "I can't do that either."

"Ann—"

She yawns. "Don't worry about it," she says. "Whatever will happen will happen."

And, right under my eyes, she falls asleep.

And she sleeps for the next two days.

Of course I'm frantic. I call Dr. Kassebaum, who is kind enough to refrain from recriminations and invites us to meet her in Springfield if we'd like to make the drive. "But I don't think I'll be able to do much for her," she adds. "My guess is she'll eventually regain her strength—and she'll be relatively well once she's in husky shape again. But I'm afraid that you'll see this pattern repeated every time she becomes human. And each time she'll be weaker and take longer to recover."

And eventually she won't recover at all. I can hear the words even though she doesn't say them.

Brody and William and I sit around the dining-room table Friday night and run through our options. They aren't many.

"I don't think I can keep her from coming here," William says frankly. "And I don't blame her. She loves you." He shrugs. Really, what else is there to say?

Brody's drinking a beer from the bottle and playing with the condensation rings it leaves behind on the table. "What about a compromise—a neutral zone?" he says. "She wants to see Melanie. Okay, makes sense. Maybe they meet somewhere else? Where Ann doesn't feel the same weight of memories pushing her back to herself?"

The suggestion makes me feel hopeful. "That's a good idea. But where?"

"Debbie's house? She knows about Ann, right?"

"Yeah, but Charles doesn't. Oh, and Debbie's having a rough time of it right now. Sick to her stomach *all* the time."

"Maria's," William suggests.

I glance at him. He looks as rangy and disreputable as ever, like the world's oldest juvenile delinquent; it's hard to read on his face what emotions might be troubling his heart. But he loves Ann, too, and this whole thing must be as difficult for him as it is for me. I wonder if it's harder or easier because he can understand, in a way I can't, the contradictory and irresistible desires that drive her.

"That sounds perfect," I say. "If it would be all right with Maria."

He shrugs again. "I'll ask her, but I know she'll be fine with it. She likes Ann. And she knows about—" He can't seem to figure out what words to use. "All this."

"So you arrive at Maria's, but you stay in dog shape, and Maria calls me, and we come visit," I say, working it out as I go along. "And Ann gets to see me, and that makes her happy, but she's in unfamiliar surroundings so she doesn't feel the same impulse to become human. And then I go away, and you guys go away, and I don't see her again until you go back to Maria's."

"It might work," William says.

"I think it sounds great," Brody says.

"As long as it's not an imposition on Maria," I add.

"She'll be pleased we thought of her."

Ann, when she finally emerges from slumber Saturday morning, is suitably contrite and just a little scared. She is pleased and relieved at the notion of meeting at Maria's and promises me she will not come back to our house before we've tried this experiment at a secondary location.

"But I still get to be human *some* of the time, right?" she says, as I French braid her hair before we all go out for pie. "Every three months? For a few days?"

"Maybe every six months," I say, trying to make the words casual. "Christmas and Fourth of July. Won't that be good enough?"

She frowns at me in the mirror. "*No*, it will *not*. Three months."

"But Annie, you see how weak you got this time—"

"But it wasn't three months. It wasn't even two months."

"Yes, but I'm afraid—"

"Three months. No more bargaining."

I heave an elaborate sigh. "Has anyone ever told you that you're a stubborn brat?"

She laughs. "Only you."

"Well, I think I'm the one who'd know."

The forty-eight-hour nap has refreshed her wonderfully.

Her spirits are high, her color is good, and our outing to Slices is delightful, despite the fact that William says very little, eats very little, and looks so much like a street person that our waitress is clearly afraid of him. But once we're back at the house, he joins the rest of us for a few hands of hearts—Ann cheating, as she always does, and getting caught, as she always does—and the evening ends with much merriment.

"Sometimes I actually think everything's going to be okay," I murmur into Brody's chest that night as we curl up together to fall asleep. "Times like today. When she's so happy, and she looks so good. I think it's going to be all right after all."

"Maybe it will be," he says.

I sigh, but I don't answer, just lay my mouth against his collarbone. He presses his lips to the top of my head. Sometimes a kiss is better than a conversation; sometimes it's the only way to communicate at all.

A nn and William leave Monday morning, already in their animal incarnations. Well, William had slipped into his habitual setter shape Saturday night as soon as he'd called Maria and gotten her instant agreement to our new plan. He'd spent the rest of the weekend prowling the backyard and sleeping on the front porch, seeming perfectly content.

On Sunday, before they leave, I take Ann to Debbie's, because who knows when she'll have another chance to visit with my oldest friend? Debbie's only two months along, not showing yet, but still complaining bitterly about her level of nausea.

"I feel fat and ugly, I'm throwing up all the time, I hate my life," she says, when Ann asks how she's doing. "Did I tell you the doctor thinks I might be having twins? *Twins!* We're having another ultrasound next week. I still can't believe it."

"Do you know the sex of the baby yet?" Ann asks. "Or—babies?"

"No, but if there's two, they better be girls, or I'm sending them back."

I wave a dismissive hand. "Eh. Girls are a lot of trouble to raise. Better to have more boys."

Ann sticks her tongue out but otherwise ignores me. "Have you picked out names?"

"We thought we'd ask the boys for their input because, you know, we want them to feel some connection to the babies from the beginning. But Simon suggested Zelda and Stevie went with Pikachu." She rolls her eyes. "So Charles and I are making our own lists."

"Zelda's kind of cool, though, even if he got the idea from a video game," I say. "Zelda Zimmer. I like it!"

"Oooh, and if you have two girls, call the second one Zoe," Ann exclaims. "Zoe and Zelda Zimmer! Zachary and—and Ziegfried if you have two boys. Best names ever."

Debbie puts a hand to her stomach. "See? This is why I feel like throwing up all the time."

When we leave, Debbie hugs Ann tightly and doesn't let go for a long time. It's clear it's a *good-bye forever* hug, though no one says so, and she embraces me for almost as long. "See you tomorrow," she says as she reluctantly lets me go. I nod, because I'm too close to tears to allow myself to speak.

And Ann and I go home, and Brody's made dinner, and we watch a DVD he picked up, and we all go to bed. And in the morning, Ann and William leave, and I have no idea when I'll see them again.

It's a shitty way to live. But right now, I can't think of an alternative.

CHAPTER TWENTY-ONE

It's a solid month before Maria calls my cell phone late one Thursday afternoon. "Hi, Melanie, it's Maria Romano. William's sister-in-law," she says, in case I could have possibly forgotten. "Just wanted to let you know Ann and William arrived a couple of hours ago."

"How are they?" I respond, since it seems polite to include William in the question, but of course Maria knows what I'm really asking.

"Good, as far as I can tell. They both had healthy appetites, and neither of them had any sores or injuries. Ann's been running through the yard, playing with Lizzie, so she seems to have plenty of energy. And so far she's kept her husky shape."

"So what's your schedule like? Are you up for company?"

"My mom and aunt are coming over for dinner tonight, but you're welcome to join us."

"Oh, no, I wouldn't want to get in the way. But tell you what. I can take tomorrow off and come out to spend the day if that works for you."

"That would be great. I'll leave you a key."

Brody's on a deadline, so I make the long drive by myself,

early enough to catch what rush-hour traffic exists along the rural roads connecting Highway 55 in my part of town to Highway 44 by Maria. The setter and the husky are sniffing at promising rabbit trails in the front yard when I pull up, but Ann comes bounding over the minute I get out of the car and frisks around my knees, barking and wagging her tail.

"You look great," I tell her, bending down to ruffle her fur and let her lick my face. "And you're being so well behaved! That's my good girl."

I pat her on the head, find the key under the doormat, and let myself in. I've brought a bag of groceries because I want to make dinner for Maria to thank her for playing hostess, and it takes me a few moments to refrigerate the perishables and organize everything else on the counter.

Then I whistle to the dogs, and we all climb into the Cherokee. It's mid-July and bidding fair to be a hot day, so I figure we should enjoy an outdoor activity while the temperature is still tolerable. We end up at Babler State Park, not far from Maria's, a place Ann and William seem to know well. I follow them along the heavily overgrown paths, swatting at mosquitoes, tripping on the occasional tree root, and calling them back a couple of times when I get completely turned around. They're never lost, though, and I enjoy the outing, the company, and the day.

Dante's waiting for us when we ma. it back to the house—at least, I assume it's Dante. At any rate, there's a pretty big German shepherd sitting on the front porch, panting a little in the heat, guarding the house with what seems like proprietary interest. He watches closely as I turn into the driveway, but doesn't seem hostile when I cautiously step out of the car. William ignores him, heading straight for a water bowl under the carport, but Ann races over and nips at his ears, trying to entice him to play. He responds with a short growl of irritation, and she dashes off again.

Yeah, pretty sure it's Dante.

I'm almost done making dinner when Maria arrives home, Lizzie in her arms. "Well, aren't you sweet!" she exclaims. "You didn't have to do this—but I'm delighted that you did."

The meal is chaotic, because Lizzie eats with us and she is *not* a quiet or easy dinner companion. But once she's full, she's content to hang out in her playpen in the living room, watching a Nickelodeon video and sticking her fingers through the mesh whenever one of the dogs presses a nose against the side. Maria and I drink coffee and eat cookies and enjoy a long, comfortable conversation that, a year ago, I could not have imagined having with anyone.

"Has Lizzie changed shapes yet?" I ask.

"Oh, God. William didn't tell you? Yes! Four or five times now."

"Kind of exciting and kind of horrifying all at once, I bet."

"That's exactly right. So far she's taken the same form each time—a little poodle puppy—you have *never* seen anything so cute."

"I can imagine. So—where did the transformations take place?"

"So far, thank God, only at home. But I've taken her out of day care because—well, I simply can't picture myself explaining this to the woman who runs it."

"Then what are you doing about your job? Can you work from home?"

"That's one solution. I've been staying here about one week a month. And Dante's human a week a month. But, of course, that leaves a lot of time when *somebody* has to watch her." She takes a deep breath. "So a few weeks ago, I decided I would have to tell my mom. She'd already asked if I would need help watching the baby, and we'd talked about moving her down here from Springfield, at least temporarily. And I knew that she might think I was crazy, but I knew she wouldn't be—*overset* by the news, if you know what I mean. It's pretty hard to rock my mom off balance."

I blow on my coffee. "So what did she say?"

Maria gives a little laugh, still disbelieving. "She said, 'Oh, I wondered if you knew.'"

"What?"

"That's exactly what *I* said! 'What?' And she said, 'Last time I was watching her, I left her in her crib and when I came back, she was a puppy. Just for a couple of hours, then she was herself again.' I mean, I almost couldn't speak. I said, 'Did it occur to you to *tell* me this?' And she said, 'Well, I thought it might be a one-time thing. I didn't want to worry you.'"

I start laughing, and I can't stop. In some ways, this is the funniest story I have ever heard. Maria's laughing, too, but not so hard that she can't finish the tale.

"So then I said, 'Well, no, I'm pretty sure she's going to be changing back and forth between animal and human states for the rest of her life. Her mother was a shape-shifter, and she seems to have inherited the gene.' And she said, 'I always thought those were myths, but I guess not.' I mean, she was as calm as if I'd told her Lizzie had inherited the ability to play the piano! So then I said, 'Aren't you *astonished*? Don't you think this is pretty *weird*?' And she said, 'I suppose. But it explains a lot.'"

I raise my eyebrows. "So did you tell her about Dante then?"

"Yeah, since she'd obviously already guessed. And she said, 'Well, that's a lot better than *some* of the things I thought he might be.'" Maria makes a helpless gesture. "I've always thought my mom probably had secrets of her own, and this makes me think they are a *hell* of a lot more interesting than mine."

"Wouldn't that be an amazing day?" I muse. "If everyone in the world came forward and confessed the one big thing they've always kept hidden. I bet your mind would explode before the first hundred people finished telling their stories."

She nods. "I wouldn't take that bet."

From the other room, I hear a dog bark once—a low, rough sound that I think comes from Dante—and Lizzie laughs in response. "So when Lizzie's a poodle and Dante's a German shepherd and Ann and William come visiting—"

"It's like a *dog park* here," Maria finishes up. "Sometimes I worry one of the neighbors might turn me in for running a puppy mill." She gives me a quick glance, and adds, "That's a joke. I love having them here. Lizzie loves having them. She's always had a close bond with William, and she *adores* Ann. I wish they'd stay all the time."

My smile is a little crooked. "I can't speak for William, but staying in one spot for extended periods doesn't seem to be in Ann's nature."

"It doesn't seem to be in any shape-shifter's nature," she agrees. "Christina—Lizzie's mother—didn't have much trouble staying put, but Dante and William were always on the move." She glances toward the living room. "Dante has settled down a lot since we adopted Lizzie, and he's here more often than he's not, but sometimes—I can tell, he just has to get out of the house, out of the neighborhood. And I just smile and let him go."

I pause to think about Brody for a moment. We're still in those early stages of love, where the other person seems damn near perfect. Well, maybe he's silently making up a list of all my defects, but so far I haven't found much about him that either makes me want to kill him or makes me fear he'll break my heart. I mean, he's stubborn, he's persistent, he'll find ways to keep asking me the same question until I answer it, and God knows he's not the neatest person on the planet. We've had a few discussions about laundry baskets and trash cans and how to put shoes in the closet. But those aren't really flaws. Those aren't deal-breakers.

I think my sister will shatter my heart before Brody will.

"I'm glad that having her around has been easy on you," I say. "Knowing that she has somewhere to come—someplace she can be safe—you have no idea what it means to me."

Her voice is soft. "Are you kidding? I understand exactly how important it is. I would have given the world to know Dante had a safe haven. I'm happy to be that haven for someone else."

I shift in my chair. "But I don't want to impose, either! I

plan to come back tomorrow, and Sunday, too, if Ann's still here—but not if you have other things going on. You have to be honest and *tell* me when it's inconvenient to have me around."

"I will, I promise, but this weekend isn't one of those times. I'll look forward to seeing you in the morning." She sighs. "Lizzie's always awake by eight, so anytime after that will be fine."

I help her clean up the dinner dishes before I spend a few more minutes sitting with Ann, patting her head and whispering nonsense in her ear. Then I'm back in the car and heading south to my place, humming along with the radio.

"You seem cheerful," Brody says, when I walk in the front door.

"It was a good day," I answer, dropping down next to him on the couch. "Everyone seemed well and happy. And I really like Maria. I feel like we have a genuine connection."

"She's like a combat buddy," he says. "Once you've gone through an intense experience alongside someone else, you bond for life at a level no one else can understand."

"Yeah, like you would know from combat."

"Hey, I survived Mr. Peterson's advanced biology class in high school. We dissected a cat and everything. The kids who were in my study group are still some of my best friends."

"You're irredeemably frivolous," I tell him.

"What, is that a character flaw?"

"And, anyway, I never hear you mention any of these people. How can they be such great friends?"

"Well, Joey moved to Cincinnati, but we still talk a couple times a year. He wants me to come visit sometime when the Cards play the Reds." He glances over at me. "Wanna go?"

"I'm not really into sports."

"You must have been the worst cheerleader ever."

I laugh. "Well, I liked jocks. I just didn't care that much about the games the jocks were playing. So what about the other people in the study group?"

"Carolyn and Joe are in Africa on a stint for Doctors Without Borders. They're married now. We trade e-mails, and I follow them on Facebook, but I haven't seen them in years."

I turn my head to get a better look at his face. There's the faintest wistful note in his voice. "That bothers you, doesn't it?" I ask.

"That they're so far away?"

"That they're doing—" I wave a hand. "Something important with their lives. And you're just hanging out here with me."

He kisses my forehead. "I consider hanging out with you to be *very* important."

"Yeah. Answer the question. You want to be one of those do-gooders, don't you? You want to save the world."

He shrugs. "I don't know that the world can be saved. But, yeah. I'd like to find something to do that's meaningful. That pays back in some fashion. I haven't figured out what yet."

"And when you do, you're going to get restless."

Now he fixes me with an unwavering stare. "Is that what you're worried about? You think I'm going to leave you?"

I laugh slightly. "God, I hadn't even gotten that far in my thought process. No, for once this isn't about me. I was thinking about *you*. I was trying to let you know that I'm not so wrapped up in my own life that I don't realize you have a life of your own, and dreams you might want to go chasing after." I lean forward and flatten my hand on his chest, then make my voice a little too soulful. "And I want you to know I'll be *there* for you."

"Well, great. When I figure it out, I'll drag you along wherever I decide to go."

I blink because, no matter how it sounded, that wasn't exactly what I'd meant. I'd intended to imply that I'd support him emotionally, root for him when he embarked on a new project, wait for him faithfully if he set off on some adventure in an exotic land. I haven't been much farther than the city limits of St. Louis in my entire life. I have no need to go traipsing off anywhere. But I want Brody to know I'm invested in his dreams. I'm invested in him.

Before I can boil that down to a coherent reply, he says, "Are you going back to Maria's tomorrow?"

"Yes. Are you busy, or can you come?"

"I'll come. I don't want Ann to forget me."

"Or William," I say, grinning.

"God, no. That would be a tragedy."

We're both too lazy to cook, so we scrounge for leftovers, which includes checking the expiration dates on a few canned goods and deciding it's probably safe to eat them. The hike in the park has worn me out, and I'm in bed by ten. I think it's closer to midnight when Brody climbs in beside me, but he wakes up when I do at seven the next morning.

I'm in an even better mood today—rested, happy, singing along with the radio as Brody drives the Cherokee down the winding two-lane highways through a landscape that is utterly and impenetrably green. It's as if summer has forgotten there are any other colors. It's hot, but I don't care; I roll down the window just to smell the scents of grass and hay and fertilizer and baking asphalt and the occasional flowering bush. Brody grumbles and turns all the air-conditioning vents to blow on him instead of me.

He taps the horn lightly as we pull into Maria's driveway, and I'm out of the car seconds later. Ann bursts out the front door, arms extended, hands joyfully waving, blond hair bouncing over her shoulders like the most disordered halo.

Yeah, she's human.

CHAPTER TWENTY-TWO

JANET

T he only thing that changed Cooper's life more profoundly than meeting me was meeting Evan Baylor,
who was not only a shape-shifter himself but connected to
a couple of dozen others in the region. Finally, Cooper had
access to a community of people who were just like him—
who understood his idiosyncrasies, his challenges, his
unconventional joys, and his reasons for despair—without
needing to have a single thing explained to them. I couldn't
imagine what that was like. I supposed it was, only in a
much more intense fashion, akin to what I'd experienced
when I finally encountered kindred spirits in college. I supposed it might be what a gay young man born in rural Mis-
sissippi would feel the first time he set foot in San Francisco.
Like he had found the place where he belonged.

Even so, it wasn't like all the shape-shifters of central
Illinois got together in a clubhouse every few weeks and sat
around sipping beer and trading stories. They were an odd,
diverse, diffuse, and not particularly chummy group.
Through Evan, Cooper met twenty or so men and women
who could take animal form, but I only laid eyes on about
half of them. Some of them were—like Evan, like Cooper
himself—perfectly comfortable in their human incarnations,

talkative and friendly and engaged, though they all exhibited a certain *oddness* that you couldn't overlook even if you never would have guessed what caused it. They were the ones who could hold down jobs, maintain relationships, speak with a sense of humor about the strange existence they had been fated to endure. Others were edgy and ill at ease when they took human shape, virtually unable to sit still long enough to eat a meal or carry on a conversation. These were the ones who lived on the very fringes of civilization and were in constant danger of slipping permanently into the wild.

For each of them, we learned, the process of transformation was unique. Some were human 350 days out of the year; they could control when and how often they turned into animals. Others, like Cooper, were at the mercy of some internal compulsion, though few of them switched so regularly between forms as he did. Some could choose what animals to become; others frequently found themselves to be creatures they had never imagined before. Some rarely traveled beyond the borders of Illinois. A handful had roamed the continent from end to end, meeting others like themselves in every state and climate. These wanderers were the ones who came back with information about places they'd discovered in their travels—safe houses and other havens where shape-shifters were welcome or at least out of danger. The homes of other shape-shifters, most often, the ones who had enough control over their lives to earn money and own property—or the homes of the people who loved them.

It was soon clear to me that I had a duty to this newfound circle of most unusual friends. I needed to launch my career, buy a house, and add yet one more refuge to the list of places where shape-shifters could pause in peace.

And I was willing—more than willing, even eager. And I realized these new friends could fill a need *I* had as well, supply a lack. The ones who learned to trust me might allow me to draw their blood and analyze their makeup. They might let me experiment with their chemistry and devise serums that reformatted their genetics. They might help me figure out the one thing I most wanted to know: how to keep Cooper human. How to keep him alive.

Five years after we met Evan, we were able to make substantial progress toward this goal. My years of obsessing about Cooper's biological changes had convinced me that I wanted to specialize in veterinary medicine, but eventually I concluded that I really wanted to conduct biomedical research. Who knows, maybe I was influenced by the fact that U of I had both a vet school and a specialty scholars program in veterinary medicine. My career interests dovetailed perfectly with my keen desire to stay in a geographic location that had become familiar to me and comfortable for Cooper. I had been accepted in both programs, but it might take me close to ten years to finish both of them. A long time to wait to start fulfilling the dream.

I was still in school when Evan came to us with a proposal. He and a few well-funded colleagues would buy a house for us as far out in the country as made sense for me to still make the daily commute to campus. In exchange, I would begin supplying free medical treatment to any shapeshifter who could make it to our land. It went without saying that we would also provide shelter to any of these half-human creatures who needed a place to stay even when they didn't need medical attention. So our property would include a house, an artist's studio, a research lab, and a few cabins, kennels, and lairs where our strange assortment of friends could bed down, no matter what shape they had currently taken.

I had initially protested what seemed like overwhelming generosity, but Evan, always blunt, had won me over. "We have no one like you among all our friends," he said. "Someone who can help us when we're hurt or sick. We have lost so many because we couldn't risk taking them to a hospital or a vet, even though they might have needed nothing more than a shot or a few stitches."

"I'm not a licensed practitioner yet," I warned him. "I need another year or two of school—"

"You're already better than any other option we've got," he said. "We want to get you set up as soon as we can. We're already looking at property."

It was impossible not to love the place Evan and his friends eventually bought for us, a rambling farmhouse on about fifty acres of land. It was close enough to civilization that it was wired for electricity, but its water amenities included a well and a septic tank. The house was old, crumbling in places, and in desperate need of updating, but otherwise it was perfect: It had two stories, ten rooms, a cellar, a garage, and a barn. A small stream wandered along its back border, and although its main agricultural products appeared to be prairie grass and the occasional stand of wild corn, it was obviously fertile enough to sustain a diverse garden of vegetables and fruits. Trees were not plentiful, but the tall grasses and occasional oak supplied enough cover for animals moving in after nightfall. We could not have asked for something better.

Evan oversaw the heavy work of renovation, dealing with contractors and deciding we needed new features such as a backup generator. Cooper and I picked the colors and materials for the new bathrooms and the remodeled kitchen, painted some of the rooms and hallways, and did all the work required for turning the barn into a studio.

"I think this is the happiest I've ever been," Cooper told me one day as we took a break from sweeping out the debris of reconstruction. It was a Sunday afternoon in autumn, sunny and warm. We sat outside with our backs against the barn, drinking soda and marveling at the colors all around us. The few trees were flaming with an insistent scarlet, but the long, thin prairie grasses had turned a subtle shade of vibrant brown I could only describe as "fawn." Cooper had spent one whole day trying to mix paints that would capture the exact shade, but he had eventually given up.

I pushed my sweaty hair out of my face. "You mean, thinking about moving out here when it's all finished?"

"Not even that. Not even looking ahead. Now. This minute. Working here with you. Working toward something.

Making—" He gestured with the hand that held his root beer. "Making a home for ourselves. Who would have thought we'd ever reach this point? That we could have so much? I didn't have anything when I met you. You gave up everything to be with me. And now look at us."

I leaned in to kiss him. "Now look at us," I agreed. "Already so rich, and poised to have so much more."

"So I just wanted to take a moment to impress it on my brain, in case someday I need to remember," he said. "This is what happiness feels like."

I was happy, too—God, how could I not be, blessed with such gifts?—but I was also anxious. Every year brought me nearer to my degree, every week brought us closer to our move-in date, every day brought me some sweet exchange with Cooper, whether he came to me as a wolf or a man. We had friends, Cooper's art career had begun to take off, and I had already started to provide medical treatment to the local shape-shifting community. I'd saved more than one life, too, which filled me with a deep and triumphant sense of satisfaction.

But I was no nearer to solving the puzzle of Cooper's blood. I now had samples from ten or twelve other shape-shifters—vials drawn when they were human and when they were animals—and I studied these under all kinds of conditions, adding heat, adding chemicals, changing temperatures, switching compounds. I had discovered, somewhat to my chagrin, that I could inject Cooper's wolf blood into a sample of his human blood and cause the whole test tube to change over to the lupine composition. If I kept the samples live for long enough—generally two weeks—the transformation would reverse itself. The two samples would separate, the wolf's blood collecting in the bottom of the test tube, the human blood at the top.

But the reverse did not hold true, no matter how big the relative sizes of the samples. The human blood could not convert the animal's. The wolf's genetic makeup was dominant.

We had tested the theory in a couple of experiments, one of them a little unnerving. I had learned from Evan that shape-shifters could rarely tolerate blood transfusions from other donors, but it had seemed safe to inject human Cooper with a serum made from his own wolf blood. He had almost immediately taken animal shape—a week before his normal schedule. To say I was horrified would be inadequate. I could not sleep, I could not work, I could scarcely breathe for the next three weeks, wondering if I had inadvertently and permanently turned Cooper into a wolf. When he came to me in the middle of the night, human again, I began sobbing violently in his arms.

"No more experiments!" I wept into his shoulder. "You're fine the way you are. *Perfect* the way you are."

But he wasn't, of course. That was the problem. I could see it already in the skin on his face, in the slow, gradual decline of his energy. He was aging. At twenty-six, Cooper should still be in the prime of life, almost as fit and healthy as a teenager. But he wasn't. Fine lines rayed out around his eyes; the flesh along his jaw had grown heavier. Every time he reappeared in human shape after two weeks in the wild, I traced a few more lines of silver in his dark hair. He slept more, had a softer stomach, complained now and then of a stiff knee. He was still healthy, still in good shape, but he no longer possessed a young man's body. He was middle-aged. He was at least halfway through his life.

But I was not halfway through mine.

I wasn't sure if he realized how frantically I worked to find a cure for his condition; I'm not sure if he knew *why*. In fact, once we moved to the house, once our lives took on the contours and rhythms we had worked so hard to attain, Cooper seemed to lapse into a state of absolute contentment. He even told me once, "I don't mind it anymore. Taking wolf shape. I even like it sometimes. Now that I know other shape-shifters, now that I see how other people live—it seems natural somehow."

"That's because it *is* natural, for you," I replied.

"I just wanted you to know. In case you can't ever find

the cure. It doesn't matter. You can stop looking if you want."

For just a moment, I felt my heart stop, my breath suspend. For just a moment, I couldn't think how to answer. *I have to find the cure, don't you understand? If I don't, you'll die, and I will never be ready for you to die.* Instead I said, as breezily as I could, "Oh well. I've put this much effort into it. Now I'm curious. Now I want to *beat* it, if you can actually *beat* a biological imperative."

"And maybe someone else will want the vaccine," he said. "If you can ever figure it out."

"That's right," I said. "So there's no stopping me now."

I was thirty-three and Cooper was thirty-two—though he looked more like fifty—when I first started experimenting with my own blood. I spent hours, days, weeks, trying to analyze how the composition of mine differed from the composition of Cooper's—and Evan's and that of the other shape-shifters I knew. I can't remember what story I told Crystal and her husband and one of their artist friends to convince them to donate vials of their blood so I could conduct additional tests in my never-ending quest to determine where the difference lay between the human and the beast.

But I do remember the series of experiments I carried out that summer when I decided to mix serums made of Cooper's blood with samples that were entirely human. I was not surprised, when I added the wolf's blood to mine, to see it undergo the transformation I had watched in the past. As always, the wolf's blood was dominant; soon the entire sample took on its composition. I stored the mixture carefully in a refrigerated container to see how long it would take for the two samples to separate out again once the transformation had run its course. I figured that my human molecules would put up a mightier fight than Cooper's since they weren't diluted and frequently seduced by the lupine influence, so I expected the reversal to come within a few days.

But it didn't. Two weeks passed, and still the transformation was not undone; a month went by. Six months. I knew the sample had degraded so much it might no longer be viable, but I was still astonished and rocked by the implications of that single vial of mutated matter.

I repeated the experiment, of course—with Cooper's blood, and samples from some of Evan's friends. I mixed them with mine and with the donations supplied by Crystal and the others. In every case, the results were the same. The animal components overwhelmed the human markers, and not just temporarily. The changes were permanent.

A person injected with a shape-shifter's genetic material would conceivably take on that shape-shifter's same animal form. And never again be human.

CHAPTER TWENTY-THREE

MELANIE

T his is the pattern we follow for the next four months.
Ann promises to be good, to keep her animal shape
no matter what the provocation. But every time she reappears in civilization, after weeks of roaming the countryside
in her canine state, she backslides. She becomes a laughing,
willful, mischievous young woman who very quickly turns
into a pale, exhausted, frighteningly weak human girl. She
sleeps away two or three days. Once she wakes up, she is
properly chastened. She apologizes, makes more promises,
and disappears at William's side.

And then the cycle starts again.

I try to thwart her. Though it nearly kills me, I decide
not to visit Ann the fourth time she arrives at Maria's. I listen greedily to all the details Maria can give me over the
phone, but I don't drive out to her house. If my presence is
the lure Ann cannot resist, I will remove the temptation. I
won't let her see me. And when Maria calls me a few days
later to say, "Well, they're gone, and neither of them ever
reverted," I think my strategy has worked.

But that night when I come home from work, I find Ann
slumped on the front porch, leaning against the siding,
already deep in that drugged sleep from which there will

be no waking her for days. I suspect she's naked under the dirty tablecloth that William must have dragged from the patio furniture out back. He's sitting beside her in human shape, wearing a pair of ragged jeans I keep for him in a bin by the front door, and he jumps to his feet as I come running up from the edge of the lawn.

"I couldn't find the key," he says. "And I couldn't move her."

He carries her inside and we go through the usual ministrations, cleaning her up, trying to get her to rouse enough to swallow some juice or water, wondering aloud what we should do. Once we've managed to get a nightgown on her and arrange her comfortably on the bed, William stands there for a few moments, just staring down at her still form. For almost the first time since I've known him, I see strong emotions on his face, but I'm not entirely sure which emotions they are. Fear? Anger? Loss? Pain? Love? All of them?

"She's careless," I say in a soft voice. "She always was."

"It's getting to be too hard," he says. Shaking his head, he steps out of the room, and I hear the front door open and close. He moves so quietly that I probably wouldn't be able to hear his footsteps anyway, but I imagine that he has melted into setter shape and gone soundlessly trotting down the road, not once looking back.

With all my heart, I hope that is not the last we see of William. But I find that I won't be able to blame him if it is.

A nn will not wake up.

At the end of the third day, when I have barely been able to get her to sit up and swallow water, I have become frantic. I break down and call Dr. Kassebaum again, even though I know there's nothing she can do. There's no answer at her office or on her cell phone, and my panic ratchets up a notch. Oh God, Ann needs medical attention, and no one else in the world can help me.

"We can take her to the ER," Brody says, for possibly the hundredth time.

"I don't know—maybe—I can't think," I reply, also for the hundredth time.

But Dr. Kassebaum calls back around dinnertime. "I'm sorry, I'm at a conference, and I've had my cell turned off," she says. "Has there been any change since you left your message?"

"No—not that I can tell. She doesn't seem to be actually comatose—I can make her take a few sips of juice or water, and she's spoken a few words—but then she just falls back into this deep, deep, deep sleep. I'm so worried. What if she—"

"Listen, I'm actually in St. Louis," she interrupts. "I can pick up some supplies and come to your house in the morning. If nothing else, I can give her an IV and some fluids. But Melanie—"

"I know. I know. It's just that she won't—she says she'll be good, then she—I don't know what else to do."

"We all make our own choices, and sometimes no one but us understands why we make them," she says.

"She's making the wrong choices," I whisper.

"Maybe not for her. Give me directions to your house, and I'll be there in the morning."

If anything, Ann is worse the next day—her skin hot to the touch, the few words she utters impossible to understand. If I had not known Dr. Kassebaum was on her way, I don't know what I would have done. Taken her to the emergency room, most likely. Thrown away a twenty-year-old secret in the desperate hope of saving her life.

But Dr. Kassebaum arrives before nine, dark and serious and professional, and despite the fact I know she cannot truly heal my sister, I am instantly calmer when she walks through the door. She's carrying a leather satchel and a plastic bag that looks like it came from a grocery store, except it has a caduceus printed on the side. Looks like she stopped at a handy medical-supply store on her way to Dagmar.

"How is she?" Dr. Kassebaum asks, but I just shake my head and show her to Ann's room.

She wants privacy, so I head back to the kitchen to make tea. Brody's gone to get groceries, and William still hasn't returned. I stand in the kitchen with the hot mug in my hand, straining to hear any sounds from down the hall. I feel as alone and abandoned as I have ever felt in my life.

Brody's shouldering through the front door, bags in hand, as Dr. Kassebaum steps out of Ann's room and heads to the bathroom to wash her hands. A few moments later, we all group around the dining table, drinking tea and eating Krispy Kreme donuts Brody picked up along with a list of healthier menu items. I eat two of them, almost without pausing to chew. My body is in such a high-stress mode that it's gone through all my caloric reserves. I feel like I'm starving. At the same time, I feel like I could start throwing up. I suppose the two reactions have the same root cause.

Dr. Kassebaum appears to be ravenous, too, because she downs a whole donut before uttering a word, then she speaks with her usual precise gravity. "I've got her stabilized. Part of the problem today was dehydration, and the IV is helping with that. But she's very weak, and I imagine it will be a few days before she's up and moving around."

I nod. "And once she is?"

Dr. Kassebaum looks at me directly. Her eyes are such a dark brown that they look too heavy for her fine-boned face. "She'll need to make some pretty big decisions. I would expect her to recover enough strength to change to her animal form again—and, in fact, I would encourage her to do so, because she seems much stronger in that state. But I'd also tell her that that should be the last transformation she ever makes."

It takes me a second to absorb that. "The last—you mean, she should take her husky shape and then never—never become human again? Ever?"

Dr. Kassebaum nods. "Every part of her human body is seriously compromised. Her heart is struggling, her lungs are struggling—they simply can't attain the size they need to sustain her in this shape. I would expect that, if she makes the transition one more time from animal shape to human, it will be the last time she changes at all. I doubt she would survive the transformation for more than a day."

I stare at her, and I cannot speak.

Brody reaches under the table to take my hand. "And if she takes her husky shape and *doesn't* shift? How long will she have in that body?"

Dr. Kassebaum considers. "It's impossible to predict these things with any accuracy. Six months at the minimum, I would think, and two years at the maximum. Most likely, somewhere closer to a year."

"That's not enough time," I say.

Dr. Kassebaum nods. "I know. There's never enough time."

Brody says, "We haven't been successful, so far, in convincing her *not* to change. Do you have any advice on what we can say this time to make her understand the seriousness of her situation?"

Dr. Kassebaum's face warms to a sad smile. "My guess is that she understands very well."

"She can't," I say. "Or she wouldn't be so—stupid. So careless."

Dr. Kassebaum surveys me with those dark eyes. "And if you were her, what would you do?" she asks softly. "Leave your sister behind?"

"Yes, if it would kill me to see her!"

She shakes her head. "She'd only stay away if it was killing *you*," she says.

"It is!"

But she shakes her head again. I wonder if she's right. If I were the changeling child, the one living the strange, shadowy double life, would I be able to stay away from Ann even if I risked death every time I arrived at her doorstep? I don't know. Maybe not. But I cannot bear to be the siren that calls that bright soul straight down to her destruction.

"Is she awake now?" Brody asks. "Can you talk to her? Maybe she'll listen to you."

"She's sleeping, but it's a lighter sleep than when I arrived. I think she'll wake up in a few hours and be more coherent. I can come back tomorrow if you like. But I'm not sure anyone but Ann is going to have any real input into her decision."

I nod. "You're right. You've done more than enough already. This is between her and me. I can't thank you enough for rushing down here and—and—just for being there when I needed someone to talk to."

"Feel free to call anytime," she says. "I probably won't be able to help much, but I *will* understand."

Brody carries all of Dr. Kassebaum's paraphernalia out to her car, so when I hear the door open again, I think he's stepped back inside. But when I glance up, I see it's William who's returned. He's in his human form, possibly even more disreputable-looking than usual. Or maybe it's the expression of misery on his face that makes him appear more tattered, more unkempt than ever.

He's standing by the door as if he's ready to bolt back outside if I say the wrong thing, but he doesn't ask me a question. He just looks at me, and for a long moment, I just look back.

"I called Dr. Kassebaum," I say, and he nods, so I guess he saw her either as she arrived or as she departed. "She says this is the last time Ann can be human. Next time she shifts from dog to girl will kill her."

He flinches—a very small motion that I think conceals a very hard blow. His voice is rough but even. "Maybe she should stay human."

"Dr. Kassebaum says she's healthier in her other form. She'll live longer—but still not very long."

He thinks that over and nods, once, slowly. "Is she still in her room?"

"Sleeping for now. But Dr. Kassebaum thinks she'll be more herself when she wakes up." I can't tell if he's waiting for my permission or not, but in case he is, I add, "You can go on in and wait with her."

He nods again and strides down the hall into her room.

This time when the front door opens, it *is* Brody. I don't say anything, I just walk over and step into him, like I would step into a closet where I want to hide. I close my eyes, I burrow into his shirt, I try to shut out the world and all its calamitous knowledge. His arms come around me, and he brings me in tight, but he doesn't speak. He is the best haven I have, but there is no safe shore. The lightless seas are storm-tossed and treacherous, and even if I open my eyes, there will be no land in sight.

It takes Ann a full week to recover her physical strength though she is laughing and joking by the end of the next day. I make all her favorite meals, one right after the other, not only to tempt her lackluster appetite but to prove to her, in some unspoken fashion, that I love her enough to invest the effort.

"Wow, chicken tetrazzini *and* double fudge cake? You're the best sister ever!"

"I've been worried about you. This is my way of showing gratitude to the universe."

The three of us decided, in one thirty-second conversation, to wait until Ann was almost back to normal before we shared Dr. Kassebaum's conclusions with her, but she knows something's up. Brody and I, at least, have been both overly solicitous and insincerely cheerful, and I haven't delivered the furious scolding she knows she deserves. Maybe William has been more honest about his level of fear and anger, but if so, he's expressed himself in private.

At the end of that seventh day, as I'm clearing away the cake dishes, she leans her elbows on the table, and says, "Okay, what gives? You've all been acting like I'm going to break apart if I so much as bump against the wall. So what did Dr. Kassebaum tell you about me?"

William and Brody are still at the table. I briefly lock eyes with each of them, then pull out my chair and sit down again.

"She said your body can't tolerate being human. That you need to change back to your husky shape and stay that way. And that the next time you shift *back* to this shape, you'll die."

She opens her eyes wide. "*Wow.* Didn't anyone ever tell you how to deliver bad news? 'I hate to tell you that your parrot's been sick—'"

I make an impatient gesture. "You don't seem to hear or understand when we sugarcoat things. I thought if I was blunt, I'd get your attention."

She tosses back her hair. "It's not much different from what she told us in the spring. Be careful. Hold my shape. Be good, or you'll be sorry."

"And you haven't been good, and now you better be sorry. If you were a cat, you'd have used up eight of your lives. I don't know how many lives dogs have, but—"

William speaks up unexpectedly. "One. One life. And you're at the end of yours."

Ann is unimpressed. "Or so Dr. Kassebaum says. She doesn't really know."

I lean across the table, my expression intense. "Well, judging by how long it took you to recover from this transformation, I'd say she's making a pretty good guess. Listen to her. Listen to all of us. Stay human a few more days, say good-bye, then change shape and *stay changed*. Don't risk yourself—*don't end your life*—by coming back to the form that your body can't sustain."

She stares at me in disbelief. "How can you say that to me? How can you tell me to never see you again?"

"I'm not saying that! I'm saying I should never see you again in this body. Come back as often as you like—in your husky form."

She makes a helpless motion with her hands. "I can't promise that. When I see you—when I see the *house*, the minute I lay eyes on it—I want to change back. I want to be me again. I'd have to stay away from this place forever."

"Then do it."

"I *can't!*"

I fall back in my chair and throw my hands in the air. "Then die."

"Well, that's a terrible thing to say."

"I guess the truth is terrible."

"You have two choices," Brody says, his voice reasonable. "You live for another few years in your canine shape, and you visit Melanie from time to time, and that makes both of you happy. Or you take your human shape again a month from now, and you're dead before the week is out. And, frankly, I think that's a shitty thing to do to your sister."

She glares at him. "This isn't even your argument."

He laughs at her. "Since I'm the one who's going to be here when you're gone, I think it is."

William speaks up again. "Is it *my* argument?" he asks, and I'm pretty sure that the repressed passion I hear in his voice is anger and pain and love and anguish. "Do you care what *I* think? Because *I* don't want you to die. Is it that easy for you to just leave *me*? If I could spend five years with you in one shape or three days with you in another shape, which one do you think I'd choose? Which one are *you* going to choose?"

For the first time tonight, I think someone's gotten through to Ann. Her eyes grow shadowed; she places a thin hand on William's arm. "I love you," she says, her voice serious and quiet.

"Then stay with me," he says, "and live."

She glances back at me. "But—"

"Stay with him," I tell her, "and live."

Now she's starting to cry. "But I'll miss you."

I shake my head. "You won't. I'll be right here."

"It won't be the same."

I attempt a smile. "We've had this argument before, haven't we?"

"I don't think I can do it."

"Yes, you can," I say. "Do it for William. Do it for me. We love you, and this is what we both want."

Now she looks at Brody. "Will you take care of Melanie?"

He puts his arm around my shoulders. "You bet I will."

"You *promise*? You won't break up with her?"

I feel him shrug. "Hey, I'll marry her this week. As soon

as we can get a license. You can come to the ceremony, then head off with a clear conscience."

That chases away Ann's tears and makes her face light up. "Yes! Let's do it! A wedding before I go."

I've slewed around in my chair, and I'm staring at Brody. "What the—is that a *proposal*? You think I'm going to marry you just to make my sister happy?"

He leans in to kiss me. "Well, it would make *me* happy, too."

"I'll do it," Ann says. She's practically bouncing in her chair. "I'll change shapes, and I'll stay that way if you guys get married before I go."

Brody is grinning broadly. "The blackmailed bride," he says. "Sounds like a good romance title, doesn't it?"

"I can't plan a wedding in—what—a week," I say, practically stammering. "And what if I don't want to get married?"

"Oh, of course you do," Ann says. "You told me you loved him."

"You told *me* you loved me, too," Brody says. He assumes a look of dejection. "Didn't you mean it? I thought—"

"Oh, hush." I take a deep breath. "Ann. If that's what it will take to convince you to go off with William and stay in your husky shape—"

"Yes," she says. "I insist. Anything less, and I swear I'll be back on your doorstep in a month."

"And Brody. If this is truly what you want—"

He kisses me again. "Oh, I want it. Give me a couple of hours, and I'll prove how much."

"Then—I say yes. And let's plan a wedding."

CHAPTER TWENTY-FOUR

It is, as you might imagine, the most scrambling, helter-skelter sort of wedding anyone could hope to put together. Debbie screams when I tell her the news, then hugs me as hard as she can with her big belly getting in the way. All three of Brody's sisters threaten him with death if he doesn't schedule the wedding for a day they can suspend the constant activity of their own lives to travel into St. Louis for the event. His parents, from what I can tell, begin packing the instant he hangs up from the phone call because they arrive in Dagmar within twenty-four hours and instantly begin helping Brody take care of the chores that have fallen to him. He gets the license, buys plain gold rings, schedules the ceremony at the local courthouse, makes luncheon reservations for the reception, and plans for what he calls the "kiss-and-a-promise" honeymoon, which we figure will be a weekend now and a real trip sometime in the future.

I buy a dress, arrange for flowers, ask Charles to take pictures, and wonder what the hell I've gotten myself into.

Ann alternates between offering her opinion on our food, clothing, and venue choices, and sleeping. I begin to understand what Dr. Kassebaum meant by saying Ann's body is struggling in this shape; it makes sense to me that she's so tired because her organs and tissues can't keep up with the demands of this imperfect body. But I know there is no way I will be able to persuade her to take her husky form before the actual wedding. And I want my human sister there beside me, wearing a blue-velvet dress, carrying white roses, and laughing. I want her in my wedding photos, dammit. I want proof to lay next to the memories I expect to accumulate, hard evidence that she is with me on this rare and special day.

And she is.

We have a noon ceremony in the historic courthouse and a rollicking luncheon at Corinna's, which closes for the afternoon to cater our private party. After the meal, Bailey's kids and Debbie's boys take off their shoes and skate up and down the wooden dance floor in their socks. Charles plays romantic musical selections on a boom box and some of the adults dance. Brody's dad makes the only toast—"Promise me you won't let this be the happiest day of your lives"—and everyone has champagne, even Stevie and Simon. Even Debbie, though she only drinks a sip. Bailey and Brandy and Bethany grab me by the arms and hustle me into the women's bathroom to tell me stories about Brody when he was growing up, giggling and interrupting each other and sometimes tearing up. The only single people at the wedding are William and Ann, so I hand her my bouquet instead of tossing it, and William wears my garter around his wrist like the frilliest sort of watchband.

At four o'clock, as it comes time for us to gather up our belongings and let Corinna prepare to open for the evening rush, we all start making our good-byes. Everyone hugs me, hugs Brody, hugs each other, hugs me again.

"Love you bunches and bunches and *bunches*," Ann says into my neck as she holds me so tightly I doubt either one of us can breathe. "I'll never forget this day."

I can't say good-bye. I can't do it. "Me either," is all I manage by way of reply.

"You'll be happy, right? Forever?"

"Right," I say. "And you? Happy?"

"Yeah," she says. "We both got pretty cool guys, I think."

"Let him take care of you," I tell her. It's the closest I can come to saying what neither of us wants to put into words. "From now on."

"Okay," she says. When she finally lets go, she's smiling. "See you around."

Bethany catches my arm and gives me a final embrace. "We're getting ready to drive on home," she says. "*Please* come down to Cape Girardeau soon and spend some time! I can't wait to get to know you better."

I have similar conversations with Brody's parents and his other sisters, Bailey lingering a moment to look around. "Where's your sister? I wanted to say good-bye. I sat with her at lunch, and she was just delightful."

I don't suppose anyone would wonder at it if my voice catches; it's been an emotional day. "She had to leave," I say. "Maybe some other time."

But part of me can't help hoping that she hasn't left yet, that she's lingering at the edge of the parking lot, having remembered one more thing she wanted to say. I step outside with the last of the stragglers, wave at people packing up their cars and backing out of their spaces, but all the time, I'm glancing around, praying for that final glimpse.

"Come on," Brody says, taking my arm and urging me over to where the Cherokee is parked in the very last spot before asphalt gives way to gravel, then dirt, then highway. He's got my keys, so I head around to the passenger side, and there, on the pavement, I spot her final farewell.

The blue-velvet dress lying on the ground, a bouquet of white roses nesting carefully in the folds.

B rody has booked a weekend at the Chase Park Plaza, a beautifully restored old hotel in the heart of the Central West End, the only certifiably funky district of St. Louis. Bars, bistros, bookstores, and boutiques cluster along the crowded two-lane Euclid Avenue, while gorgeous and shockingly expensive houses ray off along cross streets. The clientele is a lively mix of students, out-of-towners, the urban elite, medical personnel from the nearby hospitals, and a good portion of the city's gay population. I've never been here for the annual Halloween party or Gay Pride parade, but both events sound like fabulous extravaganzas.

The hotel itself has every imaginable luxury, including a two-screen movie theater just off the lobby. Our room is more truly a one-bedroom apartment, with a spectacular view of the broad expanse of Forest Park.

"Freelance writing must pay a lot better than I ever thought it did," I remark as I stroll around admiring the room.

"Nah, I gave them your credit card when I made the reservations."

On a side table is a huge spray of roses, two dozen white ones with a single red one in the center. I bend over to inhale their subtle, foggy scent.

"Did you tell them we were on our honeymoon?" I ask. "Are they from the hotel?"

He's come up behind me and as soon as I straighten up, he pulls me into his arms. "They're from me, silly. Just a reminder that I love you."

I kiss him. "Did you put these on my credit card, too?"

He laughs. "Damn. I forgot. Maybe it's not too late to get the charges transferred."

"And to think I never realized someone might marry me for my money."

"Oh," he says, kissing me, "the money was only part of it."

We spend the next two days inside the hotel room at least as much as we're outside it, though we both enjoy walking along Euclid, people-watching, and pausing for meals, coffee, ice cream, or shopping. I'm simultaneously happy, at a level so deep that I can only describe it as my soul, and profoundly, quietly sad. For so many reasons, I do not want the brief honeymoon to end.

I am loving the chance to spend every minute with Brody. He has what I can only think must be a journalist's interest in every possible topic, from the timing of traffic lights to the pricing structure at an antique store, and he frequently offers up odd bits of knowledge he's acquired in his eclectic career. These things make him an endlessly fascinating conversationalist, but it's his affection and his lightheartedness that make him so easy to be around, so necessary to my well-being. He buoys me and lights me up. During those two days, I find myself clinging to him, always finding some excuse to pat his arm or take his hand. Well, we're newlyweds, and we're in love; of course we're always touching. But it's more than that. He anchors me to an existence of normalcy and hope, where the days unfold as they ought to, and life's small disasters are easy to take in stride.

That's one reason I don't want the weekend to come to a close. The other one is that I can hardly face what I must do on Monday.

Sunday evening, we stand at our window and watch the sun go down over Forest Park. We can see the Planetarium, and of course the great maze of the zoo, and we think we can spot the art museum and the history museum and the Muny Opera, but maybe those are just breaks in the tree line. It's November now, and the landscape is a dense brown marked with spots of intransigent green and gold. All up and down the major artery of Kingshighway Boulevard, buildings and cars are turning on lamps and headlights in defiance of the oncoming night. Brody is standing behind me, his arms around my waist and his chin against my hair. I have crossed my arms over his, and I am standing as close to him as I possibly can, just to feel his heat and weight against my body.

I feel as safe and protected as I ever will, and so I say at last, in a low voice, "I lied to my sister."

His voice is low and lazy, free of shock or accusation. "Really? You don't love me?"

"Not about that."

"Then what?"

"I told her that I'd always be around. Or words to that effect."

I feel him lift his head. "And you won't? Where are you going?"

I turn to face him, still staying within his embrace. We haven't turned on any lights in the room, and the daylight outside is fading fast. We're half in shadow, but we can still see each other's faces with utter clarity. His expression is confused but open; I wonder what he can read in mine.

"I don't trust her," I say. "I don't believe she can come back to the house, and see me, and keep her animal shape. I think she'll shift, and I think she'll die."

Brody keeps one arm around my waist but lifts a hand to brush hair from my face. "I think so, too," he says, "but I wasn't going to say so."

"I have to stop her."

"Do you really think you can? How?"

It's surprisingly difficult to say the words out loud. But ever since Dr. Kassebaum pronounced her dreadful sentence, I've known what I have to do. I lean my cheek against his chest, so when I speak, my voice is muffled. "I have to invoke my superpower."

Kurt Markham's office is pretty much exactly what I would have expected. The wood paneling, enormous black desk, and trophy case full of athletic awards and framed certificates all scream *successful ex-jock with lots of money and no class*. Or maybe I would have interpreted any of his décor schemes the same way.

"Well, darlin', this is a pleasant surprise," he says when his secretary ushers me inside. At a nod from him, she shuts the door behind her. A huge picture window behind his desk admits the gray light of a stormy November afternoon and shows me his face mostly in silhouette. I prefer that, actually, to seeing his smug smile. It doesn't bother me that the harsh light falls squarely on my face and exposes every line and fleeting expression. I am beyond caring what Kurt Markham thinks.

"I'm glad to hear it," I reply.

"I understand I should congratulate you. You got married to that reporter fellow. Kind of sudden, wasn't it?"

"Sudden but wonderful," I say.

He laughs. "Well, good for you. You and your husband planning to live in that little bitty house you got out here, or is he a city man? You thinking about selling the property and moving? 'Cause I'm sure willing to make you another offer if that's why you're here."

"That's exactly why I'm here," I say coolly. I can get through this without crying. I know I can. "I want half a million dollars. I want it today. And I want the house torn down before the end of the week."

Kurt had been leaning back in his big leather seat, but at that he sits up so fast that he slams his knee into the top of his desk. "Half a million—and *what*? Slow down, darlin', business doesn't happen quite that fast."

"Well, it does, or we're not doing business. Those are my terms. Yes or no?"

"Even if the property was worth five hundred thousand—which, honestly, Mel, it isn't—it's not like I have that kind of money just lying around—"

I come to my feet. "Fine. I'll look for another buyer."

He leaps up, too, and the chair makes a faint crashing sound as it hits the wall. "Wait, wait, wait. I'm just trying to get a handle on your terms."

I've made it as far as the door, but I turn back to face him. Now I'm actually glad for the weak sunlight on my face; I hope it shows him that I'm dead serious. "Those are my terms. Five hundred thousand. Today. And I want it written into the contract that if the house is *not* razed to the ground by the end of the week, you owe me another half million."

He studies me for a long moment, letting the easy smile fade from his face while he makes cold calculations in his head. Oh, he's not doing the math on the price of the property versus the profit he can make; he's long ago performed a cost/benefit analysis and knows exactly what he can afford to pay. He's sizing me up as an opponent, trying to guess where I might be vulnerable, how he might outmaneuver me. Most successful quarterback Dagmar High School had ever fielded, and a college standout at Mizzou. Would have gone pro if he hadn't blown out his knee. Still a poker player who wins local tournaments and has made it to Vegas once or twice on the national circuit. Charles once called him a smiling shark, but he's not smiling now.

"I think we've got a little room for negotiating here," he says softly.

I lay my hand on the doorknob. "No we don't."

"Well, can I have an hour to think about it? I need to call a few folks, see how much money I can rustle up on such short notice."

"No you don't."

"Now, Melanie. Be reasonable."

"That's the offer, Kurt. Take it or leave it. When I walk out, it's off the table."

"And you have someone else you're gonna make the same offer to? Some other developer who happens to want the same land?"

I just smile. Kurt's the local boy with all the connections and the biggest land-development operation in this part of the county, but there are a couple of other housing contractors who've started building in our area, and they're eager to do business. Sure, the economy has been bad for a couple of years, but everyone expects the housing market to rebound—and here in the St. Louis area, most of the activity is in the small towns in the semirural areas, where there's lots of room for growth.

Kurt shakes his head admiringly, and his bad-boy grin slowly reappears. "You always were a ballbuster, Mel. I never should have let you break up with me."

"That's the mistake you made, Kurt. Thinking you could let me or not let me do anything. Do we have a deal? Or do I go?"

Even though he's standing all the way across the room, he holds his hand out, ready to shake mine. "We have a deal."

One week later, the house has been reduced to splinter and brick. Ann will never be able to come home.

CHAPTER TWENTY-FIVE

JANET

By the time he was thirty-five, Cooper had the body of a sixty-year-old. A well-kept, well-fed, energetic sixty-year-old, it's true, but a man in decline nonetheless. It didn't take much basic math to figure out that he would be lucky to have another ten years of quality life.

For a while, I thought I had found a way to slow the aging process, though it was counterintuitive and cost me dearly. If I injected Cooper with a serum made of his own blood, he would stay in wolf shape three weeks instead of two. Although I would have expected him to deteriorate *more* rapidly as he spent extended time in animal form, the reverse appeared to be true. In fact, the deterioration seemed to halt altogether if I gave him enough injections to keep him in animal shape for more than a month at a time. If he was a wolf for six weeks and human for two, his systems seemed to stabilize. No doubt he still aged, but at a more reasonable rate. From this I concluded that it was the transformation process itself—not just the effort required to live as a wolf—that took such a toll on his body.

But, oh God, six weeks without Cooper beside me—Cooper, the man, the artist, the lover, the gentle soul—I had such a difficult time enduring those lengthy separations. It was not as if I could not see him every day, of course. Even as a wolf, he stayed on the property. Winter or summer, we would spend evenings quietly together outside on the back porch, as we had done so many times on the deck at my parents' house so long ago. I could talk to his dark, intelligent face; I could know that he understood me; I could be convinced, literally be without a wisp of doubt, that he loved me. But it was not the same. I missed him. I craved him. I wanted him, and I could see him slipping away.

And then everything got worse.

For the past three years, I had been assisted in my lab work by Evan's daughter, a shy, brilliant girl named Karadel. When she first joined me, she was an awkward and uncertain seventeen, a homeschooled girl who would have been instantly admitted into any med school in the country except for the fact that she shape-shifted on a random basis into a truly astonishing variety of creatures. She had been an eagle, a fox, a brown mouse, a doe, a butterfly, an elephant. I sometimes thought that finding a refuge for Karadel had been Evan's primary purpose in buying property for me and setting me up with my own practice. He had kept her for a long time on his estate in Barrington, a far western suburb of Chicago with lots of open land, but the transformation to the pachyderm had alarmed him. And so she came to stay with me.

As far as I was concerned, she was a gift straight from heaven. I had hoped she might become my assistant—fill a sort of vet-tech role—but it was quickly clear that with intensive training, she could be a full-fledged veterinarian every bit as good as I was. So I approached her education as if I would one day send her out into the world to open her own clinic. I taught her everything. By the time she was twenty, she could treat and diagnose any creature who came to my office, whether true animal or shape-shifter. She had also had a little success in learning how to control her own bewildering transformations, and she worked alongside me in the lab, trying to unlock the mysteries of her personal chemistry.

Cooper adored her, and she treated him like a favorite uncle. Sometimes, when he was a wolf and she was in some compatible form, they would romp through the grassland of the property like adolescent cubs learning to play and fight. I would watch them from the windows and blink back tears, reminding myself that it was foolish to be jealous. Oh, I didn't think they harbored romantic feelings for each other, but Karadel could share with Cooper something I never could. Half of his life had always been mine—less than half now; perhaps one-quarter. And I had always wanted all of him to belong to me.

It was Karadel who first realized that the wolf serum was no longer halting Cooper's deterioration. She had spent four days as a lively little Yorkie, and she and Cooper had chased each other through the snow-covered meadow that comprised the biggest section of my land. It was mid-January, not too early to think about spring, the time the world would redeem all the promises it made every fall. *This is not the end. This is only a time for rest and renewal.*

"I'm worried about Cooper," Karadel said. They were almost the first words she spoke aloud once she was back in human shape.

"What? Why?" I asked sharply. My heart, always braced for tragedy, seized up for a moment; I felt a spasm of pain pulse through my chest.

"He seemed so much slower today. He couldn't run very far or very fast, and a couple of times he just stopped and sort of panted for breath."

"Maybe he's picked up a lung infection," I said. "I'll bring him in and do an X-ray."

"I don't think that's it," she said gently. "I don't know if you've noticed, but his muzzle. It's gone almost completely white. I think—I think it's caught up with him. All the extra time you bought him with the serum—it's all kind of evaporated. I think he's old."

I stared at her—a dark, slim girl with her mother's build and her father's uncanny eyes—and felt the edges of my world begin to disintegrate. It was as if I were standing on a sandbar in the middle of a low, sluggish river, and upstream about a mile or so I could hear floodwaters rumbling. The level of the river was already beginning to rise, nibbling away at the crumbling boundaries of my safe island. It wouldn't be long before the toxic, tumbling water would come roaring through, obliterating my life and drowning me in despair.

"How old?" I whispered.

"I'm only guessing," she said. "I'd have to examine him. But I'd say—in wolf years—eighteen. Maybe nineteen." Wolves in the wild rarely lived past ten; those in captivity might live to be twenty. Karadel's voice became even softer. "And once he's human—"

"He'll be about ninety or more," I breathed. "Close to the end."

"He's probably got a year, at least," she said.

"In wolf form," I answered.

She just looked at me and didn't answer.

"I think whenever he changes to human shape, he loses time," I added. "If he has a year, but he changes shape three times—maybe he has six months."

"You don't know that for sure," she said.

"It's not long enough."

"I don't think we ever get enough time with the people we care about," she said sadly, and I knew she spoke from experience. Her mother had died when Karadel was a child, and her father, who was now in his late forties, was growing weaker by the day. And, of course, she had lost any number of shape-shifter friends to disease, accident, and those too-early deaths. "My father says grief is the price of love," she added.

I shook my head. "I can't pay that price. I can't live without him," I said.

"You'd be amazed at what you can do," she replied.

That I knew to be true; my whole life had been a series of surprises. But even if I discovered I *could* live without Cooper, I knew I wouldn't want to.

"I want that year," I said. "I want every minute of it."

"You want to keep him in wolf shape that whole time?" she asked. "It doesn't seem fair to him. He misses you, too, when you're human and he's animal. If he doesn't have much time left, he deserves to share it with you."

"He does," I said. "And he will. But you're going to have to help me."

Her eyes went wide with shock. She had worked beside me in the lab; she knew at once what I intended.

"You don't even know if it will work," she said, her voice low and urgent. "It might kill you—it really might."

"I don't care," I said. "Without Cooper, I'd rather be dead."

In the end, and only because Karadel insisted, I put off the injections; I allowed Cooper to become human one more time. She had been right, of course. He was a very old man now, decidedly frail, but still marked by that eternal sweetness and that hard-won peace. He knew at once that he could no longer cheat his implacable internal clock. He understood right away that his choice was to go back to wolf form and stay there for a year or more, or bounce between states of existence and be dead in a few months.

"I choose human," he said. Despite the cold, we were outside, sitting side by side on the back porch, watching sunset sigh and release its golden grip on the ice-covered trees, the shorn grasses, the yawning acres of land. "I choose you."

I had my arms around his waist and my head against his shoulder, but now I snuggled closer, inhaling him like the fresh scent of a summer day. "I choose you, too," I whispered into his chest. "But I choose wolf. And I will be a wolf alongside you."

I felt him lean back, angle his head down, try to see my

face. "You want to test your serum on yourself?" he demanded. "What if it doesn't work?"

"I think it will."

Now he did pull back far enough that he could put one hand under my chin and tilt my head up. "And if it doesn't?"

I met his eyes squarely. "Then you will get a chance to mourn me the way I have always expected to mourn you."

"I don't want to do that."

"No," I said, "neither do I."

He leaned in to give me a gentle kiss. "I would love to be a wolf alongside you," he whispered. "We would have a year?"

"I think so. Close enough."

"And we could stay here?"

"Of course."

"What about your practice? All the shape-shifters who have come to rely on you?"

"Karadel is as good as I am. She can take care of them." I kissed him. "You can't possibly have any more objections."

"Only the big one. The only one that matters. That I am afraid for you. That I don't want you to give up your life for mine."

"My life has always been yours," I said. "And I'm not giving anything up. I am simply joining our lives together at the end."

He leaned his cheek against the top of my head. "Then I say yes."

CHAPTER TWENTY-SIX

MELANIE

T he year that follows is one of my best and one of my worst.

Brody and I rent a house in south St. Louis and settle in to married life. For the most part, I love it, and the easy companionship we enjoyed during our courtship just becomes easier and more companionable. Of course, there are adjustments. He's still something of a slob, he doesn't always remember that two people sharing one bathroom have to display a great deal of sensitivity to both individuals' schedules, and his sense of time rarely synchs up with that of the general population. He's as likely to want a serious in-depth conversation at 3 a.m. as high noon, and it rarely occurs to him that there might be an hour when it's too late to call. But those are minor irritations, and the benefits outweigh them a hundred times over. In many ways, I am happier than I have ever been.

On the other hand, I don't really like living in the city, in a little row house that's one of a series of row houses all marching down the street like redbrick soldiers. I like being able to walk to a neighborhood Italian restaurant, but I don't like the fact that I have to close every shade in my house at night or my neighbors will make comments on the following day about what TV shows I've been watching. I'm not used to this many people being this close, all the time. I miss my house. I miss my twelve acres. I miss my sister.

Can't think about that.

I don't mind the commute down to PRZ every morning because the rented house is only a few blocks from Highway 55. I've started listening to audiobooks to make the trip pass more quickly, and I find I like this way of consuming a novel. When the book—or the narrator—is particularly good, I even become a calmer driver, less inclined to curse at red lights and people traveling slowly in the fast lane. Yet another benefit of my new life.

Brody takes Highway 55 in the opposite direction, back into the city, on *his* morning drive. He's been rehired at Channel 5—not as an on-air reporter, but as a behind-the-scenes producer. When I ask him if he likes that better, he merely shrugs.

He has, at least for the time being, given up the notion of writing a book about shape-shifters. I'm deeply relieved, but I hate the thought that he's had to put aside even a small dream. When I ask him about it one night, he says, "I'm too close to the story now. It would be a memoir, not a work of nonfiction. And I don't want to write a memoir." The distinctions aren't clear to me, but he seems adamant. *Maybe later,* I think. *After everything's settled.*

We both have the sense that we're just marking time. The sense that our *real* lives will start in a year, maybe two, that we're in a very pleasant but still extremely nerve-wracking state of limbo, and nothing important will be launched or decided until it ends. Until something happens to Ann.

Maria Romano calls me every few weeks with updates, and I *live* for the sound of her voice on the phone. I admire the way she handles these calls, telling me every single detail she can call to mind, knowing how important each one will be to me, without sounding maudlin or depressing.

Ann looked thin, but she had a good appetite. She rested most of the first day, but then she was up and playing with Lizzie the next day. She yelped once when Lizzie pulled her

*ear too hard, but she didn't bite or scratch, just kind of
backed up and watched her for a while, as if waiting to see
if Lizzie was going to do anything else inappropriate* . . .

William usually takes human shape at least once during
these visits and fills her in on anything major that's happened while they've been gone. It's William who describes
what happened only three weeks after the wedding when,
despite his best efforts, he couldn't keep Ann from following the back roads that would lead to the house she'd grown
up in. They arrived on Bonhomme Highway at dusk and
traveled cautiously along the shoulder to avoid being hit by
cars, though Ann, as always, became increasingly reckless
as they approached the most familiar curves of the road.

*And then they got to the point where he knew your house
should be, but it wasn't there—just an empty field with a
couple of Bobcats digging up dirt—and it was like Ann
didn't know what to do, William said. At first she slowed
down, like she knew something was missing, she just didn't
know what, then she picked up speed again, racing up the
hill and around the next curve, as if what she was looking
for was just around the corner. And she kept going for
another mile or so, then she stopped, and turned around,
and retraced her steps. And the same thing happened—
she'd slow down, she'd speed up, she'd keep looking for
something. He says he's not even sure she knew what she
was trying to find. And after a couple of hours of this, she
turned away, and they headed to a park to spend the night.*

My heart breaks to think of Ann lost, confused, frantically seeking something she can't even articulate to
herself.

And rejoices—in a stern and bitter way—to think that I
have, with my staggeringly expensive purchase, bought her
another year or two of life. If I had ever doubted it, I know
for certain now that she *would* have reneged on her promise.
She *would* have come to see me, turned human again, and
died in my arms. I have outwitted her, and I am fiercely glad.

And irredeemably sad.

I carry those two contradictory, equally powerful emotions in my heart for the rest of that year. Through a sparkling white winter and my first Christmas as a bride. Through spring's shy, flirtatious arrival, one day warm and beckoning, one day haughty and cold. Through summer's expansive, self-satisfied, slow and sluggish reign. And back toward autumn's temper tantrums, stormy and beautiful.

Debbie has her twins, both of them girls—named Sasha and Sarah, not Zoe and Zelda. Immediately, she descends into a life of sleepless chaos from which she occasionally sends bulletins that roughly translate into *This is even harder than I thought it would be, but God are they beautiful.* After a three-month maternity leave and a long search for the perfect nanny, she's back at PRZ, vowing that Charles won't touch her again until he's "cut off the jewels and buried them in the yard."

Brody wins a regional Emmy Award for a program he produced, which prompts his boss to offer him a raise and an extended contract. But I sense a restlessness in him that more money and increased responsibilities won't appease. His friends Carolyn and Joe have left Doctors Without Borders to begin volunteering at a place in Tasmania that treats and educates children with handicaps. He keeps reading books about mountaineers who found schools in Asia and economics professors who start microfinance banks in Bangladesh.

"I don't want to be the guy who builds the school or starts the banks," he tells me. "I want to be the guy who *writes* about the guy who goes out to change the world."

"I have half a million dollars," I say. "We could take a year off and go to Africa."

"Maybe," he says. "Not quite yet."

Not quite yet. Not while Ann is still alive.

The call from Maria comes on a Wednesday afternoon in late October. "Ann's here," she says without preamble. "But she's struggling. Lying on her side and panting. She took some water, but I couldn't get her to eat anything. I think it's time."

For a moment, I can't think. "Okay—I'll—thanks for calling. Let me get some stuff together and—I'll leave as soon as I can."

Brody's at work, and I know he can't always answer his phone, so I text him. Going to Maria's. He'll know what that means. I stop in Debbie's office, and say baldly, "I've got to go. Don't know when I'll be back."

She's sitting behind her desk, looking weary and hot, but on the instant I have every scrap of her attention. "Ann?" When I nod, she says, "Do you want me to come with you?"

"Thank you, but no. I just want to be with my sister."

Against this very eventuality I have, for the past couple of months, kept a packed overnight bag in my car. I don't know how the next couple of days will go, but if Ann's too weak to travel, I might be staying at Maria's for a while. Part of my brain acknowledges that as a horrible imposition, and part of me doesn't care. All that matters is that I get to Ann's side as quickly as I can.

An overcast sky ushers twilight in an hour or two early; I accomplish the whole drive in a gray half-light that reinforces my sense of dread. All the lights are on at Maria's, and I push the door open without even bothering to knock.

All the people who live in the house full- or part-time are gathered in the living room. Maria's reading a book to Lizzie, and the little girl—more than two years old by now, and *so big*—is repeating words back to her. Dante and William are seated on the couch, both of them turned to gaze at me. Dante looks sober and sorry; he knows what it's like to lose a sister. And William—he looks dreadful. Pale, scraggly, rail-thin, and miserable.

He knows what it's like to lose a sister, too. And now he's learning what it's like to lose a lover.

"She's back in Lizzie's room," Maria tells me. "Dante and I thought we'd go away for the night. Give you a little privacy. You can sleep in our room—I changed the sheets this morning."

"Thank you," I say. I'm already edging toward the hall, but I meet William's eyes. "Are you staying?"

He relaxes a little, as if maybe he'd thought I wouldn't want him to be here. "If you don't mind."

"She belongs to you, too," I say.

And then I can't wait another moment, and I run straight to Lizzie's room. It's decorated in a zoo motif—perfect for a shape-shifter, I suppose—but most of the furniture has been pushed back against the walls. There's a hooked rug on the floor, shaped like a plump giraffe, and Ann's lying on top of it. The only illumination comes from a polar-bear night-light, but that's plenty. I can see that Ann is still in husky shape, and Maria was right. She's definitely struggling. Her eyes are closed, her breath is shallow and troubled, and her legs are held out stiffly from her body. But she hears me come in and she stirs, seeming to make a great effort to lift her head from the floor. When the blue eyes open, they look whitened, half-blind, and as they stare at me for a long moment, they show no flicker of recognition.

"Annie," I whisper and drop to my knees. "Annie, it's Mel."

Maybe she remembers my voice, or my name, or my scent, but suddenly she knows me. I see her face change and her body ripple as she tries to push herself upright. The heavy tail beats the floor a few times in joyful welcome. I put my hands to her face and her tongue flashes out to lick my wrist. Her nose is hot and dry, and her fur feels gritty and sparse beneath my fingers. She doesn't have the strength to sit up.

So I lie on the floor next to her, my hands still on her face, her paws scratching gently at my shoulders. "How've you been, baby?" I ask in a soft voice. "You're looking pretty tired. I guess you've had a tough few months, huh? But I hope you've had some fun, too. I've missed you. I've thought about you every day."

She makes a little whine deep in her throat and paws at my shoulder again, like she's asking me a question. "Yeah, baby, you can change now," I say, my voice even softer. "You can come back to me. It's okay if you're not strong enough. I'll just lie here with you awhile, just like you are now. But if you want to change, you can do it. You can come back."

She whines again, and I move one hand from her face to

her neck to her shoulder. Under the brittle fur, I can feel her muscles straining, almost unraveling and reknitting; she closes her eyes again as if the effort of transformation is almost too much for her. I'm afraid to speak, afraid to distract her and somehow strand her in a half-life between one form and another. Then all at once I feel the tension leave her body. Her head falls back, her legs splay—and all that bristly white fur melts away.

Lying beside me on the giraffe rug is my painfully thin, fearfully weak, radiantly smiling sister. Blond, naked, shivering, and dying.

"Annie," I breathe, and crush her in my arms.

She's laughing and crying into my neck. I feel the bones of her arms as if they are not softened at all by muscle or flesh. Her skin is chilled to the touch, so I shake free and sit up just enough to twitch a quilt off the nearby rocker, and I tuck this around her so she's covered from her chin to her toes. Then I snuggle up against her again.

"It is so good to see you," I say.

"It's been a lot more than three months," she answers. Her voice sounds a little froggy, as if she's been battling bronchitis, but I know she just hasn't used it in a very long time.

I'm surprised into a breath of a laugh. "Yeah. More like a year."

"You tricked me," she replies, but she doesn't sound angry.

"I did. I'm sorry."

"You tore the house down!"

"Sold it to Kurt."

"No! Did you get a lot of money?"

"Half a million dollars."

"But why? Why did you sell it?"

I stroke the blond hair that falls around her face. It's matted with dirt and frayed with split ends. Not so much unkempt as uncared-for. "Because I didn't want you to come back and turn human and die."

She gives a long, shuddering sigh, a sound that could belong to a dog as much as a human. "Yeah, and I would have. I wanted to. But I still can't believe you'd sell the *house*!"

"So now I have a lot of money. How should I spend it?"

"Buy a red sports car and drive it really fast."

"Yeah, and get a speeding ticket every day."

"Travel around the world. Spend a year in Europe. You'd like that."

"I've been thinking about traveling. That's a good idea."

"How's Brody?" she asks.

"Working at the TV station again. Just won some award. I like being married to him."

"That's nice," she says with another sigh, this one happier.

"So what about you? And William? How've you been?"

"Good. Really good, until a few weeks ago. We spent the winter down in the bootheel on a farm William learned about from a friend. Lots of cows and barns and warm places to sleep. I felt so good. Really strong. When it snowed, we'd just go *racing* across these open fields. We wouldn't see a human footprint for miles—just this gorgeous white expanse of snow. William said whenever I stood perfectly still, I'd just disappear."

"I remember that!" I exclaim. "The first time it snowed after we moved to Dagmar. You went out to the backyard— you were still a puppy—and you got lost in the drifts. And we couldn't see you. And Daddy and Gwen were panicked, and they started combing the backyard, calling your name and trying to find you. Daddy was sure you'd gone on into the forest and broken a leg or something."

"And I was just sitting there on the side of the yard, watching everyone run around. I thought it was a game."

"You were a little shit," I inform her, and she giggles.

"Hey, remember the time Debbie and her mom came over, and I was in the front yard, and Debbie started playing with me, and her mom was all, like, 'Don't touch stray dogs! They could have rabies!' And Daddy was *so mad*, but he couldn't say why."

"Oh, yeah, and I remember the time Kurt came over and

we were sitting on the couch watching TV and everyone else was asleep. And we were making out, of course, and you came out of the bedroom and said, 'I can *hear* you kissing, and it's gross.'"

"Well, it was, all slobbery sounding."

"To this *day*, if I'm watching a movie, and the couple makes any noise at all when they're kissing, I think about that."

"You know what I always remember?" she says. Her voice is dreamy, as if she's drifting back toward a memory or tiptoeing down to the boundary of sleep. "And it's so stupid. I was, I don't know, ten, and you wanted me to wash my face and brush my teeth, but all the washcloths were in the laundry. So you said I could wash my face by putting soap on my hands. And I didn't want to, because I was stuck on the idea that you had to have a washcloth. And you said, 'That's how cowboys wash their faces.'"

"I said that? I have no memory of that conversation at all."

"You said it," she confirms, speaking through a big yawn. "And to this day, whenever I'm splashing water on my face, I think, 'Hey, that's how cowboys clean up.'"

"Well, they probably do."

She yawns again. "I'm so tired," she says. "I've lost so much energy in the past few days."

I speak as casually as I can. "Yeah, you've gotten pretty thin."

"I haven't had much appetite. Been sleeping a lot. Just dragging in general."

"Yeah," I say again. "I think the life you've led has been pretty hard on your body."

"Yeah," she repeats, sounding even fuzzier. For a moment I think she's already drifted off, then she speaks again in that drowsy voice. "Mel, I can't keep my eyes open, but I don't want to fall asleep in your face!"

"It's all right. We've had a chance to talk."

"Will you be here when I wake up?"

"Of course I will."

"Promise?"

"Cross my heart."

"All right. Then I'm just going to take a nap."

"I think that's a good idea."

"It was *so good* to see you again," she whispers. "I missed you so much."

"I missed you more."

She manages the faintest laugh. "Love you."

"Love you more." She might have fallen asleep already; in any case, she doesn't answer. I add, "Love you, love you, love you."

She stirs, and for a moment I think she's going to add something, but she's just resettling on the rug. I wonder if I should move her to Lizzie's bed—I wonder if the hard floor will bruise her fragile bones. I'm sure William would pick her up if I asked him to. Hell, she's so thin I could probably lift her myself.

But I don't get up. I don't move away. I merely lie there for the next hour, listening to her breaths as they gradually grow farther apart. At some point I sense a presence behind me, and I turn my head to see a shadow standing in the doorway, unmoving and silent.

"I don't think it will be much longer," I tell William, "if you want to stay."

He doesn't answer, but he steps into the room and settles on the floor on the other side of Ann. I wonder if I should leave them alone together—it's a lover's right, after all, to gather up his beloved's final hours and fold them against his heart—but then I realize it doesn't really matter. Ann will have no last words to share with either one of us, so we have nothing to fight over, no reason to be greedy.

We share the night in a silence broken only by our occasional rustling motions and the sounds of Ann's breathing. Which slows, then slows again, and then finally stops. When the sun comes up, it is so blond and brilliant that it hurts my eyes. Or maybe my eyes hurt because I can't stop crying.

I spend a month grieving and a day deciding I'm going to change my life.

"Let's do it," I say to Brody over dinner one night. It's late November, a week past Thanksgiving, and only gaudy Christmas stands off in the future to paint color and hope into a world of gray shadows and endlessly threatening skies.

He sets down a forkful of mashed potatoes and regards me steadily. "Do what?" he asks.

"Move to Africa. Work at that school you're always talking about. What's it called? Faraja. You can write your book about do-gooders. And I'll—do whatever they want. They must need cooks or housekeepers or something."

"This is awfully sudden."

I shake my head. "No. You've been thinking about it for a year."

"Yes, and you've been thinking about it for five minutes."

"Longer than that. Let's do it."

"It's an awfully big change," he warns. "You'd have to get—I don't know—malaria shots. And work visas. And, who knows? International security clearance."

"Okay," I say, nodding. "Let's get started."

"Melanie—"

"I want to *do* something. I want to *feel* something. I can't just sit here and mourn for the rest of my life. You've spent the last year and a half living *my* life, so let's spend a year living *your* life. I might hate it. I might love it. But it will get me away from here, and it will give you a chance to do something really important to you. It's a win-win."

"You know it will cost a fortune."

"Hey, I've seen your bank account. You've got plenty squirreled away, and God knows I do. We can afford to take a year off." I tick off additional points on my fingers. "We don't have a house to sell. Neither of us has a job we'd be sorry to leave behind—I mean, Debbie will be sad to lose me, but I think she'd be the first one to push me out the door. We don't have kids. We don't have sick parents. We don't have anything preventing us from simply picking up stakes and going wherever we want."

He's starting to show a little excitement—tempered with

caution in case I suddenly reverse course. "It *would* be a good time in our lives to go off on an adventure."

"So let's do it," I say again.

He stretches a hand to me across the table, and I push aside the bowl of mashed potatoes so I can reach for him. "Melanie," he says. "Are you *sure*?"

"The only thing in my life I've ever been sure of is marrying you," I tell him. "Everything else has always been a gamble. But I want to do it."

He squeezes my fingers, hard, and his smile grows wide. "Then let's go to Africa."

It's weeks before we're ready to depart. Brody wasn't wrong about the shots and the visas and the extensive red tape, and then of course we have plenty of other details to take care of, from packing and storing our belongings to saying good-bye to friends and family. Some people think we're insane, others think we're heroic, but the ones who love us best are happy to see us go. Because they know all the reasons we want to leave.

We're only three days from departing when I receive a bulky package in the mail from Dr. Kassebaum. I've had a day of extended lunacy, so I don't have time to open it before Brody comes home in the evening, bearing pizza and Coke. We've completely cleaned out the refrigerator and the pantry, so we've been living on takeout and fast food for the past week.

"What did Dr. Kassebaum send you?" he asks as he gets out the paper plates.

"I don't know. Haven't opened it yet."

"She knows about Ann, right? I mean, you told her?"

I nod. I'd sent her a note a few days after the funeral, giving her the news and thanking her for all her help. Her reply had been brief almost to the point of rudeness, and at the time I'd wondered if I'd offended her in some way. But now I'm thinking there was something else going on in her life just then, and maybe this package will explain what.

Brody picks up the envelope and hefts it, as if from weight and size he'll be able to determine what's inside. "Huh. Feels like a lot of paper. Like a—" He moves his thumb along one margin. "Like a spiral notebook, maybe. A five-hundred-sheeter."

I raise my eyebrows. "Notes on Ann's case, maybe?"

"Maybe. Why don't you open it and find out?"

His three sisters beat it into his head that you don't just read a girl's mail or browse through her diary, so he won't even sort through and discard the junk letters that come to the house addressed to me. Heaving an exaggerated sigh, I take the envelope from him and pull the plastic rip cord that opens up the side. Bits of gray recycled paper stuffing float down to the table, landing on the plates and the top of the pizza box.

I pull out a green notebook with a tattered cover and a few sheets of paper that appear to have ripped free of the spiral over the years of its life and been stuffed back in. Just thumbing through quickly, I get the impression that it's a journal of sorts, written in a similar-though-evolving handwriting over hundreds of pages.

"What the hell?" Brody demands, coming around to peer over my shoulder. "Is it a diary? Is it *Dr. Kassebaum's* diary?"

"Or something like that," I say. I'm wildly curious, but I'm also starving, and I have at least five hours' worth of chores to get done tonight before I go to bed. I flip the cover shut and slip the notebook back in the envelope. "I'll save it to read on the plane."

"I bet it's juicy," he says.

"I'm sure it'll be interesting, whatever it is. Dr. Kassebaum's that kind of woman."

Brody gets out paper cups and pours two glasses of wine from a bottle that is literally the last thing in the refrigerator. "To Africa," he says. "New beginnings, new challenges, new lives."

"To Africa," I say, "and to us."

EPILOGUE

JANET

For a long time, I couldn't decide who to give it to—this
notebook where I have written down my story. My first
thought, of course, was Karadel or Evan, people who would
wholly understand the life I have lived and the choices I
have made. But I found that I wanted to put the story into
the hands of someone more like me. Someone entirely
human. I wanted to try to explain the impossible tale to
someone who would not at first believe it, and make that
reader, finally, believe.

At first I thought that person might be Crystal. She would
be shocked and astonished and perhaps horrified (and I
would certainly have to change Evan's name). But I thought
she would accept the story. She knew enough about me,
enough about Cooper, to understand how much we would
want to be together, no matter how impassable the gulf
between us seemed to be.

Then, when I met Brody Westerbrook a couple of years
ago, I thought I would give the notebook to him. He could
edit it, supplement it, turn it into a book. I smiled at the
thought. He had wanted so much to document the existence
of shape-shifters. This firsthand account by a woman who
had loved one would go a long way toward winning over the

doubters. Although maybe not. Most people would think my tale was fiction—would want it to be fiction, because they would not be able to bend their minds around the notion that supernatural creatures exist all around them, unnoticed and ordinary and real. But Brody would still like to read the pages, I thought.

In the end, I realized it was Melanie who needed the book the most. I know she struggled mightily with her own decision—the terrible choice she made for love. I want to be able to tell her it was the right choice. I want her to know that she bought Ann the only things that anyone is ever really willing to pay a high price for—love and time. The two things I am now willing to buy with my own life.

Karadel will give me the injection tomorrow. Cooper turned into a wolf last night, and I have already given him his own shots, the ones that will keep him in his animal state for at least six weeks. When he feels the urge to change come upon him again, he will return to the house, and Karadel will give him another set of shots—and another, and another, for as long as he has the strength to present himself at her door.

I cannot guess how long my own transformation will endure. I have no idea how long my body, unused to such stresses, will be able to sustain the wolf state. I may live only a few days or a few months, leaving a bereft Cooper behind to grieve for me. I may live another ten years. Though I don't think so. Once Cooper is gone, whether I am wolf or human, I expect I will lose the strength to keep on living. Karadel knows that. She will not look for me to return to the house once Cooper has breathed his last.

I imagine sometimes what Crystal would say if I had decided to give her the notebook. Perhaps Melanie would ask the same questions—perhaps anybody would. "Are you crazy? Why are you throwing your life away like this?" And all I would be able to summon for a reply is, "Because I want to be with him. Because I need to be with him. Because I love him."

There is never any other answer.

From National Bestselling Author
SHARON SHINN

THE SHAPE OF DESIRE
A Shifting Circle Novel

For fifteen years, Maria Devane has been desperately,
passionately in love with Dante Romano. But Maria
knows that Dante can never give everything of himself
back—at least not all of the time. Every month, Dante
shifts shape, becoming a wild animal.

Maria has kept his secret since the beginning, knowing that their love is worth the danger. But when a
string of brutal attacks occurs in local parks while
Dante is in animal form, Maria is forced to consider
whether the lies she's been telling about her life have
turned into lies she's telling herself...

sharonshinn.net
facebook.com/ProjectParanormalBooks
penguin.com

M1325T0513

Quatrain

From National Bestselling Author

Sharon Shinn

Sharon Shinn's "outstanding" (*Publishers Weekly*) Twelve Houses novels have fascinated readers and critics alike with their irresistible blend of fantasy, romance, and adventure. Now, in *Quatrain*, she weaves compelling stories set in four of the worlds that readers love, in "Flight," "Blood," "Gold," and "Flame."

Now available from Ace Books!

penguin.com